Also by
Elizabeth Essex

Almost a Scandal
Breath of Scandal
Scandal in the Night

After the Scandal

ELIZABETH ESSEX

St. Martin's Paperbacks

AFTER THE SCANDAL

Copyright © 2014 by Elizabeth Essex.

All rights reserved.

For information address St. Martin's Press, 175 Fifth Avenue, New York, NY 10010.

ISBN: 978-1-250-04457-0

Printed in the United States of America

St. Martin's Paperbacks edition / April 2014

St. Martin's Paperbacks are published by St. Martin's Press, 175 Fifth Avenue, New York, NY 10010.

10 9 8 7 6 5 4 3 2 1

For the Plotting Princesses:

Vicki Batman, Kathleen Baldwin, Karilyn Bentley,
Jillian Burns, Barb Han, Kathy Ivan, Chris Keniston,
Kelly Lee, Liz Lipperman, Sylvia McDaniel,
Phyllis Middleton, Michelle Miles, Liese Sherwood-
Fabre, Alisha Paige, Linda Steinberg, Pamela Stone,
Sasha Summers, and Mary Sullivan; for services
joyfully and so happily rendered in all matters of plot
and story line.

For the Publishing Powerhouses:

Vicki Lame, Kathleen Harden, Kaitlyn Henkel, Jillian Harris, Ruby Feb, Kathryn Parise, Emily Walters, Karlyn Lee, Lisa Lippman, Sylvia McDaniel, Fiona Malabari, Michelle Anne, Meg Sherwood, Talia, Alison Fargo, Lindy Steckler, Pamela Stone, Sasha Amuruso, and Mary Sullivan; for services prickly and so happily rendered in all matters of plot and story line.

Acknowledgments

It is with the deepest gratitude and wonder that I thank my ever thoughtful editor, Holly Ingraham, for making me write better books than I think I am capable of writing; my endlessly supportive agent, Barbara Poelle, for never letting me get out on a ledge; my patient critique partner, Joanne Lockyer, for reading chapters in the middle of the Australian night; and last, but certainly not least, the ever resourceful brains that are the Plotting Princesses for plotting the heck out of every story.

Prologue

Richmond upon Thames
August 1815

Tanner Evans, ninth Duke of Fenmore, should have known he would never truly be satisfied with a bride he hadn't stolen fair and square. Despite years and years of careful training in the arcane arts of being a Duke of Fenmore, the more honest and useful art of larceny still ran red and ruddy within his veins.

When the opportunity to make the inestimable Lady Claire Jellicoe his very own dropped into his hand like a pilfered purse full of shining, golden guineas, he palmed it deep into the hidden pocket next to his heart, and held fast.

He stole her from the garden of his grandmother's magnificent, ancient manor house in Richmond, during a ball, on a moonlit summer night so sweet and warm and comfortable, it never should have needed anything approaching larcenous stealth or guile. But even on such a soft evening, and even after all the years and years of training in the polite proprieties, stealth and guile came to him quite naturally. Like old friends out of the silent night.

Old friends he could trust.

This fortuitous piece of larceny came to his attention directly after the fourth couple of dances. Tanner had been standing along the north wall of the cavernous old great-room—it was one of the sacrifices he made to preserve the honor of the dukedom, this standing about against walls, just to be seen—when he saw *her*.

He saw everything, every ferocious little detail that others either didn't notice, or didn't want to see. All the things they did not want *him* to see—their nervous glances and telling looks, their nasty bad habits and impulsive, informing foibles. He saw them *think*, just as clearly and easily as if he were reading a broadsheet.

He saw the shift of their eyes and the clutch of their hands when they intended to cheat at cards. He saw their backhanded smiles and snide pleasure when they made plans to cuckold their friends. He saw them stuff silver salvers into their reticules, and stand idly by while innocent servants were given the sack. He saw them laugh and cry and flatter and flirt and lie and cheat and steal.

He saw it all.

But he had never seen Lady Claire Jellicoe do any of those things, not once, though he had watched her for years, in ballroom after ballroom, from London to Leicestershire. He was helpless not to—an informing foible *he* should have long overcome, but had not. He could not. She was as tiny and staggeringly beautiful as the fragile orchid blooms that filled his grandmother's conservatory, and just as full of wondrous, vibrant life. She was always smiling, always laughing and chatting, and serenely happy, glowing with luminous vitality—a rare white orchid he fervently admired, but could never touch.

But others did touch. Others danced and twirled and took her hand—the young lordlings who were meant to be his peers, the men who were as different from Tanner as sharp chalk was from soft cheese. Because no matter how hard he tried, or how carefully he had trained himself to become the ninth Duke of Fenmore, Tanner Evans knew he could never wash himself clean of the sulfurous stink of his years on the streets.

And so he had given up trying, and settled for being different, for retreating into the fortress of his mind, and preserving his still-savage pride behind a wall of eccentric silence.

His sister had laughed at the change in him. *Never shut up when you were a boy,* Meggs had teased.

But he had learned to hold his tongue now, and refrained from talking, though he watched them still. He watched *her* still—his lovely, luminous orchid of a girl. Because watching her gave him a pleasure so incomprehensible and inexplicable and vast, it was beyond his understanding. And beyond his power to stop.

So when Lady Claire Jellicoe turned her wide, sparkling blue eyes upon her dance partner, and smiled that smile that absolutely slayed Tanner—the smile that was warm and open and entirely without guile—the spurt of some small pain that would be very much like jealousy, if he allowed it to be, made him follow the line of her gaze to her partner, Lord Peter Rosing.

God's balls. God's bloody, bleeding balls.

Beneath his spotless gloves, Tanner's palms went damp and itchy, and his back propelled itself off the wall.

Not Rosing. Anybody but Rosing.

Tanner controlled himself enough to stop his face from contorting into a sneer, and immediately scanned the crowd. He tried to place Lady Claire's parents, the Earl and Countess Sanderson, where he had seen them last, chatting with his grandmother near one of the greatroom's arching doorways. Or her oldest brother, James, Viscount Jeffrey. One of them had to be near enough to act. One of

them had to see and know and understand just how vile
Rosing truly was beneath his charming veneer. One of
them had to stop him.

One of them had to *save* her.

Because Rosing was as slick and plausible and cunning as he was opportunistic. And he was nothing if not
opportunistic, the amoral bastard. Rosing took Lady Claire
Jellicoe's elbow in his filthy grip, and escorted her out the
tall, open doors at the foot of the room so smoothly and
quickly, no one seemed to notice they were gone.

No one but Tanner.

Tanner knew that out in the shadowed dark, where the
garden plummeted into the river, Lady Claire would soon
stop smiling her open, honest, guileless smile. Because
people were terrible, awful, cruel creatures of habit. And
Rosing was the most terrible, habitually cruel creature of
them all. Rosing indulged himself with lethal impunity.

The walls of the greatroom tilted inward—the room
narrowed to the spot where she had been.

Tanner was already moving, preparing to employ lethal habits of his own—his old friends stealth and guile.
Stealth and guile, and single-minded devotion. Because
he was devoted to Lady Claire Jellicoe, this exquisite orchid
of a young woman he had never met, never danced with,
never so much as spoken one single word to in all his years
of propping up ballroom walls.

He had never dared.

Tanner Evans, ninth Duke of Fenmore, was madly,
deeply, irrationally, and altogether secretly in love.

Chapter One

Lady Claire Jellicoe hadn't thought to protest. She hadn't thought Lord Peter Rosing would ever do anything untoward. She hadn't thought someone she'd just met on a ballroom floor could ever wish her irreparable harm.

She simply hadn't thought.

She had smiled. She had smiled because she was Lady Claire Jellicoe, pretty, privileged daughter of the Earl Sanderson. She had smiled because she was polite and considerate, and did as she was asked—she had been asked to dance with the handsome, fair-haired heir of the Marquess of Hadleigh. She had been taught to smile, and say yes.

"No" was what she said now. "No. No. No."

No, when Lord Rosing pushed her into the dark seclusion of the boathouse at the Dowager Duchess of Fenmore's lovely riverside villa in Richmond. No, when he pulled Claire's arm, and grabbed her by the neck. No, no, no, when he shoved her face-first against the rough brick wall.

The brick was hard, and hurt. Stone bit into her face. Sharp grit clawed and scratched against her skin and tasted like dust. But the chalky, bitter bile in her mouth was really fear.

Fear that for the first time in her life, she was powerless.

Powerless because she had been spoiled. Powerless because all her life, she had been pampered and cosseted and buffered and protected from all the truly ugly unpleasantness of the world. And she had never known it until that exact moment when she screamed, "No."

Because her voice was too small—shadowed with the fear pouring like acid down her throat, filling her chest with the high suffocating heat of panic.

She bit the gloved hand choked across her mouth as instinctively as a wild animal caught in a trap. Her teeth tore through the thick fabric, and the taste of blood suffused her mouth with the metallic tang of hatred and shame.

But all she got for her desperation was a low profanity spewed hot into her ear, the shifting of his grip to grind her face into the brick, and the bloody glove shoved into her mouth and held there as a gag.

He was everywhere around her, covering her mouth, standing on the train of her gown, pinning her against the wall with his weight. Closing out everything else, every hope of help, every thought of action. There was nothing but his body and his breath and his smell and his power.

And she had none.

She couldn't scream, and she couldn't move, and she couldn't stop Lord Rosing.

She could only hear the roar of her heartbeat filling her ears until she was drowning in it. She could only taste the bloody fabric clamped inside her mouth, suffocating out sense. She could only feel the wall cutting into her skin, and the grabbing and pushing and rending of her clothes as he exposed her body.

She could only think in the tiny, screaming part of her mind that was still capable of thought, no, no, no.

No, this could not be happening to her. No, he had to stop. No, someone had to stop him. Please. Please. Please.

And then someone did.

Rosing fell away from her for one suspended moment. Then his head cracked hard against the bricks two inches from her wide-open eyes. He stared back at her, his own eyes open and blank and uncomprehending for one agonizingly sick moment before they rolled back in his head, and he slid slowly down the wall, collapsing in an untidy half-clothed heap at her feet.

Claire clung to the wall, paralyzed and cold and shaking, until something inside her finally rattled free. She spat out the choking glove and scrambled back—away from him, away from the danger. But there was no room to go anywhere with the corner of wall at her back. And there was another threat.

A huge black shadow hung over Rosing's inert form like a monstrous carrion crow.

And then, without saying a word or making a sound, the shadow reared back, and stomped viciously on Rosing's splayed leg. A dull, sickening crack bounced up from the brick-paved floor, and lapped upward into the vaulted silence of the boathouse.

Everything else inside Claire wrenched into a single, tight knot of pain and misery that hollowed out her throat, and clutched its clammy way across the surface of her skin.

She shrank back into the corner, away from the looming specter.

And then the specter spoke. "Are you all right?" The voice was a dark, deep rumble she had never heard before.

"No." Her own voice was nothing but a fracture of a whisper.

"Yes" was all he said, and Claire couldn't tell if he was agreeing with, or contradicting her.

She couldn't tell anything. "What have you done?" She looked from her rescuing specter to the heap of man and tailoring at her feet who had only moments ago been the duplicitous Lord Peter Rosing.

"Broken his leg, I should think. It'll be a bloody long time—if he is lucky enough to heal well enough to even walk—before he rapes another girl."

There it was. Spoken plainly and ruthlessly. *Rape*. She had almost been *raped*.

And *another girl*. Claire's pulse throttled against her throat, but she could think enough to understand exactly what those words must mean—she was just another girl to Lord Peter Rosing, not Lady Claire Jellicoe whom he had asked to walk with in the moonlight because he found her enchanting. No matter her name, or her rank, or her fortune, or her parents, she was just another girl for him to do with as he wished. Like a maid or a shopgirl, or anyone else who was as powerless to stop him. Anyone.

The wretched knot within her clenched violently, and she had to close her mouth down around an unbecoming sound very much like a moan. Her hand rose to her throat. "I think I'm going to be sick."

"Try not to." He leaned nearer—across Rosing's prone form—as if he were trying to see her more clearly, and the dark, imposing shadow resolved itself into the tall, lean outline of a man she recognized instantly, though she did not really know him. "You haven't got time. Breathe deeply through your nose. Can you move on your own? Or would you like me to help you? I'm Tanner Evans, by the way. We have not been introduced."

It was a ridiculously enormous understatement. He spoke as if they were still within the ballroom, or in a shop, or at a musicale, or anywhere else upon the earth but standing across the unmoving form of her would-be rapist. "I know who you are."

But he wasn't some mere Tanner Evans. He was His Grace the Duke of Fenmore. The same impassive, impenetrable man she had seen at such events for years, hanging aloofly at the edges of ballrooms, and never being introduced so he might dance. She had thought him a strange, different sort of man, with a haunted, faraway look, like the men who had come back from the wars last summer with death stalking behind their eyes. Except that she knew the Duke of Fenmore hadn't gone to war. He had never done anything that she knew of, except stand around ballrooms looking chilly and off-putting.

And he was still rather more than off-putting now, breaking people's legs with such violent efficiency, though he also shook out an immaculate white handkerchief and held it carefully toward her. "You've blood," he said quietly, "on your face. Scratches from the coarseness of the mortar between the bricks, I should think. You might also want to put a cut of beefsteak or a potato on them, when you get home. You are so fair you're likely to bruise."

Beefsteak? Was he mad? Or perhaps it was she who was mad. Perhaps being assaulted by a bastard of the first rank did that to a person—drove them toward Bedlam—judging by the way she flinched from the gloved hand His Grace had extended toward her.

But he wasn't looking at her as if she were mad. He was nodding, as if he were reassuring and calming her, the way her father might do with a trembling gundog. "It's all right," he said. "I won't hurt you."

No, he didn't look like he would, though he did look rather inscrutable, with those narrowed eyes she could not read staring at her so intently. But Lord Peter Rosing's warm brown eyes had seemed charming not five minutes ago.

"Oh, God." Clearly, she knew next to nothing about assessing the character of a man.

Claire calmed her battered breathing enough take the proffered square of precisely folded linen from his hand. But her hands shook, and the brick floor beneath her feet wobbled unevenly, as if she were standing upon a floating dock, and not on solid stone.

She leaned against the wall for balance, and pressed the starched handkerchief to the part of her face that stung the most. She immediately withdrew it to see the dark staining of her own blood. Her head began to ache as if someone were scratching at it with an out-of-tune violin. "How bad is it?"

He shook his head, a kind negation. "Not too bad," he said, though the serious look in his dark eyes said the opposite. "But it were better if we removed ourselves immediately to a less dangerous, less illicit, and better-lit position. Especially before he comes to." He ducked his head out the open door of the boathouse, before he closed it, and he looked back to her. "Can you move on your own?"

As if the Duke of Fenmore knew she would rather do anything than be touched. Claire stiffened her legs with several hundred years of inherited Jellicoe pride, and tried to push herself away from the wall. Only to find the bricks shifting precariously underfoot again. The enormity of it all—of what had just happened and what had yet to happen—rocked her back against the wall.

"No." Heat built like a bonfire in her throat and behind her eyes, and her breath was seesawing in and out of her chest, but she pushed the tears away with the back of her shaking hand.

"Stay there a moment. So you might recover. I will stand here, and make sure he doesn't move." His Grace took a place on the other side of Rosing's bleeding head, where he was at a more than respectful distance. If anyone should chance upon Claire and the Duke of Fenmore in the boathouse at the bottom of the garden, they would only be seen to be conversing politely. Albeit across the unconscious form of her would-be rapist.

Yet tongues would wag even if she were seen to be only conversing politely with the Duke of Fenmore. The Duke of Fenmore did *not* converse politely with young ladies. He had never conversed politely with any young lady in all the time that Claire had observed him looming around the edges of ballrooms. He looked and he brooded and he judged, but he never conversed.

And he looked so intent now, she felt the need to explain how she had gotten herself into such a god-awful predicament. "His father asked me to dance a couple of country dances with Lord Peter Rosing. That's who he is, Lord Peter Rosing." Her voice sounded thin and small. So unlike the girl she had been until three minutes ago. "His father said he'd be obliged if I would make myself agreeable by dancing with his son. So I did. And then he asked—Rosing—if I'd like to take a turn on the terrace." *To cool the roses in those beautiful cheeks,* he had said with just the right amount of warm feeling when he had offered Claire his arm. "I thought he might try to steal a kiss."

The duke made an exceptionally unducal, rude sound of disgust. "Steal a kiss." Fenmore's gaze dropped to the inert man heaped on the floor. "Rosing was obviously intent upon larceny of an altogether grander design. As is his habit."

The duke's tone was strangely vehement. As if it were some sort of a personal affront to the dukedom that Rosing had tried to rape her on Fenmore's family's property.

There it was again, the awful, horrible, brutal word.

"I said no to him. I said—" She could hear her voice

try to scale the icy cold that was just now seeping into her bones.

"I know," he said shortly, though he did not look at her. "I heard you. And now, I reckon, so will he have done. And past bloody time. He has grown altogether too brazen."

In the strange fitful light that came from the wavering reflection of the moon off the water beneath the boathouse docks she took a closer look at the duke's face. At the rage which was only barely concealed behind the offputting veneer. "Why are you so angry?"

"Ah." His dark gaze flicked to hers only momentarily, before he looked away again. "I am not angry. I am *outraged.* Contrary to popular opinion, I happen to be a nice man. Rosing is *not.*" He snapped the word off as if he could break it as easily as he had Rosing's leg. "And you needed help."

Another ridiculous understatement. But she could only be grateful. "Yes. Yes, I did. Thank you."

He waved off her thanks with an elegant, economical gesture of his hand. "And you still need it. Your hair is coming down from its pins. You'll want to restore yourself a bit before you return to the house. Or would you rather I brought your parents down here? I would have done— brought them, or sent them to find you—but I reckoned time was of the essence."

It had been. A few moments more and—

The realization hit Claire like a shovel to the back of her head. Sick pain snaked its way around the dark edges of her skull—sharp pinpricks of light stabbed at the soft sides of her vision.

Fenmore must have anticipated what had almost happened.

"Did you *know* he was going to—" She stumbled over

the detestable word—it was like an anchor, dragging her down, down, down. Drowning her in the doubt and shame.

"To rape you? Yes. I did. Rosing is a rapist, Lady Claire. Behind those angelic looks lies a dark, twisted heart of rapine. He has made a rather execrable habit of it."

A *habit*. A hideous hive of an itch that had to be scratched.

Lord Peter Rosing might have picked anyone, anyone else in the ballroom, but she had been foolish—and maybe even, if she were honest with herself, *desperate*—enough to smile at him and consent to the dance. Even on the ballroom floor, Lord Peter Rosing must have been thinking and planning what he would do to her.

"Were he not the son of a peer, Rosing would have twisted at Tyburn long before now." Fenmore brought his dark gaze back to hers before he went on relentlessly, nearly spitting out the words, as if they left a bad taste in his mouth. "I do not know if it will comfort or disgust you to know that you are not the first young woman Lord Peter Rosing has raped, or attempted to rape. But I do mean you to be the last."

The calm surety with which he spoke sucked the last of the air from her lungs. "You mean to kill him."

Again that obsidian gaze came back to hers, so sharp it was nearly cutting. "I meant to cripple him. I *mean* that in the future, if he isn't hanged, he should find it so difficult to walk that he will find it utterly impossible to shove young ladies up against brick walls."

The same feeling of powerless shame, of helpless, hopeless, choking despair, tightened around her chest.

But she fought it back. It had not happened. Lord Peter Rosing had not *raped* her. But only because His Grace, the chilly Duke of Fenmore, had come in time.

She meant to thank him again, not only for herself, but

also for the greater population of London's women, it seemed. But she could not. The words were stuck tight in her throat, trapped there by the casual violence of both men's actions.

Within her skull, her head began to ring like a church bell.

"You are not yet recovered."

Again, she could not tell if the strange, dry ordinariness of his observation was an attempt at humor or censure. But pride was the last refuge of the weak. And Claire felt desperately weak.

So she put up her chin. "Yes. Thank you, Your Grace. You do have a penchant for the obvious."

"And you have a penchant for the dangerous," he shot back. Some of that vehemence had leapt back into his tone. "Planning to let a man like Rosing *steal* kisses."

That *was* condemnation in his low voice. Claire felt the thoughtlessness of her action burn a trail of heat down her face. She swallowed down the hot embers of her shame. "Yes. Stupid. But I think Lord Peter Rosing has cured me of stupidity."

"Good." Fenmore took an audibly deep breath, as if he were as fraught as she. "Though I suppose you could not be expected to know what he is."

"No." The admission gave her some small measure—a very small measure—of comfort. "Though if you *did* know what he is, why did you not tell anyone? Why is he still allowed to show his face in polite company? Why was he invited to your grandmother's ball?"

"A mistake." The vehemence was back. "One for which I will never forgive myself. Nor ever make again. And he was *not* invited." He spoke with such low, savage heat, she was taken aback. But his anger was all for himself.

"It wasn't your fault." The words came out of their own volition—a forgiveness she could not grant to herself.

"Wasn't it?" He seemed unconvinced. "I should have anticipated that they would come, even uninvited."

It gave her another small measure of comfort to see him doubt himself. "They?"

"Rosing and his father. Hadleigh."

"I don't see how you could have anticipated that." She was happy to find she could take a rather more normal breath. "My parents would never dream of going someplace they weren't invited."

"Yes, parents. We ought to be getting you back to your mother, so she can take you home."

Yes. She wanted her mother. She wanted to be safe in her arms, and forget this had ever happened. But it had. "We're not meant to go home. We're meant to stay the night, as guests." The worry and doubt and shame and anger wrapped itself ever tighter and tighter. "Oh, God. I don't think I can bear the questions."

"No one will question you. I'll make sure of that."

"Will you?" It was probably not the wisest thing, to allow herself the relief and sanctuary of hope. But she already had.

"Yes." This time the vehemence sounded more like surety. More like a promise.

For which she could only be grateful. "Thank you." Another small measure of comforting relief tiptoed its careful way into her lungs. And she took the opportunity to take a long look at him, this vehement man she had thought so aloof. "Contrary to popular opinion, you *are* a nice man."

A nice man who had crippled Rosing, still splayed upon the pavers.

For her. This time the heat in her chest was something more comforting than mere relief.

But there was still a man on the ground. "We can't just leave him here, can we?"

"Yes. We can. I'm not *that* nice. Someone will find him. In fact—" He came to an alertness, livid with stillness, rather like one of her father's hunting dogs scenting the air. And then he swore. "God's balls. Someone is coming. Now." He turned that implacable gaze upon her. "Lady Claire, you have approximately three seconds to decide what comes next. Stay here and be discovered with Rosing—and bear all the possible and different consequences of that. Or you can come with me."

"What?" Her heart started pounding in her ears again.

Claire pushed off the wall, and found she *needed* to move. To get air back into her lungs. To get away from Rosing. But not back to the house and the ball. Not with her face like this, still scratched and blotted with blood.

Fenmore had crossed to the narrow wooden decking that projected out over the water, and unwound a line to one of the boats from its cleat. "I can take you away in the skiff. We can slip away, out onto the river, with no one the wiser."

The idea was astonishing.

And she was truly astonished. Astonished to find the events and words and feelings of the past few minutes swirling and twisting through her head, trying to sort themselves out into something approaching logic.

Going in a boat with His Grace the Duke of Fenmore would undoubtedly be just as rash and stupid as walking into the garden with Lord Peter had been.

But the Duke of Fenmore was not Lord Peter Rosing. He looked across the narrow dock at her, and he understood. He reached behind his back, under the tail of his beautifully tailored coat, and pulled out an elegant, well-polished pistol. The shifting moonlight glanced off the slick metal barrel as he held it out to her, handle first. "So you'll feel safe. But choose. Now."

Astonishment was too tame a word for the rush of

alarm and something else—something unfamiliar and altogether off-kilter—that gripped her, once more stealing the air from her lungs. "Is it loaded?"

"Yes. Do you know how to use it properly?"

Claire didn't answer. But she did take the gun. Because it gave her her answer.

"Yes." She scrambled into the narrow boat. "Let us go then and escape. Just for a little while, at least. Until I'm ready to come back."

"Yes." The Duke of Fenmore gave her an oddly boyish smile that crinkled up the corners of his eyes, and softened his narrow face, and made him appear young and almost vulnerable. As if he were taking as big a chance as she. "Yes. Just for a little while."

Chapter Two

Tanner wasted no time. Before the rest of the rest-
less energy still coursing through him was spent, he
used it to shuck the detestable gloves that made him
into a gentleman, wrap his itchy hands around the oars,
and slip the skiff out of the boathouse. He pointed
the bow into the stream of the river, and put his back
into it.

With luck, he might be able to get well away before she
discovered his guile in inventing the intruders.

He settled into a steady, hard rhythm, propelling them
smoothly downstream on the slack tide, and calming
the jangling excitement he always got when he'd stolen
something and gotten away clean. He rowed them past
the town on the south bank and toward Richmond Bridge
at a rate designed to carry them well away from the
house for long enough to safely compromise Lady Claire
Jellicoe—albeit in a much more civilized and mani-
festly less criminal manner than the bastard Rosing had
attempted.

Just for a little while.

Because a little while was all it would take. With that
luck he had always been able to count upon—along with

stealth and guile—neither Lady Claire nor her father, the Earl Sanderson, would object when Tanner silenced any hint of scandal by making his very handsome offer for her hand.

But none of this did he share with Lady Claire. He saved his breath to cool his porridge, and acted the gentleman. He let the smooth simplicity of the river work its peace on the still-shaken young lady who gripped the thin rail of the small vessel so tightly the ridges of her knuckles stood out through her gloves.

He wanted to tell her that it would be all right, that she was unharmed and whole and safe. But he knew such empty platitudes were not the truth.

And she wasn't even safe with him. He wasn't a rapist, but he was making his play for her just as surely as that bastard Rosing had.

So Tanner shut his gob, and rowed on for a mile or so downstream. Once past the dark eaves of Richmond Bridge, which marked the end of the town, the only sounds were the steady stroke of the oars, the lapping of the river against the banks, and the thick, peaceful hush of the summer night. There was enough of a moon so that as he sat with his back to the streaming moonlight, his face remained in shadow. He could gaze at her undetected, and watch the luminous oval of her face as the quiet of the river wrapped itself around her.

She sighed as if she were trying to exhale her ordeal from her lungs. "Wouldn't it be lovely if one could always just float away from one's problems so easily?"

"No."

Her bright, wounded gaze sought his through the shelter of the dark. "Why not? Are you so cynical and hard of heart that you wouldn't allow yourself—or me—the kindness of forgetfulness?"

"I am not a cynic. I am a realist. You've still got blood

on your face. And there"—he nudged his chin at her—"on your mouth. His blood, I should think. Did you bite him?"

"Oh, God." Her voice became smaller, hiding, as if she were not at all sure she should admit to such a vicious, unladylike action. "Yes."

He would disabuse her of such a ridiculous notion. "Good. That will mark him. With luck it might fester as well. Bites are notoriously septic things."

Even bites from immaculate young ladies like Lady Claire Jellicoe, who tore off her soiled gloves, and leaned over the gunwale of the narrow vessel as if she were about to shoot the cat. Tanner shipped his oars so he might be ready to assist her if she needed support being quietly sick over the side.

But she did not vomit. She took another deep, shaky breath, and pulled her tattered composure together enough to dunk his handkerchief into the clear, dark water, and apply it to her face.

She closed her eyes as the cool wetness settled against her abraded skin. "I do wish I could just float away. Float away and forget it. As if it never happened."

Tanner heard the hurt and bewilderment in her voice, and made his own gentler. "Then that is what we shall try to do. At least for a little while." He took up the oars again, aiming to take them around the small island that shimmered darkly off the north bank. Beyond the island was nothing but empty countryside of pastures and woods. Too far for them to go this night. "But there is as much danger in forgetting, as there was in not anticipating the trouble in the first place."

But even as he said the words, he knew he liked—no, *liked* was far too tame a word. He idolized—he was *obsessed* with—Lady Claire Jellicoe precisely because she was so sweet and so optimistic and so sunny a person that she could never have conceived of the idea that Rosing could wish her such malicious harm.

Her he could excuse. But others—her father, the earl; her brother the viscount; and all the so-called men of the world who turned a blind eye to Rosing's predations because he was "one of them"—Tanner held accountable. And as for Rosing himself—

Tanner felt the black, icy rage grip him again. He should have killed the bastard. He *would* kill him if given another chance.

Lady Claire Jellicoe was not so decided. She was still trying to sort out the tangle of emotions that looked to be knotting her into a tight, miserable ball. "Yes. I know you're right. But it's just so . . ."

"So hard. Yes."

"Yes." She looked at him, and eased a bit from her cramped posture. "Thank you. For being so understanding. And for bloody well laying him out like an undertaker."

God's balls. Curse words aside, *laying him out like an undertaker* was a turn of phrase so improbable, so cant, and so directly from his own misbegotten youth that Tanner was startled out of his easy rhythm. The idiom was vulgar, street thieves' cant of a sort that an innocent young woman like Lady Claire Jellicoe ought never have even heard. "Where on earth did you learn that sort of talk?"

There, in the wash of moonlight, was the small beginning of a rueful smile—the first smile she had ever smiled for him—pressing up the corners of her lips. "I have brothers."

Tanner did not have brothers, and so did not entirely take her meaning.

But he must have frowned at her, because Lady Claire Jellicoe answered his silence. "I have three brothers, to be exact, and they are full of what my father calls 'buckish slang.' But I like the way they talk. And I liked that they

have always done that sort of thing for me—lay imperti-
nent fellows out like undertakers. My brother Will was
especially good at what one might call personal justice.
Rather like you." She stared at him for a long moment,
before she turned her troubled, wistful face up to the
moon. "But I wish . . . I wish I knew how to do that for
myself. To use my fives, as my brothers say. I had a friend
once . . . one of my sisters-in-law, now. Mrs. Jellicoe, not
the Viscountess Jeffrey, who is also my sister-in-law. Do
you know them—they're sisters? No? Well, she would
have known what to do, Antigone. She would have been
able to stop him, Lord Rosing." Another sigh wrestled its
way out of her lungs. "I couldn't. I couldn't do anything. I
just felt so . . . absolutely powerless. So entirely useless."

Useless. This he understood. It was one of his greatest
fears that somehow, someday, someone was going to find
that *he* was entirely useless—a pretender of a duke. A
sham of a man. An urchin from the streets. Nothing but a
creature of stealth and guile.

Lady Claire Jellicoe wasn't a sham. She was everything he was not. Polished and easy. Elegant and refined.
She belonged to her world in a way he never could, his
exact opposite in every way.

Which was why he idolized her. If she had not existed
precisely the way she was—beautiful and immaculate—he
could not have thought her up and made her any more
ideal.

And yet in the quiet intimacy of the skiff she looked
more real, if such a thing were possible. It was possible,
if only *because* he had idolized her from afar for all
those years—ever since she had turned seventeen and
made her come out—and never before sought to make
her real.

But up close, she looked so much less perfect now,
with her hair coming down from its pins, and the breeze

blowing one or two fine strands loose across her damaged face. It made her more approachable. More human, and fallible, and frail.

Infinitely more beautiful. And more vulnerable.

And that was his fault. He should have found a way to stop Rosing sooner, before the bastard ever set his eyes on Lady Claire Jellicoe, who was now wrapping her arms about her torso, hugging herself. She was shivering in the warm summer air, her skin shining white with gooseflesh in the moonlight.

"You're cold." She might also be suffering from the shock of the bastard's assaulting her like a ravening beast, but the effects were just the same—she was shaking.

Tanner once more shipped the oars, and let the skiff drift where it would on the outgoing tide, while he shucked himself out of his form-fitting evening coat. And then he leaned forward to wrap it carefully around Lady Claire's shoulders.

She let him, and clasped her hands into the coat's lapels gratefully, even as she looked away in embarrassment. "I'm sorry. Thank you. I just feel so . . . so stupid. So inadequate. I don't know what I would have done if you had not come."

He knew exactly what Rosing would have done— which was why Tanner had followed them. He felt the icy rage, the cold, smoldering fury, flare up within him. He leashed it, a power to use later, when he might have need of it. Not now. Not with her. "You would have managed something. You did bite him."

"Yes." Another sigh, but this one was perhaps less forlorn and more resolved. "How clever you are to have noticed that."

Tanner tried not to succumb the bitter thrill of pride welling within his chest. He knew he was clever—it was how he and his sister, who was cleverer still, had stayed alive all those stealthy, guileful years they had prowled the streets. It was why the Admiralty had kept its grappling hooks firmly in him even when he became the duke, using him much as they had his brother-in-law, Hugh McAlden, before him—making the most of his unique, larcenous abilities for the benefit of King, country, and Admiralty with no one the wiser.

But it was strange to find himself the object of Lady Claire Jellicoe's admiration for being so. And for some reason he didn't want to examine too closely, he found himself wanting to impress her even more by his cleverness. "His hand was bloody. Back there on the ground. His palm. Only logical explanation was that you had bitten him. You'd have gone on in the same vein."

"You're being kind again. And I thank you for it." Her voice grew small and tight, and she seemed to shrink into the folds of his coat. "But I'm afraid you're wrong. I don't think I could have done much else." The dark fabric swallowed her up until all he could see was the shining crown of her blond head in the moonlight. "I hate it. I hate feeling so . . . useless. Useless to help myself."

And because Tanner knew exactly what that felt like— the aching, gnawing desperation of having no good choices, or no choices at all—he could not stand for *her* to feel that way. "I could teach you."

Her face turned up toward him, and she looked at him now with the same sort of strange fascination as she had in the boathouse—as if she could not quite allow herself to believe him. "Would you? Would you really?"

"Yes." Tanner heard his voice come out of his mouth, firm and secure. Sure. As if he really could teach an immaculate, innocent young woman like Lady Claire Jellicoe how to defend herself like a brawling, barely civilized street rat. As if he did it every day of the week. "I *could* teach you to take care of yourself. To notice things—the important things—so you're never put in a position like you were with Rosing again."

"Never again," she echoed. And then her face cleared, and she looked once again like his immaculate angel. "I'd like that. I'd like that above all things."

Tanner felt a smile soften the harsh planes of his face. "Good. We can start this moment. Close your eyes."

The directive brought the clouded look back to her face. Then her eyes opened wide, staring and searching in the moonlight for a keener glimpse of him, and her hand strayed toward the sleek gun at her side, her fingertips seeking it out in the dark. "Why?" Her voice was quiet and tight.

"Because I want you to understand how to take in all the information from your surroundings. I want you to understand that you already know things you don't realize you already know." And because she did not answer, but continued to look at him with her doubt all but written across her face, he added, "I promise you no harm. And I am a man of my word."

Lady Claire Jellicoe weighed the merit of his assertion for a long time before she finally said, "Yes, I suppose you are, aren't you? All right." And she did slowly close her eyes.

But, he noticed, she took surreptitious possession of the gun. Clever girl.

He rewarded her for it. "Excellent. And you've already done the first thing to make yourself safer, taking hold of the gun. But the way you're holding it, I can see that you are unfamiliar with firearms. Actually—open your eyes." He shipped the oars and took the gun from her hands. "We'll start with this."

It was both remarkable and, from his point of view, rather criminal that her father, or one of her surplus of brothers had never taught her even the rudiments of shooting. If he did nothing else, he would remedy that.

"This is a Royal Navy, sea service–style flintlock pistol, with flat stepped locks with half-cock safeties, waterproof pans, roller frizzens, and reinforced cocks. Take hold of it firmly—point it away. The gun is loaded. Always point it away from a person—or an animal for that matter—unless you mean to aim it at them. Never aim your gun at anyone or anything which you are not prepared to shoot. And kill. Do you understand?"

"You must have a good deal of experience with guns."

"Yes." He did, in fact, have rather a lot of experience of guns, among other weapons. He had learned how to handle and fire pistols in his short stint in the navy as a boy, and he had fired hunting pieces as part of his later training in the gentlemanly art of shooting. But gentlemen generally didn't carry firearms the likes of his pistol. Or the long knife in his boot.

But he was no gentleman.

And being a lady had only served Lady Claire Jellicoe ill this night.

"It's at half cock, and the frizzen is closed. Which means that it's been loaded and primed. Powder is in the pan, under the pan cover, which is this part of the frizzen, here." He pointed to the striking plate. "That lock mechanism there, the hammer, when toggled back thusly"—he put the weapon into her hand, and closed his own larger fingers around hers, helping her to thumb the cock fully back—"means you're ready to fire."

He would have raised her arm up beneath his, in order to show her how to steady her arm and take aim. But his brain—the intricate, organized, resourceful brain that had seen him through nearly thirty astonishingly full years of use—refused to do his bidding.

Because beneath his palm, her skin was soft. So astonishingly, exceedingly, innocently soft. Softer than morning air. Softer than wonder.

And he could only wonder at how small and delicate and nearly fragile the bones beneath her extraordinary skin felt under the crude, dexterous strength of his hand.

He had never touched her, never been so close to her before. So close the damp, liquid smell of the river faded away, and there was nothing but her. Nothing but orange blossom and lily and rose, and something beyond mere perfume. Something that confused and unhinged and liberated him all at once.

He could have recited the scientific nomenclature for the oxidized alcohols and esters and compounds that gave her orange blossom fragrance the subtle welcoming hint of nutmeg, but he had no words, no knowledge, to combat what the scent of her did to his brain, and how it made him want to do more than cover her hand.

How it made him want to cover her entire body with his own, and feel every delicate bone and sweet muscle within her. How he wanted to explore every elegant sinew, and hold the fey weight of her in his arms, as if he could subsume her into himself. How he wanted to do so with a sudden swiftness that shocked him to his core. And how he knew he would no longer be able to merely worship her from afar.

And so he slid closer to her, down on his knees in front of the stern seat, lifting his elbow over her head so he could line his right arm up with hers, and show her how to sight.

All along the length of his arm, where the linen of his shirtsleeve lay over the material of his own coat covering her, he felt the heat and slight, fine-boned tension of her beneath fanning across his skin.

"And then?"

He felt, more than heard, her quiet question hum into his chest. She was looking up at him, so close the moonlight poured into her eyes, and lit her like a beacon. And he thought he really ought to kiss her.

And then she turned her head sharply away.

God's balls. It was as if he had forgotten what had happened only half of an hour ago. And that there was a gun in his hands. A loaded, primed, and cocked gun, ready to fire.

He was a cad. An armed, dangerous, guileful cad, who was not worthy of her. And he proved it by shutting down all sensation but the feel of her finger under his on the trigger. He squeezed.

Within a second, the slick sound of the flint hitting spark was drowned out in the echoing roar of the deafening explosion as the gun spat its bullet over the still surface of the water, and sped into the dark, silent wood behind the bank.

Her arm gave way immediately—she would have dropped the weapon if he had not held her there, buoyed by his strength and by his resolve to stay there, close to her, as long as possible. As long as she would allow.

But her arm, and indeed her whole body, began to tremble, and he made himself slide away from her, and take up his oars, and let her be.

"There's more to it of course—the need to have a good, well-made lock, and keep a sharp flint, and a well-tempered frizzen, as well as proper loading, priming, and a proper touchhole." He was blathering—something he never did. Or had never done before.

But he had never been so close to Lady Claire Jellicoe before.

Her nearness unhinged him, opening some heretofore-leashed part of his character. She made him a stranger to himself.

She lowered the gun to the seat beside her, and looked at it for a long moment, and he, who saw people think just as clearly as if he were reading a broadsheet, had absolutely no idea of her thoughts.

And so he—who never babbled—babbled on. "Even though the charge is now spent, you can still use the pistol as a weapon, if you take hold of the barrel with a backward grip, so you can backhand the butt of the gun across your attacker's face at a moment's notice if they make the mistake of thinking to act like Rosing."

Which was exactly the wrong thing to say.

She folded herself back into the sanctuary of his coat and turned to look over the water in the direction the gun had fired. "I hope to God I didn't hit anyone, or anything."

They were passing the along the unpopulated expanse of the Old Deer Park, the acres of former Royal hunting grounds that had originally made Richmond a retreat for the nobility.

"Only people in this wood this time of night are poachers." Who might be expected to have earned whatever stray bullets came their way.

Of course, he was contrary enough to have a rather brotherly feeling for the poachers, despite being a duke. Honor among thieves, and all that.

"Thank you for the lesson in shooting." Despite her discomfort, she was nothing if not unfailingly polite.

"I can teach you more." He hoped his offer didn't sound as salacious aloud as did in the depths of his mind.

It must not have, because she brightened a little—a star coming out from behind the night clouds—and said, "What else?"

"Just listen." With another quick glance over his shoulder, he steered the skiff toward the quieter seclusion of the trailing boughs of a tall willow tree that marked the boundary of the Old Deer Park, where the river turned toward the vast Royal Botanic Gardens at Kew.

Which meant that they had already come much farther than he had planned. Which also meant that the tide had begun its ebb, flowing downstream toward the city of

London. But the woods were soft and quiet and peaceful. And she was not ready to go back.

So he plied them along the south bank where an industrious river vole was dragging a green reed into his hole beneath the willow's roots. The trees overhead were full of drowsy insect sounds. "What do you hear?"

In the cathedral-like quiet of the willow trees' sanctuary, the river quieted until to a low gurgle.

"The water," she said. "The river, with the water lapping against the bank. And the night wind, rustling low through the trees."

"Yes. Very good. All information you can use."

"But it sounds the same as when I went out with Rosing. Were the bush crickets supposed to warn me as I went down the lawn? Did I fail to heed their warning?"

"No." He could hear her self-remonstrance and frustration, and understand how little it seemed to make sense to her. "But there were other clues in Rosing's behavior. In his look."

She had opened her eyes and was staring at him now, her eyes wide and velvet dark with something stronger than frustration. "I should have read his intent in his look?"

"Yes." There was no kinder way to say it.

He half-expected her to dissolve into sloppy tears—innumerable women had at his blunt assertions. But even that might be for the good. Many women seemed to believe quite strongly in the efficacy of what they called a good cry.

But she surprised him with her depth of character. "You mean I should have given him greater scrutiny of my own before I accepted his—or rather his father's—invitation to dance, and especially to walk in the garden. I should not have trusted that just because he's the Marquess of Hadleigh's heir he wouldn't be a bloody bounder."

He would have smiled at her cursing if he hadn't been so instantly furious. At Rosing. And at himself. "Yes. Exactly."

Because the truth was that every man was a bounder—himself included. And refined, polite young women were easy targets. It was all the confining codes of ladylike behavior—of always having to be civil and passively polite—that got immaculate, refined young women into such monstrous trouble.

This was one of the twisted coils of his obsession with her—the innocence he adored in her was what had made her unsafe.

Perhaps she was thinking the same, for she pleated her forehead into an angelic frown. "I should have paid attention to his hands. They were clenched into fists, I think, opening and closing in . . . anticipation before he took my arm. I thought perhaps he was nervous around me. Men often are."

That fucking, fucking bastard. Tanner should have killed him when he had the chance. Planning, all the time he had this exquisite young woman in his arms on the dance floor, to defile her. "Excellent observation."

"And now that I think on it, his breathing was strange. Exercised. I think I thought him out of breath from the dance. But I wasn't out of breath—it was an easy country dance. And you're not breathing hard, even though you are exercising. You're breathing evenly, in and out, even as you do all the work to ply the oars."

Tanner tried to muffle the deep sound of satisfaction her observation startled out of him. She wasn't meant to notice him—no one ever noticed him. He was the one who was meant to notice others. He was the one who was meant to pass unseen. She had certainly never *seen* him before. If her eyes had ever alit upon him, it was only in mistake, for she would look past him, or turn away, or step so that some piece of architecture, or the voluminous plumage of a matron's turban blocked her vision.

But now Lady Claire Jellicoe was noticing him, and it made him feel the need to draw air deep, deep into his lungs. It made the muscles of his arms sing with awareness, and made the skin of his palms itch against the smooth handles of the oars.

Tanner took a hard stroke to exercise such demons, and turn the skiff. It was time he took them back. Past time.

They had been away more than long enough to effectively compromise her. And long enough for her to start to trust him, so that when his offer was made, she would at least consider it in a favorable light.

And he would also need to get back to deal with Rosing before anyone else found him.

Lady Claire gripped the rail of the skiff as they turned. "Are we going back to— Oh!"

They both had to grapple for balance as the skiff rammed into something. Something large that floated out from a small side eddy of flotsam, mixed with toppled branches, and made a small dam of sorts.

"What on earth was that?" Lady Claire's breathless query sounded as if it were from far away.

Because Tanner had turned on his thwart to peer hard over his shoulder, and identify the obstruction. And he saw the one thing he had not prepared himself for this evening.

A sodden tangle of clothing.

Floating facedown in the river.

A body.

Quite, quite dead.

Chapter Three

His Grace the Duke of Fenmore let out an oath so blue Claire felt the tips of her ears turn crimson.

It brought the fear back, hollowing out her chest. "Your Grace! What was that?"

He was turned away, leaning over the side. But his voice came back to her, low and clear. And as chilly and relentless as ever. "It's a body."

Claire was sure she would have gasped if she had been able to draw breath. She couldn't manage to make a sound over the fresh horror throttling down her throat. Cold slid under her skin leaving a trail of tingling gooseflesh.

His Grace must have taken her silence for misunderstanding. He turned to look back at her and clarified, "A dead body. A woman's."

"No. Yes." Claire had to put her hand over her mouth to keep from spilling any more nonsensical idiocy in the face of such tragedy. Her hand shook against her mouth, trembling and cold. Cold like the water, and the night air, and every part of her. And then panic flared, hot and burning. "Oh, God. Did *I* shoot her?"

"No. I am quite sure—" His Grace looked away, and then back at her again, those disconcertingly unreadable eyes of his glinting in the shaded moonlight. And his mouth was curving. "You did not."

"Are you— Are you smiling?" She could hear both horror and outrage in her voice.

"Apologies." There was self-censure in his voice, but the grim little grin didn't leave his face.

"You *are* smiling." Her voice was all accusation now. "Are you glad? Are you *mad*?"

"No. I am outraged." He said it simply, as if it were a cold, commonplace fact, and not heated ice in his voice. "Just like you."

"Then why are you smiling?" He *was* such a strange, faraway man. He made no sense whatsoever.

"Because this—this dead girl—is something I know how to do something about. Because there are no coincidences." His voice held more than vehemence. It held conviction. "Now, I'm afraid we can't leave her in the water. I'm going to take her on board. Can you help to balance the boat while I do so?"

"I— Yes." Claire grasped the rails obediently. She would do anything he asked, so long as she didn't have to touch, or even look at the body.

At the woman. The poor dead woman.

Unlike her, His Grace the Duke of Fenmore was calm and composed, and surprisingly competent at heaving a dead woman out of the water with a minimum amount of fuss. Surprisingly because Claire would never have thought the man who propped up ballroom walls with such aloof disinterest could be so capable.

But there was nothing aloof about him now as he worked the sodden, lifeless bundle into the bow of the skiff. His Grace was all lean shoulders, long arms, and efficient sinew beneath his shirtsleeves. He was a different-looking fellow out of his coat, and his now-wet shirtsleeves revealed arms more like a stableman's than a duke's—all flesh and blood and bone. Competent flesh and bone.

He arranged the drowned woman's body with as much dignity as possible in the bow of the boat, and turned to impart another cold fact to Claire. "She was not shot. You may rest easy on that score." His Grace regained his seat and took up the oars. "But we will have to head back immediately. It will be difficult with the added weight, with the tide already pulling the other way—"

He looked grim and accountable, just as he had in the boathouse—the boathouse, where Lord Peter Rosing might still lie. "Yes, of course. But perhaps there is someplace for us to dock other than the boathouse?"

He did not take her meaning. "I need to take the body where she can be properly examined, and I can learn more than is already evident."

Cold skittered down her arms. His Grace of Fenmore shocked her again, and again. "What do you mean, '*examined*'? What is already evident?"

He sent her another one of his inscrutable, obsidian looks before he explained. "She is a young woman, between the age of fifteen and perhaps twenty. Young, unlined face, despite the effects of the time spent in the water upon her skin."

The effects of the time spent in the water upon her skin. The detailed observation was nearly too much for Claire. Cold heat raced up her throat. She swallowed hard against the rising bile, and tried to draw in some air.

But the duke seemed impervious. He went on methodically. "Her hands are rough with work, but from the little I could see in this light, her nails were trimmed—although the nails on her right hand are broken at the tips. The skin on her hands and forearms, as well as her face, is pale, although that could be the water. Or alternately indicating that she wasn't out of doors much. Her clothing is plain, also suggesting a working life, but she is well nourished, indicating she probably worked as a household servant somewhere where regular meals were part of her compensation. This conjecture is bolstered by her clothes— clean, with no trace of food stains—and her shoes: half boots, well kept, but with well-worn soles. Someone on her feet most of the day, but inside. Ergo an upper servant in one of the houses along the river."

"All that, in less than a minute? In the dark?" How on earth could he guess so much?

"It isn't hard, even in the relative dark, if one knows what to look for."

His words were sinking in. "A servant girl? Like the maids at Riverchon Park?" She herself had been assigned a lovely young girl to work as her maid for the duration of her stay in the manor house. A lovely, chatty girl who had worked wonders on Claire's hair, making it shine to perfection. She would never forget what the girl had said to her: *Oh, miss, you look ready to break hearts.*

It seemed strangely prophetic now. Except it had been Claire's heart, as well as her face, that was broken.

The boat moved out of the shadow, the moon moved out from behind some nebulous cloud, and for one stark moment the pale moonlight washed over the bow of the skiff, illuminating the dead woman's face.

And Claire saw her—the *girl*.

"Oh, dear God." A burst of pinpricks scattered under her skin and sharpened into a hundred points of horror. "That's her. That's Carter. Maisy Carter."

And Claire was off the seat, and reaching for the duke, unthinkingly grasping his shoulder to steady herself and look behind him, taking an awful, unbelieving look at the eerily pale body glistening in the moonlight. "Oh, my

God. It is her. It's the maid I was given, Maisy Carter. What an awful, horrible coincidence."

His Grace abandoned his oars, and steadied Claire with one hand to her elbow, and another to her hip, strong and sure. But he said, "I don't believe in coincidence."

Despite his steadying hand, Claire felt her legs give way beneath her. Her knee cracked into the bench, and the pain in her leg bled upward into the aching pain in her chest. "What do you mean?"

His Grace shook his head as if it pained him to have to enlighten her. But his voice was sure. And uncompromising. "I believe in patterns and habits and vices that led people astray. Very far astray. I wasn't sure I recognized her in this light. Are you sure? How well did you know her?"

The light touch of his hand atop hers where she still clutched his shirtsleeve was a kind rebuke—a reminder to let go. She pushed herself back into her seat in the stern.

"I didn't really. She was assigned to be my maid, at Riverchon Park. I didn't bring my own with me from town. She had the toothache, Silvers—my own abigail, who sees to me always. So I left her behind, so she might see to the tooth while we were away. And Carter was assigned to me, when I arrived, yesterday." The poor, poor girl. The cold horror was dissolving into hollow, aching sorrow. "She helped me get dressed, and put up my hair."

The duke squeezed her hand, this time a kind reassurance, as if he would give her some of his insistence and vehemence. "When did you last see her? Exactly?"

"This evening, before dinner. Just before I—before we all—went down to the drawing room. You were there." He had stood to one side of the room, haughty and inscrutable, ignoring her as she rushed in just as a tall case clock chimed the hour. "What time was that?"

"The dinner was at eight." He looked neither haughty nor inscrutable now. He looked alive in a way she had never seen before while he loomed from ballroom walls. He looked like a Renaissance painting of a saint transfixed in the grip of some holy quest—seeking God's justice.

"Then just before eight. She had finished my hair earlier, but then came back to help me into my dress. Fresh pressed." The fabric had still been warm from the iron. "She told me I looked—" Claire broke off, chagrined that His Grace, the perfect Duke of Fenmore, might think her silly and vain and self-absorbed when she was alive with only scratches on her face, and poor Maisy Carter was white and still and so very, very dead. "She made me a very pretty compliment. And I said the credit was all to her."

"It's nearing one o'clock now. But I can't really tell how long she's been in the water."

"Oh, heavens. Has it gone so late as that?" She had not meant to stay away for so long, only to get away for a brief while, to recover. But she oughtn't be thinking about herself at such a time, when poor Carter was drowned and dead in the bow of the boat.

"Yes," the duke answered in the same grave tone. "And it's going to be much longer now, I'm afraid. I don't think we ought to go back to Riverchon." He worked one of the oars to reverse their direction, and send them gliding once again downstream. "We need to go to Chelsea."

"Chelsea?" Claire was beyond flabbergasted, even as she watched the dark ribbon of the river begin to spool by. "Why on earth can't we take her back to Riverchon Park? The staff there, the housekeeper, will know who her people are, and what's to be done for her. Don't you think?"

"No. We're not going back to Richmond." He repeated

the words between hard strokes at the oars, clearly putting his back into it, as if his simple obstinacy would convince her. "I can't explain it." And then he reversed himself. "Instinct. I need to keep you away from Riverchon. Safe. We're going to Chelsea."

This time Claire did not even try to stop the sound of distress and shock that flew out of her throat. "But that's miles and miles downriver—that's practically to London," she sputtered. She'd had no idea of staying away so long. She'd no idea of anything at the time they came away. She'd only wanted some escape. "Do you mean to row all that way? On our own?"

She realized the moment she said the words how ridiculous she must sound—like the petted, pampered, buffered daughter of privilege she had only just an hour ago lamented herself.

But though His Grace of Fenmore looked at her steadily with those obsidian eyes of his he said nothing in condemnation, only, "An hour or two, no more. It will be safer. And easier than going back to Richmond on this tide."

As if it were just a decision about the tide and not about her life. She could hear in his voice that he meant well, but Richmond was where her family was. Richmond was where she needed to return. "But— Why?"

"The average speed of the tidal flow in the Thames—"

"No!" For the first time she cut His Grace off—obsidian gazes and aloof, haughty looks be damned. "Why Chelsea, of all places?" She'd never been there in her life. Never been anywhere without either her parents or brothers or abigail for accompaniment. Never been alone with a gentleman for more than a few moments when already she and His Grace had clearly been away for over an hour. The consequences—

The consequences were too much to even contemplate.

It was all too much—Lord Peter Rosing and the brick wall. His Grace and the dead body. The night had gone from horrible to horrific.

"Lady Claire, you'll be safe in Chelsea. There is a house there, where we can go, to examine the body properly. To see what we can determine about how she died."

"How she died?" The cold, creeping horror slid back under Claire's skin. "But she drowned, didn't she? We found her floating in the river."

He shook his head, calm and implacable. "The river is where we found her body. But it tells us nothing of how she died, nor how her body came to be in the water. We have as yet no evidence to support the supposition that she died by drowning. For all we know, she could have been dead before someone dumped her in the river. Indeed, from what little I can ascertain at the moment, her lungs don't appear—"

Evidence? Supposition? Dumped? Claire felt bombarded by shock after cold shock. She ached from the effort of holding herself together. "Do you mean 'on purpose'?"

His Grace did not try to soften the weight of the blow. "Yes. On purpose."

"My God." This time the tight heat in her throat was both horror and outrage—anger at everything that seemed to be happening on this too-eventful evening. At everything that she could not control. The world had gone mad around her. "Who would do such a thing to a poor lady's maid?"

"I do not know. But I will find out." He shook his head and rowed on, casting his gaze out over the dark gunmetal gleam of the river, as sure and implacable as death itself.

"How?" It was impossible. There was no way to tell what might have happened to poor Carter. Not unless someone had seen something. And they could not tell that without going back, and calling the magistrate. What on earth did His Grace think he could do alone? And in Chelsea?

His Grace was unperturbed by the prospect. Though his eyes were as dark as the night, they burned with conviction. "I have my ways."

She believed him. Even though she was not sure she wanted to. "How?" she asked again.

"With science. And questions. For example, do *you* think she cast herself into the water? That she was a suicide?"

Claire would have gasped again if she had any breath left to be surprised. But surprise seemed to be the order of the hour with His Grace of Fenmore. She was nearly reeling from the force of each of his increasingly blunt pronouncements. But this bluntness seemed to be his way.

"No." Claire tried to pull her thoughts together in some semblance of order. "She was, from what I could tell—I had her to help me only yesterday and today, from our arrival to the hour before dinner, just before the ball—a brisk, skilled, intelligent girl. Unassuming. A true Christian, she had a small cross, a gift, she said, from her former mistress before she came to Riverchon, on a necklace around her—" Claire made a gesture to her own throat before she forced herself to go on. "Around her neck. And she was kind. Sweet. Very kind."

His Grace glanced briefly over his shoulder at poor Carter. "It is not currently evident. But we shall look for it when we examine the body."

"We?" The air squeaked out of her lungs.

"There is a surgeon there in Chelsea, a friend of mine at the Royal Hospital, who can perform a postmortem. Don't you see? We have to know." His Grace seemed impatient with explanations—he shook his head as he answered—as if he thought she were deflecting him from his purpose. He immediately asked his own question: "What was her demeanor when she attended you? Was she dispirited in any way that you could see?"

Claire was too relieved not to be included in the "we" to take umbrage at his insistent tone, and she had rather think of anything besides the ominous-sounding postmortem. "Dispirited? No. I would say that she was warm, and attentive. She smiled, and complimented me. She said she was right pleased with the way I looked. Said she wished her young man—one of the footmen, she said—could see her looking like that. But she meant no harm—she was no more than she should be. I wouldn't want you to think—" Claire wasn't sure what she wanted the Duke of Fenmore to think about Maisy Carter. Or about her.

But there seemed to be no stopping the duke's thinking. "So in the hours before her death she was not unhappy?"

"No. She was smiling in that soft way that girls have when—" Claire heard her own voice growing warm and ridiculous, and stopped herself. But she would not let the chilly and aloof Duke of Fenmore discompose or embarrass her. Not when she suspected he really was a very nice, kind man behind all the glower and off-putting questions. "The way they look when they are in love. Real love that's reciprocated, and not a sham. It's easier for other people, servants and the like, to find that. It's different for people like . . ." She almost said "us." "For a person like me. A person with family expectations."

"Very different." He nodded in understanding. "But the important thing is that young ladies who are not unhappy do not kill themselves on the spur of the moment by casting themselves into rivers. And even those who are unhappy, and have great reason to be unhappy, do not often do so." His gaze founds hers in the glittering dark. "You didn't."

"No." Her chin came up in agreement—instinct, she reckoned, or those hundreds of years of inherited Jellicoe pride—as an antidote to that unhappiness, the fear, that still skittered up and down her body like an ill wind. "I wouldn't. And she doesn't strike me as someone who would either."

"No. You wouldn't. Even though you were brutally assaulted, you never would have thought of killing yourself." The conviction was back in his tone.

It was either disconcerting or strangely comforting to hear him speak so plainly and so surely of her—of thoughts to which he could not be privy. She was no saint. "No. Although I did think of killing Rosing. I wished I could. Only I had no means, or method."

His smile was small and somehow understanding—a secret communication he shared with her, alone. "So did I—think of killing him. I *did* have the means. And any number of lethal methods. But I did not do so either. Because we are not animals, you and I."

He made the statement with his usual blunt speed, but he looked at her very carefully. Hopefully. As if he were giving her some sort of examination she was not sure she was ready to pass.

She could only answer with the truth. "No. Not animals. We can choose."

He had chosen to cripple Rosing, quite deliberately, he had said. And she had chosen to come with him, making herself complicit in that choice.

His Grace had been looking at her as they talked—indeed how could he not when he faced her not more than three feet away?—but his attention was fully upon her now. She could feel the weight of his focus press against her chest, like a physical thing. "So we can. And so can you. You can help me, Lady Claire Jellicoe. You can choose to come to Chelsea with me, and help me find who killed Maisy Carter."

The skiff slid into the matte black shadow of Kew Bridge, poised above them, and a moment came again— the same feeling of breathless suspension, of the air inside her growing flat and still, just as it did before a summer storm. Just as it had in the moment before she had followed the Duke of Fenmore into the skiff. The moment she had chosen to put herself into his power.

For a little while, she had told herself then—a temporary solution. But she could not tell herself the same comforting lie, now. Chelsea was a long way ahead of them on the other side of Putney Bridge. Although the ball at Riverchon House could reliably be counted upon to go on through the wee small hours of the morning, she would have passed all that time alone, with the Duke of Fenmore—handsome, aloof, and appealingly vehement.

The truth was, she had already made her decision. Perhaps she really did have a penchant for the dangerous.

"Yes," Claire said before she could let herself regret it, and slip back into wanting to be pampered and cosseted and buffered. "Yes. I will help you. Just as you helped me."

"Pledged." He said the word, and then rested both oars in one hand while he reached forward, offering his hand to shake. "Upon my honor, I do pledge it."

Chapter Four

There wasn't much between Richmond and Chelsea but twelve-odd miles of meandering water and dark, tree-lined banks. Lady Claire Jellicoe became quiet and watchful, so Tanner kept his own counsel, and used his breath and strength to propel the skiff silently onward. By the time they passed beneath the dark arched spans of Putney Bridge, his back and arms began to feel the strain of the long spell at the oars.

But his mind was still fresh—still ticking over each word that she had spoken, each action that she had chosen to make.

She had chosen to stay with him.

But ought he have made it more obvious that by choosing to stay with him, she was choosing him in another way? That she was choosing to stay with him for good—with him as her all but pledged husband? Indeed he had given her his pledge, as solemnly and reverently as if he had been standing at an altar.

When she spoke, her thoughts seemed more prosaic. "You row well."

The observation startled him—he could not accustom himself to the feeling of being watched. But it was not unpleasant, her awareness of him. And it was only natural that she fall back upon the sort of social pleasantries and compliments at which she excelled.

"Thank you." And it was a rare thing to be complimented with sincerity. In his role as Duke of Fenmore he had grown too used to obsequious flattery and empty compliments from those who sought to curry his favor. He had grown to distrust others' opinions, though he could remember as a child an almost hunger for praise, first from his sister, and then from the captain, the man who would become her husband and Tanner's brother-in-law.

In the years since those days, it seemed Tanner had grown hard as well as watchful.

So he tried to be something less hard, something more approachable and forthcoming, to this girl whom he meant to marry—or at least offer to marry—at the end of the night. "Took it up when I was at school. First at Eton. Then at Oxford."

His savage pride would not permit him to tell her he had only taken up rowing at Eton because it was the one gentleman's sport he could manage without wanting to break someone's face. And the fact that he had been banned from other sports *for* breaking someone's face. But it had suited him perfectly, the relentless drive and determination to outrow all the others. And hurtling himself backward at speed, not seeing where he was going, had seemed an apt metaphor for his changed life.

But there was something else behind her simple compliment. Something in the wistfulness he thought he heard in her voice. And in the fitful moonlight he could have sworn he saw something like the pinch of envy on her normally angelic face. Not envy of *him,* but . . . "Would you like to give it a try? I could teach you."

Both her pleasure and her reticence were instantly palpable in her quick exhalation of breath and in the way she hesitated for a long moment before she overcame whatever qualms were holding her back. "Are you sure? It seems a little strange to— It seems a little strange with poor Carter there behind you."

He gave Lady Claire an excuse: "I could use a rest. At least for a little while. Here." He shifted over on the narrow thwart to give her room to sit adjacent to him. And in another moment she was seating herself carefully next to him. And he could feel the slight, febrile heat of her body all along his side in a way that made him feel strange and feverish and young again.

Young because the last time he could remember feeling so physically close to another person had been back when he and his sister had lived on their own, in cold rented rooms in one dingy part of the city or another— huddling together before bare hearths, and sleeping tumbled up like dogs to find some small measure of warmth and comfort.

But he was no longer twelve years old and Lady Claire Jellicoe was definitely not his sister. She was everything warm and everything comfortable in a way that was both discomfiting and remarkably easy. Her small, fine-boned shoulders seemed to fit just so against the curve of his biceps, and the delicate scent of her perfume filled his head like an opiate, rendering him young and eager and ridiculous, unable to govern either his mind or his body, which responded to her proximity with an almost-overwhelming confusion, as if he had been tumbled up by a wave.

But he was not Rosing, to let his brain be overcome by ungovernable desires. He was not an animal.

He had learned what it was to be a gentleman.

But his gentleman-like mind did not seem to want to communicate the set of steps his clever brain had instantly sorted out. The instruction simply wouldn't come, so he settled for saying only, "Watch me. Take the oar like so, and just follow my lead."

She copied his motions easily, so in another moment he turned both oars over to her, and retreated to her seat so he could give himself both the relief of distance and the pleasure of watching her. Relief because he felt as if he were electrified, like the people at demonstrations of the Royal Philosophical Society electroscope machines, with their hair standing on end—all prickling awareness. And pleasure because she was naturally graceful, rowing smoothly; but she wasn't used to the physical exertion, and soon had to rest her oars for a long moment.

For a quiet moment, they drifted along. Until she said, "You remind me of my brother."

A scoffing huff escaped him. He didn't want to to be compared to Lady Claire Jellicoe's brother the viscount any more than he wanted to compare her to his sister.

But she surprised him again. "No. He's quite wonderful, my brother Will. Quite out of the ordinary way of men, who never seem to want to let a woman do anything on her own." Her face eased into a small, private smile. "And like you, he is a realist. He's a ship's captain."

Tanner supplied the facts about her second brother without having to think. "Royal Navy. Decorated at Trafalgar and promoted to post captain last spring in consequence of the renewed threat of Napoléon's return to power, as well as meritorious conduct in several sundry victories. Received more recent acclaim for victory in the Gulf of Guinea action against slavers off St. Matthew." His mind was still occupied with the other part of what she said—the part about him letting her do things on her own.

"Fancy you should know all that."

He didn't want to appear to be keeping track of her and her family, memorizing details that were none of his busi-

ness. Like the fact that she was born on a Monday—as fair
of face as the folk rhyme would have it. So he supplied an
excuse. "I read the newspapers."

"So do I." And then she amended, "After James—he's
my other brother, Viscount Jeffrey. Do you know him?
After he reads them first, and makes sure there's nothing
in there about Will being dead, or maimed, or something
else equally horrible."

He saw her discomfort in the hunching of her shoulders inside his oversize coat, and he heard the quiet fear
that lived inside her obvious love for her family.

It nearly shocked him, to see the burden of worry settle over her. He had gotten too used to imagining her as
his ideal—perfect and untouched by the same cares as
the rest of the writhing world. But she wasn't immune to
such care. She had grown up in a country that had been at
war all her life. And she'd had a much-loved brother who
had been actively engaged in that war throughout much
of her childhood.

While Tanner had only been at war with the world, in
one way or another, almost every day of his life. "I understand," was all he could say.

"Do you?" She was looking at him again, her eyes
searching through the night.

"When I was a lad I served a very short and not entirely
successful term in His Majesty's Royal Navy myself. I
know my sister worried for me, the way you must do for
your brother."

"Yes. Did you? A duke sent to sea?" She shook her head
again. "How irregular. Did you run away then, to go to
sea?"

"No." The idea was laughable. His whole youth had
been spent as a sort of a runaway, but his stint in the navy
had been an instance of running *toward* something for
once. "I wasn't always a duke."

Lady Claire Jellicoe let out her own huff of patent disbelief. "Nonsense. Even if you were not yet the duke, you were the heir. The heir hardly ever gets to choose a military career nowadays."

"I didn't know I was the heir. My father had been estranged from his family." He parceled out his history in small bites, waiting for her moment of enlightenment. It had been over fifteen years since the Fenmore scandal had been the talk of the *ton*.

But she did not say, "Oh, yes, of course." She still frowned at him. "What do you mean, 'estranged'?"

"My father rejected the dukedom. He left his father, and all his claim to Fenmore for the church, and made a different kind of life. He made a new family, with my mother. And us. But then my father and mother died, and we were orphaned—my sister and I—and left on our own. In London. Without a real home. Without any money. We lived like beggars in the streets." The memories of those days were growing hazier now with every passing, well-fed day, though he worked assiduously to remember. To never forget.

Never forget the years of hunger. Never forget the years of hard, lonely change from one life to another. Never forget the years of slights and snide, cutting remarks.

But he was a man now, and meant to put away childish, resentful thoughts. "We managed."

But the expression on Lady Claire Jellicoe's face was one of fresh grief. "Without your family? How cruel."

He averted her pity by investing his voice with indifference. "I thought everyone knew our scandalous story. How my sister was discovered by my grandmother, the dowager duchess, at a ball."

"No." She shook her head, and frowned with sympathetic distress. "I had no idea."

"How old are you?" It was rhetorical question—he knew

to the day how old she was. But now that he was in the process of stealing her for his bride it came to him for the first time that the years might be a concrete and unbridgeable gulf—a yawning chasm between them.

And not just the years. The hunger and the slights. The savage, ungovernable pride and the cutting, unforgiving intellect. Too much experience. He was a man with a sordid, scandalous past.

She was innocent, and young in so very many ways.

"Nearly twenty." But her voice told him she did not regard her age as young. She turned her face to the side, and although it was too dark for him to see any evidence of heat, he thought he heard something of discomfort in her admission.

He thought to supply her with an explanation. "You are too young to have remembered our old scandal."

"I'm not young." She shook her head again, not disagreeing with him, but unhappy. She kept her eyes averted. "Not at all. I'm getting old." There was more than discomfort in her voice now—there was a sort of private mortification. Her next admission was no more than a whisper. "That's probably what led me to letting Lord Peter Rosing talk me into the dark."

Ah. Desperation. This he understood. This he knew as well as he knew hunger and pride.

How strange and how unfair he had been to think her remote, high upon a pedestal, untouched by the craven cares of the world, when she suffered from the temporal, grasping needs of their world as much as he. He had done her—done them both—a grave injustice.

But the long length of the soft night stretched before them, giving him time. Time to bridge the divide. Time to assuage the desperation.

Time to make her love him.

* * *

His Grace said nothing more, but took over for her when her too-soft hands became sore. He propelled them unerringly down the dark ribbon of the river, and on into the night. Claire had liked that little transfer of places, that moment when, for whatever reason and however briefly, he had held her hand again.

His touch had been sure and strong, and calming and kind. And in that moment she had felt that she was doing the right thing, the correct thing—the very thing that she ought do—in going with him. It was the least she could do for poor Maisy Carter.

And however dangerous he might be, the Duke of Fenmore made her feel safe.

But as the night cooled and the damp rose she could not help but second-guess her choice. A low, silvery mist seemed to roll off the dark banks, catching the moonlight and illuminating the night with pale, ghostly light. Illuminating His Grace the Duke of Fenmore, who looked altogether different up close—bending forward and then away with every stroke—than she had always pictured him. He was handsome, in an austere sort of way—all long, lean, relentless strength. All sharp cheekbones arcing across his face, all shadow and high relief. All penetrating obsidian eyes.

But his cool, nearly haughty looks were a visible contradiction to the warm, if vehement, compassion of the man.

And she was sure now that the vehemence was compassion. His kindness had been evident in everything he had done, every movement he had made toward her. And why else would he be rowing them all the way to Chelsea? For a dead maid? Why else would he have helped her—saved her from Rosing—if he were not absolutely filled with a very human, gentlemanly compassion?

How strange that she'd never suspected him of such tender feelings, never sensed any sort of deeper emotion in the silent, stoic man.

Who kept them moving silently, efficiently onward. In a few more strokes, the tree-lined banks of open farmland began to give way to more and more buildings, hulking shadows in the mist. Lights began to be visible on the north bank, wavering over the water. And then out of the fog the thin, rickety span of a footbridge loomed high overhead. "Are we there—Chelsea?"

"Battersea." With one quick glance over his shoulder, His Grace angled the boat toward the illuminated steeple of a church shining dimly in the watery distance. "Though Chelsea is not much further."

He rowed on until they neared the north bank, where a dark stair jutted out into the silvery water, leading upward onto the dark embankment. In another few minutes, he laid them smoothly alongside.

Claire looked up at the brown bank hulking out of the mist above, and tried to overcome the creeping unease chilling her skin and making the pale, fine hairs on her arms stand up. She'd never had the occasion to venture so far south of the city as Chelsea. She'd never wanted to. The name alone was anathema to her ears. It brought to mind the hospital there—full of maimed old pensioners, like the one-legged man who leaned on buildings on the corners of Oxford Street, holding out his hat for passing pennies.

The uncomfortable shiver seeped under her skin and into her bones. All she could think when she saw one of them—the maimed men—was that, but for the grace of God, her brother Will, who was in His Majesty's Royal Navy still, might have been one of them. Might *yet* be one of them.

She knew Will came down here, to the hospital, when he was in town—part of his duty to visit armless friends and legless comrades who had served in his crews.

But she was giving way to worry and an excess of sensibility, for His Grace had also served in the navy, it seemed, and he still had all his long, sinewy arms and legs, moving out of the boat, and onto the steep stone steps with a lithe, fluid agility that still surprised her.

He tied off the lines and came back to crouch down next to the boat, and take up the pistol she had left on the seat. "This is where we disembark." He held out his hand to assist her, as if he could sense her unease.

Claire could only hope the darkness hid the heat in her face. But still she hesitated, putting off the moment as long as possible. "Yes. Shall I get out then? Or ought I to keep the skiff steady again, so you might get the— So you might get her out more easily?"

"Ah." His quick brows showed his surprise. He cocked his head a bit, as if he were trying to see her from a different angle. "Good thinking. Yes. In a moment. But first, let me reload—and teach you how to load—this gun."

He took the pistol up with his long fingers, and turned it in his hand. The dull gleam of gunmetal winked wickedly in the clouded moonlight.

"I've measures of powder ready for priming." He reached into the folds of the coat she still wore, and pulled out a small sueded leather roll, much like the one in which her mother kept her jewelry when she traveled. His Grace's articulate fingers unfolded the leather to reveal cleverly organized little compartments with all the necessities.

He took up a small square of chamois, and wiped down the pistol's mechanism while he talked. "I have twists of paper with pre-measured amount of powder, as well as wadding"—he pulled the lock to half cock, and tapped the powder out of the paper twist; then he plucked a small piece of fabric out of the pouch, placed it over the end of the bore, and thumbed a lead ball in behind it, before tamping it down with the short ramrod—"and priming powder."

He tipped the brass tube into the firing mechanism and pushed the cover down onto the pan before he held the loaded pistol out to her in the palm of his hand. Like a particularly lethal gift.

All in less time than it would take for her to clean her teeth, or pull the pins from her hair. His competence in this, as in the other things he had already done that night, left her confounded. What an extraordinary duke he was proving to be.

"You can load it the next time."

Claire wasn't sure if she liked the sound of that—the surety that there would be another time they would need this skill, and this pistol, this night. "Is Chelsea really that dangerous?"

"One never knows. You'll have to carry the stick—to have at the ready, and keep well shut of the nypers and foysters—while I carry the body."

"Nippers and . . . foysters?" Was this buckish slang, of the sort her brothers used when they didn't know she was listening?

But the duke's cadence and ease sounded nothing like her brothers—he slid the words on like a well-worn shirt. "Nypers be thieves who might think to steal it."

Claire sent another wild glance into the surrounding mist. "Nypers be thieves? Are we like to be set upon?"

"Not if I can help it." This, however, seemed to give him some pleasure or humor, for his mouth curved again into that small, almost-secret half smile before he turned that penetrating stare of his on the dark beneath the stairs. "Cry beef there."

At that cryptic direction, a quiet, almost-disgusted voice piped up from behind the shadowy wooden slats. "You needn't rag, Tanner. It's only me."

"Ah." His Grace's smile slid sharply upward. "I'll tip you a scrope to watch the paddler whilst we're afoot. And another to keep your red rag stowed."

"Done," came the swift, low answer. "I'm no peach."

"Right so," the duke answered. And then he slanted that secret smile at Claire. "Friends are everywhere if you know how to look for them. You steady the boat. I'll get the girl."

It was as if he were a different man—a different man entirely from the aloof duke in the ballroom. Even different from the kind friend of the boat. He sounded to Claire's untutored ears as if he were quite at home. At ease in cryptic chats with thieves, and transporting a corpse across a dark city in the dead of night. It took him only a moment to collect poor Carter's lifeless body up in his arms, and then, with a sharp nod in Claire's direction, he set off up the stairs.

Claire clambered onto the bottom of the stairs in his wake, but found herself reluctant to leave what felt like the sanctuary of the boat. Which was silly. Because she did not particularly want to remain, alone on the misty riverside with whoever was sheltering under the stair. But neither was she ready to discover exactly what the bloodless word *postmortem* might mean.

And in his omniscient way, he saw her hesitation. "Lady Claire? I'll keep you safe, but you'll want to keep close. It's not a particularly unsavory neighborhood, but neither is it savory."

"Yes. I understand." But still she didn't move, hovering on the cusp of the decision. Feeling it would be irrevocable.

"The mudlark will keep a close eye on the skiff, Lady Claire. And this may take . . . some time."

Some time more than they had spent away already.

Claire could only hope her reputation could withstand the blow if the truth of the evening came out. The duke had said that no one would talk. And he had kept all of his promises, so far.

And in the grand scheme of the night, she was alive. Poor Maisy Carter was not.

And Claire wanted to have something more than a penchant for the dangerous. She wanted to have that agile competence. This was her chance to be brave. Braver than she ever had before.

Claire gathered her resolve, as if it were His Grace's coat, still wrapping her in its comfort and protection, and firmed her grip on the pistol. "I understand."

His Grace gave her his quick almost smile—a pleased tug at one corner of his mouth. "All right then? Are you ready?"

She swallowed her trepidation. "Yes."

"Good. Then follow me." And away he went into the mist.

Claire had to shove her arms through the overlarge sleeves of His Grace's coat so she could gather up her long skirts to hurry after him. But when she reached the level of the embankment, he had paused in a crouch, waiting for her, and looking around—though how he could see anything in the eerily shifting, rising damp from the river, she did not know. But he was absolutely still, and in another moment she realized he was listening, gathering information from the sounds, just as he had urged her to do earlier.

She made herself crouch down, and listen with him, and found herself sorting out the sounds. The regular lap of the river against the bank was there, but there were city sounds now, as well—the creak of a door being opened, and the splash of a bucket being emptied onto the street, followed by the closing of the door. The low rumble of a carriage off somewhere. The thin scrape of a fiddle even farther away.

"Right then." His Grace shifted poor Carter's body up and over his shoulder, and then nodded to Claire. "Hold close."

He set off across the dirt street at a steady but fast pace, moving purposefully, as if he had every right, as if there was nothing remotely wrong or sinister or tragic about him carrying a poor dead girl's body through the night.

Claire didn't know whether to be amazed or appalled by his audacity and seeming lack of compassion now. But compassion was likely to do them no good should they be caught by a night watchman or constable. This strange amalgamation of buckish swagger and ducal audacity would have to do.

Claire held her skirts up higher, away from the muddy dirt of the street, and followed as closely as she might— though she didn't like to get too close to him, with poor Carter slung over his shoulder like so much grain. But neither did Claire want to let him out of her sight. She had no sense of place slinking so quickly along these narrow lanes, no way to get her bearings.

"Where are we going?" Her voice sounded strident and overloud in the emptiness.

He turned and put a finger to his mouth, and then whispered, "Round the back and down the alley."

He led her down a varied row of tall, prosperous houses that towered over them out of the dark night, and around a corner, before he ducked into a dark, unlit alley. He steered her tight against a low brick wall, and paused again.

She sorted out the sounds—the more distant mull of the river, but now she could pick out the clack of a pot or pan or two, the slam of a door, the splash of a pail being emptied.

He seemed satisfied by the ordinariness of the sounds, and started off. "Stay close," he urged, and she tried to keep close, filling her hands with her skirts to lift the lace and silk of her ball gown well clear of the dirt while trying keep her grip on the gun, and to emulate his posture, crouching low, close up against the alley walls.

When he darted to the side for no reason, but Claire could see nothing, and so kept to her path, with one elbow touching along the wall for guidance, until she promptly stepped ankle deep into a chilly puddle that instantly soaked her thin dancing slipper through.

"Ooh, bloody hell—"

"Not a sound." His low whisper whipped at her through the dark. And then his hand found her, and pulled her up hard against his side, holding her still against him and the wall as two fellows with lanterns crossed the far end of the alley.

He had clearly put Carter's body down, because Claire felt both his hands on her shoulders holding her still. When the lantern light at the end of the alley winked out, she released the breath she did not know she had been holding.

But His Grace was not at all relieved. He muttered another blue oath before he whispered low, "Stay here. And no matter what, don't say a word."

He moved no more than a few feet away before a lantern suddenly shone in her eyes. She put up a hand to shield her gaze, and saw two men—one large and bald, and another one larger still—smiling from behind the beam of the light.

Every part of her felt stripped cold.

"Show me your hand, Your Lordship. And I'd advise you to fill it with guineas."

His Lordship did indeed show his hand, stretching his long, articulate fingers out in what Claire assumed would be an attitude of beseechment. But one moment his hand was empty, and in the next it held the haft of a deadly-looking blade that winked wickedly in the moonlight.

"Filled it with something else entire, haven't I? Something you'd better mind, Robertson, you buggering bungler."

The miscreant couldn't hide his startlement—which was second only to Claire's—or his amusement. His head jerked back before he narrowed his eyes and peered more closely into the misty murk. "Jesus God. Tanner? That you?"

"It is."

Claire could hear the sly smile in His Grace's voice, even as his hands reached back to herd her into the shelter of his height.

"Well, fuck me blind." The miscreant gave a wheezy chuckle. "Look at you all toffed up like a flash cully. Why did you not cry beef?"

"Didn't ask, did you?" His Grace's cool, amused baritone eased over the top of his crooked smile. But the duke's voice was different. Less smooth. Rough around the edges.

"Didn't, did I?" Claire saw the yellowy glint of the footpad's grinning teeth flash in the watery light. "What in seven hells are you doing out on a night like this? Though fuck me, it's good to see you again. And yer lovely dolly mort there, as well." The footpad canted a wiry eyebrow in her direction, before he reached a meaty paw out to His Grace, who actually took it.

"I'd rather not fuck you, if it's all the same to you. And neither would my lass." The cadence of his voice was sliding into the same dockside gurgle as that of his strange acquaintance.

"Your lass, eh?" The bald footpad wagged his shaggy eyebrow at her admiringly. "She looks like she could butter a man's parsnips nicely with—"

"Shut it." His Grace pointed that wicked blade at the miscreant's heart. "*My* lass. So treat her gentleman-like."

Astonishment was a pale description of what Claire felt at His Grace's words. She felt strange and tingly again, not with cold, but with warming heat—that lovely feeling of safety.

"Oh, easy, lad. That's the lay o' that land, is it?" The miscreant nodded his head respectfully toward her. "I wish you joy, missus."

"Thank you," she said because she didn't know what else to say.

"Listen to that. Quality she is, Tanner. She'll do the governess for you nice. Hain't seen no one do a governess like yer sister, and old Nan herself, back in the day." The bald man seemed to think this was a remarkable accolade he was bestowing upon Claire. "Yer man's a dab hand—a damn good knuckler, missus. Best there is. You stick with 'em. The Tanner'll see you right in the end, he will. Even if they hang 'em in his fancy togs at the end. Hang us all, won't they, Tanner?"

"Not if they don't catch us."

"Ha-ha," the miscreant barked. "Too true. Too bloody true. Stay on our toes, then, won't we? On our toes."

"Will do. Now off with you, before you ruin my rig with all your palaver."

"Ha-ha!" the man chuckled again before he shuttered the lantern. "Good to see you in the old roads, Tanner. Good to see you." And then he and his silent partner shuffled off down the alley.

In the moment after they were gone, Claire realized that His Grace had come to stand so close, she could register his heat and solidity through the material of his evening coat.

"You weren't supposed to speak," he admonished.

As if *her* speaking had been the strange thing. "I'm sorry," she whispered, because she was brought up with manners, and politeness was always her first refuge.

He nodded sharply, accepting her apology. And then if the confounded man didn't smile and toss her a wink. "Not to worry," he whispered directly into her ear. "It's all sorted now."

And then he patted her back, and was off again, slinking as sure-footed as a cat down the rutted, foggy way.

By the time she caught up with him two houses down, he had laid poor Carter's body on the ground, and was vaulting over the top of an ivy-covered wall in one single, agile leap.

And he was gone.

And Claire had no refuge left at all.

Chapter Five

Claire waited what felt like forever for him to reappear, but he did not. There was no sight, no sound. Nothing. Nothing but the empty alley, the pitch darkness, and the hard hammering of her heart in her ears. He had left her.

Claire's palms went damp and clammy. Heat prickled and then chilled her skin. Her breath sounded short and harsh in her ears.

Without His strange Grace of Fenmore, she was completely on her own. And entirely out of her depth. She did not dare to call out to him after he had cautioned her to quiet.

But she did not want to be alone. Already the hot clutch of panic was closing in around her.

No. No, she would not be a girl who needed to be petted and cosseted and attended by others every minute of every day. She would *not*. If he thought she could scale a six-foot wall, she could. She *would*. She would have courage, and take care of herself.

Claire abandoned all pretense to ladylike sophistication, and wadded up the muslin skirts of her silk-embroidered ball gown, hiking her petticoats and rucking the hems into her garters without care for the cost or fineness of the material. Nothing mattered but that she get over that wall and find His Grace.

She gripped the gun as tight as she could in her fear-slick hand and scrambled for a toehold in the ivy. She made it halfway over, landing hard on her belly on the slightly rounded crest of the wall, but the force of her landing knocked the wind out of her.

Bloody heavens, but it had been a long time since she had scrambled over a wall. Only a few years ago she had eagerly followed her brothers on rambles around Down-park, fording streams, climbing trees, and clambering over stiles. But for the past four summers such meanderings had been replaced with harvest balls and tight laces. With proper deportment and politeness. With smiles for marquesses' unworthy sons.

Smiles and proper deportment be damned. It was nearly impossible to scale a wall while wearing stays. And carrying a gun.

But the evening seemed to be one for impossibilities. And for courage.

She repeated the word to herself as she got her wind back and searched the dark garden on the other side of the wall for a sign of His Grace.

"Why, Lady Claire. Whatever are you doing? Did you think I wasn't coming to get you?"

She twisted atop the wall to find His Grace of Fen-more with his arms stretched over his head, leaning on the top of the frame of the deviously silent, well-oiled gate. The pose made the linen of his shirt draw tight against the sinewy muscles of his forearms. But it was his smile that pinned her to the wall—full across his face now, curving from one dimple to the other, making his chin look long and pointy and entirely boyish.

"Forgive me for taking too long. Not that I don't ex-cessively admire the view." He was frowning and looking at her as if she were a particularly puzzling thing he had just chanced to discover. "You look the veriest romping girl."

Heat streaked across her cheeks. Claire attempted to yank her skirts down over her ankles. "That does not sound like a good thing."

"But it is a very good thing. At least from my admittedly askew point of view." His voice was low and off-kilter enough to insinuate itself inside her. But there was also something honest and just blunt enough in his tone to be boyish and somehow unthreatening.

But she still felt quite silly on her ungainly perch atop the wall. "My point of view is not much sounder. Would you be so kind as to take this?" She held out the gun. "I'm as like to shoot myself and anyone else."

He made a shallow bow and put out his hand. "Of course," he said in that agreeably terse, obvious way of his. "My apologies. I am sorry I did not open the gate with more alacrity." But he did not look sorry. A slow curve slid across one side of his face—a smile full of complicit, confederate charm. "I am also sorry I arrived too late. I would have liked to see you assay it. Though it seems to have ruined your pretty skirts."

"Bother the skirts." Thank goodness the darkness hid the flame in her face. "I hope you do not think I am so helpless and vain as all that."

"No. Not vain. Not at all. You mistake me. Again, my apologies."

"I thought I was meant to scale the wall after you."

"No, I meant to come get you. But you seem to have done the job right, with no help from me."

Something that had to be pride replaced the heat in Claire's cheeks. "Thank you."

But she waited until he had turned away before she slithered down the wall and landed knee-deep in overgrown grass. Her shoes, as well as her white muslin skirts, would certainly be ruined beyond all repair. Her mother was going to have her head.

Claire pushed the uncomfortable thought of mothers, and fathers as well, away and set her skirts and petticoats to rights before she followed His Grace across the length of the overgrown garden, and down a short set of stairs to the low kitchen door.

He looked as if he were about to put poor Carter down again, so Claire hurried forward. "Shall I knock?"

That made him smile. "Shouldn't think that'll be necessary."

And as if he had clapped his hands and said, "Open sesame," the door did open.

A creaking voice floated out of the dark interior. "Well, would ya look at what the cat drug in." A small, pixieish old fellow stuck his head out into the moonlight, and then quickly gestured them inside.

His Grace led the way, shifting Carter's body sideways, so he might pass through the door. "Evening, Jinks."

"Speak of the devil, and up he crops." The little man's accent was Irish, all fey dips and feints. "Look like yer coming back down in the world this evening, Tanner."

"That I am," His Grace admitted, with that same ironic, conspiratorial half smile that he had just given Claire. "Looking in the low places for my friends."

"Well, you've come to the right place and all." The Irishman locked the bolts behind them. And then his sharp eyes found her. "Who is that there with ye?"

"A friend," Fenmore said. "And a body."

The little Irishman didn't blink an eye. "Not much profit in either. What game's afoot, now?"

"Don't ken yet." His Grace and the Irishman plunged down a dark hallway, and disappeared from view, but presently a lantern was turned up, and a growing halo of light revealed a spacious, well-scrubbed kitchen at the end of the corridor.

His Grace seemed to know his way around, and went immediately to the long deal table, where he laid Carter out, like a queen upon a tomb at Westminster. "We'll be needing more glims, Jinks. And coffee. Strong and hot. And send for Pervis."

The Irishman hung a second lantern from the rack of pots above the table, and took a long look at the pale, inert body laid out there. "Left it too late for a sawbones, haven't ye?"

"Send for him anyway. We'll need his particular expertise. I'm wanting this one as tight and tied as Newgate."

"Ah." The little man's eyes seemed to turn up like a lantern. "Murder, is it? Ye thinkin' to make someone dance for it?"

Claire could only vaguely follow the little man's broguish cant. But the duke seemed to understand fully. He answered in his emphatic way, "Yes. I mean for the killer to hang."

The Irishman proved himself to be curious about live women as well as dead. He turned his beady black eyes on Claire. "And 'oo's she when she's at 'ome? Quality at least—that much I can see. And what's happened to 'er?"

Claire's hand flew to her flushed face. She had almost forgotten. Almost. In the brighter light from the lamps the injuries to her face must be much more apparent. His Grace had said she was likely to bruise. And those friendly miscreants in the alley—advising her that the Tanner would treat her right in the end. Did they think that *he* had done this to her? Did *he* think they thought that?

But His Grace's level gaze steadied her. He said in his even, factual way, "She had a run-in with a Beau Nasty, whose brains were in his ballocks."

In the light from the lantern she discovered Fenmore's

eyes were lighter—the dark blue-green of the deep sea. She had never noticed the vibrant color of his eyes across the ballrooms, or in the shelter of the dark.

Behind His Grace, Jinks's face broke into a snide smile. "Serve him a thorough basting, did you?"

And out came that crooked, secret half smile, curving up one corner of His Grace's mouth. "I might have done."

"Ah." The Irishman's small eyes brightened and crinkled at the corners in amusement. "Like that, is it?"

"No." The uncompromising tone slid back into His Grace's voice like a bolt going home in a lock.

"'Tis," the little man contradicted with sly humor, wrinkling up his face.

The duke was having none of Jinks's lip. He infused his tone with chilly command—all trace of the roguish tough banished from his voice. "The deceased was her maid. I'm helping her. And she's helping me. Please get her a cold compress for her face. Then make the coffee. Then get Pervis."

Jinks already seemed to have a cold, wet cloth in his hand, and was proffering it to her, but he was squinting over his pug nose at her, and shaking his head. "What you'll want for that is a beefsteak." He clomped away toward what must be the larder, and came back a few moments later with a fresh-cut piece of red meat, which he slapped into her hand. "Put that up on yer face bone."

Claire started to do as she was bid—because she *always* did as she was bid.

But there was something about the juxtaposition of the bloody red meat and Maisy Carter all laid out as if on a slab and the idea of what they might do to the poor girl next. Claire's stomach cramped in emphatic protest. "Thank you, Mr. Jinks, but I think I'll just use the compress."

The Irishman was having none of her. "Don't be a stubborn mort," he growled, and shoved her hand, and the beefsteak it held, up toward her face. "Best thing for it. You mark my word. An' I know a thing or two about dark-lights."

His Grace intervened. "Jinks, that'll be enough of that. Fetch Pervis. Bribe him if you have to, to get him out of bed. Away with yourself. Now."

"Aye, aye then, sir. I'll go." The man Jinks finally began to act the servant, though he winked at the duke as he went toward the stairs. "But I've a mind to do you one better."

"If you've a mind, that's the first I've heard of it," Fenmore muttered in response. But his attention had already turned from the departing Irishman's guffaw of laughter to the still form stretched along the table.

Fenmore hung a third lantern on the iron rack over the table, and then His Grace wasted no more time but straightaway set about his examination of the body, putting his face up indecently close, moving her bodice clothes to inspect poor Carter's corpse in the most inde-corous fashion.

Claire grew hot and then cold when she realized that she was quite alone with His chilly, off-putting Grace of Fenmore and a corpse. "Whose house is this?"

"Mine." His Grace straightened. "Apologies. I've forgotten myself—my manners—again. I've brought you to my house, so you'll be safe."

"Oh. Thank you. But, I thought you lived in Green Park?" Everyone knew Fenmore House loomed out over Piccadilly onto Green Park the same way His Grace loomed about the edges of ballrooms. Indeed, the image had for years given Claire pleasure as she watched him not dance and not converse.

"Yes. But I keep the lease on this house as well. It was formerly the home of my sister and her husband. I like to keep it for her."

"How thoughtful."

Her mention of thoughtfulness seemed to have reminded him of how to achieve it. "Lady Claire. Perhaps you would like to . . ." He looked around the homey kitchen, as if it might give him some suggestion or inspiration for what to do with her. "Perhaps you would like to . . . see to yourself?" He gestured to the kettle on the hob. "A cup of coffee or chocolate perhaps?"

"Yes, I would." She would have crossed to the fire, but her glance was interrupted by the line of knives slotted into the rail of a dresser. A new kind of dread sliced into her lungs. "Are you—" She swallowed and made herself return his sharp regard, but her voice was losing ground with every word. "Are you going to cut her up?"

"No." He followed her glance to the knives, and back looked at her face, softening his scowl. "No, I'm not an anatomist. But I've called for the surgeon, Pervis, who may need—" He stopped himself at her instinctive and altogether involuntary little wail of distress. "I beg your pardon, Lady Claire. But it cannot be helped. Miss Carter is beyond pain and fright, but she is not beyond help."

"And you mean to *help* her by poking and slicing at her so?"

His smile turned gentler. "Ah. I see it's you who is not beyond pain and hurt. Please let your rather vivid imagination rest, Lady Claire. I mean you no harm."

"It's not just my imagination. I read the newspapers." They were full of gruesome tales of bodies being stolen or murder victims being sold to doctors and surgeons who studied corpses by dissection. Her stomach twisted tighter at just the thought of it, even as his words echoed inside her, resounding and reminding. *He meant her no harm.*

"So you do." He acknowledged her with that curt but oddly respectful nod. What a man of contradictions he was. "You needn't fear dissection. It should be enough to make a close observation of Miss Carter's more obvious injuries and bruises."

"Injuries? You mean she is not dead?" A flare of hope made her stupid. She started around him, toward Maisy Carter's pale, closed face.

"No." He stopped Claire with a hand at her waist, light but unyielding. "I'm sorry. She is quite dead. I meant to say 'injuries that led to her death.'"

"Oh." She retreated, slowly. The slight pressure of his hand, the articulation of his fingers, spread against the thin muslin of her dress front, and his thumb, upright along the line of the hard busk in her stays, was strangely comforting. It were almost as if she wanted the contact to last as long as possible. "Then you're certain now that she didn't drown?"

She looked up at him to find His Grace slowly opening his eyes, as if he were awakening from a trance—thinking hard about poor Carter, no doubt.

"As certain as I can be without— Her lungs don't appear to be full of water. I've depressed them—her lungs—and no water has come out of her mouth, nor froth. And she'd had something of an awful fight beforehand."

"A fight? How do you know?"

"Fingernails, broken—quite shredded at the end." He returned to his close inspection, taking out a small hand lens like the ones her mother's jewelers used to judge the worth of the stones they presented to her. "And there is some blood, and probably skin, beneath her nails—either her own blood, or, if we're lucky, it means she scratched her assaulter. But the broken nails mean she clawed and scrabbled hard at something." He carefully raised one of Maisy's lifeless hands up to show Claire. "Very hard. It would have hurt. But she did it anyway, either because she was beyond hurt or because she was desperate."

"I should think anyone would be desperate enough not to die."

"Yes. Most times." He looked at the hand and then closed his eyes quickly, as if he had to take just that moment to come to a decision. "I think she knew what this man—and it was a man; look at the bruises, here, across her neck."

And despite herself, despite her dread and her disgust and her fear, she did look, because he was showing her something she could see and understand. And it seemed important, and right, and grown-up in an entirely uncossetted way that she do so. That she bear witness along with Fenmore.

"He crossed his thumbs here—these darker marks," His Grace went on in his inexorably factual way, "to crush down on her windpipe and choke the life out of her." Though even as he described the injuries matter-of-factly, Claire could hear the rage—the clawing, impotent fury— rattling around behind his voice. And it calmed her.

It calmed her to know that there were men in the world who did not think like Lord Peter Rosing. Who did not think they could mistreat a girl just because she was a servant, or abuse a young woman and push her up against a hard brick wall just because she was not strong enough to stop them.

The Duke of Fenmore made her feel as if she had a friend. A good, reliable, capable friend. A friend who noticed a maid's broken fingernails, and knew the marks of strangulation, yes. But a friend Claire could trust.

What a strange duke he was proving himself to be.

"Quite purposefully, do you mean? Not an accident?"

"Quite purposefully." He looked up from under his brows at her. "There is no way her death could have been an accident. Her eyes were open when I took her from the water. Meaning that they were open at the moment of her death, which was therefore likely not in the water. And her skirt is ripped. A vertical tear from the hem up. Which points the way to her being—"

A sound of distress echoed down into, rather than out of, Claire's chest despite her effort to stifle it. Or perhaps because of it. But it could not be helped. Nor avoided, though His Grace tried to spare her feelings.

"I beg your pardon, Lady Claire. I should not have said—"

"That she was likely raped?" She took a gulping gasp of a breath, and then one more. "There, I've said it. It is an ugly word and an uglier crime, but if it is what happened to Carter, it must be said. Just as you said it almost happened to me. Though I am lucky enough to be able to thank God you came when you did. Who knows if I might have ended up like poor Carter."

"No." His response was instantaneous. "You would not have."

He said it to reassure her. But it was not the truth.

"Only thanks to you." The truth was that the duke had suspected Rosing would do exactly what he *had* been doing to her when His Grace intervened. Which was why His Grace had laid His bloody Lordship out like an undertaker. And in case she did not sound sufficiently grateful, she added, "For which I am, and will be eternally, grateful."

"I don't want your gratitude."

His voice was sharp, and Claire retreated in the face of such incomprehensible heat, her determination withering a little under the rebuke. "I don't . . . understand you."

"No." His voice was harsh—a rough exhalation. "I misspoke. I did not do it—help you—to earn your gratitude. Rather, I hoped to earn your trust."

Oh. Trust.

Relief had learned its way, tiptoeing less cautiously

back into her lungs. That was as it should be. Everything he had done ought to have earned her trust. "Yes."

As if he knew he had said too much, he turned away, returning to the business of examining Carter. But Claire had seen. She had seen that beyond the cool, aloof demeanor was a heart as fragile and vulnerable as her own.

And she didn't know when she'd been as pleasantly shocked. A low sort of warmth had kindled inside her, chasing away the aching cold.

"Thank you, sir. You do have my trust. I would not be here, with you now, if I did not trust you. And realize I can trust you to do what's right for Carter."

She looked again at the state of the poor girl's hands, one of which was clutched into a tight fist as the rigor of death began to settle upon her body. There must be thousands and thousands of girls like Maisy Carter—one for every house on this block, in block after block the length of London. And there were another thousand girls just like her, Lady Claire Jellicoe, lined up like so much expensive cattle, ready enough to dance with the Lord Peter Rosings of their world. Not all of them, nor many of the girls like Maisy Carter, had been as fortunate as Claire, to have such a savior and friend as the Duke of Fenmore.

Who was trying to deflect her attention by asking another question. "Tell me again all you know about her. Everything you can remember of your conversations with Miss Maisy Carter."

"She attended me yesterday and today—or should I say the day before yesterday and yesterday."

Fenmore was nodding, but his hand was making an elegantly silent motion of encouragement. "What would you say was Miss Maisy Carter's frame of mind? How would you characterize her?"

She said the first thing that came to mind. "She was a lovely girl. Skillful and perceptive."

"What were her duties for you? When did she execute them?"

"She helped me dress. Did my hair and prepared my clothes and helped me—" There was no way she could possibly talk about such a closely personal subject as the intimate relationship between a woman and her lady's maid. "She was a great help to me."

"Do you know anything about Miss Carter's background? Where she was from?"

"Don't you know? She worked for your family." Claire could hear the defensiveness in her voice.

"Riverchon Park is my grandmother's dower house. I know little of its management, unfortunately. And I would have warned the staff to be on guard had I known Rosing would come."

"Yes. But Rosing could have nothing to do with poor Maisy Carter."

"That has yet to be established. I told you, I don't believe in coincidence." And there was the vehemence prowling through his voice. "Did Miss Carter ever mention his name to you?"

"No." Claire shook her head, trying to understand this connection His Grace had already made.

His Grace was back over the table, leaning his weight on his hands as he looked closely at the body. "Did Miss Carter speak of any men?"

"Only the footman. I don't remember his name. But I do remember she said she was 'a good girl' when I teased her about the footman. The tall, dark-haired young man who attended in the drawing room—although I suppose they are all tall and dark haired; they'd never be hired otherwise. But when he passed us in the upper hallway, he was so obviously looking at her in the way—" The words died away in Claire's mouth. The soft, sweet, adoring look the young footman had sent after Maisy Carter was somehow too intimate a thing to discuss with His Grace. "He looked at her in a nice way. As if he cared for her. But she said she was minding herself with her fellow, and meant to get ahead in her position, like her mam wanted her to. She said she was a good girl, and was grateful to work in such a lovely house. And 'happy to have landed here out of the almonry,' she said. But I'd no idea what an almonry was or what sort of work she did there." Picking the nuts from trees, she supposed.

His Grace put his head back, and drew in a long, contemplative breath before he spoke. "The Almonry is a dirty, broken-down district of vile slum rooms unfit for habitation lying in the shadow of Westminster Cathedral. The Devil's Acre. If she came from there, she *was* lucky to get out."

Unfit for habitation in Westminster? God, but she was so bloody ignorant of the world. The world that existed less than a mile from her parents' front door. She had been to Westminster, to the lovely cathedral, and she had not known such a place as the Devil's Acre existed. She had never noticed. "She's not lucky now."

"No."

"And she does not look as if she were at peace, does she, with her hand all clenched up like that? She looks like she's still fighting, still trying to pound some justice into someone with her small fist."

"Yes, I had noticed—God's balls." This time the duke didn't even apologize for his oath. He was too busy looking at Carter with his head cocked to the side, twisting his neck and narrowing his eyes as he peered more intently at her hands. "I *hadn't* noticed properly. Why hadn't I seen that?"

"I don't know," Claire began. "Perhaps—"

But it had been a rhetorical question—one he did not mean for her to answer—as he paid Claire no more attention, but squatted down until he was at eye level with Maisy Carter's poor stiff fist.

"Hello," he said as he pried apart the lifeless fingers clutched tight with the spreading rigor of death. He came away with some little thing. "What do we make of this?" he murmured.

She looked more closely at the items in his open palm. "A little scrap of fabric, and a coin?"

"More like a seal," he corrected. "No. A coin set as a watch fob, I should reckon."

Claire felt that she could not reckon nearly as swiftly as His Grace. She felt as if she were constantly playing the catch-up. "I suppose she could she have found it somewhere—anywhere—whilst she might have been going about her duties. But you're going to tell me it's not a coincidence, aren't you?"

The Duke of Fenmore looked up at her with eyes that seemed a hundred years old, dark and full of knowledge and pity. "Exactly, Lady Claire. There's no such thing as coincidence."

Chapter Six

She really had no idea. And why would she? Until Lord Peter Rosing had put his filthy hands upon her, Lady Claire Jellicoe had never been touched by violence or vice, squalor or want. And an acquaintance of only a few hours' time had not been sufficient to introduce her to the full depth and breadth of humanity's faults and frailties.

Tanner hated to be the one to disillusion her.

It was different for him. He had known nothing but poverty and desperation as a child. They had been his constant companions—had taught him his stealth and guile.

But tonight he could only be glad of them. He could only be thankful that he had been stealthily watching her with Rosing, or it might have gone very, very much worse for Lady Claire Jellicoe.

And there really was no such thing as coincidence. Murder, like rape, was an awful, telling, lethal habit.

He stood, and strove to keep his voice low and level, to keep anything that could frighten Lady Claire under strict control. "She is clutching it on purpose, Lady Claire. She was a smart girl—clever and capable, you said. I think she tore this fabric"—he very carefully extracted the little scrap of material, and held it up to the light— "twilled silk brocade, from a man's waistcoat I should think, and grabbed this watch fob because they were the last things she caught hold of in her desperate bid to stay alive. Before this man in his silk brocade waistcoat quite deliberately choked the life out of her."

Lady Claire turned her exquisite, terrified face to his and asked, "Are you quite positive?" In grave stillness her beauty was amplified in a way it hadn't been when she was gay and animated, though she had always seemed lovely to him then. But her fineness—her pale skin as smooth as alabaster, her blue eyes wide and full of pity, her delicate bone structure carved from marble—made him achingly aware of the difference between them.

He hated that he could not give her the answer she wanted. "As positive as I can be. But as I am neither an anatomist, nor a surgeon, that is why I've sent for Mr. Pervis."

"And he is an . . ." She swallowed hard around the word. "Anatomist?"

"Yes. But," Tanner added at her frown, "he is also a proper medical surgeon. Up at the naval hospital. He will give his opinion about my conclusions, or draw his own, and then we will proceed."

"And if he, too, thinks she was murdered?" She had turned her head, asking both directly and carefully. "What will you do about it?"

He could only give her the truth. But he hesitated, because the words he wanted to say—the words that were in his head shouting for their chance to be heard—were ugly and brutal.

He wanted to tell her that he was going to hunt whoever had put his hands around this poor, powerless, defenseless girl's neck, and he was going to track them down like a bloodhound, and make them pay at the tight end of a noose. That he would see justice done, whether within the law or without. That he would choose whichever course of action, legal or not, would serve when the moment came to avenge Lady Claire. To make her feel safe.

He was an old hand at skirting the law—that was why the Admiralty came to him with their unsolvable problems. He would not shy away from the doing of dirty, necessary deeds.

But she, who had so little experience of the world outside the *ton*, would not be able to understand this about him. She still thought he was a duke—that he would cleave to propriety out of loyalty to his family name and honor.

"You're going to help her, aren't you? You're going to find out who did this?" Her voice held an urgency he shared.

"Yes." Tanner spoke carefully, though he had already decided to involve himself—the moment he had decided to take the body on board the skiff he had been involved. And he would see it through to the bitter end.

She nodded in relieved agreement, her face still and beautiful even with her bruises, and he saw for the first time that she was looking at him not with curiosity or fear but with admiration. "Thank you, sir."

His pride—his damnable savage pride—was like to crack his chest wide open with the pleasure he felt at her regard. But he had learned not to show himself so incautiously. "You do not have to thank me. A great wrong has been done, and justice must be served."

"Yes. But not every man, nor certainly every duke, would feel that such efforts needed to be made on behalf of a mere maidservant. And that is why I thank you." She gave him another of her small smiles, a demitasse of sweetness. "Besides being a nice man, you really are rather remarkable."

He knew he was remarkable for the differences that separated him from other men. He was different for the way he saw the world and the people in it. Different in the speed and acuity with which his mind leapt from one detail to the next, drawing out connections and patterns. Different but never before remarkable in her eyes.

His chest was not going to crack open—it had already melted under the warm sun of her regard. But he allowed his mouth only to say, "You are kind," even while his mind was silently shouting, Yes, yes. I am remarkable.

If only because this remarkable, exquisite girl had said it was so.

He would do anything—anything for her. Anything she asked. And she did not even have to ask. It seemed impossible that she did not know this—know the power she had over him.

"Yes," she acknowledged, "I hope I am kind but also truthful. I've never met anyone like you." She smiled again—a small, almost-shy curving of her lips that stopped just short of being coy. "And I haven't even properly been introduced to you."

Claire's very real danger had been all the introduction he had needed. But she was kind and polite, and lived with a different set of rules from the ones he held for himself. "No. We've met rather improperly. But impropriety has its own rewards, don't you think?"

"Yes." And then her expression changed, and the kind regard slowly fell from her face. "No. Impropriety has more costs than rewards. If I've learned nothing else, I've learned that tonight. And so has poor Maisy Carter, though I can't think that anything she did was an impropriety. But whatever it was, it resulted in her . . . death— No." Claire shook her head as if she could will herself into acceptance by dint of determination. "I'll not shy away from the ugly words anymore. Her murder. Rape and murder. I suppose I should be thankful that Rosing only tried to rape me when someone—someone in Richmond—murdered Maisy Carter. And she couldn't do anything about it, and I can't do anything about it. But you, you're a man of influence and power. And you see things the way they really are, not just the way you wish them to be. You see and you understand. You see things I can't see, and can't understand. And with your power and authority, *you* can find out who did this. And you can make them pay." Her voice sounded tight and breathy—on the verge of tears—and in her distress she reached out to grasp his hand. "Please, Your Grace. Would you please do this for me?"

She did not need to beg. She did not need to even ask—he had already said yes. But for her he would do anything. And everything. She had no idea—she had never experienced anything of life beyond the confining, rarefied circle of the *ton*—of what he was capable.

But she was asking as if it were the greatest favor in the world. And she was holding his hand—this exquisite, fragile flower of a girl he had been afraid to presume to touch.

And it was enchanting to be asked. It was beyond enchanting—it was bewitching. His chest was bursting with something more than mere pride. It was rude, impolite joy.

It was a dangerous joy to feel that she was counting upon him.

"Lady Claire, your wish is my command. But you are wrong. You can do something about it. You can help me. You can stay, and help me." And then he said a word he had rarely used. "Please, Lady Claire. Please help me."

She did not answer as he had expected—right away. Her glance skipped away from him and took a short trip around the room—from her torn gown and muddy, ruined shoes, to Miss Carter's corpse, to his hands—before she looked back to him. "Why?"

Because he wanted her. Because he did not want his time with her to come to an early end. Because he wanted her compromised so completely in the eyes of society that she would accept the inevitable and marry him. Because he needed more time to convince her to do it willingly. "Because I need you," he lied.

And he turned her hand within his own, and raised it to press a kiss to the center of her palm. Her skin was soft and supple beneath his lips, and still delicately scented with orange blossom and lily and rose, and still far, far too fine for the grubby likes of him.

But she did not tell him so. She did not disdain him.

Instead, it was as if a light had been kindled inside her. For the first time that evening, she looked incandescent, transformed back into the luminous girl he had worshiped. Her wide blue eyes softened, and she looked, if not exactly happy with her bruised, scratched face, then happier than she had been thus far that night. "Yes," she said finally. "I'd like that. I should very much like to help you."

"Thank you." He gave her hand—her sweet, fine, bone-china hand—a gentle squeeze of thanks before she drew it away, and folded it up with her other.

She spoke so low, he almost didn't hear her say, "Thank you for needing me." But then she physically shook off any further hint of melancholy with a brisk little toss of her blond head and asked, "Where do we start?"

Tanner had to pull his attention back to the task at hand. "With Mr. Pervis, and with this fob."

Tanner held the gold piece up to examine more closely in the light of the lamp. The piece had all the appearance of being a Roman coin—it was impressed with the image of a man riding a horse, standing on top of a triumphal arch, and some Latinate words—but Tanner was certainly no scholar.

His thief's instinct told him only that the coin itself was valuable, and the ornate gold setting of the fob was expensive and well made. Experience told him it would fetch a pretty penny with a fence he knew up on Jewin Street.

But he was no longer in the business of fencing stolen goods. And the fob had far greater value as information about the killer. It was a well-crafted, expensive piece. The kind of ornament only a rich and powerful man would wear. Not a footman. "Have you seen this before?"

"No." Lady Claire creased her perfect brow into a frown, and moved closer to peer at the object before she took it from his hand. "But if I remember my history lessons aright, it will be from the reign of the Emperor Claudius, made in commemoration of the conquest of Britain, somewhere near the year 45, or was it 46?"

Lady Claire's governess had been thorough and extraordinarily well versed. His well-educated goddess pointed to a particular mark. "You see here, the obverse side, where it says: *De Britann*? That's us, I should think, Britain, or—forgive my ignorance—more correctly 'of the Britons.' I believe—that is, if I recall correctly—they have found some coins like this in the excavation of Pompeii. They were shown in that exhibition—" Two tiny vertical lines pleated themselves between her brows as she concentrated, closing her eyes, and shaking her head again, as if she might loosen the thought to tumble down upon her tongue. "Oh, I don't remember where—Somerset House, or Sir John Soane's, or somewhere."

That she was clever as well as kind and beautiful had not seemed possible—too much for a man like him, who lived so entirely at the behest of his relentless brain, to hope for. But the realization that she clearly had a first-class mind hidden behind all that astonishing beauty excited him more completely that all of his inchoate longings from afar never had.

My God—he could *talk* to her.

"Excellent. Have you seen this fob before? Think of all the gentlemen you've danced with in the past week or so." Tanner himself was sifting through the catalogue of each and every man with whom she had danced in the vast archive of his mind, reviewing mental image after mental image of men with stickpins and fobs gleaming from the fronts of their waistcoats. Family crests, school insignias, regimental badges, honors and seals of office, one after the other, until he came to Lord Peter Rosing.

The catalogue spilled out of him. "Expensively tailored evening clothes. Coat of darkest green superfine from Schweitzer and Davidson on Cork Street—judging from the style of the buttonholes and shining gold buttons. Immaculate white linen and cravat. Snowy satin breeches to catch the light." Everything designed to appeal to the eye. Dressed to lure. Dressed to rape.

Dressed to kill.

Tanner could calculate to the farthing what that rig had cost and exactly how much it would all fetch at a rag trader's in Black Swan Alley when Rosing's valet deemed it was out of fashion. Enough to feed a family of four for a year.

But that waistcoat had been covered almost entirely by the high cut of Rosing's coat. Tanner's normally infallible memory provided him with an image of a fashionably white waistcoat—white to match Rosing's linen and cravat. Not gold-threaded brocade.

Fuck all.

Tanner did not want to believe the evidence. Because

he wanted it to be Rosing. Tanner wanted another inexcusable, irrefutable reason to hate the bastard and take his revenge.

Lady Claire was looking at him closely again, the short, sharp lines of a scowl marring her perfect face. "Fancy you should know all that. I never notice what men are wearing. All men have watch fobs, don't they? How can that mean anything?"

"Everything means something. Everything. Not *all* men have watch fobs. All the men of *your* acquaintance, meaning your social peers, who are rich and have the money for such ornaments, have them. Not your butler, nor your footmen—nor Miss Carter's footman. Jesse Lightfoot, I should think," he added offhand. "No. Whoever wore this fob, and assaulted Miss Carter and killed her, had money."

Tanner bent down to take a second look at the bruises upon Miss Carter's neck, looking for some other mark, for a blot of blood beneath the skin that might have been caused by a ring on the hand of her murderer.

And there, low across the sinew, where her shoulder met the right side of her neck, was a larger spot of bruising, but it was not distinct enough to draw any conclusion as to being from a particular crest.

"There. Do you see this?" He directed Lady Claire's glance to the spot. "This darkened, wider mark likely came from a ring. On a man's left hand. Thus, a married man, rich enough to wear a ring and have a gold watch fob."

Which also left Rosing—who was unmarried—unequivocally out, damn it all to hell.

Tanner tried to deflect the sharp stab of disappointment sliding between his ribs, by making himself continue to look for other evidence. Because both his gut and his formidable mind were in agreement that the killing of the maid and the assault on Lady Claire were related.

The evidence would be there, somewhere, if only he were clever enough to see it.

But he could see nothing at that moment, with Lady Claire so close beside him, following his gaze, looking herself, and wanting answers. At least half of his brain was taken up with cataloguing all the things about her that he had guessed and dreamed about while watching her from afar.

The subtle scent of orange blossom and roses, of sunshine and bright happiness, that wafted off her body like perfume from a flower was not new, yet Tanner let his eyes slide closed as he took a deep inhalation of the now-familiar scent.

But there was more, more he had not been able to see in the uncharted depth of the moonlight on the river. He opened his eyes to fill them with the sight of the lamplight shining off her blond hair, long and fine, falling across her shoulders now that it was released from its pins. It looked soft to the touch, and he nearly put his hand out to let the loose tendrils sift through his fingers. She reached up and tucked it back behind her ear with an efficient flick of her delicate, fine-boned wrist.

And he was struck again by how warm and *real* she was, despite her air of wide-eyed, delicate fragility. She was herself, and not the figment of his obsessed imagination.

So real that when she returned the coin to his hand he had to steel himself for her touch—for the havoc the fleeting press of the tips of her fingers against his palm would wreak. Even with just the whisper of her warmth, she could nearly knock him over.

She was not in the least similarly affected. She was all clever inquisition. "How can you see all that? And before, what you said about her? How can you know all that?"

He dredged his mind back to the here and now. "I

made a logical assumption from my observations. Things are there for you to see, if you learn how."

"Goodness. Is this what they're teaching at Eton and Oxford these days?"

Her question surprised a short bark of a laugh out of him. "No. Not at all. Perhaps some."

"Then . . . how? How do you know? How did you learn?"

"I correspond with people. Scholars in France and . . . elsewhere." And then he made himself abandon this patent ploy to prove himself more learned that he was, and give her the truth. "And I learned at an altogether different sort of school. A kidding ken—a school of baby thieves. I told you, I wasn't always a duke."

"Yes, you said that. I don't exactly understand."

He might have let himself prevaricate again—he could lie readily enough. But it seemed important that she know exactly what sort of man she had gotten for herself when she had agreed to get into his boat. "I was a thief. I was the Tanner."

"No." For a moment she stared at him as if she could not conceive of him in such a role. Nor could she imagine it as anything but a tragedy. "How awful."

It ought to have been awful, but it wasn't. If he were honest with himself—and if he told the truth to no one else, he told it to himself—it had been a lark, really, the stealing. His sister had borne the weight of the moral compromise and unending worry. He had found it all a grand game, ready to be played. He had *liked* the challenge of the picking of pockets and the pilfering of unguarded lour. He had nourished himself on the thrill of picking out and sizing up a mark. He had very much liked to steal. Still did, even though he had learned it was wrong.

"I thought everyone knew I was a terrible scandal."

Her smile spread out across her face like a warm sunrise over the river—pink-tinged dawn. "You, the lofty, silent Duke of Fenmore, a scandal? No. I can't imagine."

"Can't you?" He felt his own face curve into a corresponding smile, as if he were powerless not to answer the joy in hers.

"No. Will you not tell me?"

For the first time, he was truly tempted to retell the old story in all its gory fullness—and especially to her. How his sister had taken up stealing to feed the two of them. How old Nan the kidwoman had taken them into her fold, and turned them both—but especially his sister, Meggs—into accomplished pickpockets and picklocks. How stealth and guile had been their bread and butter. How they had stolen because their hunger—their very lives—had depended upon it.

And how he had loved every dirty, exhilarating minute of it. How he had missed it when he had been made to stop. Missed it like a dead friend.

And so he hadn't stopped. Just switched sides.

But now was neither the time nor place, standing over Miss Carter's pale corpse, to reveal his work for the Admiralty. "No. It would bore you. Suffice it to say that I have a range of rather felonious skills not taught at either Eton or Oxford that I find come in rather handy. Like picking locks, and sizing people up. And while I am sorry that our time on the river should have brought us here, and exposed you to the seamier side of life, and not given you the peace you so dearly desired, I'm not sorry that we were the ones to find Miss Carter. Without our having done so, there would be no chance to bring her killer to justice."

"Yes." Claire nodded in agreement. "Justice. I like how that sounds. And I like how you call her Miss Carter, full of respect. It's lovely."

And she smiled at him. Not the contented, guileless

smile she wore in ballrooms but something smaller and more personal and therefore more poignant. Because it was a smile for him, and him alone.

And it absolutely slayed him.

And he, who was always armed to the teeth, who had learned to kill with knives and guns and his own capable bare hands, could summon no defense.

But Lady Claire carried on as if she hadn't rendered him incapacitated. As if he hadn't already had a full heaping of her praise. "And thank you, again, Your Grace. Thank you for doing what's right. I've learned it is a rare man who will do what's right and just, especially at some personal cost to himself. I daresay you didn't mean to stay up all night doing this." She spread her hands to indicate the room around them and the whole entirety of their strange circumstances. But still she smiled.

Tanner could feel a bonfire of pleasure swell within his chest at such praise. Enough pleasure to push away more responsible thoughts of how he had not, in fact, meant to stay up all night, nor to keep her up all night with him. For once, he didn't disagree or try to slough off her praise. He let himself bask in it, if only for a moment, like an alley cat in a sunbeam, content for a small while to be petted and purring and happy. And he smiled back.

In response, she extended her hand for him to shake. As if they were equals. As if he were truly a man for whom she felt a measure of esteem.

"Thank you," she said again. "Thank you for everything you've done for me this night. And the things you've shown and taught me. For asking me to help you. I want to help you catch this killer."

The night had already gone on far longer than the half of an hour he had planned to steal from her. And catching a killer was going to take far longer than one night and would expose her to things too far out of her depth.

His conscience, which had thus far remained docile and silent in the face of his larcenous plan to steal her for his bride, at last demanded to be heard. She'd had enough of drama and death for one night. He needed to be the gentleman she thought him. He had to be content with her esteem, and hope when he made his proposal that it would be enough.

"Lady Claire, that is very kind of you, and as much as I want your help and assistance, it really is past time I got you back to your parents. They'll be worried about you."

The lady's eyes lit with a spark of something he had not see in her before—something hopeful, and quite determined, and entirely fractious. "I'll send them a note. Say I've gone home, to the London house."

She took him aback at the readiness and facility of her solution. It spoke of an agile mind that was entirely at odds with the rather more pristine image he had built of her in his head.

And it was even more alluring than her immaculate innocence. "Why, Lady Claire. You surprise me. And do you assay such notes to your parents often?"

"No." She slid her shoulder up fractionally in an attempt to be nonchalant. "But I see other people doing it all the time. And they say that when you lie you should cleave as close as possible to the truth, and the truth is that I am well, and unharmed—thanks to you—and in London."

"It will not be a lie, because I *will* take you home. But best leave out any mention of me, I should think, in your note."

"Why not mention you?"

Oh, but he liked her affronted indignation. It was utterly delicious, her regard. So much more delicious than he had ever imagined. And he had imagined it more than he ought.

"My dear Lady Claire, I'm hardly the sort of fellow a

parent would think of when they need their lovely young daughter escorted safely around London. Though you may not know my scandal, I'm quite sure your parents do."

"Nonsense, Your Grace. You're exactly the fellow who *has* escorted me safely into London. I wouldn't have come with you if you weren't. And I wouldn't be going on with you otherwise."

"Going on with me?" Did she understand, then, the full ramification of their solitary sojourn? Did she not object to tying herself to him so permanently with the marriage he would be duty and honor bound to propose?

"I mean to go on with you in finding justice for Maisy Carter. We started this together, we found her together, and I think we should go on together. Justice must be done, you said. I heartily agree. And what did you say before? 'Past bloody time.'"

He could see the excitement, the sheer, bloody, hopeful, innocent determination shining in her clear-sky eyes.

And he was tempted—sorely tempted—to keep her with him just so he could bathe in the warm light of her regard for a while longer. And cement both the bond that seemed to be forming between them and the inevitability of their having to marry to stifle the potential scandal.

But a stolen hour, or even four, to keep her safe and with him, had been one thing. It would be entirely another if he were to continue on with her and take Lady Claire Jellicoe on a jaunt into the dripping, stagnant stews of London in the wee, dark, thieving hours of the morning—that would be larceny on an altogether grander scale than even *he* had ever imagined.

Chapter Seven

"Please." She turned the full hopeful force of her smile on him, and all at once he understood that her hopefulness, her expectation—and his own corresponding desire not to let her down—was being wielded like a weapon against him.

He had never before thought himself so easily disarmed.

"I can help you," she insisted. "I can talk to people. I know I can. And I've been to Westminster. I'm sure I can go to this Almonry place."

"Lady Claire." He tried to make his voice firm and even frosty, but he was afraid he could not hide his own desire to keep her with him. He ought to dissuade her. "The Devil's Acre will certainly be beyond your experience of Westminster. It will be like nothing you have ever seen, or smelt, before."

Tanner knew he had to put aside his own wants and needs and plans, and do what was right for Lady Claire, not what she wanted in the heat of the moment. She was too caught up in the thrill of the new and different and forbidden. She had to understand she really couldn't go to a place like the Almonry, and emerge unscathed. He would not ask her to even try. He would not make her his accomplice.

"You could stay here instead," he hedged, "while I—"

"No." She shook her head, growing more determined before his eyes—putting up her chin and drawing herself up to her full height, this tiny teacup of a young woman. "No. I don't want to stay behind, safe and protected. You said you could show me. You said you would show me what life was like, so I wouldn't be so willfully ignorant and susceptible to bounders like Rosing."

"Lady Claire. You are not willfully ignorant, only unlearned." His hand came up of its own volition to smooth a loose hair off her porcelain face. "And Lord Peter Rosing is more than a mere bounder. You know better than anyone what he is capable of. And it is far too much of a coincidence to think that the execrably flawed guest list for my grandmother's ball would have included more than one rapist, although I can't vouch for it." He withdrew his hand before it touched Claire. He could hear the venom—the ferocious anger and self-loathing—in his tone and feel it roiling in his gut. Lady Claire and Maisy Carter were two more girls on his conscience. He did not know if he would be able to keep the violence locked deep within him from his touch.

"You can hardly hold yourself responsible—you said yourself Lord Rosing wasn't invited."

"No, but—" The rest of his apology was swallowed in the sound of Jinks clumping his way down the kitchen stairs carrying the surgeon's black leather satchel.

Tanner stepped away from Lady Claire, so propriety still had a place between them. "Back so soon? I had expected it to take—"

"Got a bit of a surprise for you, Tanner. There's yer one." The Irishman gesticulated over his shoulder at the man entering the kitchen.

But it wasn't the surgeon Pervis at all. It was Jack.

"Jack Denman, as I live and breathe." Tanner held out his hand to his oldest friend. "My God, it's been an age. Good of you to come, man. I had no idea you were in town."

"Tanner." The younger man shook his hand and greeted him easily—they had known each other far too long for the formalities of titles. "Good to see you as well."

"Sorry to pull you out of your bed this time of night."

"Anything for an old friend." Despite the late hour, Jack's eyes were bright with amusement. "Especially for one rich enough to endow chairs at the Royal College of Surgeons." The surgeon's handshake was as firm and steady as ever. "I know where my bread is buttered, Your Grace."

"Aww now, don't ye start 'Yer Gracing' 'im," Jinks complained. "Don't want anyone to be hearin' that kind 'o talk from this 'ouse. Rot the Tanner's brain, it will. And ruin me reputation as well, it would."

Tanner had to smile at that. As one of only five people on earth, besides Jack, who had known him before he became a duke, Jinks felt it his particular position to treat Tanner as the hungry, thieving boy he once was. God knew the banty Irishman still kept the larder well stocked just on the off-chance of feeding Tanner up. "What were you doing up at the hospital?"

Jack had done well for himself, albeit with a little help from the Dukedom of Fenmore, in the years since Tanner had first met him—at the rail of a Royal Navy cutter when they were both infant midshipmen.

"I wasn't up at the hospital, but in fact up the stairs. I gave a lecture at the hospital yesterday"—he squinted at the clock on the wall to check the time—"and didn't want to head back to town. And you and your man Jinks here keep such an excellent cellar."

"And that's why we keep it—to lure you home. You know you are always welcome here. It's the least I can—"

"Much appreciated, Tanner. As are your rather staggering recent donations, to both the Royal College and the hospital. I know"—Jack held up his hands to stop Tanner from speaking—"the donations are meant to be anonymous. While I did not give my opinion on the name of their generous anonymous benefactor to Their Lordships of the board, or to the Fellows of the college, I reckon I have a pretty fair idea of who gave those funds. If only to ensure himself of my appearance to do his bidding before dawn."

There was the puckish, teasing smile. Tanner could feel his spirits ease and lift, as they always did when Jack was around.

"As well he should," Jinks agreed stoutly. "And who else should benefit but the service that done everything for him, and made him a man."

Other things besides the senior service had made Tanner—and Jack as well—a man. But it wouldn't do to argue with Jinks. Not when there was evil afoot and work to be done.

"Exactly, Jinks," Tanner agreed. "We'll say no more of that, Jack. Except that if I'd known that a donation was all it would take to ensure your appearance, I'd have given years ago."

"Never fear. You've done enough." Jack chuckled. "But what have we here?" The anatomy professor and surgeon in Tanner's old friend made him step forward, and begin a cursory check of the body laid out on the table.

Tanner filled in the required information without being asked. "Last seen alive at approximately eight o'clock last evening. Found the body in the river, a few miles east of Richmond, just before one this morning. Strangled, I think, before she was . . . put in the river. Also . . . assaulted, I suspect."

Jack Denman's gray eyes met his, and then slanted meaningfully toward Lady Claire's.

"My apologies. Lady Claire Jellicoe, if I might have the honor of introducing Mr. Jackson Denman, learned professor of anatomy, and surgeon, late of His Majesty's Royal Navy, and current scholar and Fellow of the Royal College of Surgeons, Lincoln's Inn."

Jack's perceptive eyes flicked back to Tanner. "Not late of His Majesty's Navy, *Your Grace*. I've a endeavor—a voyage of discovery in the offing. But all in all"—he bowed very correctly—"your servant, my lady."

Lady Claire did them both the honor of not shying from the introduction, even though surgeons were not considered gentlemen, and Denman was well below her socially. And even though she was clearly in dread of what the good surgeon might do—her eye kept darting nervously to his brass-buckled black leather bag. "Mr. Denman." She curtsied gracefully and extended her hand.

"My lady." Jack bowed over her hand. "An honor."

"Lady Claire was acquainted with the deceased. It was she who identified her as Miss Maisy Carter, a maid at Riverchon Park in Richmond."

"Your grandmother's home? I see," Jack said, though the look he sent toward Tanner—all high arched brow—said that he did not see at all how a young lady of Lady Claire Jellicoe's pedigree was so completely involved in the death of a servant. Or with Tanner.

And without his own desire for her company to cloud his vision, Tanner began to see how odd—how strange and even wrong—it was that he had kept her by his side.

And how she could not possibly stay there as Jack took up his examination.

Jack clearly thought the same. "Perhaps the lady might like to . . ." He was gesturing in a gentlemanly way—far more gentlemanly than Tanner, who had not been thinking of her sensibilities at all after her sharp intellect and insistence to accompany him—toward the stairs.

"Yes. Of course." Tanner touched Lady Claire's elbow to turn her away from the table, if only for the pleasure of feeling the soft slide of her skin beneath his fingers. "Let me show you above. I'm sure you'll want to refresh yourself before we depart. Jinks, the coffee. And bread and cheese will do." It was going to be a very long night, and Tanner and Claire had already missed the supper at Riverchon. She was going to need her strength. They were both going to need strength.

"And the body, Your Grace?" Jack asked quietly. "Have any arrangements been made for where ought it be taken for burial?"

"I'll see to it," he responded. "Jinks will help with the necessary details."

But Lady Claire was not yet satisfied. "You'll see to it yourself, surely? See that's she's taken to a reputable undertaker, and not someone who would be tempted to sell her off to a resurrectionist—"

Lady Claire stopped abruptly, clearly not wanting to insult Jack with any kind of accusation, but also clearly feeling she had to say something. The papers seemed to delight in relating ghoulish, although true-enough, tales of the bartering and stealing of bodies.

"Yes, my lady. I will do." Tanner shifted his gaze to Jinks. "Send round at a decent hour to Deed Brothers."

But having attained her object did not seem to put Lady Claire at any ease. "Ought we not ask her family, when we go to them?"

In front of the other men, Tanner made sure to keep his voice even and factual. "I doubt any family who resides in the Almonry has the money for a burial, Lady Claire. If we leave it to Miss Maisy Carter's family, it is likely that her body will end in a pauper's grave. I will see to the expense."

"Oh. I did not realize." She colored—a wave of pink washed across her pale cheeks. "Yes, of course. Thank you."

"And we will certainly abide by her family's wishes, if they have any." Again, speaking of family— "And in the meantime, Jinks will deliver a note to your parents at Riverchon House, to let them know you are safe and sound."

"Aww, now." Jinks began his usual palaver. "That's all the way down to Richmond. At this bloody time o' night, I—"

"Will either take the note yourself or will arrange for an express rider. Which will no doubt take as much time and effort to arrange as it would to carry it yourself. But one way or another, the earl and countess will not be made anxious one minute longer than absolutely necessary."

And then Tanner saw it in her face—the doubt and embarrassment and fear that could not be hidden in the harsh light of the kitchen. Two spots of high color burned in Lady Claire's pale cheeks, and her beautiful blue eyes were wide with anxiety.

It had already been too long a night for Lady Claire. He could not be so selfish as to ignore her needs at the expense of his own. The time they had already spent away was more than sufficient to secure their betrothal. "Perhaps if you had rather simply go yourself, Lady Claire, I will completely understand. We'll send for a carriage and suitable accompaniment from Fenmore House, and have you back to Riverchon within the hour."

"No." Lady Claire spoke in a rush, as if she wanted to

get the words out before she could think better of the idea and change her mind. "I want to go," she said again, infusing her voice with determination, as if she still needed to convince herself. "You should have someone who knew Maisy with you when you speak to her family."

"Lady Claire, I hardly think you—"

"Are capable?" She exhaled a little sigh of pent-up frustration. "No. I know I'm not. But I want to be. And how shall I ever become capable if I do not try? If I do not attempt to do the things I ought? You said I was not ignorant, only unlearned, and I'm tired of being unlearned. Of being incapable. I want to learn. You said you would teach me. And a few hours more at this point will hardly matter."

After such an extraordinary speech in front of all of them, it was everything he could do to keep himself from pulling her into his arms, and kissing her. She was so much more than he had ever thought her. She was worthy of so much more esteem than his mere infatuation would allow. "I honor you, Lady Claire. But I hardly think your parents would approve."

He doubted her parents would approve of any part of his and Claire's night together, much less a final jaunt into the Almonry at dawn. He could picture the Earl Sanderson's normally impressively controlled expression now, his face slowly growing crimson with parental outrage.

But by now the Earl Sanderson's outrage could not be avoided—it could only be put off for a short while. And perhaps Lady Claire was right. Perhaps it *would* be good for Lady Claire Jellicoe—for all the young ladies like Claire Jellicoe, too ignorant and too sheltered for their own good—to see how the greater portion of London's population lived. To see the real, all too miserable lives of the people like Maisy Carter, who made the young ladies' lives so immaculate and beautiful.

The pigs on Claire's father's tenant farms likely had a cleaner, less distressing existence.

Jinks couldn't resist throwing his tuppence worth of opinion into the pot. "You're never going Almonry way in them flash togs, are you, Tanner? You'd be a mark and pillock in no time, traipsing across London in ball clothing. They'll never know you was the Tanner. You'll be tipped, stripped, and left for the rats before Lady Bountiful there can cry beef. And 'er—they'll do more than strip and pip 'er. Why—"

"Mind your alehouse jaw, Jinks." Tanner's voice instinctively lowered to a growl of warning.

But Jinks was as tone-deaf as he was stubborn. "Well, you'll look like a cull, you will."

Tanner didn't even bother to hide the annoyance in his voice. "Never you fear, Jinks. I wasn't born at the damp end of a pumpkin patch. I know what's what."

Jinks was still his too-opinionated, grumpy self. "Don't know if you do anymore," he muttered, "bringing ladies 'ere, when there are others more deserving, as could use your attention."

"Jinks." This time Tanner spoke with the silent strength of a lash. "That will bloody well do. Shut your gob and mind the bleeding coffee."

Tanner let his stare bore down through Jinks's thick hide before he turned back to Lady Claire. "As I said, you'll need different clothes. You'll not want to dirty your skirts in the Almonry's filth." Indeed she had been hampered considerably by the lacy layers of her exquisite, white-on-white embroidered ball gown when they had traversed the alley behind the houses.

"You think me vain and shallow."

"No. I told you before, I don't think you're particularly vain. At least not for holding your skirts out of the muck. I thought you were practical to do so. And being practical will also involve taking a rest and some food before we venture out into the Almonry."

"All right. All right, I will." She gave him a smile so relieved and grateful and luminous, it made the promise of the coming dawn seem pale and wan in comparison.

A dawn that would illuminate such misery as she had never conceived. He looked her in the eye. "Don't thank me yet."

After that rather extraordinary conversation, His Grace returned to his cool, urbane, self-contained former self. "Lady Claire." His manners were all polished Duke of Fenmore as he gestured politely toward the stair. "Please allow me."

He led her up the kitchen stair, and into the quiet but comfortable house. Above stairs she could hear the patter of the light rain that had evolved from the heavy damp of the night.

"It will be light in about an hour." His voice had lost that rolling, rough cadence of his directives to Jinks, and returned to the blunt formality of the Duke of Fenmore. "We'll wait only until then. Why don't you see if you can get some rest?"

Claire was quite determined not to be put off. She felt herself on the verge of something new and, if not exciting, then perhaps better. More adult. More self-determined. But she needed his help to become so.

"I don't need to rest. I'm quite used to town hours." For once Claire was thankful that her mama had insisted, as she always did, on Claire taking a nap in the late afternoon, before the evening's festivities. "In this, at least, I can take care of myself."

"All right," he confirmed in his brusque, factual way, before he led her up the main corridor to the elegant stairwell where he lit a branch of candles for light. "My sister still keeps some things here. Although this is my house now—I keep the lease—it was her home first," he explained. "Why don't you see if you can find some cleaner and plainer clothing. You look to be of a size—you look like you'd make spare change from a hundredweight. Her clothes may seem worn, but they are all quite clean. Are you all right?"

Claire nearly missed the next step on the stair, and her cheeks had grown hot and uncomfortable at the rather startling idea that His Grace had surreptitiously sized up her body like a tailor. "Yes. Quite. Does your sister live with you at Fenmore House now?"

"No. Sadly—for me, not her—she lives on New Providence Island in the Bahamas, where she is closer to her husband, who is an admiral of the West Indies Station."

"Oh, I see." She had never heard anything about any of His Grace's relations besides his grandmother, the dowager duchess, who was still a fixture in society. She had never heard anything about a sister or an admiral. But she had not heard of an old scandal either.

It had to have been years ago, when he was a young boy, for despite his mention of age, he was clearly a man in the prime of his life, in full command of a rather amazing set of faculties. He looked to be of an age with her oldest brother, who was not yet thirty.

But thirty was still young in a man. She would be ancient when she reached his age.

There it was again—the ashy taste of failure and shame and doubt in her mouth, burning up her throat and heating her eyes, telling her it was her own fault.

Planning to let a man like Rosing steal kisses. She could hear the duke's scathing set down as if he had just said it. And he was right. She had been stupid and accommodating and desperate. But she would be no more.

She was determined.

She put up her chin and swept past the Duke of Fenmore when he showed her to a lovely, if somewhat spare, room done up in warm cream-colored walls and furnishings.

"My sister's." He lit the candle set ready on the table nearest the door and pointed his chin at the large wardrobe. "Her old things will be folded at the bottom, I should think. And there should be writing paper in the little lap desk, there."

"Thank you. Your coat—" She divested herself of his evening coat and folded the elegant garment to hold it out to him.

He looked at it for such a long, silent moment, Claire thought perhaps he meant not to take it. She was on the verge of asking him if something were wrong—more wrong than finding a dead body and traveling to London, and being alone together—when he finally took the coat from her hands.

Without saying another word, he bowed and disappeared through an adjoining door, presumably into his own room to change clothes.

And Claire was alone again. "Bloody gracious."

It felt good to swear. It felt good to say what she oughtn't. It felt good to be alone with her thoughts—to *think*.

That was how she had gotten herself into this awful mess in the first place—not thinking. Not thinking about what she wanted instead of what people asked of her. Not thinking that the worst could happen to her.

But the worst had *not* happened to her—it had happened to Maisy Carter.

His Grace thought that Lord Peter Rosing—Lord bloody, bloody bastard Peter Rosing—was somehow responsible for what had happened to Maisy Carter, as well as to Claire.

And she wanted him to be right. She wanted Lord Peter

Rosing to be responsible. And she wanted to help His Grace prove it. She wanted Lord Peter bloody Rosing to be brought to account, and shamed and punished and excoriated in public so no one else *ever* smiled and said yes, and walked out into the dark with him *ever* again.

Propriety be damned—Claire wanted justice.

She wanted it so badly she could almost taste it—and it tasted a good great deal more palatable than the chalky, bitter bile of fear and humiliation.

Let Lord Peter taste *that*. Let him choke on it.

She would help His Grace, and help herself and Maisy, even if she had to force herself past her own faltering limitations.

But she wouldn't falter anymore. She wouldn't.

Claire followed His Grace's instructions and found a set of clothing—a simple round gown of some faded dark greenish color, plain practical undergarments and stockings, and a soft shawl—on the shelves of the lavender-scented wardrobe. And again, she was reminded of how privileged, how spoiled, she had been. She had never been dressed in anything that hadn't been handmade expressly for her. She had never worn a stitch of clothing that wasn't in the absolute first stare of fashion. She had never worn such a shapeless, rough garment in all her life.

But it seemed to be a night of firsts.

Yet the moment she decided to take action, and put it on she did falter. She had no means of putting the clothing on, because she had no method for getting herself out of her current dress. Indeed, she had never, not once in the entire course of her life, gotten herself in or out of a gown on her own. She had always had some assistance, some nursemaid, or lady's maid, or borrowed attendant like Maisy Carter to lace and unlace her as the need should arise.

Bloody, bloody useless.

Claire wasted more than a few moments trying in vain to reach the laces at the center of her back, but try as she might, it was impossible. And impossible to ring for assistance—she was sure there was no one else in the house but the two of them, the surgeon, and the man Jinks.

She searched the wardrobe and then tried the drawers of the dressing table, in case there were a scissors or some other thing she might use to cut herself free. But the dressing table also had a mirror, in which could she herself clearly for the first time.

Despite the cool bath of river water and the cold compress and the beefsteak, her face was clearly already starting to bruise. Her left cheek, where the scratches sliced across the skin as if a cat had raked her, was already pink and slightly swollen, and puffy to the touch. There was no way she could conceal her attack. Not from her parents— not from anyone.

Not unless she didn't go home.

The thought was as frightening as it was liberating.

She had never been off on her own. Never before tonight, when His Grace the Duke of Fenmore had laid a man out like an undertaker and shown her how to row a boat and fire a gun, and had reminded her that she could climb a wall. He had shown her that there was another world out there, where balls and gowns and polite, perfect manners didn't matter.

And he had pledged to help her. Justice he had called it, being a duke and a gentleman. But revenge was what it would be, for herself and for Maisy Carter.

He would give her what she wanted, even if she was afraid. Afraid of death. Afraid of dark, dangerous places like the Almonry. Afraid to be useless.

But His Grace would never let her be hurt. And he would get her out of this damned dress.

Before she could change her mind, Claire went to the connecting door and rapped soundly, though she did try out different excuses and explanations on her tongue. But before she could come up with the most efficacious way of explaining herself, His Grace opened the door.

He frowned at her in his oblique way. "You haven't changed. Are you having second thoughts?"

At that moment she was having third thoughts. About him.

He had changed into worn, but clean, linen. He had turned the cuffs of his shirtsleeves back from his bared forearms, which, along with his face and dark hair, bore the glistening remains of a recent washing.

The hair at his temples was damp with beads of water, and the knowledge that she had interrupted his washing seemed almost too intimate somehow, even as she stood there about to ask for help with her lacing. Claire felt heat blossom across her cheeks and down her neck. Which no doubt made her unattractive and splotchy. Which was ridiculous—the strange awkwardness was all on her part.

"No." She firmed her thready voice. "I'm afraid I require some assistance. I can't get myself out of this gown."

It took no more than a moment for His Grace's changeable eyes to reflect his understanding of her predicament. "Ah. Your laces?"

"Yes." She cleared her throat again, and made herself speak louder than a whisper. "If you would do me the service."

He made another one of those silently elegant gestures of his—twirling his finger slowly in the air—so that she would spin around, and give him her back.

She did so but put a hand to the bodice of her dress in

the front to hold it securely to her. Through the material she could feel the erratic tattoo of her heartbeat, throttling against her ribs. But it was silly to be nervous with His Grace. He was not like other men. He was strange and aloof, and wholly and completely a gentleman.

She spoke again to cover her ridiculous sensibilities. "The laces are tucked in, I believe. Carter—Maisy Carter— was quite particular that the ties not show. If you would just pull them out and untie them, I can do the rest."

She had expected that he would make short work of it, his fingers as efficient and capable with this task as he had been with all the others—the handling of the skiff, and his detached examination of Maisy Carter. But he wasn't.

He was all closeness and slow, almost-fumbling care, as if he were making an examination of how a lady's laces were tied—as if he were taking mental notes of how it had been done, and how he might improve upon the style of lacing or knot Maisy Carter had made.

He moved closer to Claire's back—so close she could feel the heat emanating from his body. So close she could feel each gentle tug as he pulled the laces slowly free, drawing them one by one through the eyelets, pulling the fabric so that the material of the bodice hugged tight against her chest. Her chest, which she now noticed was rising and falling rapidly, as if she were frightened again. But she wasn't. She was something else.

Something new and different in an altogether personal way.

Something light and suspended and breathless, like a dream where she didn't have to breathe.

And then he touched her. She felt the pressure of a single finger tracing the line of her spine, from the base of her neck downward to a spot low between her shoulder blades, leaving a trail of tingling heat and sensation that burrowed beneath her skin, and nestled deep into her bones, and stopped her from speaking. It all but stopped her from breathing. She closed her eyes to try to shut out the feeling, but beneath the layers of smooth lawn fabric Claire felt her breasts tighten into peaks.

Another shock of heat suffused her face and neck and spread downward, melting into her. Turning her bones liquid and light. Claire had to put her hand against her bodice to assure herself it was still in place, and preserve her modesty. Beneath her hand, her pulse battered against her palm.

She stepped away, putting distance between them. What was wrong with her?

His Grace remained his usual cool, reserved self—as practical and kind and unaffected as he had ever seemed. Everything a duke ought to be.

He cleared his throat and said, "I hope that is satisfactory."

"Thank you. Yes." Claire kept her back turned to him. Not that the posture did much to preserve her modesty, as the gown was gaping open in the back, exposing her underclothes to the man. "I think I can manage now."

"Yes. Then. Yes. I'll go."

"Thank you. But—" She called to him over her shoulder, "I was wondering if perhaps you also had—or there was somewhere—some rice powder. For my face. I shouldn't want to appear in public looking like this."

She didn't want everyone to see her shame.

He looked at her damaged face and then stepped closer, as if he would examine her in the same close way he had Maisy Carter. But he didn't. He looked grave and solemn, especially when he turned down his mouth with a sort of small, ironic smile. "You won't need it where we're going. Better maybe if you do look a bit roughed up."

"Better? But what will people think?"

Then he did come closer and reached out with one careful hand to take her chin and turn her cheek to the light. "They'll think I'm a brute," he muttered under his breath, as if she couldn't hear him. As if she weren't right there watching his eyes turn dark sea green in the candlelight. "But it will serve our disguise, and even help. If people think I'm such a reprobate as would hurt a beautiful young woman, they'll know I've no compunctions whatsoever about giving a thorough basting to anyone else."

"But you are not a brute. You are a true, perfect gentleman." He had *chosen* to be so.

But he stepped back from her abruptly. "I am sorry."

Claire wasn't entirely sure what he was apologizing for until he said, "I never should have let him get near you. I'll make him pay for this, Lady Claire. So help me God I will."

His vehemence no longer astonished her. It comforted her to know that he understood. "Thank you, Your Grace."

"You are welcome." And with that, he bowed and removed himself and quietly closed the door behind him.

And left her glad at what a strange, strange, interesting duke His Grace of Fenmore was proving himself to be.

Chapter Eight

Tanner did not know how his feet carried him from the room, nor how he managed to close the door.

On such matters his mind was alarmingly blank.

Because it was full to bursting with other things—the entrancing way Lady Claire Jellicoe's spine had curved down from her shoulders. The shadowed dip of skin behind her shift and stays. The astonishing elegance of her stays themselves—beautifully made with exquisite attention to detail.

It had been everything he could do to to keep himself from letting his fingers stray all the way down the long, elegant line of her spine. It had been everything to make himself speak like a gentleman. Everything to simply remember to breathe.

He did so now, taking a deep, deep breath—inhaling the memory of her warm perfume the same way he had inhaled the scent of her body from his coat as soon as he was safely behind the door of his chamber.

Orange blossom and rose. Exquisite.

And he was going to take this exquisite bloom of a young woman with him into hell.

He must have run utterly, hopelessly mad. Because he

was filled with the same sort of excitement—a physical hum of readiness in his body—that he remembered as a boy, out stalking rich culls to dip with his sister. His professional acumen had remained—he could still spot a goldfinch at twenty paces—but he'd lost that jangle of excitement that used to grip him hard when his sister, Meggs, had tipped him the nod and set him after a mark.

The intervening years had left a different sort of mark. Hunger no longer hollowed out his belly—the dukedom had seen to feeding him up. But the plenty had left a different sort of fire in his belly. A fire he had never been able to slake. A fire that flared ever stronger in the presence of Lady Claire Jellicoe.

The need to prove himself worthy.

Tanner folded the evening coat Lady Claire had returned to him and set it carefully aside—an act of sentimentality he decried in himself, but was powerless to resist. He would likely never wear it again, nor surrender it ever to be laundered, because it still held the warmth of her body, her scent.

Would that it always could.

Yet he knew it would not. So Tanner took another scalding gulp of the coffee Jinks had finally delivered—as aromatic and as dark as the peat bog Jinks must have originally come from—and let the hot jolt of urgency set his blood to pumping, before he proceeded to change the rest of his clothing into what he thought of as his Seven Dials rig. He discarded his satin breeches for the rough buckskins and well-worn, heavy boots that were his usual companions when he ventured out into London's meaner streets.

And mean they would be this morning. The meanest.

Which meant rechecking the gun he had retrieved from Lady Claire and adding another to his waistband, along with the knives in his boots.

He was as ready as he could be. He could only hope she was as well.

Tanner left his bedchamber to return to the kitchens, where Jack was recording his observations into a notebook in his careful, precise hand. "What have you got?"

The surgeon didn't look up. "Death by strangulation, just as you supposed. Throttled her as effectively as if she'd been hanged. Choked off the blood flow in the jugular vein and carotid arteries first—evidenced most easily in the petichiae here in the whites of her eyes."

"Pinprick dots of red. I see." A new fact to tuck into the orderly file room of his mind.

"Yes. I was about to remove her clothing, but I wanted to make sure there would be no other viewers." Jack gave him a rather particular look—a look that asked a different question from the one he had just voiced.

"You mean Lady Claire?"

"Yes, Lady Claire." Jack tipped his chin to the side, always a sign that he was rampantly curious but too well mannered to blurt out his question.

Unlike Tanner, who countered his friend's curiosity by bluntly concentrating on the practicalities. "Do you need to anatomize the girl to know what happened?"

"No." The surgeon shook his head. "Not likely. The signs are clear that she was murdered."

"But was she raped?"

"Ah." Jack's head went back slowly. "You wouldn't ask unless you had good reason to suspect so stored up in that fiendishly clever brain of yours. Further examination will be necessary. Which will necessitate removal of the clothing. Which would be easiest to accomplish before the full rigor mortis sets in. Which brings us back to Lady Claire Jellicoe. And whether or not she is likely to reappear in this kitchen."

"We'll leave directly."

"To take her home?"

"Later."

"Later?" Jack's look was cautiously probing—narrowed eyes under one raised brow, along with that characteristically questioning tip of the head. "How much later? And I have to ask, what on earth you were doing alone with Lady Claire Jellicoe in the first place?"

Tanner was not going to answer the question. He would not expose Lady Claire in that way. "We were not *doing* anything. I told you, Lady Claire identified the body as that of her servant Maisy Carter."

"You do realize? Even *you* must realize what must occur if you've had that girl—*that* girl, the daughter of an earl—out on the river all these hours?"

"Even me? Careful, Jack."

"Yes, even you. Tanner, you have to realize that there are some social conventions that are set in stone. Not even the silent, frosty Duke of Fenmore could hope to silence or endure such a scandal."

"I can endure anything."

"But can Lady Claire? Will she want to? Do you want her to?"

No. He did not want Lady Claire to suffer at all. That was how the night had begun. But he was saved from finding the answer by the arrival of Lady Claire herself, who stooped down to peer cautiously under the lintel as she came down the stairs. "Your Grace?"

"Yes, my lady?" he answered automatically. And in that moment he realized that he would do almost anything it seemed to make her his lady in actuality. Even take her to the Almonry.

He really did have a stupendously stupid amount of pride.

Lady Claire came down the last few steps, and stood at the bottom of the stairwell, awaiting his approval. She was dressed much as he, in worn dark clothes, sturdy fabrics, and heavy boots. But if he had thought the drabber dress his sister had left behind from her days of working the dub would have diminished and dulled Lady Claire's beauty, he was wrong.

Even without silk and muslin, she was exquisite. And even more so because the dull, rough fabric of the gown made the fineness of her beauty stand out more starkly. She looked both the same, and entirely different—a younger, far less polished version of herself, from the days when she must have rambled over her father's country estate, climbing trees and chasing after her brothers. She looked like a wild wood nymph from some ancient story, earthy and natural, and, dare he say it, free.

Free to come with him.

Her long, shining, golden hair was also freed from its pins, swirling loosely into a knot at her nape. The messy coil was an attractive nuisance—it was all he could do not to plunge his hands into the bright strands and disrupt the whole thing.

But his practical, organized mind reasserted itself. "You'll want to wear a shawl to cover your bright hair. And to remove your earbobs. They'll make a temping target, and I should hate to have your lobes ripped as a result." He meant to scare her. He meant for her to completely understand what she was getting herself into. Her costly earbobs, jeweled with diamonds and pearls, were valuable enough to keep half of the Almonry's residents in gin for a ten-year.

"Oh. My. No." She quickly unpinned the jewels, and held them out to him in the palm of her hand.

"Did you find the pockets sewn into petticoats?" The jewels would be safe enough in Meggs's deep pockets. His canny sister had hidden the entirety of their wealth there many a time.

"No. I kept my own chemise—" A swath of color swept across the lady's cheeks. "No. Perhaps you might have a safe place for them here?"

"Yes. Of course." Tanner had at least two caches hidden in the old walls, and he suspected that Jinks must have several more he could be made to divulge in a pinch.

"Thank you. And I have the note. To my parents."

As she handed him the earbobs and the unsealed note, her fingers brushed against his palm, and Tanner was again reminded of how soft her skin was. She had the hands of a lady—hands that had never done any kind of manual labor or rough, uncomfortable work. Hands that would only find exercise in piano sonatas or embroidery work—fingers long and supple and fragile. She was a fine china teacup, suitable for taking life in manageable sips. Entirely unsuited to the education he was giving her now.

But she wanted more, she had said. She wanted to be competent and capable and self-determining in a new and different way.

"You're welcome," he said stupidly, because he no longer remembered what he was thanking her for. And he stood there awkwardly for another long moment, because he couldn't seem to stop himself from looking at her, and marveling that he appeared to be living through a waking dream. A dream wherein everything he had ever fantasized about Lady Claire Jellicoe was coming true—she was with him, away from society, and looking at him with a sort of hopeful cheerfulness that told him she really was as mad as he.

"Are you ready?"

"Yes, I'm— No. I can't lie." She looked at him, her wide blue eyes open and guileless. "I must admit, I'm afraid." She caught her lip between her teeth to quash her smile. "And excited, perhaps? But definitely afraid. But it will be all right, won't it? You do know what you're doing, don't you?"

"I do. Come with me, and I'll show you."

Her glance went to the corridor to the kitchen door.

"Not yet. First, let us have a look at the clues the tenacious Miss Carter left us—the fob and the scrap of fabric." He unhooked one of the lamps, and led her into the labyrinth of small rooms and offices off the kitchen, to the small room that used to house the laundry.

It was here that he kept his scientific instruments—the bright lime-washed walls reflected light, and helped illuminate the instruments at night, when he was most often in Chelsea. He pulled the felt cover off the beautifully made brass microscope, and moved the lamp closer to the reflecting mirror so he would have plenty of light.

Beneath magnification, the fabric revealed itself to be a creamy and glistening silk. Rich and enticing. But he resisted the lure, and moved aside to let Lady Claire take a look. "Have you used an optical instrument before? The image you'll see is magnified—made larger—through a number of progressive lenses." He also resisted the urge to lecture. She was a smart girl—she would figure it out.

Lady Claire moved to the eyepiece and copied his stance. "Oh, heavens. I can see—how marvelous."

"Tell me what you see."

"Ivory-colored twilled silk, with fine gold tissue woven in."

"Yes. Exclusive and expensive fabric. The kind of fabric only a rich man could buy."

"Yes. I see."

"The kind of fabric only three or four tailors in the city of London would keep in stock. An old-fashioned fabric, used by an established, old-fashioned tailor, who had made their reputation on the elaborately brocaded and embroidered waistcoats of the previous era. That narrows it down to two—three at most."

"And any of those tailors would likely be more than happy to furnish the lofty Duke of Fenmore with a list of their exclusive clients, don't you think?"

"I do." Oh, how he liked it when the hunt was afoot. But the rush of pleasure filling his chest surprised him. It went beyond that jangling excitement of the hunt. It went beyond anything he had heretofore experienced. It was almost . . . happiness. How extraordinary.

"Shall we visit them all?"

"No." As much as he wanted to do just that, he knew couldn't expose Lady Claire Jellicoe so publicly as to take her on a tour of *tonnish* tailors—she was too well known in society, and was like to be recognized. "I'll send a man while we're in the Almonry." He would send Jinks to put Beamish, the majordomo nominally in charge of Fenmore House, on to the task. Beamish knew a thing or two about taking the lay of a ken. "We have other tasks to undertake."

"All right. You know best."

He did. But she not only looked at him—she also looked to him. She looked to him as if he could take away her fear, and fill the empty space it left with something easier.

But he had nothing. Nothing of finesse and grace. Nothing to ease her fears but his cleverness. Nothing but himself.

And Tanner found he was as selfish a creature as Rosing. Because he wanted to show her his cleverness. So he would take her by the hand and lead her into hell.

He said the only thing he knew that was true. "Trust me."

She smiled. That small private smile that seemed as if it were only for him. As if he were everything important and trustworthy in her world. "I have," she said. "And I will."

He knew it for the gift it was. But he nodded, all confident brusqueness, and said, "Right then. Shall we go?"

He could see her fill her lungs with silent resolution. And then she gave him that quick, bright smile, full of wobbling Dutch courage. "Yes, please."

He pocketed the fob, gave his instructions to Jinks, and led her out of the house. They went out the same way they had come—through the kitchen door and back down the alley—and headed back to the water stairs just as the first faint flush of dawn pinked a ribbon in the eastern sky. It was the best time to be up and about. All the dirty business of the wee small hours of the morning had long since been done, and villains and victims alike had quit the street to find their respective sanctuaries. Gone to ground like foxes to their dens.

The muddy funk of low tide rose off the water to greet them. The tide was almost full out, but the skiff was still in the water where he had left it at the far end of the plank way. After he had handed Lady Claire in, Tanner took a moment to search the shadows beneath the stairs for the urchin he had bargained with to keep it safe.

"Lark?"

"Aye, Tanner." A small shadow moved in the murk beneath the stair until a thin face became visible in the watery light. "Lukey come round, looking to make a quick snatch. But I gave him the caution, and said it were yourn."

Tanner fished the promised pennies from his pockets, and tossed them to the urchin, who snatched them up from the air as quick and silent as death. He didn't like the pinched hollowness in the urchin's face—the stoic acceptance of a life so mean and tenuous a stiff gale might blow it all away.

"Come with us?" He oughtn't let pity color his judgment. But then again, if he couldn't put his judgment at the service of the pitiful he was less than half the man he thought himself. And far less of a man than he wanted Lady Claire Jellicoe to think him.

"Come with us," he offered again. "We're Westminster bound. There's another bit of lour in it."

"How much?"

Tanner named another paltry sum but added, "And more if you look sharp and mind the skiff all through the day."

The offer was lure enough to the hungry. "Done" was the immediate reply.

"Whitehall steps, and then you return the skiff here when the tide turns."

"Right." The pile of rags resolved itself into the thin shape of a tall young girl—taller than he remembered.

Tanner did the maths in his brain. She must be nearing six- or seventeen—hard to tell without parents who remembered—though she looked both a hundred years older and a hundred years younger than Lady Claire. Hunger did that to a body.

But he'd been doing his best to keep her fed. "You've grown."

"People do that, don't they, when they've food." Her answer was all scrappy sarcasm that he recognized all too well.

He kept his voice even. "And you've food enough from Jinks, now?"

"Don't like charity."

"Don't like being hungry more." Only sharp, insistent logic would convince her. "And it's not charity when you're working jobs like this one."

"Huh." A huff of breath was her only response, but she promptly began to make ready to shove the skiff away from the planks. She scampered over to untie the painter, and then seated herself nimbly and silently in the bow as Tanner swung the boat out into the stream of the river.

Lady Claire accepted the raggedy girl's appearance just as silently. But he could see her trying to peer around him in the thin dawn light to try to make the girl out.

"This is the River Lark," he said by way of introduction. "From time to time, she looks after boats and such for me. Lark, this is . . . a lady friend."

The Lark proved just as curious about the lady. She flicked a cutty-eyed glance at the stern. "She *your* lady friend? Special-like?"

"Very special." Tanner kept his eyes on Lady Claire to see what she made of this particular piece of flummery.

The lady just gave him a quick squeeze of a smile before she introduced herself, all exquisite manner and gentle politeness. "Yes, I'm Claire. Very nice to meet you, Lark."

"Huh."

The poor child had likely never been spoken to by a lady of Lady Claire's rank. At least not kindly. Behind him, Tanner felt the girl's disbelieving glare, but soon enough her swift attention turned back to the river.

"Barge coming out from Battersea, Tanner."

"Ta." Tanner steered them more toward the west bank, out of the main stream of the river, to avoid larger vessels as the traffic began to pick up.

"Tanner?" Lady Claire asked. "Is that your Christian name?"

He had been waiting for the soft question. "A childhood name."

She smiled, a small show of some private delight. "I didn't think men like you had nicknames. Unless they are terribly bad and rakish, and are called Beau or Hellfire

Harry, or some such. Or are very good, and are called Parson. But I've never heard anyone call you anything but F—"

"No." His injunction was swift and low. Although the Lark and other people like her on the damp, dark margins of London life probably knew more of him than he had ever let on, he tried to keep his identity as the Duke of Fenmore as separate as possible from his streetwise self. "'Tanner' will do. A tanner is a coin—a sixpence—which I used to steal quite a lot of. My sister was called Meggs, for the guineas she was so good at stealing."

"Oh, I see. From your sad childhood."

"It wasn't sad." He said it too quickly—she was looking at him with that terrible combination of concern and pity. "I had what I needed." Provided for him by his sister. Unlike Lark, who had no one. But this wasn't the time to expound upon his one-man crusade to help London's abandoned children. So he changed the subject. "And if I may call you Claire? Or perhaps you've another, more familiar name you'd prefer to be called?"

"It does seem a little strange at this point to hold to the proprieties. Of course you may call me Claire."

Another spate of pleasure warmed his chest. "Thank you, Claire. The next lesson in protecting yourself will be acting like you've already got all the protection you need. Like you belong. Swagger." He let his voice go rough-and-tumble. "Piss and vinegar. Do you see?"

She pleated that line between her perfect golden brows and shook her head. "No."

"When we get to Westminster, you'll need to act like you're my lass, and I, your man. For protection, if nothing else. The world is not, as you so roughly learned from Rosing, a kind place. And this city—and the part of the city where we're going—is unkinder still than even Rosing."

"Oh. Yes. I see." She nodded and sat up a little straighter. "I understand. You mean to pretend, for show. Like that extraordinary show in the alley when you put off those two footpads."

"Ah. Mick and Duffer Robertson."

"You know their names? Oh." Those lovely golden brows shot up. "From your childhood?"

Tanner almost gave her the truth. He almost said, no, it was not for show—it was very much for real. He almost said he did not know those men from his criminal childhood. But guile—he was full to his back teeth of guile, and he meant to take advantage of each and every inch of ground he could cover with her, even if it meant taking advantage of her pity—told him not to. So he asked, "Will it be such a burden to pretend to like me?"

"No." She said the word carefully, as if she were still mulling it over and wanted to draw the denial out long enough to make up her mind. "I don't think it would be a burden, Your Grace—"

"Tanner."

"I don't think it would be a burden to act as if I like you, Tanner." She tried the name out, like a new taste in her mouth. "Because I do like you. I trust you, even though we've known each other only a few hours."

And he'd known her—or thought he'd known her—forever. And yet, as he looked at her steady, uncompromising gaze, he realized that didn't know the true Claire Jellicoe—the girl behind the elaborate facade of "Lady Claire" that he had constructed for her—at all.

She was infinitely more than her aura of glistening, golden perfection. She was capable of using her mind. She thought. She understood. And she seemed to understand and accept him. A little, at least. Enough to be going on with.

And God knew not even his own flesh and blood had ever completely understood the clockwork tickings of his mind.

"Will it be—" She straightened her chin and began again. "Will it be a burden for you to pretend to like me?"

This he understood a little better, this small sign of vanity. It was kin to his own savage pride. He would reassure her. "It's no imposition to smile at a lovely lass, Claire. No imposition at all."

He watched her smile and look away and then color, her pale cheeks turned rosy in the inky purple light of the dawn. But the smile didn't quite reach her eyes. He couldn't quite read her. And for the first time in his life, he actually wanted someone to tell him what they were thinking. "Claire?"

And he liked saying her name, if for nothing beyond the calming pleasure of it.

"I just realized that you must do this all the time. With these clothes at the ready, and how you were with the men in the alley. You weren't surprised. You must do this all the time, with other people. Other girls?"

This was more than vanity or pride surely? This was . . . personal. Tanner lowered his voice and leaned toward her. "No. Not all the time. I've never acted like I was anyone's man before, Claire. Nor like anyone but you was my girl. This day is special in that way."

The smile that grew up from her lips was small and trying not to be pleased, but quite pleased nonetheless. "Now you will make me feel vain. But I suppose any lass likes to think she's special."

"Ain't that the truth, missus," Lark added in a rueful aside from the bow. "Ain't that the bleeding truth."

Tanner made no other answer. But all he could think, as he rocked back and forth with the rhythm of the oars, was that he would make Claire feel more special yet.

Chapter Nine

Dawn spilled slowly over the purple rim of the horizon to the east. Other colors seeped into the morning sky—deep orange-soaked pink rising to push back the purple. The mirror of the river spread the colors over the surface of the smooth water. Only around the banks was the land separated from the sky by a swath of moving mist, swirling around the humps of buildings and wharves along the banks. The morning was breathtaking and stunning in its vibrancy.

And His Grace's face, silhouetted against it all, still in gray shadow, looking cool and collected against the riot of warm color.

But Claire knew now that there was nothing cold about him. Nothing placid or unfeeling. The facade he showed the world was just a high wall, designed to keep all the vehemence within from spilling out into the streets. His aloofness was a bastion of gentlemanly reserve designed to hold the world at bay, and keep his feelings private.

But he looked nothing like a reserved gentleman now, in a loose old redingote that had seen far better days, over plain spun-linen shirtsleeves, a dark suede jerkin, and rough-looking breeches. He had traded his smart Hessians for heavier, treaded boots and leather gaiters. He completed his ensemble by covering his too-well-groomed hair with a slouchy hat and shrugging himself into that loose old redingote the color of spring mud.

He looked like one of the rough-and-tumble fellows her mother would have termed a swell—tough and disreputable, and altogether far more male and potent than he had ever looked looming around the edges of ballrooms. And he had looked potent enough then.

But now he was rather thrilling, actually.

Back in the house at Chelsea there had been a moment when he had looked up at her from under his brows when he had heard her tread upon the kitchen stair. He had done as neat a double take—looking away absently and then cutting sharply back—as she could ever hope to see. And a thrill had clattered its silly way down the length of her spine, leaving her flushed and nearly giddy. His regard thrilled her.

He thrilled her.

Until she reminded herself it was not a time for foolish thrills or giddiness. The night had already seen enough naive foolishness—that her face was so scratched and bruised was evidence enough of that. And they were on a solemn mission, bringing the woeful news to Maisy Carter's poor family.

They alighted from the skiff at a place called Deval's Wharf—a faded sign was painted on the side of a building, spilling out on to the narrow south yard of the old Palace of Westminster. As soon as they stepped off onto the embankment the Lark took the oars, and pulled silently away southward.

"Won't we need the boat to get back to Richmond?"

"No." His Grace was already moving purposefully forward, making a silent come-along-and-follow-me gesture with his hand. "By the time we're done here, the tide will have turned."

Claire moved as close as possible to him. The neighborhood looked ominously gray and dreary. Full of moldy menace. "Where do we go next?"

His Grace—Tanner, she reminded herself—stopped and turned back to her, toe to toe. He looked her in the eye, his deep blue-green gaze intent and penetrating. "Are you still determined? You do understand it won't be pretty? It will be close and damp and reeking and very, very shabby. As shabby as you've ever imagined." He paused as if he were waiting for her imagination to catch up with his description. "Shabbier. Dirtier. Poorer. Much, much poorer."

"Yes, all right. I understand." Claire also imagined his words would prove to be an understatement. "But I *am* determined." She said it as much to convince herself as him. "We can do no less for Maisy Carter, don't you agree?"

"I do." But he didn't look glad of it. He looked unhappy, and burdened and dangerous, with his eyes shifting right and left, scanning the way ahead. "Right then," he said. "Follow my lead. Let me do the talkin' as needs to be done. You're my lass, then. Special-like, as the Lark said. My mort."

"Mort?" It was not a word she knew.

"My woman." He took her elbow, and guided her backward until she came up against the wall at the corner of the street.

The moment her backside hit the brick, the cage of her chest tightened, and her hands came up, her cold-slick palms open wide, ready to push him off. Ready to stop him.

But he did not come any nearer. Still, she felt the loom of him, the physical dominance of his position, the imminent threat of his mere presence. Her heart thundered in her ears, filling her up until she started to feel as if she could drown in it. Her chest began to rise and fall in great gulping gasps.

But he came no nearer. He stood his ground and looked at her from under the dark brim of his hat. "We'll need to be close, Claire. To be safe." His voice was a low rumble. "But you'll tell me if I get too close. You'll tell me if this distresses you."

And because he said it, because he seemed to know what she was feeling, some of the tight, strangled feeling eased. Her heart was still pumping too fast, but she was no longer breathing like a leaky bellows.

She nodded her understanding, and he stepped nearer and reached out to touch her, as if he had a right to touch her freely, sliding his hand along the line of her jaw and fanning around her nape. As if he were about to kiss her.

Claire flinched, her head smacking the wall smartly, knocking some sense into her. "No."

He stopped immediately. The brim of his hat brushed against her temple, enclosing them in a tiny, close tent of privacy. And then he waited. Waited for her to accustom herself to him. Waited for her to protest or say she'd had enough. His touch at her nape turned even more gentle and careful—almost reverent, as if he feared she was fragile and might break. As if he thought she needed his protection.

But she would not break. She was determined.

And so was he—determined to take his time. Determined to be controlled and light and careful. His left hand came up to barely caress her elbow. "All right?"

"No." She was all right, even if her voice did sound small and breathy. "Almost."

She needed—

She wasn't sure what she needed, besides more time—

which they didn't have. But Tanner didn't rush her, so Claire took her time, and let her instinct be her guide and clasped his elbow just as he had clasped hers and swung herself around.

So he was the one with his back to the wall and she was the one who was free and could choose how close to him she wanted to be.

He accepted the reversal with an easy grace. He relaxed back against the wall and waited, holding his hand carefully at her nape so she could follow him if she chose. And in another moment she did choose to lay her hand upon his chest, resting lightly against the front of his coat.

He touched her face again—that soft, gentle, reverent touch—and she let him. Let the warmth of both his fingers and his regard chase away the lingering cold within.

It was nothing like before. He was nothing like Lord Peter Rosing. Tanner was protecting her. Teaching her.

And it was nice. He was nice. He even smelled nice—of starch and cedar spice from the chest where he must have stored his clothes. Homey and practical. Safe.

So unlike the chilly, aloof Duke of Fenmore.

This Tanner was warm and confident. "Are you ready now, lass?" His voice regained the low rumble of roughness, tumbling across his tongue like an agile acrobat.

Claire found herself looking at his mouth, watching his perfect lips form the imperfect, mangled words and still make then sound so compelling. "Yes."

"That's the girl." And then he pressed his lips to her forehead—a quick benediction and encouragement. "Stay close to me so we'll look like we're together, see? Like we're a . . . couple."

Like they were intimate was what he meant. Like they were lovers.

A new heat blossomed deep under Claire's skin and made her feel flushed and tingling and discomfited. Every

nerve in her body was awake and, if not exactly uncomfortable, then alarmed.

But she could no longer deny her attraction to him.

He showed no such susceptibility. He was only playing
a part, putting on the role of intimate just as easily as he
had put on the worn redingote and the casual, rangy stride
that took up the greater portion of the narrow roadway,
and made people pull back to let them pass.

But there was something still of the duke in him—
though he certainly looked humbler, rigged up in such
worn clothes—something, if not of privilege, then of command. Yes, if anything, the rough-spun clothing made
him more masculine, more powerful and commanding in
an entirely different way than the sharp, clever tailoring
of his perfectly cut evening clothes ever had.

But this was not a place for evening clothes, for polite
euphemisms and flattering, soft talk. This was a place for
the sort of cagey swagger and quiet bravado that clung to
him more surely than his highwayman's jerkin.

And he seemed to know this city, these dark, festering
places, like he knew the sharp lines of his own face. He
walked with authority, moving as if he knew exactly where
he was, when she could barely keep conscious of which
way was east the moment the crowded buildings blocked
out the sight of the rising sun.

The crooked buildings soon loomed over them, until it
seemed as if they were walking back into the night. There
was nothing familiar now. The farther they moved off
the river, the thicker the air seemed to become, though
no less damp, laden with the gritty stink of the fires that
coughed out of listing chimneys leaning against the low,
dirty hovels.

He urged her closer with a hand at her elbow, though
she was nearly walking upon his heels in an effort to stay
near. "Snug up close, lass."

"Oh, yes." She needed little urging to take advantage of the comfort of his sheltering height, as the fetid stink from the gutters assailed her nostrils, and the acrid smoke stung her eyes. But then she came to a fuller understanding of His Grace's meaning when he slung his arm across her shoulders, and pulled her flush against his side in the casually rough way of the stevedores and their girls working in the Hungerford Market down near the river, or the carters working Shepherd Market near her father's house in St. James's, where she sometimes went in the morning at her mother's request.

How remarkable it was that she felt safe in the Duke of Fenmore's roughly casual embrace—in what he had proclaimed to be one of the worst slums in London. She felt safe, when she had felt exactly the opposite with Lord Peter Rosing in the seemingly safe environs of a wealthy estate.

How astonishing. And how dangerous.

Claire's pulse quickened and began to keep time with her footfalls upon the dank cobbles. No. Tanner was nothing like Lord Peter Rosing. Everything Tanner had said and done had already proved that true. Everything.

Tanner angled then toward the side of the narrow lane, where what her buckish brothers would have called a likely-looking chum was splayed low against a barrel.

"Lookin' fer a ken." Tanner looked down at him from under the brim of his slouchy hat. "Carters live along 'ere?"

The greasy little chum squinted up at them but didn't move another muscle. "Whot's in it fer me?"

Tanner pushed his voice so low it raked the gutter. "Mebbe me not darkening your daylights. Mebbe a copper if you can furnish it sharpish-like."

The speed with which he devolved to casual violence shocked her to her core, and sent a sharp wedge of doubt prying into her fresh convictions. Despite his injunction to stay close, Claire pulled herself back from him. She had conveniently forgotten how ruthlessly Tanner had broken Rosing's leg. How coldly and efficiently it had been done. Despite the fact that Rosing certainly did deserve it.

But neither Tanner nor the chum paid her crisis of confidence any mind.

The chum evinced a sour smile. "There's a Molly Carter takes in washin' up Union Place way. Mean-eyed old mort. I'd watch my baubles with her, if I was you."

Tanner turned up one side of his mouth in a tight smile. "Obliged." And with a flick of his fingers, he sent a single copper coin spiraling through the air.

In the dimness Claire couldn't see if it were caught, but she didn't hear the penny drop.

And had to smile to herself.

This was what His Grace had been talking to her about—about how she knew more than she knew she knew. How she knew the chum had caught his penny because she never heard it hit the ground. How astonishing.

Tanner led her in his meandering, loose-limbed way down the meanest, most filthy, most stinking streets she had ever encountered. And every step brought them somewhere meaner and filthier and more stinking still. They came along the back wall of Saint Margaret's workhouse, where the place stank of stale sweat and something stronger—desperation. Claire had to put her hand across her face to combat the stench.

"Don't, if you can help it," he leaned close to rumble into her ear. "It will draw attention to you if you look like you can't stomach the odor. Lean in to me. Jinks launders what he keeps for me, regular-like. Or hide a bit in your shawl. Even cut up, you're too bloody beautiful for the Almonry."

The offhand compliment warmed her cheeks and restored her faith in His Grace's essential kindness. He might be violent and vehement, but he was violent and vehement on her behalf. It certainly was not what she might have expected from the aloof and chilly Duke of Fenmore, but it certainly was serving her well now.

Without his stunningly swift violence, she would have been raped. And perhaps murdered.

The grim reminder made her hitch the plain-spun shawl higher over the crown of her head. Her abigail, Silvers, would have an apoplexy if she ever saw Claire looking like a worn-out shopgirl, with her hair sliding loose from its pins.

But despite her misgivings, she didn't feel worn-out. She felt alive and exhilarated by the exciting newness of it all.

Her guide had another low word with an old slattern propped against a semi-derelict brick building on the ill-lit corner of Orchard Street—semi-derelict only because people were streaming in and out of the place even though it looked as if it were about to fall down on top of them. The old trull pointed them around a corner, and in another few moments they turned into the darkly narrow confines of Union Place.

"It's a dead end," Fenmore said low into her ear. "In more ways than one. Look sharp. Stay behind me."

Claire wasn't entirely sure how she might look sharp, other than keeping her eyes wide-open and trying to remember the way they had come. She began to count the number of footsteps they took into the dim little court.

"Carters'?" Tanner growled his inquiry at an urchin, who simply pointed to the open door of number 10.

Tanner steered Claire across the gap where a thin gutter ran down the middle of the lane, whereupon he knocked on the door frame with the side of his fist.

Claire peeped around Tanner to see a middle-aged woman with a uncapped head of fair hair, a face red with exertion, and a cynical, distrusting look in her eye come to the door. "Whatta you want?"

"Lookin' fer Molly Carter," Tanner said.

The sharp-eyed woman narrowed her gaze. "'Oo's asking?"

"A friend o' your daughter, Maisy."

The woman cut a sharp eye over him and shook her head. "My Maisy ain't got no friends as look like you. She's a good girl, she is, and not for the likes of you. There's summat off about you, like four-day-old fish."

The woman made as if she would slam the ramshackle door in their faces until Claire stepped quickly forward.

"We've come from Riverchon Park, ma'am. We need to speak with you."

At the sound of Claire's voice the woman stopped, and took another look from Claire's face to her skirts and back. "Yer no friends of my Maisy." Her eyes were slitty with suspicion.

"No, ma'am." Claire swallowed over the sudden heat in her throat. "I'm so very sorry, ma'am. Despite present appearances, we have come from Riverchon Park, and we must speak to you. I'm afraid it is very bad news."

Molly Carter's red face fell pale, and she put her hand to her chest to steady herself for the blow. Tanner put a hand to Molly Carter's elbow to support her and urged them both over the threshold in uncompromising tones. "Inside. Private-like."

Even as she stepped into the dimly lit, grim interior Claire could see the fear darken Molly Carter's eyes and hollow out her features. And in the way of her kind, fear made the woman pugnacious. She shook off Tanner's assistance and rounded on them threateningly, snatching up a rusty pair of scissors. "What have you done to my girl?"

In his blunt, straightforward way, Tanner did not try to cushion the blow. "She's dead."

The scissors clattered to the wooden floor.

"No." The mother's denial was no more than a whisper, but it went through Claire like a blade.

But Claire did the only thing she knew how to do—she took the hand the woman had clenched into a fist and held on tight. "I am afraid we've found her, ma'am. But too late."

"No." The poor woman clasped on to Claire's hand and gripped harder, till her knuckles were white. "Not my Maisy."

"I'm so sorry."

The poor woman shook her head, as if the action could stave off both the tears and the terrible truth.

But it was impossible. Molly Carter began to cry. Loud, wailing sobs that tore Claire's heart to absolute bits. And all she could do was bleed with her, and hold on.

Chapter Ten

Maisy Carter's mother was a washerwoman. Tanner had instantly taken in her raw red hands—chapped from constant dunking in the lye soap vats that no doubt littered the small yard at the rear of the house—and rheumy, squinting eyes, and concluded her profession. Her face looked as rough as her hands. And likely her withered old-before-her-time soul. He recognized the face of a cynic. He had looked in the mirror often enough.

And the inside of the hovel, though canting dangerously to the north, was scrubbed within an inch of its life. Scrubbed so viciously there were scrape marks in the uneven wood-plank floor.

Molly Carter hated the dirt. But she must have loved her daughter.

"She were marked for something better," Molly Carter said between sobs. "She were free of this place."

He hadn't expected her tears. He had expected the kind of cynical stoicism that only a place like the Almonry could produce. He had expected Molly Carter to be what she appeared, cutty eyed and deeply distrusting, hardened and worn to a dull blade by care and ceaseless work.

There was nothing more that could be done. He and Claire had done their Christian duty and given the poor creature the awful news, but hysteria was taking over. The woman's sobs racked her stout body. They would learn nothing more from her now.

And weeping had always made him uncomfortable.

"Claire." He touched her elbow to show themselves out.

But Lady Claire Jellicoe wasn't listening. She was rounding her delicate elbow out of his grip and reaching toward Molly Carter, instead of away. Lady Claire Jellicoe moved close to Molly Carter and took up the woman's hand where it lay pressed flat and white against the bleached and battered table.

Lady Claire made one of those strange wordless sympathetic noises. Like a well-bred mourning dove, making an empathetic coo. And then she took the hard-boiled harridan who was Molly Carter into her soft, pale arms, as if she were giving the woman a lifeline. As if she would save her from drowning in her sorrow. And somehow, she was.

Molly Carter was clinging to Lady Claire's slim shoulders as if she were the last piece of flotsam in the whole of the sea. "God help her, miss," the woman sobbed.

Tears were sliding down Lady Claire's cheeks as well. "I can't speak for God, madam, but I can speak for *him*." Claire's eyes met his. "He will help her."

"How?" the washerwoman howled.

"He will find out who did this," she pledged. "He will find who did this, and he will avenge her."

Avenge. Such a bloodthirsty word from such an immaculate girl. But he liked it. It suited his plans. Because it gave him permission to do just as Lady Claire wanted, and avenge her as well.

"Nothing will bring her back," Claire was saying.

"And nothing will compensate you for her loss. But we promise you, we will put this right."

"You mean my girl was murdered? You can't never put that right." Molly Carter clenched her hands, as if she would rail against fate.

"No." Tanner spoke. "But I can promise you that I will make the man who did this pay. I will find the miscreant who did this to your daughter. I will hunt him down, and see that he is hanged by the neck in Newgate Yard, if it is the last thing I do."

"You do that. Do you hear me?" The woman pushed herself away from Claire and wiped her face on her apron. "You find him, whoever the hell you are. You find the whoreson that took my Maisy, and you get him. And you send me word when you've got him, so I can curse his soul to hell, and watch him dance." And then all her defiant anger seemed spent, and she collapsed down into a chair with a silent, gasping sob.

Tanner looked into her red-rimmed eyes. "Madam, you have my word upon it."

It was done. He turned toward the door. "Claire."

But again, Lady Claire Jellicoe was proving to be a great deal less predictable than he had expected. She had her arms wrapped tight around Molly Carter's shoulders again making those soft, sympathetic noises.

And then she did the most astonishing thing of all. She lied.

Her face was as fresh and open and honest as it ever had been. But she lied through her teeth. "You should know she didn't suffer, Maisy didn't." Her voice was as smooth and soothing as a balm.

A balm Molly Carter wanted to hear. "Thank God." The woman looked upward, as if in entreaty to a God who had clearly forsaken her, and tried to catch her breath, but tears were still streaming down her cheeks. "Thank God for that."

"Did she come home, here, to see you often?" Lady Claire's voice was soft and kind and encouraging intimacy, a much more subtle weapon than any he knew how to wield.

"No, I didn't like her to." Molly Carter shook her head, and mopped at her face again with the apron. "She'd gone on to better, hadn't she? Didn't like to have her come back here."

"But she did anyway?"

"Yeah. Yeah, she did, bless her." Molly Carter was nodding and smiling and crying and wiping her eyes all at the same time. "Said I were her mam and that were that. Came on her half days, at least once a month. Always made sure I had a piece of cake for her here, though I'm sure she had finer up at Riverchon Park."

"Yes. They treated her very well up there. Just as they ought. She was a hardworking girl. A good girl. And such a good girl likes to come see her mam, no matter if she's gotten used to better, doesn't she?" Lady Claire consoled. "When was the last time she came here?"

"Tuesday week it were." The admission brought on a fresh spate of tears, which Lady Claire dealt with by rubbing the space between the woman's hunched shoulder blades.

"She came to visit regularly, because she was a good girl."

"She were. The best," Molly Carter confirmed on a watery wail. "She were the best. It's not right."

"I know it's not right, Mrs. Carter. I know. That's why we've come. To find out everything we can, and make it as right as we can. To find out everything we need to know about your Maisy."

Claire kept up her rubbing of the woman's back and patting her hand and wrapping her arm around her every few minutes to give her a squeeze. And she kept talking, kept on with her soft kindness. "Did she say anything about her work at Riverchon Park? Was she happy there?"

"Excited, she were, that she were to help to see to some very grand ladies soon. Ambitious, she was, my Maisy. Sharp and quick. Could see that when she were but a girl. Too sharp and too quick for the likes of the Almonry. Would've ended up in some bleeding kidding ken, with a kidman working her rough till she were stretched for a handkerchief."

Tanner could envision such a life clearly—it had been his own.

Molly Carter banged the flat of her hand against the table in emphatic denial. But the truth could not be denied, and Claire held on, and never stopped rubbing her heaving shoulders. "So I got her out. Got her into service with a lady I did washings for. Trained her up. Moved her on. Bigger houses, better positions."

Until last night, Maisy Carter had indeed been lucky—lucky to have had such a mother who could see a clear-eyed way out of a place like the Almonry for her daughter, even if she could not for herself. Not many other children were as lucky, or as loved.

"How she was getting on at Riverchon Park?" Claire probed gently. "How did she like the other staff?"

"Working her way up, she were. Told me she were going to be a housekeeper someday, she was. Had her eye on the higher prize. Saved all her wages, too—never one to spend it on cakes or ribbons and fripperies. Too smart for that. Brought me most of it. But I wouldn't take it. Wanted her to keep it."

A penny had a different value here than in Mayfair or Richmond.

"You were very good to her, just as she was very good to you."

"She were," Molly Carter repeated. "The best."

"And she was a very pretty girl. So what about young men? Was there anyone, anyone special, she talked about?"

"She was, wasn't she? Very pretty." Molly Carter reached out her coarse, chapped hands and cupped Lady Claire Jellicoe's soft, bruised face. "Remind me of her, you do. Same blue eyes, and sweet pale hair."

That someone might think Lady Claire Jellicoe resembled anyone else in the world was an idea so foreign to Tanner that his mind—his constantly, inexorably scheming mind—simply ground to a stop. Because Lady Claire Jellicoe was too unique, too much her own special luminous self, to resemble anyone, especially some poor murdered maid.

"You are so kind." Lady Claire was smiling, as if Molly Carter had given her the greatest possible compliment, although her cheeks were also wet and shiny with tears. "I imagine Maisy's prettiness brought her admirers."

"It did. Had to watch her close when she were a little one—keep her from the kiddy snatchers. And only put her in service with good houses, where I knowed she'd be looked after."

"Did she ever say she had admirers at Riverchon Park? I thought the footman . . ." Claire turned her wide, guileless eyes upon him.

"Jesse Lightfoot," he supplied.

"Yes, thank you. Jesse." She turned all her attention and comfort back to Molly. "A very handsome young man. He certainly admired her."

"Told me about him, she did. But she weren't that kind of girl as has her head turned." Molly fished out a thin, worn handkerchief, and mopped at her nose. "She were ambitious, she were, my Maisy. Wouldn't have wanted to let any man get in the way of her plans. Saw what happened to me, didn't she?"

That there was no Mr. Carter in residence was evidence enough of what had once happened to Molly Carter.

"Hmm. Yes." Lady Claire was all agreeable sympathy. "So she wasn't walking out with him?"

"Could be. If'n he accepted the way it stood with her. Could be they came to an understanding."

"Yes." Lady Claire nodded. "But a girl that pretty. Men don't often take no for an answer, do they? They often insist, don't they? More than insist."

Tanner heard the tremor in Lady Claire's voice—the uncomfortable emotional aftershock—and saw the slight shaking in her hand, though she kept trying to comfort Molly Carter.

Molly Carter saw it, too, for this time she put her own hand over Lady Claire's. "God rot 'em. Never leave you girls be, do they? Take what they want, when they want it, and be damned if they ask. The bastards." Again her rough, reddened hand came up to gently cradle Lady Claire's face. As tenderly as if Lady Claire had been her own daughter.

Remarkable.

"Yes." Claire's voice was small and tight. But she kept her clear gaze steady on Molly Carter. "I don't imagine a girl like Maisy would put up with that."

"No. Did he do that to you?" Molly Carter gave him a cutty-eyed look and tossed a defiant chin his way.

"Oh, no. Not Tanner, ma'am. He's the one that saved me. Kept it from going any further. Broke the beau nasty's leg, he did, and cracked his head as well."

"Good," Molly Carter said with some small relief. "Good." Though her eyes lingered on him as if he were a marker for all the evil no-good bastards of the world.

"Did Maisy ever have trouble with gentlemen, like I did?" Claire pushed on, though her voice was so thin she had to swallow to speak. "Did she ever find herself . . . imposed upon?"

He had always thought of Claire as naturally open and honest, but for the first time Tanner could see that it took a sort of bravery he didn't understand, for her to be so. A strength hidden beneath the delicate surface of her skin.

Molly could see what it cost her as well, for she was the one to put her arm around Claire and rub her back now. "Bless you, no, I shouldn't think so. I'd warned her, hadn't I? Told her how. She kept her eyes open, my Maisy. Kept away from that kind of gentleman." Molly Carter still thought him somehow responsible—still a stand-in for all unworthy gentlemen. She narrowed her eyes at him again, as if she could see under his raffish clothes and see the unworthy gentleman hiding somewhere underneath.

Funny. He usually feared it being the other way round—that under his gentlemanly tailoring someone would discover that he was nothing more than an impostor. Playing at being the duke until they found him out.

"She must have gotten her smarts and cleverness from you." Despite her own emotions, Claire was still working to ease Molly Carter's distress.

"Bless me," Molly said on a rough half laugh, "but you're kindness itself."

"I wish I could be kinder still. I wish I could have given you better news. I wish we had met under different circumstances."

"Bless me, child. Had Maisy not been murdered, we'd never have met under any circumstances at all. Quality, real quality, you are, despite the fact that you're here in the Almonry. And with 'im."

"He only *looks* that way, Molly. He's really as sweet as pudding underneath that fierce exterior, which he will put to good use finding Maisy's murderer." Claire gave him a quick smile before she asked him, "Speaking of, ought we to ask Molly about the fob?"

Tanner fished out the gleaming ornament. "Have you ever seen this?" he asked the washerwoman.

"Dunno." Molly Carter turned down her mouth and shook her head. "Where'd it come from?"

"From Maisy," Claire explained.

"Some gentleman give it to her?"

Molly Carter was as clever as she was heartbroken and weary. She had immediately grasped that any man with such an ornament had to be a *gentleman*.

"Oh, no," Claire was saying. "We think she took it."

"Never. She weren't no thief, my Maisy. She'd too much pride to lower herself. Pride I gave her, God help her."

"No, ma'am." Lady Claire took Molly Carter's hand again. "We think she took hold of it because he was trying to kill her."

It was too much for Molly Carter. But by now her sorrow was mixed with a more characteristic fury. "Oh, damn him to hell. Had to have been one of those bleeding nobs, then. Toffs think they can do what they want, don't they?"

Tanner saw Claire close her eyes, even though she nodded. "Yes, Molly, they do."

It took every bit of restraint he had to ignore Claire's quiet distress. But she had gotten Molly Carter talking and they needed more information. "Why do *you* say that, Mrs. Carter?"

"Stands to reason, don't it. Never was one of those boys she worked with at Riverchon. I'd stake my reputation on it."

"Why?" he probed again, taken by her absolute certainty.

"You wouldn't as' if you'd ever a met the housekeeper, Mrs. Dalgliesh, out to Riverchon. Runs that house and her staff right and tight. Never would have stood for a footman or anyone a'messing with my Maisy. Made me that promise the day I took my Maisy down there. Looked me in the eye, Dalgliesh did, and said it would be so. And so Maisy said it was. No. Had to be one of the nobs. Had to be someone even Dalgliesh couldn't cross, or was afraid of. Here, let me see the thing."

This time, it was Molly Carter's hand that shook as she reached for the fob and peered at it close, stretching her mind to its limit to think. "Poor lamb." She wiped away more tears with her apron. "I don't know—you know it brings to mind a gentleman I seen once or twice. I takes washing from his dolly mop up on Little George Street. She's no more than she should be for a whore, and remembers where she come from though she's over in Sloan Square now."

"His name?"

"She called him Taffy, if you can believe that. But when he's respectable, he's the Honorable Mr. Edward Layham."

The name set off an alarm bell clanging in Tanner's brain. The name was familiar. But he couldn't remember ever having come across Mr. Edward Layham before— couldn't remember if he had been on the guest list of Tanner's grandmother's ball—or put a face to the man. A mystery.

But he would certainly search him out now.

They would search him out now.

"Obliged to you, Molly Carter." Tanner touched the brim of his hat and set his mind forward, toward a murderer.

Chapter Eleven

They left Union Place and Molly Carter with assurances
that Maisy's body would be delivered unto her mother,
and all the expenses of a decent burial paid for. Claire
was especially reticent to leave Molly Carter on her own
to bear the burden of her daughter's death, but Tanner felt
they had already spent more time than he had planned
with the woman.

In the long hour they had spent with the washerwoman,
morning had broken across London. The summer sun
was up, and somewhere, either in Mayfair or in Richmond, a murderer was still breathing freely, enjoying the
morning in a way that neither the dead Maisy Carter, nor
her mother, nor even the damaged Lady Claire Jellicoe
ever would again.

Tanner had not imagined the way she had flinched
away from him. He had not imagined the febrile heat of
fear that left her cold in his arms. He had seen and felt it,
and it slayed and enraged him all at the same time. But it
gave him purpose, that flinch.

"The game has been afoot for hours, and the trail is
growing cold," he told Claire. "Every minute that passes
since the moment Maisy Carter was murdered means it will

be harder to find answers. We have to act, and act swiftly. Thanks to you, we have a new name, and a new direction."

"You are most welcome." The small pleasure of her smile was a gift to him. But Lady Claire must have heard something else besides praise in his voice. "Did you not expect Molly Carter to be able to help us?"

As much as he derided the glaring faults and weaknesses he saw in himself, he had to acknowledge them. And one of his faults was that he always assumed his way was best—he always assumed he was the most clever person in any room, in any given situation. The only person he had ever deferred to was his sister. The only person he had felt his equal in intellect was Jack.

And now Lady Claire Jellicoe had just proved that intellect was not enough. She had gifts that were entirely different. And entirely lacking in him.

And he needed to acknowledge that. "You handled Molly Carter superbly. Far better than I had expected. Far and above what I would have accomplished on my own. I never would have gotten her to talk. And if you hadn't gotten her to talk, she never would have seen the fob, and never would have mentioned the Honorable Edward Layham."

Claire's pleasure added warm color to her already livid cheek. "Thank you. I wasn't thinking about the information, really. I just did what I felt was right, but I'm glad it yielded a good result."

"A very good result. Come." He steered her around a corner. "This way."

To free them of the Almonry's narrow, sloping streets, Tanner turned them east on Orchard Street, moving swiftly into the wider, less dangerous stretch of Dean Street. Claire kept his pace, striding along by his side, looking decidedly more confident than she had an hour ago going into the Almonry. Her head was up, and she was gazing more

resolutely at the filth and poverty now, though in the
sharp morning sun the scratches and bruises on her cheek
looked far more livid than they had in the gray light of
dawn

And with her confidence came her formidible intelligence. "I've been thinking about that fob, Tanner. I've
been thinking that there can't be too many places, or
dealers perhaps, that deal in ancient Roman coins."

So had he. But she had just called him Tanner, and the
appellation set up a buzzing in his brain that extended
outward from his chest. God help him, but her acceptance
of him—glaring faults and all—excited him as much as
her cleverness. His attraction to her was a itchy, warm
vibration that worked its way down into his gut and back
out to his fingertips. An excitement that could only be assuaged by easing his arm over her shoulder and urging
her snug up against him.

He liked this leaning down to speak low into her ear.
"Yes, exactly. That kind of gold work—custom fitting an
irregular ancient coin into a framework—would take skill.
There are only four or perhaps five firms in London that
deal—honestly—in those kinds of rare numismatics."

She was more amused than excited, but she did not object to his presumption—she relaxed her slight weight into
him readily enough. "What a compendium of London's
firms you must have in that head of yours. So, we should
visit them first, one by one, until we find the right firm?"

"I have another idea. I know a fellow in the City who
should be able to tell us exactly what we need to know."

"And what a compendium of interesting people you
know, as well. Not at all the usual acquaintances for a
duke." She was smiling and shaking her head in her
amusement—for the first time truly at ease with him.
Happy.

Yes. The welcome jolt of fist-clenching pure male triumph that shot through his chest was more than just his savage pride. More than mere physical arousal. It was bone-deep pleasure for her sake as well.

And it made him want to please, and amuse, and put her at ease even more. "I told you, I wasn't always a duke. And because of that, the Honorable Edward Layham has heretofore escaped my rather encyclopedic eye."

"But not mine."

Unlike him, Lady Claire inhabited society as a familiar. She would naturally see things and people very differently than he. He was learning that it was very useful to have another person's opinion as a comparison.

She pleated her pristine forehead with that adorable little frown of concentration. "I am not formally acquainted with him, but I know him by sight. Rather short man. Looks like a small badger."

"Excellent. What else?"

"Solid country gentry, if I recall correctly. Suffolk. Middle-aged, married man. Wife stays in the country. Third or fourth son of Lord Layham, whose heir has sons of his own, so I don't think Mr. Edward is in any real line for the title. Don't think he's an ally of my father's in Lords. Don't think he's political at all, really. He's too young to be one of my father's set, and too old to be one of my brothers'."

"You see? You knew more than you thought you did. That was a very clever assessment." He gave her the compliment not only because it was true but also because it gave him the opportunity to watch her cheeks grow pink with becoming color. He gave her the compliment because it gave him the opportunity to be a better man. For her. "So those are our choices at the moment—find out more about the fob, or find out more about the man."

He turned his head to face her. "Claire, what do you think we should do?"

Claire stilled—or would have stilled if his arm had not been around her shoulders and not carried her along with his momentum. But she felt light and suspended again, as if the entirety of the earth had just narrowed to the two of them, alone together in the middle of the wide churchyard of the Abbey. She could barely feel her feet touching the ground. And all she could see and feel was this strange and wonderful and warm man asking her what *she* thought they should do.

It was an idea and an offer so foreign to her existence that for the longest moment she could do nothing as the pleasure slid through her, as slow and warm and golden and sweet as honey. And she knew that something within her had shifted. She knew that she would never be the same girl she had been last night—that she was somehow older and wiser. Because she knew without a doubt that she was falling in love. With His strange, wonderful Grace the Duke of Fenmore.

All because he had *asked* her. And protected her. And laid Lord Peter Rosing out like an undertaker.

"Claire?"

And she was falling just a little bit in love with him because she thought she understood what it cost him to ask for her help, and her opinion. He was a man of ferocious intellect, a man who was quite used to making his own decisions—who was quite used to drawing his own correct assumptions, and making his own lightning-quick decisions. For him to ask her, to solicit and consult her opinion, seemed entirely out of character.

Or was it? "Why are you asking me?"

He tipped his head from side to side as if he were uncomfortable—stripped of his usual surety like a schoolboy caught doing something he knows he oughtn't. He frowned, a ferocious scowl clawing its way between his brows, and then shrugged as if it didn't matter. But his answer was telling: "Isn't that what people do when they respect each other—ask their opinion?"

Oh, it was lovelier still, this feeling of gratitude and esteem and pride all blossoming in her belly in a spate of warmth and happiness. His esteem was indeed a heady, heady, intoxicating prize.

In her world, *respect* was a word that meant money and position and power and reputation. It was the water on the surface of a pond—one's job in life was not to ruffle those waters, to make it all look effortless and easy. This past night and morning, which might yet see her reputation in tatters, she had done nothing but agitate the waters—allowing herself to be compromised by a known debaucher, running away with His Grace, involving herself in the investigation of the murder of a young maid, traipsing across the countryside and half of London Town. She had done everything her upbringing had told her not to do.

And still, somehow, he esteemed her.

It was as if she had been fed a food she had not known she craved. It left her hungry for more.

"Yes," she answered him. "That is what people who esteem each other do. Thank you. I am very sensible of the honor you do me." And she returned it. "So how to decide?" she mused aloud. She took a deep breath, as if the damp morning air could clear both her mind and her lungs of the lingering aftereffects of such unsettling pleasure. "It seems to me we don't know where to find Mr. Layham, while you *do* know where to find your friend who knows a thing or two about Roman coins."

"Yes. But my friend is all the way in the City, which will mean another ride downriver, while Layham ought to be closer at hand in Mayfair."

"But if we need to go by river—is the tide still running out?"

He smiled—that sharp little smile of admiration that told her she was right. "Just."

"Then I suppose we'd best go with the tide while we can. And then we can return to Charing Cross and Mayfair more easily after the tide turns and runs upriver." First the Almonry and now the City. The financial district at the heart of the ancient city of London was, in the Jellicoe family, the sole purvey of the earl and his heir. Claire doubted her mother and even her two other brothers had ever had occasion to go into the City. In Mayfair, the City came to them, rather than the other way round. But today she was determined to be brave. "Well, I've never been to the City. It seems a good day for it."

And frankly, she did not want to go to Mayfair. Not yet. Mayfair was almost too familiar, and she was too familiar in Mayfair. Even dressed as she was, people were bound to recognize her.

Tanner did not try to dissuade her. "All right." He accepted her decision with equanimity, and pointed the way up the street. "We go east, back to the water stair."

"Oh, but I forgot Lark may have gone, and taken the boat."

"Ah. Yes." His smile broadened across his face. "But there are other ways. Have you never, in all your days in London, taken a wherry?"

"No." She had never traveled by any accommodation but private carriage. She had never set foot inside anything so humble as a hackney carriage, let alone a boat for public hire. But it was a new day. "But it seems an excellent adventure."

His smile was deeply amused, and entirely complicit. "That's my girl."

Was she his girl? She hardly knew—he said it so casually, so in tune with his rough-and-tumble persona, that she could not tell what he was thinking.

"Wooden Bridge Stairs." He strode onward, his long, swinging stride eating up ground.

She had to skip to keep up, but the happy, bouncing stride suited her expansive mood. "I am glad we are doing this. Glad to be doing something instead of sitting at home, letting other people do things for me."

"I can't think of another lass who would have done so well. You've been very . . ." He paused, as if he were searching for the right word. "Courageous."

A very flattering word. But, alas, not entirely a true one. "Not I," she declared. "My heart was pounding away the whole time we were in the Almonry."

"And that is courage," he insisted. "And I admire you greatly for it. And your compassion. Talking to Molly Carter like that—getting her to talk to you and tell you important things—"

"Were they important things?"

"Everything you got her to say was important. Even if it confirmed things I already knew. Everything has value. Everyone has value. You're a rare genuine person, Claire. And I admire you greatly."

It was a lovely thing to hear. And very lovely to feel valued for who she was, not just for her face, or her station, or her family's fortune. "I'm glad." It was a very heady thing, his admiration. It was lovely and warm and easy. "I admire you as well."

They approached the water steps and Tanner took her hand to help her into the vessel, but she held on to it as long as she could, liking the warm feeling of connection. Liking his calm, reassuring touch.

He gave their destination. "White Lion Wharf."

The boat felt almost familiar now. Or at least the motion of the vessel was familiar, though this one was for public hire, with two weathered old watermen at the oars, squinting at her in the cool morning light, as inscrutably as the Duke of Fenmore ever had.

But Claire was no longer willing to be intimidated by their stares. She put her chin and bruised cheek in the air, and looked inscrutable right back.

They shot out into the swift water at Westminster Bridge, and around the great sweep in the wide river toward the City. The city—her city, in which she had lived for a good half of the year, every year of her life, and the city she thought she knew—looked incredibly different from the vantage of the bright, gleaming river. Across the water, the low, hulking outlines of the buildings were illuminated by the crystalline light that shimmered along the reflected surface of the water. It was magical and different and made her feel alive, and happy and privileged to live in such a place—the center of the entire world.

The euphoric feeling might also have been due to the fact that she was snugged up close to Tanner, who retained the rough-and-tumble persona he had employed on the street when he had pulled her close, and told her she was to be his girl.

His nearness made her feel as if she had drunk too much of the chilled summer wine they had been serving on trays at Riverchon Park. But she hadn't drunk any wine. She was drunk on his presence, his attention. His esteem.

"Where are we headed?" she asked him as the the gray stone arches of Blackfriars Bridge rose in the distance.

"North." The rough intonation was back in his voice—a caution not to give up her role in front of the watermen. "Along the well-trodden paths of the ancient city."

"And your friend will see us this early in the morning?"

Tanner smiled his piratical smile that curved up one

side of his mouth. "The rest of the city doesn't stay abed till noon like the nobs."

"No, I don't suppose they do." And the evidence was all around her—every sort of craft, from small wherries like the one they traveled in to small sailing ships and barges plied the waterway.

"Why did you lie to her?"

His question surprised her. "To whom?"

Tanner tipped his head back upriver in the direction of the Almonry. "To Molly Carter. Why did you tell her that Maisy Carter didn't suffer?" he pressed. "It won't have done any good. She'll see for herself the bruising when she sees the body."

"Perhaps. But I thought it would give her at least some small ease of mind, at least for now." She could feel her shoulders slide up into an apologetic shrug. "Because that's what people do. At times like that, sometimes people need to be told what they want to hear. And maybe when the time comes, she'll see it for the kindness it was intended."

"I hadn't thought of that." He spoke as if he were slightly baffled. As if he never thought of saying the expected thing. As if he had only ever dealt in hard truths and uncomfortable realities. What a strange, hard life he must have lived.

"We'll head up Bennet's Hill and Godliman Street to Paul's Chain, and then round the back of the churchyard toward Aldersgate."

It was as if he could measure the precise distances between the turnings. "Do you carry a map around in your head?" She was trying to tease him, but he was so different from anyone else of her acquaintance that she had to ask.

"Yes. Don't you? You always need to have two ways in and at least three ways out of every situation."

"Every situation? Is that something you learned in your childhood?"

"Yes," he said in his emphatic way. "But it would have suited— It is good advice for everyone."

He meant it was good advice for her. That she would have been much better served to have thoughts of ways out of walking with Lord Peter Rosing. But she hadn't.

But she couldn't linger on that rather morose idea, as they had come to the arched spans of Blackfriars Bridge and neared the north bank of the river, where fingers of wharves and piers reached out over the muddy banks exposed by low tide to find the water.

"White Lion, gov'nor," the wherryman nearest the bow called out.

Tanner slipped some coins into the oarsman's callused hand. "Up close there, to the ladder."

A ladder at the end of the pier descended into the shallow water, and led directly into the structure above via a trapdoor. Tanner jumped out of the wherry with an ease borne of long familiarity and had the trapdoor unlocked in a trice.

She clambered after him when he ascended the rickety rungs. "What is this place?"

"A wharf. Business of a friend."

"He must be a very good friend indeed to give you keys and let you walk though his locked-up warehouse." A friend whom Tanner must visit often, judging from the ease with which he navigated the dim, crowded interior. He wove his way around crates and stacks of gunny bags as dexterously as a cat.

Claire began to fall behind. "Tanner, wait."

And then he remedied the situation by simply taking her by the hand. "Actually, the warehouse is mine. Fenmore's, more accurately. As Fenmore, I bought up all the places where I used to live."

He used to live here in this dingy warehouse?

But Claire did not have time to ask or ponder the difference between a warehouse and the splendor of Fenmore House, because he was moving forward with her in the dark.

She could not have said which way they went or how they made their way through the darkened building, because the entirety of her mind was consumed by the feel of his hand holding hers. His hand was long boned, and rather finer than she might have thought, but the feeling of his warm, sleek, muscled flesh pressing intimately against hers was so different from all of the times she had held hands with other gentlemen in dances, through the interference of cotton and kid leather gloves.

Tanner fanned his fingers to mesh with her and hold her securely at his side in a way that made her feel both held and free. He had held her hand briefly on the street, but this felt different. This felt close and intimate and personal in a way that had nothing to do with playing a role for public consumption. Indeed, they were entirely alone and in the dark. In more ways than one.

They burst out onto the sooty, twisting streets along the river. Despite the fact that the church bells were tolling out the seven o'clock hour, the streets were already crowded as they made their way around a small church on the corner of Thames Street, and up a narrow lane past the George Inn and an official-looking courtyarded building that bore the sign of the Herald Office. Public houses and gin mills alike spilled their patrons out onto the streets in the warm summer air.

Claire had never really walked on the street in London. In the country she might walk and ride freely, but not in London. In London one did not want to be seen walking more than a few leisurely blocks. She had strolled a short distance up Oxford or the new part of Regent Streets on her own power, but shopping trips had always

been made with the Sanderson town coach idling alongside, at her mother's disposal.

Encountering the world as a pedestrian, navigating wet
gutters and pungent horse droppings, was certainly different from watching the world pass by from the privileged vantage point of the windows of a coach. As they
made their way up the long reach of Aldersgate, dodging
daytime drunks and cits alike, Claire hoped she never
took such a ride for granted again.

And she was rather disappointed to find that here, in the
narrow, well-ordered streets of the City, Tanner did not
drape his arm across her shoulders. But neither did he let
go of her hand when they turned into the strange stairstep
configuration of Angel Alley.

Tanner evidently knew his way here better than he had
in the Almonry, because he did not need to pause for direction but went right to the rear door of a house that
fronted on Jewin Street, and knocked.

As they waited, Claire could hear a mumbled shuffling
sound nearing the door.

"Who is it that bothers an old man so early in the
morning when half of London is still abed, and before he
has broken his fast?"

"Elias, it's the Tanner."

A small peephole in the wall to the right of the door
sprang open and then shut with a snap. And then the door
opened, revealing a gray-bearded old man in a nightcap
and dressing gown.

"Tanner, my boy. Come in, come in. And tell me what
you're about." The old man's wiry eyebrows rose when he
saw Claire standing behind Tanner. "And company, as
well. Well, this is a special occasion. Come in, come in."

The old tradesman picked up a taper from the small
table in the entryway, and shuffled off down the corridor
into the gloom. Tanner plunged after him with the ease of

a familiar, and Claire once more had to move quickly to keep up or be left behind.

The old man led them through an unlit workroom, and up some narrow stairs into a small sitting room brightened by high windows, and made comfortable with several well-used upholstered chairs. "Have you broken your fast? Come have something to eat. Let me offer your friend a chair. It's a long way from the wharves to Jewin Street."

"Thank you. Elias Solomon, this is my friend Claire. Claire, Elias Solomon is a goldsmith of some repute."

"Miss Claire." The old tradesman made a courtly, gentlemanly bow. "Any friend of the Tanner is a friend of the Solomon brothers."

"Thank you. Likewise, I'm sure." Claire returned his manners with a curtsy of her own, and looked about the small room over the workshop. A small table positioned nearby, with decanters of water and wine and a plate of fruit. And no trace of a brother.

The goldsmith must have followed her gaze. He gestured to the table. "Come have some watered wine," Mr. Solomon offered.

"Thank you." She took a tentative sip, knowing it was only right to accept the man's hospitality, but she noticed that Tanner did not. And then she did what she always did when she felt nervous or out of place; she made small talk. "How did you know we had come from the wharves?" It was as if everyone saw things she couldn't see.

Her question elicited a chuckle from the goldsmith. "Because he comes in the back, with damp shoes and damp hems like he always does." He flicked a gnarled finger toward Tanner's redingote. "And no carriage in the street in front of my shop, where it would do me some good to attract customers. And he brings with him such a pearl, I know he must have found you in the South China Sea, and come straight from his ship to me."

Claire laughed at such charmingly fantastical praise but was more pleased to see that Tanner smiled along as well. "I found this pearl in Richmond, actually."

"Farther up the river." Mr. Solomon waved his hand. "But a pearl from the water all the same. Now tell me why you've come."

Tanner did not prevaricate. In his usual abrupt manner, he produced the watch fob and thrust it at the man. "What can you tell me about this?"

"Ah. This." The tradesman's eyes narrowed. "Where did you get it?"

"From a murdered girl."

The older man heaved out a sigh, and made a face like soured milk. "This is what you bring me, murder before breakfast? Who can eat with such things going on?" He squinted at the golden fob in the light from the window for a moment before he shook his head. "I don't like it. We'll go downstairs."

Mr. Solomon led the way back down the stairs, and into his dark, meticulously organized workroom, to a table with scales, small crucibles, and pan weights lined up along the top.

He lit several lamps before he drew a high stool to the worktable, and turned the fob over in his hand. "Tell me what you already know."

Tanner glanced at Claire and then said, "Gold aureus of Emperor Claudius, minted around the year 46, commemorating the conquest of Britain."

"Yes." Mr. Solomon made a considering face, with his mouth turned down at the corners. "Stamped *De Britann* with the equestrian mounted over the triumphal arch. But you didn't come to me for a history lesson."

"No. Miss Claire has already provided me with one." Again Tanner's sharp, conspiratorial gaze found hers. "What can you tell me about the fob itself?"

"Typical, nothing special. Looks like something from Field and Parker, goldsmiths and gunsmiths they call themselves, on High Holborn. Jumped-up tinkers, if you ask me—and you do ask me. This is why you come to me." He picked up a pair of spectacles, and perched them on the end of his nose. "Who would buy jewelry from such men, who do two things badly?"

Tanner slapped his hand against the flat of the workbench. "Field and Parker," he repeated, as if he were adding the name to a catalogue in his head. Or perhaps just accessing the catalogue that was already there. "Their guns are fair enough. So a countryman with money but no discernment? Or someone of the *ton*, who is canny, and knows Field and Parker will do the work quickly and cheaply, since he already buys guns there?" Tanner fired off his deductions with rapid-fire surety and conviction. As if it were obvious, and not guesses he had made within a split of a second. "High Holborn is just far enough out of Mayfair to make him feel like he's got a bargain."

It was astonishing how absolutely he could draw such conclusions.

Mr. Solomon was more amused than amazed. "This is good. A likely story. Now." He examined the coin more closely, turning it over and over in his wiry fingers.

Tanner's tone grew sharp with impatience. "What else? What can you tell me about the coin?"

"Tell *you*, who sees everything, and knows so much? What do you think I will tell you?"

"You know things I don't. You see things I can't. This *is* why I come to you first thing in the goddamned morning, when dawn is in the air and half of London is still abed."

"The lazy half. This is true." The old goldsmith held up a gnarled finger, and then gestured dismissively to the watch fob he set on the table before him. "A trinket for a nobleman. As you say."

"A girl has been murdered, Elias. By the man who wore this fob. Look again."

The reminder of murder sharpened the old man's eye. He took up a small hand magnifying lens to amplify his vision and examine the watch fob more closely.

He held the ornament close to the lamp, and squinted down the eyepiece. "I have seen this coin. No." He held up a finger to correct himself. "No."

Tanner crowded closer to the workbench, as if he would try to see exactly what the old man could see.

The old goldsmith took the hand lens down from his eye and turned the fob over in his hand, frowning and turning the corners of his mouth down into his gray beard. "There's"—he paused and narrowed his eyes again at the fob—"something that's not right. Must the fob be preserved?" He looked to Tanner. "Are you attempting to return it, or may I remove the framework of the fob to release the coin within?"

"Yes."

"I will of course repair it and return it to its original state. Neither the owner, nor Field or Parker"—Mr. Solomon said the names with amused contempt—"will know what has been done."

Tanner was typically to the point. "Do it."

The goldsmith took a small pair of snips off his worktable and had the framework of the fob off in a trice. And then he did the most astonishing thing. He put the coin up to his nose and took a long, indecorous, quite audible sniff at the thing. And then he cast it down upon his table, letting it bounce and roll around in ever smaller circles until it dropped.

"It doesn't ring true." He shook his shaggy beard. "I smell a fake."

Chapter Twelve

"Smell?" Claire did not understand.

"And taste." The old goldsmith put the coin in his mouth, and kept it there as he reached across the workbench to take up a heavier pair of metal snips. He spat the coin from his mouth into this hand, before he plied the tool to snip a small wedge out of the coin.

"Mala fide," the old man muttered into his beard, and passed the split coin to Tanner, who was fairly bristling with barely contained energy at the sight.

"What does that mean?" Claire looked from Mr. Solomon to Tanner.

"Mala fide." Tanner explained, "Made in bad faith. A forgery. Fake."

The goldsmith turned his mouth down in distaste. "A thin layer of gold fused over a core of lead, and then struck. Worthless."

"Not entirely," Tanner countered. "Only if discovered."

"Ah. True." Mr. Solomon chuckled into his beard. "They're good." He looked at the tiny cut he'd made into the body of the coin again through his hand lens. "Damned good. Proportions correct. Attention to the detail. The formation of the equine pose, the depth of the lettering. Whoever they are, they're skilled."

"Whoever?"

The old goldsmith shrugged, and took a long pull at his beard.

Tanner helped him along. "Who could make such a thing, in London, Elias? It's not like making flimsies—forged banknotes," he added for Claire's benefit. "It takes a different kind of skill. And space. Lead, you said, and gold fused together. Working hot? Lead smelting isn't something that can be hidden in a garret room like paper notes. Whoever did this has materiel, space, and skills."

"A skilled hand to forge the molds, but then—" Mr. Solomon made a disparaging sound. "Half of Rotherhithe is heavy with the sulfurous stink of lead."

"But I'll venture not half of Rotherhithe has the skill for this kind of gold work. Who could have had the skills to cast the molds to strike something that could so easily pass for the real antique? And what have you heard of goldsmiths who were down on their luck, or not keeping their custom, who suddenly seemed to have bounced back?" The relentless questions poured out of him, as if from an open tap. "What lead manufacturers were badly operated or on their last legs and have had a sudden resurgence? Who could be bribed into taking on this kind of work? Who was vulnerable or in debt? Walker and Maltby on Red Bull Wharf? Or Reynolds and Wilkins in the Barbican? Who?"

"Got your ear to the ground, haven't you?" The old man chuckled, but he was serious enough. "There are goldsmiths enough with skill, including myself, and making a cast for a replica is not a crime—maybe even Parker and Fields can make a replica for a client who wants to wear such a coin as a fob, and wants to preserve his original."

The old man took another long moment, as if he were considering how much to say, before he made a little moue of decision. "But no reputable goldsmith makes a replica out of lead. And the lead—passing the lead coin off as gold—is where the crime occurs. Now that I put together a little of this, and a little of that, I'd say Walker's *son*"—Mr. Solomon said the name as if the word itself might be poisoned with the fumes of lead—"fell out with the old man. Went into business on his own just recently. Set up down St. Catherine's Dock."

Tanner was watching the old man's face, reading his expression. All but quivering in his excitement—like one of her father's gundogs who knew exactly where to find the fallen grouse. "Yes. What else do you hear?"

"I hear he was back telling his old man he didn't need him, or his ways—that he had plenty of business. But I hear the old man doesn't believe it, and says the yard he took at Parson's Stairs is decrepit, the shot tower falling down. And for myself?" Here Mr. Solomon made an ironic little shrug. "Since the peace, lead yards are not doing the custom they did during the war. Not such a demand for bullets. The peace is bad for business. So, what is he doing in his decrepit yard in St. Catherine's Dock? Perhaps Walker's boy is pouring something other than bullets. Perhaps."

"Ah." Tanner drew the word out, thinking and looking up at the low ceiling meditatively, his expression a sort of agonized ecstasy of a Renaissance saint. "St. Catherine's Dock. Where the traffic of the Goodwyn, Skinner and Thornton brewery might mask an havey-cavey business they've got going on. Ingenious. Yes, I'll find out."

"But what about the real coins?" Claire asked.

Both men turned to her, as if they had forgotten she was there. But only one of them smiled—Tanner. "Go on," he said.

Thus encouraged, she said, "Does it stand to reason that someone has to have the real coin in order to make a copy? Could it have come from someplace like the Royal Academy, or Sir John Soane's house, where the artifacts from Pompeii have been displayed, and someone could see it, and then make his own copy?"

"I see why you like her." Mr. Solomon offered Tanner his own sharp, conspiratorial smile. "But I *have* seen the original coin from which *this*"—he tossed the fake upon the table—"was copied."

"You're sure?" Tanner was still bluntly inquisitive.

"Oh, yes. Gold the color of Damascus honey, soft and buttery, and as ancient as time. Only a few legitimate dealers in London would have such a coin. So I ask a question or two, but Goadly and Berry, up on Cornhill—who are the ones who would know—say they've never dealt that coin. So it wasn't bought in London."

"But it was genuine?" Claire was still trying to follow. "Something from which someone might strike—is that the right word?—strike these replicas?"

"Fakes," Tanner insisted. "Made of lead to deceive."

"It was genuine. As genuine as this one is not." Mr. Solomon was emphatic. "This I know."

"But the question is who brought you the coin?" Claire was thinking out loud, trying hard to understand. "And if that is the same person who is striking these fakes?"

"Oh, oh." Mr. Solomon clapped his gnarled hands together. "I can see why you like this one, Tanner. Very clever. She's like you. She's special."

She was special. She was clever.

She was his.

"Yes," he answered but met Elias's eyes, willing his attention back to the pressing question that he had not yet answered. "Who brought you the real aureus, Elias?"

"Customers." His answer was vague and evasive. "Discerning gentlemen who know better than to take their custom to tinkers on the High Holborn."

It wasn't like Elias Solomon to be so cagey. "Elias?"

The old man looked at Tanner and then let his eyes travel very carefully to Claire before they came back. "If I might have a private word, about my fee?"

The telling glance would have been enough without the additional mention of the fee—Elias knew damn well Tanner would compensate him for his trouble. He always had. So something else was afoot.

Tanner gestured toward the doorway. "If you'll give me a moment, Claire?"

"Of course." She smiled, nodded, and curtsied politely to Elias Solomon and then moved just outside the doorway of the workroom, so Tanner might turn his back and speak to the goldsmith privately.

"And?"

"The names." Elias lowered his voice to something just heavier than a whisper.

Tanner's impatience was about to crawl out of his body. "Yes?"

"Be careful, Tanner. These are powerful men."

The warning was out of character for Elias, whom Tanner had known for so many years, he had lost count. "I always am."

His brusque assurance wasn't enough. "Be more careful. Especially with her." Elias's eyes cut to the figure in the doorway. "I don't like to think I have to worry about you."

"With her? You don't." Was this meant to be some sort of fatherly advice to act the gentleman? "What is it you're trying to tell me?"

Elias Solomon gave him another long look over the top of his spectacles, his eyes old and sad and tired. "Tanner.

Several men have come to see me about this gold coin of yours. Each more powerful than the next. First was Mr. Edward Layham, a monied squire from Suffolk."

That it was Layham satisfied Tanner's brain. The pieces of the puzzle were finally beginning to take shape.

"Not a regular customer," Elias Solomon went on. "It's real, I tell him. Then next comes Sir James Kersey, a baronet who has never darkened my door before. Asks the same question. Gets the same answer."

This was news of a different sort. Sir James Kersey was known to him. Amiable, social, a man who liked his cards for recreation but was not a gambler. The kind of man who did not lead but followed. But Elias was not done. "And?"

"And the last, my dear boy, was the Earl Sanderson."

The words fell on him like a cold dousing from a bucket. His skin went cold and clammy, his palms damp.

And while his brain's reaction was more controlled than his body's, the result was the same—every fiber of his being was alert.

"The Earl Sanderson." He repeated Elias Solomon's words, trying them on for size, giving his brain time to sort out this particularly unwelcome piece of evidence, and make the connection backward, from the coin to the fob, and from the fob to Maisy Carter's dead body.

He could find none.

But he understood one thing very clearly. Things had just gotten complicated. Very complicated.

"I will proceed with all due caution," he assured Elias Solomon. Caution in some areas and greater speed in others. "I need a ring."

"A ring?" Elias Solomon echoed his words as if he did not understand.

"A ring. Gold. Beautiful. Delicate. Fitting."

"Fitting?" Elias took another meaningful glance toward the doorway. "I see. May I be the first to wish you happy."

Tanner didn't bother to read the man's tone—warning or disapproval, it made no difference. His course had been set since the moment he followed Lady Claire Jellicoe out the doors of his grandmother's house. "You may."

"I do wish you happy." Elias took out an iron ring full of keys and began to select one out. "But will I be reading about you in the tittle-tattle of the scandal sheets, or will there be a formal announcement from her father, the earl, in *The Times*?" Tanner's old friend's tone was still quiet and careful. As if Elias Solomon were the one who were unsure of *him*.

"I honestly don't know." Indeed, he no longer knew exactly how he was going to achieve his object, only that he must do it rather sooner than he had planned. And perhaps differently. "How did you know who she was?"

"Come now, Tanner. I may be an old man who rarely leaves my quarter of the city, but I read the newspapers. I see the drawings in the print shop windows. She is one of the beauties of the age—one of the Swans of Society, they call her. And her father, the earl, is a discerning regular private customer. I would have to be blind and deaf not to recognize her. Even in her present state." With another glance at the doorway, Elias Solomon tapped a careful finger across his hollow cheek. "Are you going to tell me how *that* happened, or am I going to have to be vulgar, and insist?"

As the Earl Sanderson was a respected client of Elias Solomon, it behooved Tanner to make one thing perfectly clear. "A man named Lord Peter Rosing thought to try to rape her. I stopped him."

Even as he said it, Tanner could hear the pride, the savage satisfaction, in his voice. He made an effort to tamp it down. He needed to think—if Elias Solomon had recognized her, who else did? Was he exposing her scandal even as he planned to protect her from it?

"God blight him. Although I'm sure you already have." Elias Solomon leaned down and unlocked a drawer. "In that case . . ."

Elias Solomon retrieved a sueded pouch from his drawer, and from it handed Tanner an exquisitely wrought band of jewelry, composed of gold and scrolls and petals. It was a creation of air and stunning, delicate beauty. "It's perfect."

Elias Solomon smiled. "Of course. I *know* you—I have since you were eight years old. At eight and twenty you haven't changed all that much. You have good taste. You always have. You still like the things beyond your reach."

It *was* fatherly advice, after all. Fatherly advice no one else would give him.

Tanner's mouth felt dry and tight, but he made himself ask. "Are you saying she is beyond my reach, truly?"

"No." Elias leaned forward again and looked into Tanner's eyes. "I am telling you to reach very, very carefully, and for the love of God, boy, don't get caught."

"Ah." Tanner let air back into his lungs, and felt some of his confidence swagger back. "I won't. I never have."

"Then take it with my blessing, and go. Leave an old man to break his fast in peace."

"Thank you." Tanner hid the ring in the pouch he wore from a string around his neck under his clothing, safe next to his skin. Old habits died hardest. "Keep your ears open. Send word if you hear anything I should know."

"Chances are you'll hear it before I will, but you have my word. Now go. Take that girl home where she belongs."

Tanner couldn't. Not now.

And as he couldn't agree to something he knew he would not do, Tanner only nodded and took his leave. He found his breath and his wits again once they were outside, in the open air of the close confines of Angel Alley.

Claire turned toward him with a smile. In the warming light of morning, her porcelain perfection was disrupted by the frown pleating her forehead. And by the damn bruises scrawled across her cheek in obscene color.

He should have killed Rosing—Rosing was the one person Tanner was absolutely sure was an unrepentant villain. He should have held his hand across the man's face, and smothered the useless life out of him when he had the chance.

"Tanner? Was everything all right with Mr. Solomon?"

Tanner willed the rage to leach away. "Yes," he assured her, the falsehoods falling easily from his tongue. "That is just his way. I didn't like to pay him in front of you. He might have refused the money. Pride always asserts itself more strongly in the presence of a beautiful lady."

She shook her head and pulled her scarf up over her head as they passed their reflections in the dusty window of an antique bookseller. "I'm not beautiful today. I feel like I never will be again."

The hot surge of rage came back so instantly, he had reached out to stop her with an almost-rough grip at her elbow before he could stop himself. "Claire, you will always be beautiful. Even when you are old and frail and gray, you will still be beautiful, because you are good and kind. And that is the kind of beauty that lasts."

He realized too late that he must be hurting her—her gaze had gone to his hand at her elbow—and he let go.

But she did not object or chide him for his boorish behavior. She hugged her elbows lightly to her middle and gave him that lovely bittersweet quick little smile. "My goodness, Your Gr—Tanner. I do believe that is the nicest compliment anyone has ever paid me. Thank you."

Ask her now, his brain told him. Ask her now, before there are fathers, and talk of scandals, and imperatives about what must be done. Ask her now, when her heart is open, and her eyes are wide, and looking at you with something more than regard or affection. Something close to worship.

Ask her.

"Lady Claire—"

"Oh, come now. *Claire*, if you please. We're friends now, are we not?"

Ah. The word went through him like a sword—sharp and effortlessly lethal.

Friends.

"Yes." He answered because that was what a gentleman did. A gentleman did not howl on the pavement like a wounded beast. A gentleman did not haul her to him, and tell her what she could do with her talk of friendship. Tanner did not.

He used his brain and he made another plan. "You will not be surprised to find that the Honorable Edward Layham was the client who came to visit Elias."

"Was he? Well, I confess I *am* surprised. I rather thought he was the countryman who didn't know the inferior work up on High Holborn. Why would anyone who was having a fob made at an inferior place like—what was the name of it?"

"Field and Parker."

"Why would a man like that bring a real coin to Mr. Solomon?"

Here Tanner was on firmer ground. "A man brings a gold coin to someone like Elias Solomon to have it authenticated. To make sure it is real."

"But we know someone—perhaps Mr. Layham, perhaps also Lord Peter Rosing—has a fob, set by Field and Parker, with a fake coin in it?"

"We know only about Layham." As much as he would like to accuse Rosing, Tanner was bound by the cold facts.

"Well, it all just makes no sense. At least it doesn't make sense to me. I'm sure you'll have worked the whole thing out."

"No. I have not worked the whole thing out. I have the same questions, and no answers."

"And for answers we need to go to St. Catherine's Dock? I saw your face back there, when Mr. Solomon mentioned Walkers's yard. You lit up like a Guy Fawkes bonfire. Is that where you think we should go next?"

He did want to go. There was nothing he liked better than following one piece of evidence into another and amassing the facts. It was what he did.

It was what he did *best*.

And they were already more than halfway across London. It would take little time to make their way to Parson's Stairs.

But he learned his lessons well. He had learned better.

"You tell me, Claire. Where do you think we should go next?"

Chapter Thirteen

"Where exactly is St. Catherine's Dock?" She felt stupid asking—clearly it was somewhere within London. But he didn't seem to mind educating her.

"A few miles southeast." In fact, it was as if he were merely waiting for the opportunity to consult the map in his head. "From here at Cripplegate, down the length of the old London Wall to Bishopsgate." He made those silently elegant gestures indicating the direction. "Then across Cammomile Lane, down Houndsditch, toward Whitechapel. And south down Minories past Little Tower Hill, and on to Wapping."

It was the other side of the world. "Wapping. It sounds so far away. As far away as . . ."

"A West Indies island." He smiled and laughed with her at the absurdity of it all. "Yes."

"Well." She followed his direction and turned east down Jewin Street. "I've never been to the West Indies."

He fell in beside her. "Nor I," he admitted. His smile was all over his face, from his dancing eyes to his laughing mouth. He looked entirely boyish. And entirely irresistible. "Wapping is as exotic as I get."

It was too funny. And then she remembered. "Oh, no. Your sister lives in the West Indies. I'm sorry."

"So am I," he admitted cheerfully. "But I hate to sail."

"Do you? Oh, goodness—" She covered her astonished laugh with her hand. "And you said you'd been in the navy!"

"I was, God help me." Yet his face was nearly cleaved in two by that boyish rapscallion smile. He was as unguarded and open as she had ever seen him. "I was awful. Completely hopeless. The worst."

"But you're so good with boats."

"Rowing. I've learned to be. But I nearly got Jack killed back in the navy. Thought I had done, actually, for years."

"Oh, no. No." She reached for his arm, as if she could reassure him. But they were both laughing so hard they were leaning against each other, easy and natural. "You poor thing."

And it seemed as if the most natural thing she could do was reach up on her tiptoes and kiss him, right there, on his laughing cheek.

He had a dimple, and her mouth landed right there in the lovely, laughing crease.

There in the middle of Cripplegate, with God and everyone in the world watching. It was nothing really, just a quick buss on the cheek—but it was somehow everything. Everything she was feeling. Everything that rose up within her, and had to find expression in action. Everything she wanted to say and couldn't.

And so she kissed him.

His skin was rough with the barest rasp of whiskers against her lips. She had pulled back and turned away before she had time, or thought, to register anything else. But not before she had time to see the almost-stunned look upon his face, and see him bring his hand up to touch his just-kissed face.

Heat boiled out of her, basting her from the top of her

head down to the toes of her sturdy boots. She was mortified and pleased, and sorry and not sorry, all at the same time.

So she did what she always did when she did not know what to do. She made small talk.

"I went to the Tower once. When I was a girl. To see the lion there."

He recovered his equilibrium enough to say, "Me, too. Used to sneak in often, or as often as I could get away from my sister. I'd sneak in one gate or another—always thought it a grand lark to sneak *into* the Tower. But I'd go there, and eat my meat pie."

It was almost as if he were taking pity on her and making small talk himself. Except that his talk wasn't small. It was quite big. Nearly fantastical.

"I loved meat pies. We didn't have a home where we could cook, so we bought food ready-made from carts and cookhouses. My poor sister. I was always hungry. And I'd look at that old lion there at the Tower, and he looked hungry, too. And I'd throw him a bit of my meat pie, in solidarity. The keeper used to get after me. Threaten me with his pike." And he acted it out for her, miming the clumsy oaf of a keeper coming after young Tanner with his imaginary pike. "What a life."

"What an extraordinary life." And she was glad.

Glad she had kissed him. Glad he was with her, laughing and having the silliest, easiest fun. Glad he was such a strange, wonderful sort of duke, who had stolen his way across London, and been chased by keepers in their Beefeater reds, and lived his extraordinary life to thrive and be with her. And help her.

And chase after a murderer.

"Oh, God. We're laughing and Maisy is dead. She's not even cold in her grave, because she's not even in a grave yet. And . . . And it's all so . . ."

"Hard. Yes." His words were exactly as they had been

in the boathouse. "It is hard. Life is hard. All the more reason to laugh while we can, Claire. Don't you think?"

"I suppose. I suppose I'm just being silly. You must think me mad, laughing one moment, and sober and Friday faced as a preacher the next."

"Now that," he said with another charmingly boyish smile, "is another phrase of the fancy that you ought not to know. Friday faced. I can't imagine your very thorough governess taught you that. Your brothers, I assume?"

He was teasing her. "Yes, my brothers. They're as mad as me. Madder."

"I don't think you're mad, Claire. I think you've been up all night, and half the day. I think you've been rowed across one half of the county, and walked across the other half of London. And been shoved up against a brick wall and almost raped. If anyone has an excuse to act mad, it's you. It's been one hell of a night."

Claire took a deep, deep breath of London's coal-singed air and took his hand. "And a day. And it's not over yet."

St. Catherine's Dock lay along the river in the shadow of the Tower, clinging to the edge of the river while the dark ribbon of water in the middle of the muddy channel curved eastward toward the bigger, more important docks to the east.

But his entire world was boiling down to a single point of warm, physical contact. Because she had caught up his hand in her own, and smiled at him as if he had done her the greatest favor in the world.

No one had ever held *his* hand before. At least not since he was young. He had outgrown that kind of oversight very early—it would have been nigh unto impossible to pick a pocket if he were holding someone's hands. And harder to eat if he were not stealing.

But he liked holding her hand, for no particular reason

that he could fathom. Again he thought of the almost-puppyish physical relationship he had had with his sister, sleeping rough and clinging to her for warmth and support. Perhaps that sort of need had been trained out of him when he became Fenmore, though his grandmother had always been and remained staunchly supportive of him and physically demonstrative—a great one for gentle touches was his grandmother.

But this—this voluntary press of Claire's flesh against his for no other reason than mutual comfort—or perhaps satisfaction—was worlds different. And he liked it.

He liked her.

She was useful to him, in a way he had not imagined. He had thought it would be him showing her what life in the Almonry and the City were like, teaching her as he had promised. But she had schooled him just as effectively, showing him that she, with her tangible empathy, was an equal counterweight to his clever analytical mind. Together they were better than they were apart.

How extraordinary.

She smiled at him, blithely unaware of the havoc she was wrecking within him.

They reached the river at Iron Gate Stairs where the busy wharf was full of the local ironmongers and their trade. There were empty vessels aplenty beached in the mud beneath the stairs, and Tanner was in such an expansive mood, he didn't mind simply stealing one.

"Hop in."

When Claire was seated, he dragged the vessel through the slippery mud along the rotting plankway until they reached the water.

"Is this yours, this boat?" Claire asked quietly as they slipped out into the thinned stream of the river.

"It is now. And I'll pay whoever owns it handsomely for its use when we return—*if* he notices its absence."

But Tanner's ethical slipperiness brought no censure, just, "How casually larcenous you are."

She had the truth of it there. "You have no idea," he said almost to himself.

But Claire was listening and she was quick to answer. "I'm getting a better idea, with every minute that passes." But she was smiling in her lovely teasing way. Almost as if she didn't mind his stealing.

Almost as if she didn't mind him stealing her.

Now *he* was the one who had gone mad.

Tanner rowed them slowly down the line of wharves at St. Catherine's Dock, taking a long look at the buildings, counting and measuring off the distance as he went. Making sure he could see two ways in and three ways out of every place he passed. The old habits died the hardest.

But his old habits had saved his neck more than a time or two. And he was glad of them when he spied what had to be a decrepit lead works—a rickety rectangular structure rose about a hundred feet over piers that extended out to the edge of the water.

The ramshackle building had all the makings of a less than successful shot tower, being too short—a good shot tower needed to be about two hundred feet in height to produce rounded lead shot by the water drop method—and in a general state of disrepair. Broken panes of window glass had not been attended to, and the wooden framing had weathered and warped out of alignment. For all that Walker was supposed to be new in the business, his yard had all the looks of a place on its last legs. Young Walker was clearly in trouble.

Tanner's careful perusal of the place also yielded a forgotten trapdoor under the pilings. He rowed them beneath, and found that the trap was locked with a padlock on the inside—he could raise the door just enough to feel the pull, and hear the thunk of the lock against the hasp.

"So here's the plan," he said to Claire as he methodically checked his weapons again, running his fingers over the pistol, and touching the knife in his boot. Touchstones for this kind of life. "We'll row to Parson's Stairs, where you'll drop me off, and then I want you to row back here, slow and casual like, and wait directly under that trapdoor."

He saw her try to gauge the distance. "What if I'm seen?"

"You'll be fine—just a girl out for a row. No one's business but hers. If you have to wait, lay low in the bottom of the boat, as if you're sleeping—taking a bit of a kip, all lazy-like in the morning sun. Just be ready when I open the trapdoor."

"Ready for what?"

He could feel his face curve into a smile. "Ready for anything, darling. Ready for anything."

He could see the quick-fire excitement—the heady, jangling energy that always gathered within before a job—start to take hold of her. Her eyes were wide and glistening blue against the river and sky, and she did look as if she were ready. As if she were up for anything.

Which was good, because they might find anything in that yard. Or nothing. And that was the way he liked it.

His sister liked to plan. She liked to be careful. She always cautioned him to look sharp.

He did look sharp—always. He couldn't stop looking, even if he wanted to. Even if he wanted to go to a ball and *dance*, and not *see* everything, he couldn't.

His sister would have also cautioned him to ask the Lark—to find out everything the urchin and the rest of the mudlarks who roamed the Thames's muddy riverbed at will might know about goings-on down St. Catherine's Dock. And he would ask—send a message though the network of eyes and ears he had positioned all over London—later. At the moment he needed to act.

He needed to act because he liked to work on the spur of the moment. He liked to ride by the seat of his pants and feel the reins in his hands. He liked to take a chance.

And he liked it best of all that Lady Claire Jellicoe was going to take that chance with him.

They arrived at Parson's Stairs in less than half a minute. "Are you ready?" He nodded at her to make sure. "I'll cover the street and you cover the river. Two ways in and three ways out of every hole. I'll feel better knowing you'll be here, floating just beyond the piers, if someone comes. Just don't let anyone else near the boat." He shoved a gun butt first into her hands. "Shoot to kill."

After a horrified second, she pushed it back at him. "I couldn't. You keep it. You're better off with it, and I'm better off without it. I'll have my hands full enough with the oars. I'll row away if there's trouble, and then come back. Just be as quick as you can."

"I will." But he didn't like to leave her defenseless. He stripped off the pouch hanging from the string around his neck, and handed it to her in lieu of a weapon. "That's yours if anything should happen. Any—" He didn't know what else to say. He felt like a gravedigger—up to his arse in the business with nowhere to turn. "It's yours."

"All right." She took the strange necklace, and looped it around her own neck, thankfully without asking for any further explanation. "If you're sure."

"I'm sure. Here we go."

Tanner jumped out of the skiff as it scraped against the plankway, strode across the mud flat up onto the water stairs, and purposefully onto St. Catherine's Lane. The entry gates to the brewery were directly across from Parson's Stairs, and so there was plenty of custom and carts in the lane to cover his approach. He counted off the yards until he reached the gate below the shot tower.

He turned directly toward it and rattled the gate, as if he had regular business there, and was surprised to find it shut. If anyone were watching, they would see a normal, typical reaction from an honest businessman.

But he wasn't an honest man. He was a thief who was drawn to the brassy new padlock that hung on a new iron chain, like a pennant advertising that there was something within worth stealing. Like a gilt-edged invitation.

An invitation he meant to accept.

He walked around the corner, and then ducked against the wall, hidden in the shadow, as he waited another few moments for any signs of interest or pursuit—there was still time to say he was lost, and walk away. There was still time to avoid any cur dog they might have left loose about the place. Better than any lock, a cur dog. Cur dogs had teeth that couldn't be picked with a rake and file.

But they were careless, and had no dogs. There was nothing. The place was shut up as tight as a pensioner's purse.

It was his sister who was a dab hand with a lock, but he was a rooftop man, and without so much as breaking into a sweat he found a handhold along the far corner of the shot tower, and scaled the rickety, uneven walls as easily as if he were walking down Bond Street.

Once on the roof, he paused again. Below him lay a small, deserted yard, no more than twenty square feet in area—crossable in a few strides—with open sheds arrayed on three sides of the tower. A hint of sulfur, a light tinge of the funk of heat and chemicals floated on the stale air, even though the works were cold, and all the fires put out. Or perhaps they had never been lit.

He stayed put for a long moment, keeping quiet and blending in with the shadow of the tower, listening hard for any noise. There was only the steady lap of the water against the piers below, and the hissing ejections of steam, and the clatter and chatter that came from the Goodwyn, Skinner, and Thornton brewery across St. Catherine's Lane.

Tanner dropped silently to the dusty yard and went immediately into the tower building. The trapdoor was his first order of business—he needed to secure it should he need to make a speedy exit.

The lock on the trapdoor was iron—rusting, old, and forgotten. It took longer than he would have liked to pick it, but he was out of practice, and he wanted to make a clean pick, leave no indication—like a broken lock—that he'd been on the premises.

"Tanner?" The low whisper slid under the planks as he jimmied the rake in the lock.

"Here." Stronger pressure against the rake finally yielded results, and the iron padlock clanked open. Tanner threw open the trapdoor to find Claire's face floating like a small buoy just below.

He had never been so glad to see another person, if for no other reason than it was Claire, and she was there exactly as she had said she would be. He'd never had an accomplice, a partner, on his illicit and illegal adventures. Not since his sister.

And Lady Claire Jellicoe was not his sister. Not by any bloody means.

Tanner extended his arm, and without thinking she reached up to clasp his hand, and he hauled her straight up.

"Bloody—" She stifled the rest of her curse, and lowered her voice. "I thought I was supposed to stay with the boat?" she asked in a breathless whisper.

"You were. And you did so. Now, we're on to part two—I need your help with the search."

"My help?"

"Two eyes are better than one, and four eyes are far better than two." He was bantering. Bantering with her in the middle of a bloody job. Clearly, he was the one who was mad. "Is the boat tied securely?" he whispered back.

"Yes."

"Good girl." He liked this whispering. A man had to be close to a girl to whisper.

"What are we looking for?"

He was too happy for caution; he steered her to the doorway of the tower. "Just look. But there's only one thing worth looking at in the whole place. The shed with the new lock."

He stood her in front of him, facing forward, so her back was flush against his chest. Her head just below his chin. Her question hummed through his torso. "How do you know it's a new lock?"

"Look at it." He brought his arm around to point the way across the small yard to the shed tight next to one of the small stone furnaces. "Shiny. Bright. New. When everything else is dusty and dilapidated. Look at all the other ovens. No ashes in the fit pits, no tongs, no buckets and ladles."

"That one"—she pointed her chin toward the furnace next to the locked shed—"has been used. See the brick is blacked by the heat and charcoal of a more recent fire."

"Well done, you." His pleasure was a physical thing, stretching and rolling contentedly deep in his belly. "And look at that small stack of lead pigs, stamped *Mendip* for their place of origin, left in a haphazard heap against the shed." He was thinking out loud, letting her into the halls of his rather encyclopedic brain. He took an audible sniff. "Can you detect the lingering poison vapors of lead and sulphur and arsenic in the air? It means they are smelting something. But judging from the dilapidated state of the tower, they aren't making shot. And judging by the dead ash in the furnaces, they aren't making much. Just enough. Just enough of the kind of work that turns an easy profit."

Another check of the yard, and he whisked her across the small open space. "So the shiny, new padlock gleaming from its old, rusted hasp calls to us like a beacon. Like a broadsheet announcing something of much greater value than the surroundings is within."

"What a strange way you have of seeing the world," she murmured. "As if everything, each and every piece of existence, or dust, or could be catalogued and made useful." They were so close, he could feel the shy fluttering of her breath against the side of his neck.

"Ah. But it can. Everything can be useful. Remember that, Claire."

"I will. I won't ever forget."

He was too full of buzzing energy, too full of that unruly enthusiasm that gripped him in a job, and intoxicated by the pleasure of having her with him, to do much more than carrom onward. "The lock is good brass, but I could probably have the hasp off in a trice with a little pressure from a lever. But I want to leave no trace that we've been here, so we'll have to clean pick the lock. A delicate job, that."

"We? How could I possibly help you?"

"I thought you said you wanted to learn?" He was teasing her. Luring her deeper into his larcenous net.

"How to take care of myself," she said carefully, as if she could not gauge his mood, "not how to pick locks."

His mood was still too expansive to be daunted. "Well, you never know when you'll need the skill. So pay heed." He positioned her in front of him, so he had to reach his arms around her to work the lock. "This is the rake." He held the slender piece of tooled steel up for a moment before he slid it into the lock. "Hold that there. Keep pressure on it. Strong. Yes."

"And now we introduce the pick, very carefully." He inserted the second tool, and, leaning in to her, closed his eyes to better visualize the tiny metal serrations and tumblers within the mechanism. Feeling his way carefully. "My sister used to say that good locks are like old maiden aunties," he mused. "They know how to keep secrets. But these aren't good locks. They're brassy bullyboys meant to serve as a warning—*I'm too secure; you'll never get by me.* They're obvious, and simple. And there."

The lock fell open under the pressure.

Inside the shed was exactly what he wanted to find—a small working furnace with small lead blanks stacked by an anvil with a cut-out hole on its upper face.

"That space is for a coin die," he explained, crouching down to examine the surface for any remnants of gold foil. "The dies are metal—usually brass—cylinders upon which the two different sides of the coins' faces have been wrought. One goes here, in the anvil, and then the blank is inserted. This lead core"—he picked up one of the blanks—"around which the gold is fused. Fused hot, Elias Solomon said—hence the small furnace. Then the upper die is positioned over it, and struck with a hammer, and the hot coin is flipped into the bucket of water."

He held out his fists to illustrate the process.

"There's nothing in the buckets at all—not even water. And where are the incriminating dies?" She poked into the corners of the shed, toeing the dirt with her boot as if they might turn up.

There was nothing. Not so much as a strongbox for him work to show off his cracksman's skills. "Maybe they are too valuable and too incriminating to leave about someplace as badly secured as this yard. Or maybe the owner of the dies doesn't trust the owner of the yard and only supplied the dies when the work was being done and then took them back? That is a far more likely scenario."

"Well, I must say I'm disappointed," she admitted, with her delicate arms fisted on her hips. "Are you sure—"

Tanner didn't hear the rest. Because he had heard a different sound, and was already shoving Claire out the door of the shed, slapping the lock against the hasp and slamming it shut, and bolting across the yard with her before he thought to explain. "Someone's coming."

Someone who wasn't quite as stupid as Tanner would have liked, after all. They did have a cur dog—he could hear it thrashing and gnashing at the end of its leash as the animal was brought along St. Catherine's Lane.

Claire was a clever girl who needed no further instruction. She grabbed up her skirts and ran like a hangman was after her with an empty noose. She was through the door of the shot tower and sliding across the plank floor and down through the trapdoor like a seasoned, lifelong crackswoman. And Tanner was right behind her, stopping only long enough to slap the iron lock onto the hasp and hope it looked bolted when he lowered the trapdoor.

Claire already had the line free, and Tanner sprang to the oars, pulling hard to take them out into the stream of the river, and away.

The tide was just beginning to flow, but it was enough to move them far enough off. He had the vessel turned into the steam of the river a hundred yards off the wharf when a face appeared at the broken widow of the shot tower.

He eased up at the oars, making it look as if he were just out for a Sunday sort of row. "Don't look," he instructed when Claire instinctively turned toward the shot tower. "Look at me. Look like we're just out for a lark. Like we've a thousand better things on our minds than breaking into a lead yard. Look at me as if you—"

She came forward onto her knees, gripped her fist in his lapel, and pulled his lips to hers.

Chapter Fourteen

He knew what it was to be filled with the physical exhilaration of the chase, of success, and of the sheer bloody thrill of being alive. It was like an opiate in his blood, that elation, that slippery burst of joy at having done the illicit and survived to run and steal another day.

And he could see it, too, on her face, the giddy delight and shock and pleasure at the thought of what they had gotten away with. And she was turning that happy joy toward him, tilting the pale moon of her face up to his so that she could illuminate him with her joy.

It was heaven and hell, torture and bliss.

He closed his eyes. He closed his eyes and stopped looking. Stopped thinking. He gave in to the pleasure of having the sublime weight of Lady Claire Jellicoe nestled against him in the narrow, close confines of the boat, and slid down to his own knees, so the long length of his thigh was pressed to hers.

He wanted to touch her, to pull her tight against his chest, but she drew back, looking up at him with her wide blue eyes huge in her face, and he had to tell himself that this was all as new and faraway, as his sister used to say, as a West Indies island.

And he had to take his time.

Lady Claire Jellicoe was in his arms. And he meant to keep her there.

Tanner carefully raised his hand and turned it, so the backs of his fingers caressed the sweet curve of her cheek. He had never thought the back of his hand could have been such a repository for sensations, but now he knew it could contain a world of feelings. Of softness and warmth, and fragile strength.

"Yes." Her voice was all cotton wool, soft and tangled as if in sleep. As if she were suspended on the nebulous remnant of some dream. Open and guileless, and his.

His to hold. His to treat with wonder and care. His to adore.

Her look was slow and tentative. As if she could not make up her mind. But he saw the almost-imperceptible tilting of her head as her soft gaze fell to his mouth. He saw the parting and pleating of her lips as she made her untutored decision.

Her decision.

He said the words over and over in his mind—this was her decision.

Just as it needed to be. Just as it should be. Because it was a decision he could not have made in a hundred years, no matter how soft and plush and enticing her lips looked.

He could no more kiss her than he could ever have danced with her. The gulf was too wide. The chasm between them too deep.

But she was coming nearer. And nearer still.

He ducked his chin stupidly, trying foolishly to hide himself from her solemn, angelic regard. But on she came, and he made himself still before her, though the effort to control himself cost him, especially when she reached the soft tip of her finger to draw across the line of his lower lip.

But her touch was not a burden, a thing to be momentarily endured.

Her touch was exquisite, a feeling of intense pillowed pleasure that stilled his mind, and bound his breath up in his chest so that he could not have spoken if he had wanted to. But he didn't want to. He wanted nothing but the warm contact of her hand against the side of his face, and the warming heat that spread rapidly from his chest throughout the rest of his body.

He opened his eyes to savor the moment, to take this small sign of her favor as the gift it was, before they fell shut—pushed closed on a wave of longing.

He had never done this—this intimacy, this kissing.

His carnal adventures had always been conducted as transactions—strictly business with no time or coin spent on osculation.

Ah, but what had he missed?

He felt the change in the air between them as the subtle heat of her body came ever nearer. He opened his eyes just in time to see her lids fall closed, and her mouth land like a butterfly upon his lips—soft, tentative, and fleeting.

Her kiss was light, the barest brush of her lips against his, and for a long moment he wondered if this was all that there was. If he had been right to think kissing, for all its storied mention in poems and novels and songs, was an overrated figment of the carnally excited imagination.

But her lips settled more thoroughly upon his, and a whisper of something more promising shuddered down into his chest when she took his bottom lip between hers, and tugged gently. And then again upon his upper lip. And again at the corner of his mouth, where the skin was surprisingly sensitive.

And he was following her lead, and kissing her back, moving his lips upon hers in the same fascinating fashion. And breathing in the fresh water-laden scent of her—summer and rain and lavender all in one.

And then she was within his mouth, and the taste of her, of wine and water and sorrow and joy, suffused his mouth, and he was lost to the rising need to take another taste, to take another kiss, another breath. His hands had moved from his sides to her arms, and up around her back, and into her hair—her soft, glorious halo of hair—pouring it through his fingers, surrendering to the need to touch and taste and experience all of her, every part of her small, supple body that he could reach without losing track of himself in the process.

Without losing track of the fact that he was meant to be a gentleman and treat her like a lady when all he wanted was push her down in the boat and take her six ways from every Sunday.

He had to loosen the fist he was beginning to make in her hair, and stroke down the silken length gently, softly.

It was only a kiss.

Only a new world.

He was no stranger to carnal knowledge. He had had many a game girl. And he remembered every last one of them, the Kaths and Bettys and Annies who gave and took comfort in the messy friction of their bodies. But he had always wanted to get to the heat of the matter instead of lingering over the soft curve of a lip or the sweet, tart taste of a tongue.

Kissing Lady Claire Jellicoe was nothing like he thought it would be, and everything he had dreamed. Every sense was engaged; every muscle in his body was singing with purpose; every part of his being was consumed with the sweetness and pleasure and pure, unstinting bliss.

Her kiss was everything he had never had, and always wanted. He had wanted to kiss her—soft, sweet Claire Jellicoe—and no one else in the world.

But he couldn't lose control. Not now. Not with her. She must have had enough of men trying to do more than kiss her.

But it seemed not to matter. She was the one who was kissing him. She was the one to hold him. She was the one to run her agile questing fingers up the back of his neck, and around the contours of his skull, and pull him close. She was the one who made animal pleasure and seraphic delight course through him in a way that he never could have imagined—not in a hundred nights of dreaming of his soft, sweet Claire.

He could only be both grateful and jealous for however many kisses she had let other men steal in darkened gardens, if it meant she could kiss him so, in a way that nearly made his soul rise out of his body with sheer unbridled, unfettered joy.

He was stunned and helpless to do or say anything but look at her in wonderment when she slipped away from him on a sigh, and sat back upon the distant stern seat. He had to find his eyes, and look about, and realize that they had kissed their way down the river, drifting past the Custom House Quay.

"The bridge is coming up." Her voice was small and quiet and a little shy, but her eyes were smiling, and she tipped her head just to the side again. As if she might be considering kissing him again.

But she did not. She sat still, and waited for him to take up the oars again, and steer them safely under London Bridge and onward.

"Are you disappointed?"

"No" was his immediate answer. How could she think he was disappointed in—

"In not finding the dies, in the lead yard?"

Ah. The truth was, he was disappointed at *that*. He would have liked to have found the dies. He would have liked to take them back to Elias Solomon, and let the old man's knowledgeable eyes pore over them while he pondered who could have cut such dies.

But evidence was complicated. "Even if we had found them, we don't know who owned them—it was certainly not Walker, who is just a skilled pawn."

He paused for a moment to let the thought spin out in his mind, looping out to its conclusion. "This is somehow about money. And that is a skill I don't possess—I can't follow the money. But I have men of business who can hunt down a sixpence as if it were as obvious as a Bengal tiger."

Tanner shook his head, wanting to explain his suspicions more fully but knowing he couldn't. Not while the Earl Sanderson's name was still tied up in all this.

"So I can't follow the money. But I can feel it. And I can feel it flowing out of that decrepit yard, back down the length of this river, back to Mayfair."

"So Mayfair it is, and the suspected Mr. Edward Layham?" Claire couldn't exactly follow Tanner's rather labyrinthine thought process, but she understood the end goal.

"If we can find him."

"Well, I should think the best way to get information about any man is to find his club." She was trying to be matter-of-fact. Clever and intriguing to cover her rushing pulse and heated skin in the wake of kissing Tanner. "So St. James's Street?"

And it worked—Tanner was intrigued. "Ah. Very good idea. Except that I already know that Mr. Layham is not a member of the only club to which I would be granted admittance. And to put another damper on the idea, I should have to go to such a place as the Duke of Fenmore. Which at the moment"—he held out his hands to indicate their current raffish, muddy attire—"I am not."

The truth was, he was the commanding, knowing Duke of Fenmore no matter what he was wearing. But he had a point. One that distracted them both from kissing. "To which club do you belong?"

"Brooks's."

Claire allowed herself the pleasure of a smile. "I should have known you would be a Whig." She was teasing him, of course, but to make sure he knew it she added, "What else could Your Grace of Tanner possibly be? So our Mr. Layham is either a Tory, as might fit if he's a countryman—and I could ask my father since he's a member of White's—or perhaps the Honorable Mr. Layham fancies himself a sportsman as well, and will be found haunting the halls of Boodle's."

"Ah. I thought we agreed to have no mention of fathers?"

"Did we? I don't recall such a promise—only a suggestion to leave your name out of my correspondence with my parents. Which I have not done. I am contrary in that fashion."

She watched the very edges of his mouth turn up with pleasure, but he said nothing in reply, so she gamboled on. "Well, Your Grace of Tanner, then there's only one thing for it."

She let him dangle off the end of her line for a long moment. Just to see what he would do.

He turned, and looked at her with that blazingly sharp focus, as if she were a species of animal he could not quite categorize. She loved making him ask. "And that thing is?"

"In advance of the Goodwood Race Meeting, and the general retreat to the country for the summer, any gentleman with pretensions to the *ton* will be at the yearling sales at Tattersall's Repository. The only other place besides a club where London's gentlemen can be reliably counted upon to gather in numbers in July is at the sales. I know my older brother was making noises that he meant to come to town to enjoy the afternoon there."

"Ah." His small smile broadened, razor sharp across his face. "Very good thinking. Actually, it's perfect. I meant to go there for the sales myself."

His delight and satisfaction hit her like a physical thing—a blossoming pleasure that knocked the need for air right out of her chest.

"But Tattersall's will require another sleight of hand. And a change of costume. Tattersall's is not the Almonry. We cannot stroll into the hallowed oval while in our current state of sartorial dis-splendor. Someone will be bound to call the constable if we do."

The mental image of anyone calling a constable on the Duke of Fenmore brought another smile. "So what's to be done? Back to Chelsea?"

"No. Too far afield." The corners of his mouth curved deep into his cheeks. "Tell me, Claire, have you ever been to a rag trader's?"

"No." She knew what the rag traders were, of course. Her abigail, Silvers, went off to a specialized shop to sell Claire's cast-offs—anything she had worn out in public more than a few times or that had gone out of fashion—but there were other, less exclusive shops that dealt in secondhand clothing all over London.

"It was a favorite ploy of my sister's," Tanner explained. "Nipping into a rag trader's yard on the fly to change out her clothes in the constant running battle to stay at least one step ahead of both the constables and the kidmen. 'Can't find you if they don't know who they're looking for,' she used to say to me."

Claire could hear his admiration and his love for his sister in his voice, in the warm way he spoke of her. And how often. "How ingenious." Claire decided she liked his sister, if for no other reason than her fierce cleverness in providing for her younger brother.

"Very," Tanner acknowledged with that sly private smile he wore when he spoke of his sister. As if what they had done, the way they had lived, had been a great joke, a marvelous adventure. "As a consequence, I know no fewer than six excellent rag traders who would be happy to kit us out for Tattersall's, and Tilly's is up off the Strand at the Hungerford Stairs."

"Excellent." She smiled at him. Never mind that both their homes stood between the Strand and Hyde Park Corner, where Tattersall's was located. Never mind any of that. "I've never been."

The horse sales, as well as the rag traders', was another place that had been off-limits to her. Not that a visit there had ever been expressly denied to her, but there was a sort of unspoken rule that a place such as Tattersall's was the sole purvey of gentlemen, not ladies—a rule she had never sought to challenge.

Tanner rowed them easily on the inflowing tide back the way they had come that morning, under Blackfriars Bridge, and on to the great bend in the river to the Hungerford Stairs.

The stairs marked the entrance to a great open-air market where goods and produce from all over the city came to feed the households of the West End. It was busy and bustling, and no one paid them the least bit of mind as they left the stolen boat behind, and wove their way through the stalls.

"Hungry?" Tanner asked, picking up an apple.

"Famished." It must have been getting on for noon. "Lord, yes."

They bought food with money from the sueded pouch

she returned to him. Apples and bread and cheese—simple foods for the simple people they were meant to be. But the apple was crisp and fresh and the cheese sharp and tangy. Ambrosia.

Ambrosia because she was sharing it with Tanner.

Who leaned against a wall and ate his bread and cheese as if he were the simplest, happiest, easiest man in the world and not a duke masquerading as a ruffian in order to catch a murderer.

How strange and unpredictable her life had suddenly become.

When they had eaten the bread and cheese and apples down to the last crumb—Tanner even ate the core—he led them onward, onto the Strand, and down a narrow street into the rag traders' court.

The yard looked idle in the midday sun, but Tanner knew the place well enough to lead her around to the back of the shambling wooden sheds, to where a thin line of mellow light shone under the door.

He rapped the backs of his knuckles against the door. Claire drew up close behind him, listening with him as footsteps from inside the darkened hovel shambled closer. A solid shadow blocked the light from under the door before the latch on a large peephole cut into the wooden portal was pulled back.

" 'Oo's there?" a querulous eye demanded.

"The Tanner, Tilly," he answered, and slid his gaze back to Claire, much as he had in Chelsea. "And a friend."

The eye behind the door narrowed upon Claire's borrowed ensemble. "That shawl cach-a-mere?"

"You're as sharp as ever, Tilly," Tanner acknowledged with a polite tug at the wide brim of his hat. "We're looking to trade for the cashmere shawl."

The calculating eye narrowed, then squinted shut. "Come you in then."

The door creaked open, and Tanner led the way into the dim interior, where the pungent, earthy funk of well-worn clothes permeated the air. Claire followed Tanner through the warren of narrow corridors piled high with heaps of clothing of one sort or another, and dense with the smells of wool and sweat and dirt and use—a towering, multicolored maze of clothing.

Claire could only hope that somewhere, farther on perhaps, was a place where the clothing was all washed.

"Tilly Wheeler, this is my friend Claire."

No response followed, but in a few moments they came into a more cheerful, slightly less piled little room, lit and heated by the glowing light of the fire where the enormous woman finally heaved herself breathlessly down into a chair. "Let's have a look at that shawl."

Tilly Wheeler appeared to be a heavyset woman in her late middle years who rarely left the confines of her own yard—her face and skin were pale from lack of light, and she wore down-at-the-heel carpet slippers on her swollen feet. How she had made it through the narrow canyons between the precarious piled mountains of clothing with her girth Claire had no idea.

The moment she made the unconscious assessment, Claire wanted to share it with Tanner. To see if she were right in her judgment of the woman, to see if she could earn more of that heady, wonderful praise.

But this was not the time—and this was certainly not the place—for a private conversation, especially when Tanner's hand found the small of her back, and gently propelled her forward. She pulled the shawl from her shoulders to offer it up to the rag trader, but her mind and the body housing it were occupied elsewhere.

Who knew such a wealth of feeling could be had by a back—beneath the layers of homespun fabric her skin fairly clung to the lingering warmth of his hand.

The rag trader drew the shawl through her calculating fingers before she held the material up to the light. "Good quality. No moth holes. I'll go a few bob, you bein' a regular an' all."

Clearly the woman had a shrewd eye and a strong nose for business, if not for the pungent odor of used clothing. But Claire was instantly outraged. "It cost five times that." Not that she had bought it—it was Tanner's much-loved sister's—but Claire knew the price and value of a well-made shawl as well as or better than the next young woman. And she and Tanner would never be able to purchase better clothing if they were not afforded a fair price.

The woman gave her a shrewd, sour smile. "It's five seasons out-of-date."

"Three," Claire countered. "But yellow is all the rage this season, and will carry into fall. This shawl will pair beautifully with York tan gloves in the autumn." She pulled a twisted pair of the used, eponymous gloves out of a nearby basket and smoothed them out before she laid them over the yellow fringe of the shawl. "You see?"

The canny trader's wiry gray and black eyebrows rose in consideration. "You lookin' for a job?"

Claire felt rather than heard Tanner's wry chuckle from behind her.

"No, ma'am. I already have one." Helping His Grace of Tanner solve a murder. "I only want a fair price for the shawl."

Tanner added his support. "Need at least a bull for the cashmere, Tilly."

"Aww, now." The big woman made a show of scoffing. "Do you think I'm made of money?"

"Do *you* think I am?" Tanner countered, with that sly, clever hint of a smile lighting his eyes.

The big woman let out a wheezy chuckle. "Oh, now, Tanner, I do. You know I do."

"Put it from your head. I've no more to my name than what's in my hand. And what's on my back." And right then and there he began to unselfconsciously shuck his clothing. "Selling coat, linen, Belcher cravat—the lot. I'll want a trade for a decent set of livery—and boots. The toploftier the better."

"Livery?" Claire could not imagine why he should ask for livery. The Duke of Fenmore could not appear at Tattersall's in livery any more than he could dressed as a back-alley tough.

The rag trader didn't bat an eye at the sight of His Grace stripping down like one of the prizefighting fancy. "All of it—redingote, jerkin, hobnails, and gaiters?"

"All in the best repair," he assured the woman as his redingote fell to a pile at her feet. "And you know if you set them aside, I'll buy the lot back within the week."

"And hers as well?" Tilly Wheeler asked, shifting her calculating gaze to Claire.

"All," Tanner answered in his blunt, straightforward way, though he was smiling that wry private little smile. "Although my friend will want to keep her own small-clothes, I should think."

The rumpled linen shirt swept over his head and was tossed toward the rag woman.

Claire felt heat sweep across her skin with all the finesse of a runaway grass fire at the sight of his long, tall torso as bare as the day he had been made. Thank heavens an intervening pile of clothing obstructed the rest of her view.

Claire whipped herself around. But she had seen, and the image of his pale, sleek, animalistic body was burned into her brain.

She felt warm all over still, just at the mere *thought* of his unclothed body. And she could still see the growing pile of clothing out of the corner of her eye.

"We'll want something dark, and well made, and inconspicuous for her." Behind her, he continued to talk. "Something in the respectable lady's maid variety, I should think. Exercising her prerogative of her mistresses' cast-offs, but as fade-away as a maiden aunt."

Claire's last hopes of a more appealing set of clothing fell by the wayside as abruptly as Tanner's clothes seemed to be falling off of him. For some reason that she could not fathom, he wanted them to dress as servants.

"Got a lovely set o' livery here, just as you like." Old Tilly heaved her bulk out of her chair, and picked her way across a small hillside of clothing. "Set them aside a while ago. Had to fend off some trades to keep 'em clear for you."

"Good of you, Tilly," he offered as his leather jerkin and gaiters landed atop the pile Claire watched out of the corner of her eye. The moment his smallclothes were added she was going to . . . She was going to go . . . She didn't know what she was going to do.

But she knew she had to do something.

"It's a good thing yer a tall lad," the rag trader added as she puffed and shuffled her way across the room, "or you'd never pass for a footman."

Claire could only marvel at the thought of a duke dressed as a footman. The very idea was ridiculously amusing. Yet here he was, contemplating such a masquerade as if he did it all the time. Perhaps he did. "Do you really intend for us to pass as servants?" she asked over her shoulder.

His answer was as sure as it was terse. "I do."

"See how you like these." The rag trader was back with some clothing she must have presented to him, for the next thing Claire heard was a booming laugh filling up the tiny crowded space.

Tanner—the man whom, until last evening, she had

known only as the cool, detached Duke of Fenmore—
was laughing like a schoolboy. "God's balls, Tilly. You've
outdone yourself."

The rag woman was chuckling along with him. "Thought
you'd like that."

Claire peeked over her shoulder at the woman, who
smiled and tipped her head in Tanner's direction, as if she
were telling Claire she really ought to have a look.

So she did.

He was not naked. He was holding up a bottle green coat
with elaborate multi-colored ribbon facings and scarlet lin-
ing in front of him so that he was entirely covered by the
garment.

And Claire was too preoccupied with making sure she
saw no more of the man's naked torso to understand the
great point of the joke.

And then she realized it was a coat she had seen many
times through the years.

It was the livery of himself, the Duke of Fenmore.

Chapter Fifteen

"The surest way to pass unseen," he assured her, "is to look obvious, like a part of the furniture. Especially a loudly dressed piece of furniture. People will see this livery and never bother to look, really look, at me, or see my face. The safest place to hide is in plain sight."

"But why must we hide?" Claire had never felt so conspicuously inconspicuous before in her life. The frock Tilly the rag trader had thrust upon Claire was even plainer than the last—a respectable steel gray brushed cotton, covered by a plain white muslin apron and cap.

She had never felt less herself.

In contrast, Tanner looked more himself than ever, even dressed as his own servant. There was a strange grace to him—an unaffected frankness to him—that was more than appealing than even the rough-and-tumble rogue of the redingote and jerkin. Appealing in an entirely different way.

For the first time in their acquaintance—although *acquaintance* was a pale word for their rather interesting and very unusual association—the Duke of Fenmore looked entirely at ease. He looked satisfied even—laughing at himself as if dressing as his own servant were the greatest joke in the world. He looked like the naughtiest of school-boys, having a marvelous time at his own expense—young and happy and amused in an entirely unaffected way. As if he simply couldn't help himself. As if for this one small moment he had stopped *thinking* and simply let himself be content.

Claire wanted to be content—to be happy—as well, but she could not entirely silence her qualms about their present masquerade.

"We hide so we can find the Honorable Mr. Edward Layham and learn his secrets. Dressed like this, people will treat us as if we were invisible. They will see only station, and think us too unimportant to bother looking at our faces. And when people don't see us, they will *say* things. Revealing and important things."

It was hard to resist his obvious enthusiasm. She followed him out of the rag trader's yard, and, after a few blocks along the Strand, around Charing Cross and down Spring Gardens behind the Admiralty. He was easy but aware in an alert sort of way—watchful, even as he ambled along the pavement. After a few minutes they came out of the streets and headed down the long, shaded expanse of the Mall between Charlton House and St. James's Park.

At this time of the morning there was only a smattering of nannies and their young charges strolling about the lawns and pathways of the park, and despite Claire's feeling as if she looked entirely out of place, no one paid her and Tanner the least mind. For all the world, they looked like a footman and his lass walking out in the park.

But she had never walked out with a footman before. Or a duke.

They carried on in silence for a few long minutes, walking slightly apart along the line of trees. He did nothing to resume their previous intimacy, and she took it as a lesson to herself—his regard was a product of the role he played and nothing more. A role he must have played fairly often.

"Does Tilly Wheeler know that you are Fenmore? Does Mr. Solomon? Does everyone?"

"Not everyone. I've endeavored to be circumspect about it. But Tilly must know. She's known me for years—since long before I had to become Fenmore."

His words caught Claire's ear. "Had to become?"

"Ah." He tipped his head to the side again in his considering way, but he did not look at her. He looked away, out over the open field of the park. Some of his ease evaporated. "I suppose it must seem very strange to you, but I was not at all a willing recipient of my grandmother's benefice. Not that I minded the food, or the soft bed, but I minded the rest of it. The relentless schooling, the endless lists of dos and don'ts. The obligations and expectations. The bathing. Good God, you can't imagine how I hated the bathing. It all seems quite silly now, but I was vehement enough about it then."

It was not hard to imagine him as such a boy—he was still vehement enough now, only about other things. "It must have been very hard." It was hard enough for her to live up to her Jellicoe family expectations and obligations, and she had had her whole life to become accustomed. And she did not have to become a duke. "What of your sister?"

"She managed more gracefully. But she also married and moved away with her husband to start a new life, entirely out of society."

"Ah, yes. The West Indies."

"Yes. Rather too faraway to help ease my way with her practical, rather forceful logic. I had to manage the change on my own."

She heard what he had not said just as clearly as if he

had been able to articulate his particular experience of loneliness. "Well, you've done a rather magnificent job of it, if you ask me. I never knew you were anything but Fenmore."

"No one is meant to know. At least not in society. And they are not meant to know that I am still rather more than just Fenmore."

He stopped and looked at her then. That piercing, straightforward, intelligent gaze that made her feel as if she were the only person he could see in the entire world when she knew it wasn't true—he saw *everything*. Every tiny, telling detail. Every bruise and cut. Every blush and stammer.

It was just part of his particular genius to make her feel as if he were looking only at her.

He broke his gaze and quickly looked around, and then lowered his voice, even though they were entirely alone. "You ought to know this, Claire. That I do this—go off, on my own, not as Fenmore. For a reason. It's not just a lark."

She knew she was frowning at him, scowling really, but his tone—everything about him—was making her worry. "I know it's not a lark. It's to help Maisy Carter, isn't it, and bring her murderer to justice?"

"No." He shook his head, and his grim vehemence was back, just as strong and startling as it had been in the first moments she had met him. "Not just today, for Maisy Carter. I do it all the time, really. Whenever I'm needed."

He was still looking at her rather intently—waiting in that way that made her feel that what he was saying was a sort of a test. Her chest began to feel tight. "Needed by whom?"

"The Admiralty, mostly. Jack Denman is the only other person who knows the whole of it."

The creeping unease she had been able to hold at bay

was back, skittering up her spine and down her arms, and wrapping itself tight around her chest. "The whole of it?"

He was frowning too now, leaning down toward her, as if he were willing her to understand. "I inherited the job from my brother-in-law. He did it before me—the difficult, impossible, illegal things that need to be done sometimes. Find things or people. Like murderers. People and things that the Admiralty or other parts of the government can't get for themselves. So I get them. I steal things for them. Whenever I can."

Claire hardly knew what to say. "Good heavens."

"I keep my hand in. Keep up the old connections, the old habits and places that are still useful to me. Like those footpads. And the Lark, and Elias Solomon, and Tilly Wheeler. All of them. So it's not just a lark, a game, all this." He spread his hands out before him, much as he had before. "I do have a purpose. I just thought you ought to know. That's all."

As if her opinion of him, her esteem for him, mattered.

She had thought him a strange, different sort of man—haunted like the veteran sailors and soldiers. And that was what he was—haunted by a criminal past he could not give up.

But there was one more thing she had to know. "And do you like it? This helping and stealing and finding murderers?"

"Ah." He let out a great draught of air, as if he were relieved to get the whole of it off his chest. "God, yes."

Tanner had never felt so exposed. He had never felt less disguised, even rigged up in livery. Everything that he was, was laid bare to her. And he didn't know what he was going to do about it, because he had no idea in the world what she was going to do about it.

Her face—her tiny, heart-shaped orchid bloom of a face—was entirely blank. Or perhaps it only seemed blank because so many different, conflicting emotions ran across it at once—horror and pity and astonishment and fear.

But she didn't say anything about horror or pity or astonishment or fear. She nodded and said, "You like it." Then she asked, "Do you like me?"

"Yes." He said so immediately. This at least he knew. "Yes," he said again, in case she had not heard or understood him.

She nodded again, solemn and troubled and wise. "And are you doing this for me? These illegal things?"

"Yes." He would do anything for her. "You should know that. I will do whatever you need me to do. Always. No matter what." No matter if she rejected him. No matter if she never spoke to him again. He would always watch out for her and help her, any way he could.

Always.

She smiled then. A small, ironic little smile. "As if I'm a sort of a private Admiralty?" she asked in a way that gave him hope. "Or are you my private naval force, ready to vanquish all comers, just as effectively as you vanquished Lord Peter Rosing?"

"Yes." Anything.

She turned and faced down the length of the Mall. "Then, Tanner, tell me how we are going to vanquish Mr. Edward Layham, or whoever it is that murdered Maisy Carter?"

There it was again—his name on her beautiful lips. The name he gave himself in the privacy of his own mind. When she smiled at him and called him Tanner, whatever else he had meant to say was drowned out by a wave of pleasure so incomprehensible and inexplicable and vast, he was hopeless to resist. And so he didn't. "Stealthfully."

She looked as neat and respectable as a pin, in a plain gray frock, white apron, and starched cap. She looked as if she had just starched her mistress's sheets and had wandered out into the sunshine for an illicit meeting with a footman. But under all that respectability was the heart of determination—the heart of a thief.

He held out his hand. "Come with me. And let's go steal a few things from Tattersall's."

When they came nearer to the Queen's Buckingham House, he cut them across into Green Park, where he found a willing urchin to take instruction to his home, Fenmore House, standing in the distance across Piccadilly.

"I've sent for a horse," he told Claire. "Easiest thing to walk into Tattersall's Repository at the lead end of a horse."

She smiled, but she looked across the park toward Piccadilly and Fenmore House for such a long moment, as if she could see up White Horse Street to her own home at Sanderson House.

The short distance between the two gated town houses had tantalized him for years. When he had been a raw youth, struggling to find his place at in society and Eton, he would return to ground in London. He would sneak away from Fenmore House, eluding tutors and minders alike, to return to wandering the streets as he had when he had been a hungry, ambitious boy. But even then, he had always gravitated toward young Lady Claire Jellicoe's orbit, toward the Earl Sanderson's wedding cake of a house behind the wrought-iron gates on Curzon Street, in the hopes that he might see her, coming or going, the pale, blond moon of her face looking out at him from the window of her family coach, or riding her pony under the supervision of the huge, protective coachman in the wide front yard.

"Still determined?"

She turned back, and he could see her resolution writ across her face, in the clarity of her gaze and in the firm line of her jaw. "Yes. Quite. As you said, past bloody time."

He liked when she swore. He like the passionate incongruity of foul words coming out of such a pristine mouth. It amused him. And it reminded him that she was a great deal more than he had ever thought her. She was unique and special, and he needed to have a care with her.

A stable lad from Fenmore House met them at the Hyde Park turnpike gates, all wide eyes and gaping mouth at the sight of his master clad as a footman. But the lad knew enough to mind his jaw and not ruin the rig.

But the boy did sidle close and whisper, "There's goings-on, up to the house, sir. Powerful lot of folks looking for you."

"Are they?" Tanner kept his voice calm and reassuring. "Not to worry. Turns out I'm looking for them, as well."

He might have thought to say more or make further inquiry of the boy, but they were so close to Tattersall's he could see the well-dressed crowds and feel the pull of that jangling excitement he got before a job. His fingers nearly itching to get to work. But he also knew some of his excitement was a sort of raw happiness at having told Claire. At having her still by his side in the aftermath.

He led her down the long court off Grosvenor Place and through the milling crowd toward the back side of Tattersall's famous ring. He'd run a number of different scenarios through his head about the best way to find Layham. The easiest would be to find a central vantage point from which Claire could identify him.

"Stick close. It may be very crowded. We'll make our way across the yard to a better vantage point." There was a wagon, still loaded with hay, parked up flush against a wall—a number of younger boys had already clambered aboard in search of a way to see over the crowds.

"I don't think I can go in there." Claire swallowed hard, and shook her head, and he could see that her face had gone pale. "All those men. What if one of them recognizes me? I know most of them. And what if my brother sees me?"

Tanner could hear the panic edging into her voice. "Easy, Claire. Hush. The animal will give us some room—no one will crowd her." Then he pointed the hay cart out to Claire. "We'll go there, and be sheltered. You can stand on the whiffletree or some such, and I'll stand in front to screen you. You can hide behind me. Will that suit?"

She nodded, but he could tell she was still overwhelmed. More than overwhelmed—scared. And he couldn't blame her. She ducked her head and raised her hand to cover her bruised cheek.

But without her he had no way of identifying Layham. He put his arm around her shoulder and used the animal to cut a wide swath through the crowds, but even before they had reached the wagon he heard mutterings in their wake.

"Did you see? Fenmore's livery," some sharp-eyed sportsman said, turning to his friend as they passed.

"Is he here? Did you see him?"

"No. Why?" another asked. "What have you heard?"

Tanner slowed as best he could, letting the horse put her head down to whuff at the grass, making the crowd jostle and buffet around him, so he could keep listening.

"I heard he killed a man," the first one said.

"I heard he's cut and run," a second sportsman reported, "with the Earl Sanderson's daughter."

"Eloped with Lady Claire? Fenmore? Is he mad?"

"Must be. The earl's likely to gut him. But they do say Fenmore's peculiar."

They had no idea just how peculiar he was, nor how peculiar he was prepared to be. Not that he particularly minded for himself—he was quite at home living on the fringes of respectable society—but it was nearly killing him to walk on by without revealing himself when he heard people speak of Lady Claire in such gleefully malicious tones.

He wanted to gut them, and leave them bleeding on the manicured grass. He wanted to grab them by their starched, pointy collars, and haul them up close so he could tell them to their ugly, smug faces that they were base bastards unfit to even speak her name.

But he shut his gob, and moved on, because beneath his hands that same Lady Claire began to tremble. He gathered her closer against his chest, and leaned down to tell her, "Be brave. Keep going. We're almost there."

He could not read the look she gave him—incredulous and hurt and something else unfathomable. In another moment they were able to take shelter in the lee of the hay wagon, and he got her out of sight, where she could lean against the big back wheel. "Better?"

"Did you hear what they said?" Her voice was thin and more than scared—it was devastated. "My God. You were right about us being invisible."

But he had forgotten to warn her that one of the perils of invisibility was that one didn't always hear what one wanted to hear.

"Yes. I'm sorry." And it surprised him, frankly, that the news had traveled so far, so fast. The Earl Sanderson had always struck Tanner as a circumspect, prudent man, who ought to have done a better job to keep such a report from circulating. And her parents would know that Tanner hadn't run off with her to Gretna Green—they ought to have had her note by now.

Not that it mattered to him. The outcome was still the same—she was his. He had stolen her fair and square, and would make his offer as soon as he judged it would be met successfully.

But clearly he had misjudged it, and left it too late.

"Don't listen to them. They don't know the truth."

"I don't care. It's awful, the way they were talking about you."

"Me?" The accusation, and all its implications, didn't do anything other than cause him mild surprise—a minor hitching of his breath.

Perhaps he had hit Rosing harder than he thought. And even if he had killed Rosing, Tanner felt no remorse. The man was a monster. He had hurt Claire—probably more than even Tanner knew.

He would kill him again in a heartbeat.

Claire was not so sanguine. "Yes, you. The truth is that I ran off with you, not the other way round." Her lovely brow was all pleated up with indignation, but there was real worry there, in the dark shading of her eyes. "But what the other man said, about killing a man?"

What if he lost her because he had in fact killed Rosing? What if he had, and it disgusted her despite all the companionship and all the esteem and all the gentle kisses?

And the thought of submitting himself to the less than gentle care of magisterial authority was not appealing. And it would cock up his ability to find out exactly what had happened and exactly how Maisy Carter was connected to the counterfeiting at St. Catherine's Dock.

"We have to do something, Tanner. We have to get you out of here and protect you."

As a declaration of love it lacked a certain passion, but

it was a good start. It was more than he had a right to hope after only one night and half a day. But he needed more than protectiveness. More than her admiration and more than her esteem.

He wanted her to marry him willingly. Immediately.

It was the only thing that would save them both.

And it was what he wanted.

He wanted simply to be with her. He wanted to hold her hand, and walk along beside her. He wanted the comforting pressure of her body snugged up tight against his. He wanted her soft, fine hair to brush against his neck, just so, when he slung his arm over her shoulder, and she leaned her head against his chest.

He wanted her as his lass for however long it lasted. For however long he could make it last. For however long he could have the privilege of holding her hand.

"Don't worry about me. You saw; you heard. We *are* invisible."

"Tanner, but for how much longer?"

"Long enough to do what we came here to do," he told her. "And then get the hell out. We have to find Layham. If you stand here, behind me and the horse, you'll be sheltered from view, but you'll be able to see men as they come to view the ring." He took up a position in front of her, standing like a sentry.

A bell across the yard clanged out its warning that the first lot of the sale was to begin. The sea of faces turned almost as one.

"God. He's there. Right there." She jumped down to the ground and hid behind Tanner as she pointed at a man not more than eight feet away. "The little man with the bushy eyebrows that make him look like a badger. The man standing in front of my brother."

God's bloody balls.

Tanner shifted the position of the horse so Claire was

completely hidden. And so he could take a harder look at her brother the Viscount Jeffrey, the heir of the Earl Sanderson, to see how well he knew the Honorable Mr. Edward Layham.

As for Layham, he did indeed have very dark eyebrows that rose from his eyes at such a sharp angle that he looked very much like a badger—a well-dressed badger who was turning away, against the tide of men looking toward the ring.

Viscount Jeffrey—who looked like hell, with dark circles under his eyes and a grim line to his mouth, not at all himself—never looked at the badger or noticed him leaving. The viscount's eyes were looking elsewhere, off into the middle distance, as if he were looking but not seeing. As if he were there for form's sake only.

Damn all. Something had gone seriously wrong.

And there was still Layham to track. "Come" was all Tanner had time to say to Claire.

She nodded sharply, and that was all the answer he waited for before he slid through the crowd in Layham's wake.

It wasn't very hard. In fact, the man made it easy, because he clearly wasn't interested in the horses or the sales. He was there to chat. All Tanner had to do was lead his horse nearby, as if he were showing the animal off for his master, and no one—not even the men who bandied his name about so carelessly—gave him so much as a second glance.

But he gave them more than a glance. Especially the monied squire from Suffolk, from whose waistcoat a golden coin fob hung from a ribbon.

Fuck all. Fuck all his theories, which tangled into a knotted skein in his brain.

Disappointment leached through him like acid, corroding his confidence and control. If Layham still had a fob, chances were he was not the murderer. Not unless he had a stash of the ornaments ready-made. But someone presumably *did* have a stash of fake gold Roman coins ready-made. But who?

But then another man spoke to Layham, and gestured to his fob. Layham fondled the ornament on its ribbon, and then unhooked the fob, and held it out for a brief examination. But Tanner could only catch snatches of the conversation until he moved nearer.

"Best advice," Layham was advising in a superior sort of tone. "Quite sound, gold. Best thing to do, I'm convinced, in advance of the recoinage. You do know about the recoinage, don't you?"

Tanner knew, even if the other man did not. In the wake of the peace at the end of the long wars with Napoléon, the government was planning to stabilize the weak economy by the passage of a Recoinage Act, which would oversee the reintroduction of new silver coinage, and a change in the gold coinage from the gold guinea, valued at twenty-one shillings, to the slightly lighter sovereign coin worth twenty shillings. The theory was that the use of silver coins, which were thought to become debased, would be limited to transactions under forty shillings. And matching the silver coins to a single gold standard for transactions of all sizes would provide stability.

What rumors about the Recoinage Act also created in advance of its passing was a climate of fear and paranoia and profit taking. Tanner didn't follow 'Change as closely as a City trader, but his clever, analytical mind took delight in complicated financial transactions and the making of money—hence the Dukedom of Fenmore's robust financial strength. But he had also taken note of the new breed of fearmongers, who exploited investors' uncertainties about the recoinage to advance their own political agendas or reap massive profits in speculations on the price of gold. Men like Layham, perhaps, who were advising or had been advised to move their resources into gold.

Claire tugged on his coat. "Tanner. Look. There." She pointed to another middle-aged lord, who approached Layham's group. "Lord Quincy Edwards is wearing the same gold aureus-coin watch fob."

Fuck all.

Disappointment and confusion tasted like ashes and dust in his mouth. He hated getting it wrong. Hated it.

Tanner circled the horse, and tried to think. And keep a watch out for Claire's brother. Or, God forbid, her father—though if the rumors that were already in circulation were indeed what the Earl Sanderson believed, Tanner doubted that the earl would put in an appearance. More likely he was scouring the Great North Road with a troop of the King's horse.

Over the top of the filly's head, he saw a familiar face bear down on Layham's group, and the pieces of the puzzle began to sort themselves out into a more recognizable shape. Sir James Kersey, an elderly baronet and slight acquaintance of Fenmore's, strolled up, also wearing the same gold aureus fob.

So the fob was likely a token of an investors' club or some sort of financial syndicate. But did the men wearing them know they were fakes? Or was the fob meant to be just a token, a symbol of their financial acumen? The possibilities had narrowed and expanded all at the same time.

One thing was certain. The fob in Maisy Carter's possession was not a singular piece. Despite his dislike of the fact, Tanner's list of possible murderers had increased at least threefold.

But the three men in his sights were likely not part of the murder, as they all still had their fobs. Which might or might not be fakes.

There was only one sure way to find out.

He hadn't cut a purse in months, but the situation could not have been more perfect—Tattersall's was packed and jovial, with people and animals all going in a hundred different directions across the crowded space outside the oval.

He could take one fob easily. Even two.

Oh, hell. He could hear his sister's voice in his head—*while you're about it, best to do the job proper-like and take them all.*

Tanner felt his face curving. The slippery burst of itchy excitement was back. His fingers danced at the end of his hand.

But Claire was still with him, and as tempted as he was by his savage pride to show her his larcenous skill, he knew deep down that it would be wrong. And dangerous—he hadn't bungled a job since he was twelve years old, but there was always the chance. She couldn't be involved.

"Start for the gate. I'll be right behind you."

Claire needed no further instruction but put her head down and hurried toward Grosvenor Place while keeping anxious watch on her oldest brother's back.

And there was nothing left for Tanner but the job.

It would be easy, he assured himself. Confidence. Patience. Subtlety. Timely application of force. Natural reaction. As easy, his sister used to say, as taking gin from a dead whore.

It was easy. All he had to do was wait patiently for another few moments for the small group to disperse. Then Tanner walked forward with the horse on his right side, his left hand on the rein, and his right higher, on the bit of the bridle. Then a touch of elbow into Layham's paunch, and the restive movement of the horse interposing itself between them, while Tanner's left effortlessly plucked the bauble off its loop.

Then a few smooth strides onward to Edwards just as someone called his name and he turned, oblivious in the crowd. A twist of the wrist and done.

Kersey was the hardest. He was older and more cautious in the crowd. He was nervously patting his coat, as if he had more money than he ought to spend in his pockets. Tanner resisted the temptation to relieve him of the lot of it.

And there it was, a fully formed image in his brain—a map of England. London, and then northeast, across Essex to the border of Suffolk, where the villages of Layham, Edwardstone, and Kersey lay in a ring around the larger market town of Hadleigh. The Marquessate of Hadleigh.

Rosing's father.

Tanner felt a calm, certain reassurance, the way he did when the tumbler of a recalcitrant lock clicked into place. There were no coincidences. Rosing was in up to his neck.

And Tanner was full of that aggressive certainty now, and used the horse to better effect with Kersey, swinging the poor obedient beast into the man, and knocking him down, just so he could help him to his feet. And let his clever fingers relieve the man of his gold fob.

Done and away.

Chapter Sixteen

Claire wanted to run. She wanted to run like a child, and hide herself away. Away from prying eyes and careless mouths and sly, bruising innuendo. She was bruised enough already.

But she didn't run. She walked.

She walked down the lane because she had come too far, and done too much, to give in to the desperate, infantile wish to be cosseted, and have someone else take care of all the truly ugly unpleasantness. If the unpleasantness—the horrible events and the ugly rumors and the mortified feelings—were to be overcome, she would have to vanquish it herself.

She allowed herself the respite of breathing easier when she reached the open street. She crossed over Grosvenor Place and turned toward Piccadilly without thinking, only wanting to put the safety of distance between her and her brother. Which made no sense—her brother was not the enemy. Until last night, she had never thought she had an enemy in her life. But her life had changed.

She had changed.

She was glad she had seen her brother. Glad. Because it reminded her of who she was, and who she had been until last night, and who she wanted to become. She was

Lady Claire Jellicoe finder of murderers now, not just the pretty, obedient daughter of the Earl Sanderson. Not just a marker for her father, or her family's influence and power.

Yet she had unthinkingly headed across the corner of Green Park toward home. But perhaps it was time. She couldn't traipse about London with the Duke of Fenmore indefinitely.

And perhaps he felt the same way. Tanner was no more than twenty yards behind her, walking the yearling filly purposefully along the edge of the street, striding up Piccadilly toward Fenmore House just as if he really were a servant out on an important errand for his master. Just as if he weren't Fenmore himself.

It was all mad. She was mad. He was madder.

She fell in with him along the pavement, all prickling curiosity to understand why he had looked so grim and elated all at the same time, back there, in Tattersall's. "What did you do?"

He was still grim, in his understated way. His long jaw looked as if it were carved from stone. "Took them all."

"The fobs?" Claire didn't know whether to be astonished or outraged or terrified. She couldn't help but look back across the street, just to check to make sure there wasn't a constable trailing after them, truncheon raised. "What happened?"

He cut a shard of a glance at her, and then strode on, looking straight ahead. "I stole the fobs."

He said it as if it were a simple statement of fact. As if stealing *one* fob, let alone *all* the fobs, weren't a crime that could see him hanged. "And? What did they do?"

His mouth twisted ever so slightly into that secret, piratical smile. "Nothing."

She *was* astonished, she decided. The breath had gone hot and still in her throat. "Didn't they realize they were gone?"

"No." He turned down the corner of his smile and shook his head. "They never do. Not if I've done my job right."

Now she was astonished and impressed. "Good God. You must have done it very right. No one's coming, anyway." She chanced another glance behind. Nothing. She couldn't contain the spurt of irrational giddiness at the thought of what he'd done and gotten away with.

She had to make herself take a deep breath. And make herself not think about the slippery morality of being happy a thief had just stolen from honest men. Because they had no idea if they were honest men, did they? Indeed, all the available evidence indicated otherwise. "Can you tell if they are fakes?"

"No," he said. "Not yet. It's bad form to look at your lour after you've just stolen it."

She tried to match his grim humor with her own. "Good to know. I'll remember that, shall I, when I pinch Mrs. Layham's handbag."

But that was the absolute wrong thing to say. "Don't try it, Claire." His tone was sharp and testy. "You're not meant for that sort of life."

She could not gauge his mercurial shift. "I was only making a joke." She tried smiling at him, so he could see and understand.

He was having none of it. "It's not a joke, Claire. It's serious. Deadly serious. One girl is already dead." His voice was as low and lethal as the long knife he had stashed in his boot—sharp, inflexible steel. But then the blade of his criticism turned inward. "I can't believe I exposed you to that. I'm taking you home."

"No." She tried to sound firm, but her voice had already turned pleading. "Because I got scared?"

"Because I never should have taken you there. God's balls, Claire." He pulled the filly to a halt on the corner of

Park Lane and turned to Claire. His voice was low and oh, so vehement. "It's wrong of me to have brought you *anywhere*. It was wrong. You need to be home. Your parents need to know where you are. You can't be a part of this."

Despite her own distress, she heard the wretched fear and frustration darkening his voice and she tried to understand all the urgent, unspent, frustrated energy pouring off him. She could only imagine what a toll—the training and skill and sheer, bloody nerve—it took to steal something well enough so that no one even noticed. He must be coming out of his own skin. But he couldn't exorcise his demons on her.

She had to make him understand her nerve, and her resolve, too.

Claire scrubbed the hot, itchy feeling out of her eyes and swallowed hard over the tight heat in her throat. "But I am a part of this, Tanner. I was a part of being raped, wasn't I? I was a part of finding poor Maisy Carter's dead body, wasn't I? It's too late for me *not* to be involved. It's too late for *you* not to be involved."

"I'm different."

She hated the self-loathing she heard in his voice. "Maybe," she admitted. "But do you regret it? Are you sorry you helped me, and stopped Rosing?"

"No."

His answer was unequivocal, solid and sure. Something she could lean on. "Are you sorry that you hurt him so badly, you may have killed him?"

"No."

Another immediate answer. But he threw his head back and looked up at the blazing summer sky, as if he were seeking divine guidance. Or retribution. And his voice was laced with something stronger than regret—shame. "I do know that I should regret it, Claire. I do know that if I were good—if I were a true gentleman—I should regret it. I know that. I've been taught better. But I don't regret it. At all."

She had been taught, too. She had been taught to smile and say yes. No more.

"Are you sorry that we found Maisy's body?"

"No."

"Then there you are." She took another deep breath and forged on. "I don't regret any of those things either. But I will regret it, if we stop now—if we let that man, whoever he is, get away with murdering Maisy, and go free so he can rape and murder another girl. *That* is not something I care to have on my conscience."

And she had to make this right—for herself, as well as for Maisy Carter. Because if she and Tanner didn't find out what had gone so very wrong at the ball, if they couldn't know that Lord Peter Rosing was never going to be able to rape another girl again, Claire could never hold her head up in public or trust another person. If she went home now, she might never have the courage to leave her father's house again. "I have to find out who did this, Tanner. Please understand, I *have* to."

He was silent for a long moment, thinking with that clever, clever, encyclopedic, labyrinthine brain of his— weighing each and every one of her words, to see if they could tip his scales.

"Almost," he said at last. "You were *almost* raped."

So correct. Insisting on being both protective and right. She'd give him that. "Yes. Because you stopped him."

He winced up one eye. "Ah. I've been lucky, Claire."

"No. I've been lucky. You've been vigilant and skilled." She was sure of this. "And you're going to keep on being vigilant and skilled." She took ahold of his hand and led him onward. "And you promised me, Tanner. You said you would do anything for me. Anything I asked you to do."

"God's balls." But even his curse sounded accepting. "I did."

"You gave me your word," she pressed, "so you'll just have to keep it."

"God's balls," he swore again, but he was smiling now. "You sound just like my sister."

It was as close to agreement as Claire was like to get. The warmth of relief made her expansive. "I'll take that as a compliment."

He heaved a pent-up chuckle out of his chest. "You're nothing like her."

"No?"

"No." He shook his head and rubbed his hand across his mouth, as if he could erase the feeling. "I never wanted to kiss her."

She felt it again—that suspended moment when the rest of the earth seemed to stand still and there were only the two of them. Every hint of fatigue vanished. Every weary nerve came alive and tingling.

She turned her head and looked up at him from under her lashes. "And do you want to kiss me?"

He shook his head again, as if he would still try to deny it. But he said, "It's *all* I want to do."

Heat and something far more unruly blossomed deep under her skin. Something unfettered and entirely unrefined. Something daring. "Then you'd best do so."

He didn't kiss her immediately, there in the middle of a public thoroughfare, but clasped her hand and pulled her at a run down the pavement. The startled filly pranced along beside them, but as soon as they made the corner, and could slip into the narrow reach of White Horse Street, he looped the rein over his elbow, and reeled Claire around into the soft ivy covering the backside of the Fenmore stable block.

He took a long look at her there, at her face and eyes and lips—such a long look that she thought he might have changed his mind, and be thinking of reading her another lecture.

But what he did instead was put one hand flat against the wall over her head, and lean in, just a little. Just enough so his breath fanned across her temple. Just enough so she tilted her face up to his.

Within her chest, her heart had kicked up, keeping time with her shortened breath.

When she had kissed him in the boat, it had somehow seemed right—the natural thing to do. But he had been slow to respond, and hesitant. As if perhaps he might not want to be kissed in the middle of a busy river. Or by her. And so she had stopped. And pulled away.

But now it was he who was bending down from his great height to kiss her. He who was sneaking his hand around her waist, and pulling her near. He who was finally appeasing the near-painful ache of longing.

His lips were less tentative, less passive, though they moved over hers carefully, slowly, gauging their welcome.

She would leave him in no doubt.

She slanted her head, and took his taut bottom lip between her teeth and bit down gently, delicately, holding him captive, baiting him with the promise of more. Teasing him into complicit compliance.

But in the next moment she was almost sorry she had teased him so, for she was unprepared for the force of passion she had awakened in him. His hands cupped her chin, and he sank into her kiss with abandon, drinking in her lips, pushing her back into the verdant cushion of the ivy.

And she was lost. Lost to everything but the smooth shock of his lips and the comforting rasp of his incipient beard against her skin. Lost to the feel of his thumbs fanning across her cheek, urging her to open to him and give in to the decadent soft tangle of tongue upon tongue. Lost in the depth of the hungry ache within her that grew instead of being assuaged.

Hungry for more of the fresh-rain taste of him. More of the cedar-spice scent of him. More of the careful, decorous feel of him.

She looped her arms around his neck and held him tight, pressing herself into the comforting heat and pliant solidity of his chest while his tongue touched and caressed hers. While his lips lulled and enticed with growing heat, drugging her with sweet need.

His hands delved into her hair, cradling her nape, holding her head at just the right angle. And she followed suit, running her hands into his tousled hair, knocking his hat to the ground behind him.

But he didn't care, and neither did she. She only cared that he was kissing her with want, and need and hunger. As if *she* were a taste he had not known he craved and was still hungry for more.

On and on they kissed, giving and taking, asking and exploring, until the filly grew bored and restive, and tugged him away with a toss of her impatient head.

He and Claire broke apart, gasping for breath, and Tanner stepped away, and swept up his hat before it could be trod under the horse's hooves.

"That was instructive." His voice sounded amused and baffled and surprised. "I like kissing you." He said it as if it were a revelation, as if he had not been sure he would when he had first set his lips to hers.

How like him, to be so blunt and honest.

Joy was a heady, giddy, generous feeling bubbling through her. "Oh, I like kissing you, too."

She was rewarded by that lovely can't-help-himself

boyish smile. "Lady Claire Jellicoe. What am I going to do with you?"

She smiled back. "You're going to take me back to Richmond, and catch a killer."

All Tanner could do was agree. And smile. It was as if having tasted her lips, his mouth wanted to do nothing else. But he had to take care of a more pressing matter first.

Like proposing marriage. Best to get to that straightaway.

"I will do that, just as I promised. And then I'm going to kiss you some more. But I need to get this filly back to the stable first."

And all of those things were going to be bloody, damned difficult.

Because as he had so thoroughly kissed and been kissed by Lady Claire Jellicoe up against the stable wall, he had heard the unmistakable sound of a carriage being driven through the gates and into the very private grounds of Fenmore House.

The short hairs at the back of his nape stood to prickling attention, as if he were a cur dog. And he was a motley cur dog of a duke, slinking around his own back alley, watching the premises. And the more he listened, the more strongly his instinct cautioned him toward stealth.

And he had long ago learned to trust and rely upon his instinct absolutely—it had never let him down.

And the situation called for extra caution, because this time he had involved another person—Lady Claire. And if he got this wrong—this delicate and incredibly difficult navigation of human interactions—she would be the one who would suffer the most.

Wariness flooded his skin with pricking, itchy heat, and he led Claire and the filly toward the end of White

Horse Street, where the Fenmore House mews gate met the lane just as it widened into Shepherd Market, with caution riding hard on his back.

He was all watchful vigilance—his palms were sticky with apprehension. And with good reason. There was an inordinate amount of bustle in the stable yard—inordinate in this case being any bustle at all, for he was not in residence.

And there ought not be a carriage with the crest of Sir Nathaniel Conant, the Beak of Bow Street, idling in the yard, nor a red-breasted Runner milling about Tanner's gate.

His body reacted even before his brain, sending a rush of blood through his veins, and his pulse kicking hard against his chest.

He had miscalculated badly. A very different game was now afoot.

"Keep moving. Into the market."

Claire was acute enough to obey him instantly—following him into the anonymous comfort of the milling shoppers picking through the afternoon's produce. "What is wrong?"

Nothing he wanted to speak of in a public place. Tanner wove his dextrous way through the market stalls, winding around produce sellers with their bushels of leeks, and poulterers with their crates of fluttering guinea fowl until he reached a vantage point where he could see both the gates of Sanderson House, to the north up Chapel Street, and the mews gate of the ducal home, Fenmore House, east at the far end of the market at the top of White Horse Street.

Sanderson House was quiet, but Fenmore House was not. There were two Runners, presumably from Bow Street, idling about—one leaning against the wrought-iron gatepost, and the other milling about the yard, talking to his stablemen. Who were all—he would wager his last groat—loyal to a fault. They would say not a word, as they had little respect for the law. No doubt they were all petrified of the nick themselves—Fenmore House was rather overstaffed with what could only be described as former members of the criminal classes. Thieves, rogues, whores, and cutpurses alike.

It was an interesting life.

The coach idling in the drive looked, if not official, then magisterial in all the senses of the word he had learned at Eton and Oxford: masterly, authoritative, and commanding. They did not look like they had come to give him a commendation of any sort. They looked to bid him no good.

But Tanner was a creature of stealth and guile. And he knew a thing or two that all the magistrates in London did not.

"Stay here," he instructed Claire. "Buy some food." He pulled out his sueded pouch again and fished out some coins. "Something we can take with us downriver. And keep this." He looped the leather cord around her neck. "If I'm not out again in ten minutes—take what's inside, put it on, and go home."

"Take what?" She reached up to feel the contents through the soft suede of the bag.

This was not the time or place, but he had run out of time. There was nothing for it. "Look. I am an idiot. Here." He took the ring out himself, and held it up before her. "This ring. With it, we are betrothed, and you are protected. Whether I come out of there in ten minutes or not. But I will come out eventually. I will sort it out, and I will come for you. But in the meantime, you will be protected."

He could not read the look on her face—another one of those combinations of shock and excitement and fear and, he hoped, happiness that left her pale and trembling.

"Whatever happens, I'd be much obliged if you would wear the ring, and consider us betrothed."

As a declaration of love it lacked a certain finesse and passion, but it was the best he could do. And as he himself felt such a confusing mixture of fear and dread and excitement and hopefulness humming through his veins that he thought his heart would pound its way right out of his chest, he shoved the ring into her hand and ran.

Except that he didn't run. He pulled his hat down low over his eyes, and proceeded to walk across the market with the unhurried, confident air of a man who knows what he's doing.

Which was the biggest lie of them all.

But it worked, for he walked unmolested by the Runner at the gate in his blue coat and scarlet waistcoat until he was safe in the stable yard, out of sight of the robin redbreast.

"Pip," he called to a stableboy hauling water.

"Shite." The boy all but bit his tongue. "Ye scared me there, Yer Gr—"

"Stuff it, there's a good lad." Tanner spoke to the lad with a casual tone, and kept moving down the row of stalls. "Walk along with me, as if you're going to help me with the filly. How goes it with the carriage pair?"

The boy was disconcerted by the bland, nonsensical question. "Fine, sir. Do you want me to have 'em put to harness? Or fetch a horse for you? They say they're after you, sir."

"Do they now? That's fine. Fine and dandy." Tanner edged a bit of Billingsgate Irish into his voice. That'd help the redbreasts see and hear what they expected to—an Irish groomsman fresh back from an errand. Just as he wanted them to see. "And in a bit, I'll be after having you find Beamish for me. No, don't look at him"—he kept his own gaze away from the second fellow who sidled into

view and leaned on the side of one of the idle coaches—
"just keep on with me, there's a good lad."

He handed Pip the lead rope, divested himself of his
livery, and donned a sturdy, checked stable apron.

Pip did his damnedest to comply, but Tanner could see
he was nearly bursting at his worn seams with both questions and information.

"So what do you know, then, Pip?" he asked once he
judged they were beyond earshot.

"They come for you. Word is you done something awful bad."

"Hurt a man, perhaps?"

"Worser. They was saying murder, sir. They're talking
the noose."

Fuck all. So he had killed Rosing after all.

Tanner was surprised to find himself feeling something
that had to be remorse—his chest felt tight and achy. But it
was remorse for the fact that he now seemed to have involved Claire in not one, but two, murders.

But he wasn't hanged yet, and wouldn't be if he kept his
wits about him.

He would need a diversion. "Right then. Best ask
Moore to put the tall bays to the town carriage," he instructed Pip, "and await His Grace the duke at"—Tanner
consulted the map in his brain—"at St. Giles Churchyard
this half hour."

St. Giles Churchyard was located a convenient distance
away in the middle of a godawful slum. But Tanner had no
doubt that Moore could handle both himself and the high-
spirited bay team, and that the jaunt there might pull the
constables and Runners crawling about the place in the
opposite direction from where he himself intended to go.

And it was always lovely fun to mislay the law.

"Yes, Your Gr—" The lad stymied himself, and tugged
the brim of his cap. "Done."

"Now get along, and speak to Moore all on the quiet, mind you. And then send Beamish to me."

Tanner kept on with the filly, taking up a curry brush and rag to stroke her down, until Beamish found him.

Beamish was a mostly reformed, one-handed former thief who acted as majordomo and all-around fixer at Fenmore House, and who didn't so much as bat an eye at the sight of his master the duke dressed as a groomsman. He'd seen stranger, and he knew well enough how to run a rig. "Jesus God. There y'are."

"What's the lie, Beamish?"

"Ah, Tanner, Yer Grace. Fook me, but I'm glad to see you, lad. There's a raft of beak coves idling about the ken. Looking fer you and a mort."

"She's safe. Safe as houses. It's all my eye and Betty Martin."

"Dunno." Beamish winched up one side of his face with doubt. "They're talking the drop, they are. Mean to see you in Newgate, if they dare. They're after saying you've kidnapped two ladies, and all but kilt a man. There's talk of murder."

"Is he dead?"

"Which fooking one?" What Beamish lacked in deference for the dignity of the dukedom he more than made up for in loyalty.

"The one they say I nearly 'kilt.'"

"Bashed up awful bad, they say, but not so nears death as he couldn't screech like a ha'penny whore and name you to the beak at Bow Street."

There it was then. Tanner could feel the anger growing in him like a weed—anger at himself for not anticipating such an accusation. He had been so blinded by his own plan to steal Lady Claire Jellicoe that he didn't see anyone else's plan coming. "Well, damn me. So."

"So?" Beamish gaped at his understatement.

"So Lord Peter Rosing has laid evidence—if he was capable, which I doubt—so perhaps his father, the bloody Marquess of Hadleigh, laid evidence in his son's name for a charge that I tried to rape a lady, and that Rosing tried to stop me? And that failing to rape her, I kidnapped the lady against her will?"

"You've the gist of it. Complete shite. Anyone knows you knows that."

"I imagine there's a magistrate or two in the drawing room who say otherwise."

"The Beak of Bow Street himself. They've a warrant, they say. Writs and the like. A lot of fooking palaver, if you ask me."

Tanner had to smile at Beamish's colorful language. With such a majordomo, life at Fenmore House had never been boring. But Tanner couldn't laugh at the charges, spurious though they were.

The Beak of Bow Street would be Sir Nathaniel Conant, a well-respected man, with a reputation for fairness but also mildness of person. Just the sort of man whom someone with a reputation for authoritative behavior—like the Earl Sanderson—might be able to take advantage of.

"This is indeed a right tight jam."

"Bloody well right it is."

"And there'll be a load of work and mischief unraveling it all." Work that was already under way. Across the yard the bay pair was being put to the traces of the small town carriage. And both of the Runners were on their feet, watching avidly.

"Put out word on 'Change and with Elias Solomon that I'm after some profiteers—profiteers in gold specie in particular. A club, or a syndicate of gentlemen, hedging their bets against the recoinage."

"Gentlemen," Beamish scoffed. "Them that can breaks the law by bending it to their will."

"The very same, Beamish. Just that type." Another thought struck hard between Tanner's eyes. "And have Levy follow the money from young Paul Walker's yard at number eighty-nine St. Catherine's Dock. See if he can find who holds the lease. Or who paid for a load of Mendip ore."

"Right ho. I'm right on to it."

"Take your time. I'm off to Richmond, but I'd rather know I've a cushion of time before they think to look for me there. Send me off to the market sharp-like for the Runners to hear, to get a bushel of eels. And then keep the Beak busy. Assure him I'm expected back anytime."

"Ah, yer a right lovely bastard to think of that, so."

Tanner retrieved his coat. "And I'll wager His Worship the Beak is bound to be needing a drop or two of sherry after waiting all that time."

"Aye, he might do. They do say hanging is thirsty work."

Chapter Seventeen

After such an extraordinary speech, and after such extraordinary kisses, Claire felt depleted—so physically and emotionally wrung out that she was brittle with exhaustion. She felt numb with weariness, but when she looked at her hands they were shaking from fatigue.

At least that was what she told herself. That it was the effect of being up all night and all day that made her legs weak, and her breath ratchet unevenly in her chest. It had nothing to do with the ring that she gripped so tightly it began to dig into her palm.

She opened her hand to stare at the ring again. To marvel at its delicate loveliness and its old-fashioned charm—a poesy ring inscribed *No other but you*. It was the most beautiful, most heartwarming ring she had ever seen, and she wanted nothing more than to put in on.

But only if he did not come out, he had said. Only for her protection. He had said nothing of his own feelings—only that he wanted to protect her.

Granted, he was probably the only man in England who was strong enough to marry her and protect her from the inevitable scandal—the scandal that was clearly playing out across the market at Fenmore House. Even she knew that the shifty-eyed fellows in the scarlet waistcoats watching the duke's carriage made ready were Bow Street Runners, and that their presence could bode no good.

Claire returned the ring to the pouch, took out the few pence needed for a meat pie, and made her stiff legs carry her to find a pie seller's stall, and then sat herself down to wait.

Be ready, he had said. *Ready for anything.*

Anything turned out to be nothing much at all. The lovely town carriage rolled out of the mews but did not come for her where she sat like the veriest urchin on a stack of discarded crates, as she had somehow imagined and hoped it might. Instead, the coach took a sharp right and exited the market via Sun Court with the scarlet Runners red faced in pursuit.

And then her Tanner simply walked out the gate of the stable yard, and made his slow, meandering way toward her across the market square.

"I bought you a meat pie."

His smile was full of slow delight. "You remembered."

"Hmm. I'm clever that way." She handed it to him as he hitched his hip onto the edge of the crate, right next to her. "And I'm clever enough to see that something was going on over there. What's all the trouble?"

He took his time answering around bites of pie. "Nothing I couldn't handle."

There was not another duke in the world who would eat a pie from a stall while sitting on a crate in the street with so much gusto. It was entirely boyish and inordinately charming. So charming it nearly put her off her point.

"Which means you're not going to tell me. Which is annoying." She looked back the way the coach had gone. "Nearly as annoying as not getting a ride. I will admit to being done for. If I sit too much longer out here in the sun, I'm going melt into a puddle of Claire."

"Then we won't sit here any longer." He brushed his hands together to rid them of crumbs, and then offered to pull her to her feet. "And anyway, it's coming on to rain."

"How can you say that?" She laughed. "There are only a few clouds."

"Because we live in England. Come on. Let us away to the river."

She let him haul her to her feet, and took the opportunity to keep possession of his hand as they started down one of the many small side streets that branched off the market.

"Tired?" he asked, and then answered his own question. "Of course you are. I am. We've been on our feet for nearly twenty-four hours. Come."

As soon as they came out onto Piccadilly, Tanner put his hands to his lips and let out a piercing whistle, which immediately summoned a hackney carriage.

An antiquated carriage with two indifferent horses pulled up to the pavement, but she supposed it was the best they could hope for, dressed as they were.

Tanner must have seen her looking askance at the carriage, because he laughed as he handed her in. "I assure you it's a fine example of the species. One of the finest."

It was still stale and musty and not at all like the private carriages in which she had always ridden. "Do you take hackney carriages often enough to know? But you're a duke. You have a stable full of every sort of carriage known to mankind, and horseflesh fine enough to make half of Newmarket weep with envy."

He tipped his head sideways in a little tic of acknowledgment. "It's as I told you—I'm not always a duke. Even now."

"But you are. Even now. Even as we drive by your house—your house." She pointed out the open window at the gated facade of Fenmore House as the carriage took them up Piccadilly. "Even now, dressed in cast-offs from your own servants, you *are* the duke." It was inescapable—a simple, inescapable fact of his life.

He said nothing to that particular piece of insight. He watched the house roll by before he looked away, out the opposite window. "I know."

The realization hit her—much more softly than a shovel to the back of the head, thank goodness, but forceful nonetheless for all its quiet truth. *He wanted escape.*

As he would say, Ah.

But as she had no further insight into how she might fit into his particular version of escape, she had nothing, not even small talk, to add. As she had already noted, "It's quite a day for firsts."

He gaze flicked back to her. "Your first hackney carriage?"

"Indeed." She decided to be charming. He liked it when she was charming. "I am totting up quite a list today—skiff, wherry, goldsmith's, lead yard, stolen vessel, rag trader's, Tattersall's Repository, and now a hackney. But I shall not account the day a triumph until I have learned how to whistle."

He rose to her bait faultlessly. "I could teach you if you like."

She rewarded him with a genuine smile. "Yes, please."

"Easiest thing in the world," he said. And with all his usual focused intensity, he began to do just that.

"You put your tongue out like this"—here he demonstrated the proper sticking out of the tongue—"and curl the end of it up with your fingers. And your fingers have to be just so." Again he demonstrated the proper position. "And the force and flow of the air through the vortex created by your fingers and across the surface of your lips should sound like—" He let out a little toot.

Claire copied all his movements and positions, and

attempted to follow his directions on airflow, but by the time they reached the Haymarket she had produced only a slight wheezy sound, and had gotten herself out of breath and rather dizzy.

And Tanner was staring at her, with his mouth ever so slightly open, as if she baffled him.

"Am I doing it wrong?"

"No." His brows arced with denial over his blank surprise. "You've very clever—you're doing it right."

"Then why are you looking at me like that?"

He did not say, "Like what?" He did not pretend to misunderstand. He said, "Because now I want to teach you to do other things with your clever mouth."

In that moment, Claire began to have an inkling as to what it was to feel powerful. But she was equal to his honesty. "Things like kissing?"

This time he did not immediately take her bait. And he was not entirely honest. "Perhaps." He turned again to check out the open window as the hackney moved onto Cockspur Street.

Claire felt her smile spread across her face. She would have to try harder. "Perhaps, I want to learn more about kissing."

This time, it was his smile that stretched full across his face. "Somehow, I knew I could count on you."

And then he was kissing her, and nothing else mattered.

Nothing but warmth, and texture and scent. The warmth of his body, as he pulled her closer to him. The texture of his smooth lips, and rasp of his cheek against her. The male scent of his body, of cedar spice and horse and saddle soap.

She leaned in to him, and he pulled her flush against the long strength of his body. His hand spanned the small of her back, fitting her to him until there was no breath of space between them. Nothing but pleasure and comfort and glorious need.

His hand rose to her nape, cradling her skull, angling her head to his liking, bringing them close and closer still. She had thought she was melting in the sun, but it was nothing to what she was feeling now—pressing heat and pulsating need turned her liquid and pliant, flowing into him with every kiss, every breath, every touch.

"Claire." His voice sounded foggy, as if it came from far away, and he had to clear his throat to speak again. "Claire, the carriage has stopped. We're at the Whitehall Stairs."

"Whitehall?" Parliament, where her father spent so much of his time, was in Whitehall. Though she and her mother had been set to head to Downpark directly from Riverchon, her papa was bound to stay in London until Parliament adjourned in August, another few weeks away. All of which meant that her father might very well be about. "What if my father is here?"

Tanner looked, if not startled, then somehow conscious. "He won't be here, Claire. If what we heard at Tattersall's and what I learned at Fenmore House is true, your father may think I've eloped with you. I rather think he's searching the Great North Road."

"But I sent him the note."

"I know." He shrugged and held out his hand to help her exit the carriage. "We won't know for sure until we return to Riverchon."

But as they made their way down the Whitehall Stairs to the flotilla of waiting wherries, the sky did what it was nearly always threatening to do in England, and what Tanner had so sagely predicted, and began to rain. A hard, soaking rain that instantly pattered on the surface of the water, and washed away all other sound.

Tanner engaged a wherry to take them as far as the

Chelsea Embankment, and as soon as they were seated in the stern sheets he stripped off his livery coat and held it over their heads. For herself, she was enough of a country girl not to particularly mind the rain, but it was entirely lovely to have an excuse to snug up close to Tanner. He was lovely and solid and warm.

And then she yawned again. A big, indecorous, cannot-be-hidden yawn. She was truly exhausted. And it felt good to lean against him, and pretend that he wasn't a duke and she wasn't an earl's daughter, and that they hadn't been missing from the world to which they belonged for nearly an entire day.

She closed her eyes, and let herself pretend.

In the stark gray afternoon light, her face looked more than tired. Her eyes were red rimmed, and there were purple smudges beneath them as well as across her cheekbones. She looked entirely unequal to the task that awaited them in Richmond.

"You're exhausted."

She gave him one of her quick smiles, without even opening her eyes. "There you go again, with your penchant for the obvious. But it's of no matter. I'll get my second wind yet."

She was teasing him. He could tell because those lovely china blue eyes that fluttered from behind her lashes were soft and warmed by her smile. And he wanted to stay right there, basking in the warmth and easy camaraderie of that smile for hours and hours on end.

Perhaps the thought of the coming reckoning made her quiet, or perhaps she really was exhausted past all conversation. Because by the time they had passed Lambeth her breathing had evened out into the short, relaxed rhythm of sleep.

She was asleep. On him.

Tanner wrapped his arm about her shoulder carefully, so as not to wake her, and eased her into his arms, cradled safely against his chest, so he might keep looking at her face, inches away, illuminated by the dappled light glancing off the rain-darkened water.

And then he did what he never did—he relaxed.

At least for a few moments. It was bliss to let go of whether he was the Tanner or the Duke of Fenmore, and simply enjoy watching her through half-closed eyes. Dreaming of what it might be like to do this every day. To have the right to hold this woman in his arms, stroking her face, running the backs of his fingers gently down the line of her chin. Letting the pad of his thumb just barely graze the sublimely soft edge of her bottom lip.

It was a quiet half an hour before they arrived at Chelsea, where the wherry brought them to the rickety stairs at Cheyne Walk. The skiff was there, just as it ought to be, covered with an oilcloth to keep the worst of the rain out, but of the Lark there was no sign. He could only hope she had taken refuge at the house a few blocks away, and that even now Jinks was feeding the poor girl up.

But the Lark wasn't his responsibility. The girl in his arms was. "Claire."

He felt her breathing shift cadence, and he spoke to her again. "It's time."

Claire came slowly awake, floating her warm way out of sleep. She blinked up at him, her blue eyes slow and trusting, accepting that she was in his arms.

He stilled, as if he were still the boy he had once been, caught with his hand in someone's pocket. "You're awake," he said unnecessarily.

"Where are we?"

"Chelsea." He heard the words came out of his mouth off-kilter and slightly off-key. He cleared his throat. "You fell asleep."

"Oh, Lord." Heat rose across her face as if she were embarrassed. "I'm so sorry."

"Not at all. You were exhausted."

"What time is it?" Claire began to straighten up, and he let her go reluctantly. His arms felt empty the moment she regained her seat.

"After two."

"Oh." She sat up straighter. "Oh, goodness." She put a hand to her bruised cheek. "At least it's not Riverchon yet."

That was anxiety about the reckoning that was coming. "I promised you no one would question you. I'll make sure of that."

"Thank you." She pushed her hair back from her face and gave him one of her sweet, small smiles. "But not even you can hope to stop my mother."

No, he couldn't. Nor did he want to. But the wherryman needed to be paid, and she and Tanner still had a long trip downriver, which needed to be undertaken immediately if they were to catch the last of the tide.

"Claire, do you have the money?"

She handed over the sueded pouch without a word. Without any comment on its contents or clarification about his intent. He was about to make just such a clarification, to remind her of what he had said, and leave her with no doubt as to his intentions.

But he didn't.

He wasn't exactly sure why. And it was unlike him not to say exactly what he thought. It was unlike him to be unsure. But he was. A little dousing of doubt had chilled him more effectively than the rain.

They transfered themselves to the skiff without any further conversation, and in no time they were headed upstream, gliding into the soft summer air. The rain that had lulled her into slumber had slacked to one of London's well-worn combinations of warm fog and falling mist. While not ideal for a long row down the river, it was at least tolerable.

Claire was just as quiet in the skiff as she had been in the wherry, and as for him, he let the hard, regular rhythm of the oars and the strain of physical exertion free his mind to turn over each and every piece of information in his brain, to prepare himself for what he was likely to find at Riverchon. And what he was likely to have to seek.

"What are you thinking?"

In front of him, Claire shifted back into focus.

"That we will need to find my grandmother's guest list to see if any of the men from Tattersall's—the men with the fobs—were present. We will need to find what has happened to Lord Peter Rosing—where they have taken him, and if he still lives. We'll need to see if we can speak to the servants to see what they saw and what they heard the night of the murder, because as we know, they are invisible and will have heard or seen something that will be of use."

"Maisy wasn't invisible. If she were, she wouldn't be dead."

He had no argument, no soft words, to counter that. "No. She wasn't."

But what then had made her visible? What made someone notice her? How, in the middle of a busy evening's entertainment, had she both become become visible and gone unnoticed?

There were facts and details and questions enough to ponder the whole of the journey, and it was late afternoon by the time they came abreast of the Riverchon boathouse. Which he approached with caution—who knew if there were Runners or thief takers stalking the perimeter of Riverchon, as well as Fenmore House?

As it turned out, there were no obvious Runners skulking about the shrubberies, but the wrought-iron gate had been lowered across the entrance to the boathouse, barring access to the manor from the river. That made the choice easy enough. And after his earlier experience at Fenmore House, Tanner was in no mood to take chances. He did not want to add the scandal of a public apprehension to his list of sins.

He rowed them past Riverchon, to the adjacent property, where he hid the shallow boat in the long grass along the riverbank. The property was out of both use and repair, and was helpfully overgrown—they could traverse the length of the long brick wall separating the properties without fear of being seen.

Tanner's boots were wet from the long grass, and Claire's skirts were soaked by the time he found what he had been looking for—an old gate set into the side wall of his grandmother's property, nearly hidden by bushes and overgrown vines.

He gave the latch on the gate an exploratory rattle. "Locked."

"Why," Claire asked from behind him, "if I may ask, all this secrecy? Why the hidden garden gate?"

He gave her his patent answer. "Always pays to know two ways in and three ways out of every place."

"But this is your grandmother's house." Claire was wet and baffled after being stopped so close to her destination. She sounded just a little bit put out. But she was a clever girl, and took all of two seconds to work it all out. Her eyes widened and her brows rose as her face cleared. "You expect trouble. There is more you aren't telling me."

He had thought to spare her the worst of it, for no other reason than some misguided, primeval instinct to protect her. But being spared and protected from the world had been what had gotten her—gotten them both—into the position in which they now found themselves: crouching in the wet grass outside his own family's home.

"Someone, and I have to assume it was Rosing or his father, has laid evidence against me with the Magistrates' Court at Bow Street that I assaulted or killed Rosing—it's not clear—and made off with you, and potentially Maisy."

She laughed. A helpless spurt of disbelieving laughter that sounded overloud in the quiet hush of the rain-drenched trees. "But that's patently ridiculous. And untrue."

"Yes. That is what we now have to prove. Along with finding out who killed Maisy. And why."

"But I'll just tell them what happened."

"Will you? Are you ready to tell them all?"

His question was met with uncomfortable silence. But he wouldn't press her. He had promised her that no one would question her. The time of reckoning would come fast enough, and she would have to make her decision then.

He stepped close to have a more professional gander at the lock. It was an uncomplicated ward lock opened with a simple skeleton key. He would almost pick it with his teeth.

"What do you plan to do?"

"Two choices—no, three—boost you over, stand back, and watch you give it a go just as you did in Chelsea, or"—he looked at her and gave her that smile she liked—"pick the lock."

She did like. "What an astonishing assortment of skills you seem to have, Your Grace." She said it with just the right amount of amusement and admiration, and smiled back. A watery little smile, but she was rallying. "Pick the lock, if you please?"

"Yes." He did please. Anything to have her with him. Anything to keep her as his co-conspirator. "Don't tell anyone."

"I wouldn't dream of it." She breathed out another

shaky little laugh. "I wouldn't dream of telling anyone anything about our night. Or our day."

That stopped him cold. He left off rummaging in his pocket for his picklocks and looked at her. "Claire. You're going to have to give some explanation."

"I meant about us, and— I'm sure there's more than enough to tell with Maisy, without all the rest."

"Ah." That was instructive. She would share the awful details of her near rape sooner than she would tell them about him. Well.

"The rest is important, Claire. Rosing won't be stopped—not even by a cracked head and a broken leg— until someone finally does say something. Someone who is beyond reproach. Something that will stop him."

"But you already did. And if you've already killed him, I won't have to say a word."

Chapter Eighteen

Tanner didn't laugh. He didn't say anything. He was his terse, focused self as he instructed her on the finer points of picking a lock. "It's a ward lock with a simple single bolt within." His voice was clipped and instructional. More duke and far less Tanner.

She had said the wrong thing. "I'm sorry," she said instantly.

"Nothing to be sorry about." But he didn't try to snug up close to her as he had in the lead yard.

She had envisioned him working with her, close and intimate, but he had her stand on her own, working the tools herself. She didn't know whether to be thankful that he thought her independent and clever enough to accomplish the task or be put out that he no longer seemed to want to be close to her.

He kept his own counsel, and handed her the two long, thin pieces of metal he had used in the lead yard. "It's all right. Insert the pick, the pointed one, and feel for the tumbler, the piece of metal, like a tooth, inside."

Claire pushed aside her confused feelings, and concentrated on his instruction, inserting the pick into the keyhole. She fiddled around a good bit, feeling her way, probing, as he said, for a tooth. Wanting very badly to get it right. To impress him. "Oh, yes." She felt the tumbler, just as he said.

"Good. Then just feel for which way it needs to fall—usually away from the side the door opens on—and pin it back the other way. It might take a fair bit of tension to—"

Claire leaned her weight into her hand, just as he instructed, and the bolt scraped into place with a rusty squall. "Is that it?"

He thumbed the latch and pulled open the screeching gate just enough to show her she had, in fact, done it. "Well done, you."

"That was brilliant." She was numbly elated, standing there in the grass with her feet clammy and wet. She had impressed him, but more important, she had impressed herself.

"Yes. Very clever. You can give those back to me now."

She didn't feel clever with Tanner so patently unhappy with her, and she wanted to feel something better. "No. I meant you. You told me exactly what I needed to do. That's the brilliant part." But she was still buoyantly happy and pleased with herself. "Now I want to do it again. I shall doubtless be at all the locks on your doors with a hairpin the minute I'm free."

Finally he smiled, and Claire felt as if some of the pressing weight of unease had been lifted from her chest. "The minute you're free," he echoed. "You're welcome." But he still kept his distance.

He eased himself through the gate, checking in both directions, before he motioned her through, and pushed the gate almost closed. So he would have another way out of the place, she supposed. Just in case.

What a strange, clever duke he was.

And he was cleverer still, standing still and listening before he spoke. "Claire. There look to be a fair number of guests still here."

The hidden gate gave on to the narrow side lawn toward the side of the house. But when she stopped to listen with him she could hear snatches of conversation over the thick hush of the summer mist. "Pray God they aren't talking about us."

"No bet. Chances are they are." And with that cynical—he would undoubtedly say "realistic"—remark, he led the way toward the front of the house, where a path led to a servants' or tradesmen's entrance set low, a half story belowground.

"This should be quiet enough." He led the way, checking through the door for other people, making sure that they were alone as he led her in, and then down an empty corridor. "I thought we'd head for my grandmother's private sitting room. It's the most likely place—"

She thought he might have said more, but instead he shucked off his livery coat and left it on a peg along the hallway, and then showed her up one of the smaller side stairways to the baize green door that separated the servants' world—the one to which she had belonged for most of the past twelve hours—from the family's.

"Are you ready?"

It was the same question he had asked last night, as they were about to set off from Chelsea, and the same question he had repeated at the lead works. "Yes," she answered, putting all her determination and resolve into her voice. "I'm ready for anything."

"Excellent. And remember, Claire," he murmured low. "The danger lies not in the remembering, but in the forgetting."

He had said that before as well, when they were first

out on the water last night. It seemed a very, very long time ago.

"I'll remember."

And then the lovely, magical time was over and they were no longer alone. No longer alone in the world with only each other.

"Your Grace." Doggett, the Riverchon butler, with whom she had been on nice terms—she had always made it a point to learn servants' names, even when visiting other houses—emerged from somewhere down a corridor and stood uncharacteristically flat-footed, gaping at them. "My lady, we've all been so concerned."

Gratitude, mixed with the hot sting of guilt, filled her. She had thought only of herself, and then her parents when she sent her note. She had not thought of how her disappearance might have affected all the other people who lived at the periphery of her life.

"Thank you, Doggett. You are very kind to worry after me. I apologize for your fears. But as you can see, I am back now." She was careful not to say "we," careful of the proprieties that she had so enthusiastically brushed aside for the past twelve hours.

Tanner—His Grace—led the way past Doggett. "My guest would like some refreshment. Coffee, and a good deal of tea. And I should also like you to notify the earl and countess that Lady Claire awaits them in Her Grace's parlor."

His voice was all chilly, formal Duke of Fenmore, as if he had just chanced to find her wandering the halls, lost and wearing her absurd maid's costume. Indeed, if she had not experienced the past hours with him, she never would have believed him capable of being anything other than the chilly, aloof Duke of Fenmore.

But Doggett looked relieved to have his master back.

"Yes, Your Grace. But the Earl Sanderson has left, Your Grace, and has journeyed to London."

"Oh." Claire brightened. It would much easier than she thought. Lord only knew what her father would do if he saw her in her present state—and Fenmore as well, looking like his disreputable Tanner self. Not that she was going to have an easy time with her mother.

"I believe he went to Fenmore House on the advice of Her Grace," Doggett was clarifying, "to see if Lady Claire might be recovered from there."

"Recovered from Fenmore House?" she parroted. "There is no need for 'recovery.'"

Beside her, His Grace of Tanner made a soothing but somehow impatient sound—a subtle warning not to give away too much. "Where is Her Grace?"

"In the drawing room, Your Grace, with her other guests."

"Would you be so kind as to request her to attend me in her parlor at her earliest convenience."

"Of course, Your Grace."

The man bowed and headed back down the corridor the way he had come until Tanner—His Grace—said, "The countess first, if you please, Doggett."

"Very good, Your Grace." Doggett bowed again and headed in the opposite direction, toward the main staircase. Claire's mother was presumably above.

"Actually, I think I had rather just go to my mother, now. I think that would help, if indeed, as you suspect, she did not get my note. I don't want to make her wait any—"

Before Tanner could answer, a door banged open at the far end of the entry hall.

Claire turned to see her father burst into the house, stop in his tracks, and then stride directly toward her. "Claire. My God." Her father enveloped her in a crushing but brief embrace. "My God. Are you all right?" He pushed her back at her elbows to take a look at her. "Are you unharmed?"

"As you see. I'm quite—"

He did not let her finish but pulled her back against his chest, and Claire was once again enveloped in the strong comfort of her father's love. "Where in hell and gone have you been, young lady?" The words rumbled through his chest. "And why in hell did you not send word for me to come get you?"

Her poor father. He would not be swearing at her unless he had been well and truly frightened. "I did send word, but—" She had been too busy finding Maisy Carter, and doing what needed to be done. She had been too busy staying with her Tanner. But she was quite sure her father did not want to hear *that*.

"And what in the name of God are you wearing? Your mother will have another apoplexy if she sees you in this. Has she seen you?"

"I am sorry, Papa, but—"

"Why have you not gone to her?" Her father released her and immediately started toward the stairs.

"But what about His Grace?" Claire turned to indicate her companion and savior. Surely her father would want to thank him? And discuss whatever other agreements the houses of Sanderson and Fenmore might want to come to regarding a betrothal? At least she hoped so.

Only to find His Grace, her Tanner, was gone.

Claire looked about, rotating a full circle, with her father staring at her as if she had lost her mind. But she had not. Tanner had been right *there*.

He could not have left her. Not now when she needed him most.

"Where did he go?" She looked at her father.

"Who?" her father demanded.

"His Grace of Fenmore." She turned back to Doggett,

who appeared from down the stairs. "Where did His Grace go?" She needed Tanner's calm logic, his factual way of saying things.

"He is here?" Her father closed his eyes as if his sight gave him pain. "Almighty God."

Claire couldn't tell if he uttered an epithet or a prayer. "What is the matter?"

"Search the grounds," her father commanded Doggett. "Now!"

"No. Papa! You don't understand— You can't—"

"What in God's name were you doing with Fenmore?" Now it was her father's uncompromising gaze that centered on her, narrow and intent.

"Conversing." The lie slipped out before she thought of anything better to say. And it wasn't a lie, strictly speaking. She and Tanner had conversed. And for some reason she could not explain—especially in light of her father's belligerence—she felt protective of His Grace. She might want to curse him herself, but she could not bear to hear others do it.

"Conversing? For seventeen hours, while we turn the world upside down looking for you? Have you no idea what has happened here? A maid has gone missing—we could only assume that she had gone with you—and Lord Peter Rosing is all but fatally assaulted and left for dead, presumably at the hands of Fenmore, and you tell me you have been *conversing* with him?" He cut himself off and passed his hand over his eyes. "My God, Claire. You can have no idea what I've been made to do."

"No idea of what?"

Her father shook his head while he answered. "His Grace stands accused— No. I won't discuss this now. Not here. Not when your mother has been beside herself with worry. And that distressing bruise across your face is only going to make matters worse." His voice rose as he vented what could only be a monstrous amount of worry.

Claire had to tell herself it was a mark of love that her papa was still so worried for her that the unruffled calm that had been always been the hallmark of his character—and had stood him in good stead through the raising of her three rambunctious brothers—had so deserted him as to make him raise his voice at her.

"Any other woman would have taken to her bed with the hysterics, but your mother has stayed up all night waiting for some word of you. Quietly pacing back and forth. Convincing me to travel the length of the Richmond Road in the dead of night in the hopes that you had somehow made it back to our home in London. And then you just simply appear with the bloody Duke of Fenmore, who then promptly disappears? What in hell am I supposed to think? You're not the sort of child who tears off on a lark."

"No, sir. It wasn't a lark." Guilt made her defensive. But at the mention of the Duke of Fenmore she looked around again, as if surely, surely he was just hiding in plain sight, being quiet against a wall, listening and waiting for the storm to pass.

But he was not.

There was only the butler, Doggett, who was trying to show them into Her Grace the dowager duchess's parlor, so they might continue this distressing dressing-down in a more private setting. "The countess is on her way down, my lord."

Claire's father propelled her by the elbow into the lovely rose pink sitting room and deposited her near a chair, but she couldn't sit. She couldn't. Guilt, shame, and the unexpeced desolation of being abandoned by His Grace of Fenmore began to burn a raw hole in her chest.

But she made herself speak. She had come too far to go back to being pampered and cosseted and obedient now. And she had known what she was doing. "It wasn't a lark. It was . . . necessary." She chose the word carefully.

"Necessary?"

"Yes. Absolutely necessary. To do the right thing." Yes. She said it again, to firm the idea in her mind. "The absolute right thing."

"Necessary." Her father took a too-sharp breath. "Did he force you to marry him?"

"Fenmore? Good God, no."

"Did the Duke of Fenmore hurt you?"

"No. Not at all." She said it more forcefully, resentful on His Grace's behalf, willing her father to hear her and understand. "His Grace was a perfect gentleman." He was only hurting her now with his absence.

Her father closed his eyes and took a deep breath. "Claire."

She was astonished, and brought entirely out of her own selfish pain to see the almost-haggard expression on her father's face. The lines around his mouth looked deeper than they ever had before, graven into his cheeks, aging him by years instead of hours. "Papa, please listen to me."

"Just tell me." He took her hands between his own. "Just tell me what happened, and I will make it all go away. I will fix whatever it is that happened."

Before last night she would never have heard a thing wrong with his words. Before last night she would have gratefully let him fix whatever it was that needed fixing. She would have smiled and said yes.

But no more. And it was already fixed—fixed before Lord Peter Rosing had had a chance to hurt her beyond all repair. And she had fixed the rest, herself. Almost. But with the help of His Grace of Tanner, she had at least learned to stand on her own two feet. "Papa, I am well. I am not hurt."

"I can see your face, Claire. Just. Tell. Me. What did Fenmore do?"

"No. You've got it wrong," she assured her father. But she wished Fenmore were there to say what he had done himself. She had no idea how much to say—she had no idea if he really would be brought up on charges for assaulting Rosing.

But her father was waiting; nearly twenty years had taught her that he was not a man who could be lied to. "His Grace of Fenmore helped me."

Her father raised his head and fixed her with a steady, probing eye. "Helped you?"

Claire felt her resolve waver under the unrelenting pressure of his stare. It was too much. Too private. Too full of her own foolish, vain, desperate stupidity to do anything more than assure him that she was not hurt, or ruined so badly as he feared.

She tried to find a way to find the courage to say what was necessary. "Yes. I . . . asked His Grace to take me away from the party for a little while."

"You asked him? Good God, Claire. You're nearly twenty years old, now. You should have long ago learned better than to—" He broke off for a moment, searching for words. "Than to trust a man like Fenmore."

No matter how carefully chosen, her father's words stung like a slap. Heat and humiliation scalded her cheeks. She *had* trusted the wrong man—but not the wrong man her father thought.

She pulled her hand away and found a chair, putting as much distance between them as she could. "You are wrong about His Grace. Fenmore was entirely trustworthy. *He* did as I asked. *He* helped me. And then we found the body—"

"Body." The shocked whisper stopped them both, and Claire turned to see her mother, the Countess Sanderson, in the doorway.

At the sight of Claire, her mother took a deep, almost gasping breath, as if she had not drawn air into her lungs for hours or even days. And then she rushed to take Claire into her arms.

And there was nothing Claire could do but burst into tears.

Once she had begun, it was impossible to stop. It was as if all the remarkable and horrible and interesting and life-changing things that had happened to her over the long course of the night hit her all at once, like a cricket bat to the back of her head.

"I'm sorry." Claire hiccuped her way back to some semblance of better self-control. "I don't know what came over me. Truly, I am fine."

But her mama was not nearly so sanguine. "Oh, my sweet girl. Oh, look at your face." She cradled Claire's jaw and turned her face to the light. Everything in the countess's countenance spoke of concern.

Claire had to shut her eyes against the heartbroken pity on her mother's face. "I'm fine, Mama." Claire took her mother's cold hand from her face. "I am so very, very sorry for all the worry I caused you."

"Hush." Claire could not tell if her mama was speaking to her or to her father, because Mama was wrapping her arms around Claire as if she were loath to let her go. "You don't need to explain."

"Unfortunately, she does," her father insisted.

Claire wiped her eyes on the lawn handkerchief her mother passed her and sat up. "Yes. I feel that I must."

Across the room the door opened, and Doggett showed the dowager duchess inside.

Claire immediately stood, as she had been taught as a child, in deference to the small, delicate woman's age and stature.

"No, no." The bird-like old woman gently waved Claire

back. "Please don't let me interrupt what is clearly a family reunion. But my girl"—she reached to take Claire's hand between her own—"I am so relieved that you are returned to us. As I am sure is your mother."

"Yes, Your Grace," Mama assured her. "Thank you again for all your support."

"Say nothing of it. It only matters that Claire is back, and safe and sound."

"Yes." Claire took the dear lady's arthritic hand gratefully. "Thank you. And I am so very sorry for Maisy's loss."

The dowager and the countess looked from each other to her and back again. "Loss?" the duchess asked, her face white and drawn with dread.

There was nothing to do but tell the heavy truth. And tell it gently.

"Yes. I'm so sorry." Claire felt again all the extraordinary inadequacy of her words, just as she had with Molly Carter. "Did you not know? Did no one tell you?"

"Tell us what?" The duchess's hand had risen to her throat as if she were preparing herself for a blow.

And it would be a blow—the dowager no doubt saw Maisy a great deal more often than even her own mother. Claire held on to the dowager's soft, gnarled hand. "That Maisy Carter's body was found. We found her, last night, the Duke of Fenmore and I. That's where we were. We recovered her from the river. But it was too late for Maisy. I'm so very sorry to have to tell you that Maisy Carter is dead."

"No." The duchess visibly wavered, and Claire was sure the delicate old woman might give way to a faint. Claire immediately put her arm around the dowager's shoulders, to help her to a chair.

"No, no. I'm quite all right." The dowager rallied. "But you, my poor girl. I can't think of what you must have been through. We must think of you."

"I'm fine, Your Grace," Claire assured her. "Quite fine, for I had your grandson with me. His Grace of Fenmore was an extraordinary support and friend to me."

"Fenmore? Your friend?" Her Grace's tear-bright eyes and querulous repetition gave her all the appearance of a tiny owl.

"Yes, Your Grace," Claire assured her.

"How extraordinary. I think we had best ring for some brandy, as I think I *will* now faint."

Claire's father moved to the bellpull, and Doggett appeared nearly instantly with the tea that Tanner—His Grace—had ordered earlier. "Brandy as well, please."

"Yes, my lord."

Mama passed the dowager a dish of restorative tea, and in another moment Papa felt the elderly woman was sufficiently recovered to hear the rest of it. "May I ask what you and His Grace were doing when you found this girl's body?"

"Yes." Claire tried to think of how best to couch what had happened, in a way that would be acceptable to him, while she returned to her chair. "We were conversing. Talking about my brothers, and shooting pistols. But then we found her. And we had to take her out of the river, and notify the authorities so they might do a postmortem. And notify her family as well—because I knew that is the sort of responsibility that a Jellicoe should take." She wanted her father to know this. It was important to know that it hadn't *all* been a lark. "And His Grace felt much the same way about the responsibility."

"*We*? His Grace?" Her father's weary eyes, blue and steady and unrelentingly kind, did not waver. "I did not think you were acquainted with His Grace of Fenmore." He shook his head and looked up to the ceiling. "Your pardon, Your Grace, I did not think *anyone* was acquainted with the Duke of Fenmore."

The dowager duchess waved away any implied insult. "I know, I know."

"No. I wasn't. We met last night. And one thing led quite naturally to another." This time, it was Claire who took her mother's hand. "I am very, very sorry to have caused you both so much worry. I did try to send a note. But it seems to have been mislaid. But I don't know how I could have done otherwise."

"Claire." Her mother heaved a sigh so full of exasperation and frustration and parental love and relief that Claire felt as if she needed to hug *her* and tell *her* it was going to be all right. "You were out all night."

"Yes," she hedged. "But it was not as if I were alone. I had the Duke of Fenmore's escort and assistance."

"Claire," her father repeated, and smoothed his hair, a gesture she knew was his way of showing that he was calm and in control when likely he felt neither. "You have a livid bruise across your face. However much you may want to cast the evening in an innocent light, there is something you are not telling us. And unfortunately, this situation has already erupted into a lurid scandal, even without the sad addition of the maid's death. It was a scandal simply when you went missing. It will be a greater scandal when it is found that you seem to have gone with the Duke of Fenmore willingly. The Duke of Fenmore, whom nobody knows. Who doesn't dance or speak at parties. Who doesn't vote in the House of Lords. Just as much of a scandal as if Fenmore had carried you off as Lord Peter Rosing swore he had."

"Lord Peter Rosing swore His Grace carried me off?" Claire was almost too astonished to do anything other than echo her father's words. "Why, he did no such thing. Rosing was the one—" Any hurt she had felt at Fenmore's sudden abandonment fell away under the hot press of indignant anger that rose within. "Lord Peter Rosing is a no-good liar. And worse." She flung the words at her father as if he were the one to have made the charge.

But it was all too much—the brutal assault, the shocking murder, the long night, the head-spinning kiss, and the final humiliating abandonment. That awful mixture of worry and doubt and anger and shame came back with frightening speed, and she began to shake again—little tremors in her hands and legs—as if Lord Peter Rosing had assaulted her mere moments before and not more than twelve hours ago. As if Fenmore had not come to her rescue. As if the worst had actually happened.

And a voice in the back of her head whispered that it was her fault, that she should have known better, should have never danced or gone out into the dark night with Lord Peter Rosing. If she hadn't said yes, he would never have been able to ruin her.

She felt ruined, even if the worst had not happened. She felt bereft without her Duke of Fenmore, His Grace of Tanner, at her side with all his cool, calm logic and sensible, unflinching advice. Without him, she felt abandoned and as powerless as she had felt when she had been pushed up against that wall.

No. Not again. Not ever again.

"Lord Peter Rosing tried to rape me."

There. She had said it. Just the way His Grace would have—a fact clearly and forthrightly stated.

Everyone stopped—every movement, every conversation, every thought—and stared at her. Especially Mama, whose face held an expression not unlike that of His Grace the Duke of Fenmore when Claire first saw him, across the unconscious body of her assailant—fierce and deeply, deeply still.

"I will kill him," her mother said.

It was rather a lovely thing, Mama's focused, elegant fierceness. In her Claire could recognize that it was love.

"But he did not succeed, Mama. His Grace of Fenmore intervened, and carried Rosing off me. The worst did not happen."

There was another long silence—of overwhelming relief. Mama was again the first to speak. She turned to Claire's father and said in a voice that was as strong and unforgiving as she had ever heard, "I told you so."

Papa's face was like flint.

"Thank God, Fenmore was there." The duchess was still pressing her hand to the hollow of her throat, but she rallied again to cover the horrible silence that had descended. "But that's just the sort of thing he would do, appear in a crisis."

Yes. It was lovely to see that someone else also had faith in Tanner. It helped Claire believe that a man as vehement and clever as the Duke of Fenmore must have his reasons for leaving her without so much as a good-bye or any explanation to her father.

But she needed that calm vehemence of his that made everything so logical. She wanted him to explain that Lord Peter Rosing was an habitual rapist. That it wasn't because she had been desperate enough to ignore the quiet warnings her mother had long ago whispered about Lord Peter. That it wasn't because she was about to turn twenty years of age and was still unmarried while fresh-faced sixteen-year-olds she had shared her come-out with were now married and having their third child. That it wasn't her fault.

But she very much feared that it was.

She swallowed over the acid burn of her shame. "Lord Peter Rosing was *not* telling the truth."

"Lord Peter Rosing is *crippled*," her father finally said. "And on his deathbed."

"His Grace of Fenmore did nothing wrong," Claire insisted. "He is an honorable man."

Her father leaned back against his seat and regarded

her—working furiously to control herself and hold back the tears that burned behind her eyes—for a long time before he spoke. "Be that as it may—"

"No." Claire's voice was a croak—her throat was hot and tight, aching with the effort not to cry. "Trustworthy. Loyal. And honorable. I know *it*."

But she had nothing by which to prove it except her hopes.

"I see." The Earl Sanderson regarded his daughter anew, as if he really were seeing her for the first time. "In that case, I shall wait with whatever patience I may have left for His Grace of Fenmore to call upon me."

Chapter Nineteen

Tanner breathed a deep, satisfying lungful of air into his chest. He should have long ago given up listening at doors, but it was a useful, if filthy, habit and had served him well.

Claire had done it. She had told her parents what had happened. And she had defended him. It gave him a warm feeling in his middle that was suspiciously like happiness.

There was nothing for it then but to propose properly. And very carefully.

Some instinct beyond self-preservation—the guile that had served him for so long and so well—had made him abandon her. An instinct goaded by the thunderous, frightened rage etched into the earl's face when he came through the door of Riverchon House. But whatever it was, it cautioned Tanner that the Earl Sanderson needed to be approached quietly and privately, without the pounding instability of the potent combination of anger and relief that had all but poured across his face at the sight of his daughter.

Such a man had to be met as an equal.

And so Tanner took the time to change into proper

clothing, suitable to the honor of the occasion. Attired in the Duke of Fenmore's ruthlessly elegant tailoring he was more than equal to cornering the Earl Sanderson in his grandmother's magnificent two-story library. If his grandmother had one great pleasure and indulgence besides her gardens, it would have to be her books and the room she had built to house them. It took up an entire wing of the house, with a balcony that ringed its second floor.

Tanner knew the room well, for his bedchamber was above and connected to the library by a winding spiral stair. So it was on the balcony that he awaited the earl, utilizing all the symbolic advantage of descending from a height to meet his adversary.

The Earl Sanderson came into the room with a purposeful stride but said nothing in greeting as his gaze flicked over Tanner's figure, silhouetted against the lighter backdrop of the window, a position Tanner had chosen quite purposefully to give him the advantage—the earl's face would be well lit and easier to read, while his remained in shadow.

The earl didn't close the door behind him but stood in the middle of the room, and contemplated Tanner with decided ill favor. "By rights, I ought to have you horsewhipped."

Tanner descended slowly and stayed on the bottom step of the stair. Sanderson would have to look up to meet his eyes. But the man had a right to his anger. Tanner accepted that. But he was a man as well—a man with a savage pride.

Tanner kept his tone mild, conversational even. "You can try."

Which only served to rile the man more. "I may yet see you taken up for a charge of murder."

"To do so would be precipitous, as well as ill advised."

Riverchon was not Fenmore House and Doggett was not Beamish, but Tanner had his ways of finding things out. "Lord Peter Rosing lives yet."

"Rosing can rot for all I care. I'm not talking about him—I'm talking about the maid. This is England, sir, and not even a duke is so above the law that he can murder a young woman."

Ah. This was a charge he had not seen coming. He had assumed the charge against him would be based on some fact; he *had* assaulted Rosing, so he thought the charge must stem from that. But he was wrong.

"I did not murder Maisy Carter. I have spent a considerable portion of the past day and night trying to find out who did. So, if I may ask, who laid such a charge?"

He wanted more of the particulars from Sanderson's own lips. But Tanner had already learned something valuable—whoever had laid that charge *knew* that Maisy Carter had been killed. No one but Tanner and Claire and later Jinks, Jack Denman, and Molly Carter had known that the girl had died. And until that afternoon, no one but those five people knew that her body had even been found.

No one but the murderer.

"You can take that up with the magistrate," the earl informed Tanner, his belligerence ebbing not one whit.

"I don't intend to do anything with the magistrate," Tanner informed him coolly.

"No," the earl snapped. "I imagine you don't, what with your history. It's a wonder you're accepted at all into society."

"Ah." It was too predictable a slur to do more than glance off his hide. "Been listening to gossip, have you?"

"I've been listening to my daughter, sir." The earl's voice began to rumble like gathering thunder. "My daughter, who was missing for an entire night and morning."

"Who, I have every faith, will have told you exactly

what really happened." He knew she had. He was damnably proud of her for it. "And whom I intend to protect at all costs from being questioned by the magistrate. Think of her, before you talk of charges."

"Which brings me back to having you horsewhipped."

Tanner felt his mouth stretch into a wide smile. Oh, yes. He liked this—the ferocious matching of wits. He could feel the nearly primeval thrill of contention come over him like a physical thing—a pleasure that soaked down into his bones and made his life worth living.

But he forced himself to remember that it was never a good idea to antagonize a man one wanted for one's future father-in-law. So Tanner accepted the earl's point with a small inclination of his head. "Point taken. But I didn't come here to argue."

"No? What did you come here for? Eighteen hours overdue, I might add."

"I came here to propose." Tanner was pleased his voice was level and smooth and did not betray the mad leaping of his pulse—whether from trepidation or hope he did not know. "Which I would have done eighteen hours ago, but I did not think you would be any more receptive to my suit then than you are now."

"I will tell you plainly, Fenmore, that you are the last man on earth I would choose for my daughter."

Tanner had to give the Earl Sanderson credit for not purposefully misunderstanding him. "Acknowledged. I am deeply aware that I am not worthy of her, sir. But circumstances being what they are, your daughter has chosen me."

"Chosen? You stand here, threatening to drag my daughter's name through the mud of scandal unless I intervene with those who have laid the charge, and you—"

"No." Tanner stepped toward Sanderson before he could stop himself. "No. That is the opposite of what I am saying. I will do anything, even *face* a charge, rather than see her exposed in *any* way. I was not the person who made this"—he spread his hands in angry frustration—"a public scandal. I took her away from Rosing so no one would know what occurred. So she would be spared the vicious pleasure your *society* seems to derive from others' misfortunes."

"You took her out of a boathouse, out of your grandmother's house, without so much as a by-your-leave, sir, and you disappeared for an entire night. You took an innocent girl, who was in circumstances so far beyond her experience, and you led her away from everything and everyone that she knew. And you did not bring her back until well into the next day. Are you mad? Or suicidal?"

"Yes. Yes to all those things. But the fact still remains, she was not so bereft of all good sense that she did not know that she chose. And she chose me. Quite emphatically."

The earl's face blanched white and then went red. "By God, if you have touched one hair on my daughter's head, I will—"

"I have." He had touched her hair, stroked its silky length. He had held her in his arms. He had kissed her as if he were a dying man and she a drop of water. He had done as much as he dared.

Sanderson took a threatening step toward him. "You bastard."

Tanner felt his own volatile temper begin to heat and took his own step forward to meet the man toe-to-toe. "I am not a bastard in breeding, nor in action. And if you have been listening to your daughter, *sir,* then you will know that I saved your daughter. *I* saved her. Where were you, sir, when Lord Peter Rosing was dragging her down the length of that lawn?" He raised his hand to point to the exact spot where Lord Peter Rosing had wrapped his meat hooks around Lady Claire Jellicoe's delicate white arm. "Where were you when he smashed her lovely porcelain face into the wall? Where were *you*?"

The quiet lash of Tanner's accusation was met with utter, charged silence. The Earl Sanderson could obviously think of no suitable retort. But neither did he acknowledge his nearly fatal mistake.

"I was there," Tanner reminded him. "And no matter your horsewhips, and your insults, and your distaste for me as a son-in-law, I would do it again in a second. Without thinking. I would do it for her."

For a long moment there was no sound in the room but the storm of Tanner's indignation and the answering strain of the Earl Sanderson's tightly controlled remorse. Neither spoke. They stood there, facing each other, inches apart on the carpet. Each of them, he thought, equally full of regret and hope.

Tanner pressed his skeletal advantage. "The vile rumors must be stopped, and stopped now. I will not stand for her name to be besmirched for another moment." He made each assertion a statement—there could be no further debate. "I will be her husband."

He said it to convince them both. But it was nearly frightening, saying the words, admitting to himself that marrying her was everything he wanted—everything he had dreamed and plotted and schemed for the past twenty-four hours to make happen.

And he wanted it settled, one way or the other, *now*. "Every moment that you delay hurts her more. Think about that while you're still trying to blame me for your lapse in oversight."

Still the earl resisted. "She has not yet agreed."

"But she has been asked. She knows my intention. She has my ring. I did not do her the dishonor of asking her for her answer, as I thought it best to do *you* the honor of making clear my intentions. But I will ask her for her answer. I am compelled to."

"And if she says no?"

Tanner could not contemplate such an outcome without going stark, raving mad as a rabid cur dog. But he knew the answer he had to make. He would be a gentleman. "I will abide by Lady Claire's choice. And by yours. Not to do so would do her a dishonor. But there will be a scandal, greater by far than the rumors snaking their way across society's forked tongues now. But you will have to ask yourself what purpose such a scandal will serve. You will have to figure out just why your lovely daughter was a target of Lord Peter Rosing, who usually prefers to rape servants—girls who have no power and no protection—in the first place."

The Earl Sanderson's face whitened as if Tanner had struck him. And indeed he had. He had struck right at the heart of the matter. But the earl withstood the blow and kept his own counsel.

But Tanner was not yet done. He played his most telling—and most wildly speculative—card.

"You will have to ask yourself if Lady Claire or *you* were really the target of Lord Peter Rosing's rape. You will have to ask yourself just how far you are willing to go for your interest in counterfeiting gold coins in St. Catherine's Dock before the cost is the sacrifice of your daughter." Tanner gave him one last piece of advice before he turned on his heel and marched purposefully up the sinuous spiral of the stair. "You will have to decide, sir, whose side you really need to be on."

Tanner retreated—although in truth he ascended—to his chamber, like a clever fox going to ground. A clever fox who has clever friends.

He found his clever friend Jack awaiting him, drinking

his friend the Duke of Fenmore's fine French brandy, and going over his meticulous notes.

"Hello." Jack looked up over the top of his spectacles. "Where have you been, dressed like a pallbearer?"

"Proposing. You?"

"Nothing so dangerous."

"How did you know where to find me?"

"That girl—that walking mudskipper that Jinks calls 'the Lark.' Ridiculous name. She told us you'd come here."

"Clever girl." But Tanner had no time to waste. "Jack, tell me what you know. Did Maisy Carter drown?"

"Cause of death in my opinion?"

"Yes. Whose else?"

"Shut up." Jack flipped the notebook shut and looked him in the eye. "She never drowned herself. Her windpipe has been crushed. Quite thoroughly. Quite purposefully. I've seen convicts less hanged than that girl appeared to be." Jack's mouth was turned down in an expression of pained distaste. "And her nose had been broken. There was some swelling, and considerable bruising all up into her eyes, so it was not an old injury. There was some bloodstaining remaining on the edge of her shift, despite her time in the water. Noses bleed profusely. And blood stains."

"Ah." This Tanner knew, but he let that information seep into his brain and sort itself out where it belonged. "Yes. So by the time I found her, the river had washed most other traces of the blood away?"

"Yes," Jack agreed on a sigh. "But there was enough. In my opinion, whoever did this was violent, and knew what they were doing."

"For power or pleasure?"

"Christ, Tanner." Jack turned his weary old-before-his-time eyes away. "The questions you ask."

"Questions that need to be asked." Tanner didn't have time for useless, interfering sentiment. "Well? Do you have the impression that it was done for power, or for pleasure?"

"I'm a man of science," Jack countered. "I don't form impressions."

Tanner was impatient with his friend's quibbles. "Of course you do. You said whoever did this knew what they were doing. That is an impression. And no doubt a correct one."

Jack shook his head and passed Tanner a small china bowl with some items in it—his own bowl, nicked from Sanderson House the only time he had even visited. He had been a boy and new to being His Grace of Fenmore. His seventy-two-year-old cousin, Charles, who had been Fenmore before him, had taken him to meet the earl. Tanner had stolen the bowl then. An early keepsake of his attraction to the house of Sanderson.

"She had money in her pockets," Jack told him. "Six shillings. Not an inconsiderable sum for a housemaid."

"Ah. Just the right amount for a generous vail from a visitor she had been assigned to assist." It made him fonder of Claire than ever to know that she was a considerate employer.

But Tanner's mind also leapt to two other conclusions instantly. "Whoever killed her didn't want her money. Any professional worth his salt would have turned out her pockets before she had even breathed her last. And she must have been interrupted—and murdered—before she had a chance to store it away. It was simply too much money for her to be carrying around. What else?"

"Earbobs. Or one earbob."

Tanner picked up a small piece of jewelry from the bowl.

"Earbobs," Jack repeated. "Ladies wear them, as jewelry, in their ears."

"Don't be an ass, Jack. I know what they are." And he

knew whose they were as well. He had spent years watching Lady Claire Jellicoe. He had seen these dangling aquamarines on many occasions—a subtle counterpoint to the sparkling blue of Lady Claire's eyes. "They are Lady Claire's."

"Are they? But there was only one of them. In the girl's other pocket. The money was in one, and the earbob in the other. So it rather looks like theft on her part, except why would she be strangled for theft?"

"Which one?"

Jack frowned and shook his head in confusion. "Which pocket?"

"Yes." Tanner tried to keep the edge of impatience from his tone, but it was impossible. "Which one?" he demanded. "Tell me you noted it. Or tell me you have the clothes, still. Tell me."

"I have the clothes, still. I thought that you might want to see them again." Jack was regarding Tanner as if he were mad. But he wasn't mad. He was on to something. "Where?"

"There. I judged her clothes too ravaged and too distressing for the body to be dressed in for her mother to see. Jinks and I found some other clothes."

But Tanner wasn't listening. He was rifling through the neat stack of clothing so he could turn out the pockets. "The right pocket has a hole in it. The left does not. Was the money found in the left?"

Jack consulted the notebook he brought with him. "Yes."

"She was right-handed."

One of Jack's brows rose over a narrow-eyed look. "I could determine that, were I to examine the muscle attachment of her arm bones, but how do you come by such a conclusion?"

"Callus. On the inside tip of her right index finger. Presumably from sewing, as one of the most important skills required of a lady's maid is the care and repair of clothing. There was no callus on the left."

Jack bent to his notes to see if he could find the same observation, but Tanner's mind was already speeding ahead. "What sort of maid, who is said to be meticulous, and very good at her job, who is ambitious, and wants to move up in her position, maybe become a housekeeper someday— What sort of competent professional servant throws it all away to steal an earbob, and put it in a pocket she knows has a hole in it?"

Jack was giving him another baffled, squinty-eyed look. "Wait a moment. How do you know she knew her pocket had a hole in it?"

"It was her job to take care of clothing. The rest of her appearance is neat, her clothes in good repair. And the hole is small, and formed by the unraveling of the seam, here"—he showed Jack the loose threads in question— "not by any wear in the fabric. So it was a recent thing, this splitting of the pocket seam, perhaps by a small scissors if she was doing mending." He shook his head to pull himself back into his train of thought. "It doesn't matter how; it only matters that it was fresh—or else she would have repaired it."

"Come now," Jack objected. "This is all conjecture."

"No!" Tanner could hear the aggravation invade his voice. "Think, man. She is right-handed. She would have normally put her coins in her right pocket, where she would have access to them. But the coins came from the left pocket. So she put them there because she knew she had a split in her right."

Jack stared at him. "And so?"

"So, don't you see? She never would have put valuable earbobs in her right pocket. She knew it had a hole."

"So?" Jack's voice had risen with frustrated aggravation.

"She didn't put the earbob there. Someone else did. But why? Why?" His brain immediately ·supplied two very plausible answers. "To make it look like she had stolen them. But we know she could not have stolen them, because she never would have put them in a pocket with a hole in it. And who would steal just one of a pair?"

His hands were already examining the hems of Maisy Carter's now-dry skirts, feeling all the way around the edge. When he didn't find what he was looking for, he put aside the skirt to examine the thicker cotton petticoat, running his hand down the length of the fabric, feeling for any anomalies, any bumps or unexpected knots in the material, until—

"Hello." Tanner turned the quilted skirt of the maid's petticoat over and turned back the flat seam where it had been pressed apart, to reveal the mate to the aquamarine earbob, hooked on a stitch. "And there's the pair."

"But what does having a pair mean?" Jack was leaning forward, curious and aggravated at himself for not seeing what to Tanner was so obvious.

"It means that someone—and I can only assume it is our murderer—placed these earbobs in her pocket as some sort of diversion."

"A diversion from what?"

"From the true nature of the crime. From the murder. If all he did to her was murder?"

Jack looked at Tanner in his sharp, incisive way. "You frighten me sometimes with the way your mind works, you know that?"

Tanner was too impatient to be insulted or even concerned. He knew his mind worked in ways that other people thought strange. It was why he was cleverer. "Just tell me if she was only strangled."

"You are right, damn you. She was raped. Quite forcibly. From behind, I should think. The pattern of bruising . . ."

Jack simply shook his head. "I've never seen the like of it on a deceased's body before."

But Tanner felt the blow ring through him like a bell, clear and resonant. "Fuck all."

Jack took a weary breath. "Well, that's one way of putting it."

"No. I—" He thought not to say it. He didn't have the right to tell anyone if she did not want him to. But she had already told her parents and his grandmother—and he could only pray that the belligerent Earl Sanderson would have the moral fiber to do the right thing with that information. Because if a man of the Earl Sanderson's reputation and power and authority—a man whose position was unassailable—spoke against the rapist perhaps, perhaps, something might at last be done about Lord Peter Rosing.

But Tanner was getting ahead of himself.

And Jack was catching up. "He also used a ligature of some kind to choke her, possibly during the rape. There is a deep but narrow line of a bruise in a perfect semi-circle just above the collarbone which is different from the marks from the hands that crushed her windpipe."

"Her necklace—a cross upon a chain. He would have grabbed it from behind." Tanner could see it in his mind's eye as if it were happening in front of him. "Fisted it tight to control her, or even make her black out." And he could still see Rosing's hand clamped across Lady Claire Jellicoe's mouth. See her china blue eyes wide and dark with panicked fright.

He should have killed Rosing when he had the chance.

Jack squinted into the air to contemplate the possibility. "Seems about right." His detachment pulled Tanner back out of his rage, back to the facts that would help him put the bastard Rosing away.

"And how," Jack was asking, "if I may be bold enough to ask, does your Lady Claire Jellicoe fit into all of this?

And don't bother to tell me 'coincidence'—I know you don't believe in it either."

"She's not my Lady Claire." Not yet. Not if he weren't very, very careful and very, very clever. And very circumspect. The lady's story was hers to tell.

But if there were one man in all of England he could trust, it would be Jack. "I stopped a man from raping Lady Claire. From behind. Shoved up against a rough brick wall with a bloody glove stuffed into her mouth. Last night at Richmond."

Jack let out a long, low whistle. "Two girls, one rape and murder, followed by an attempted rape? All in Richmond? That is . . . disturbing. Too damn disturbing to be coincidental, don't you think?"

"That is exactly what I think. I believe the two are connected."

"I believe in science and facts. Does either the science or the facts prove the two are connected, or even who did this?"

"The facts are yet unfolding. And here is one fact—the girl Maisy Carter was clutching this piece of fabric." Tanner fetched the delicate scrap wrapped in a twist of paper out of the leather pouch still secreted around his neck. "And what's more, she also held this coin. It was in the form of a fob—the kind of fob such as only an aristocrat or a monied member of society would wear. Not a laborer or a footman. Or me. The fob held a Roman coin—which, I have come to find, is a fake. A modern counterfeit made to look like an ancient Roman coin."

Jack fetched a hand lens out of his waistcoat to examine first the fabric and then the fob. "But then—correct me if I am wrong and my logic is faulty—if she took this from the man who killed her . . ." He looked at Tanner in question.

"Or the man who raped her, assuming they were one

and the same. She was clutching it in her hand. There were threads of the same fabric caught in her broken fingernails—yes?"

"Yes. So whoever she took it from was in front of her, not behind. They could not belong to the man who assaulted her."

Tanner gave it only momentary thought. "Not necessarily. He could have tired of her fighting, and manhandled her around." That was exactly what Rosing had done to Lady Claire to shove her face-first into the boathouse wall. "I saw him do just that—manhandle a girl against a wall—to Lady Claire Jellicoe. And I know for a fact that he's done it before—raped girls—the man who tried to rape Lady Claire."

Jack looked at him over the top of his eyeglasses. "A habituated rapist? Are you going to tell me his name?"

"Rosing. Lord Peter. Heir of—"

"The Marquess of Hadleigh." Jack let out another long, low whistle.

"Ought to be hanged." Tanner did not bother to keep the vehemence, the bone-deep loathing, from his voice.

"My sentiments exactly. But you can't hang a man just for being a bastard." Jack rocked back against his chair. "Christ, Tanner, but you can pick them. Rosing is a thoroughgoing bastard—speaking in terms of character, not lineage, although his father is a bastard of the same stripe if you ask me."

"I do ask you. What do you know of either of them?"

"Knew Rosing at Oxford. You had taken your degree by then," Jack said to Tanner. "But Rosing was sent down. Had been several times from what I recall. But I didn't pay much attention. Good riddance, was all I thought."

So Rosing had been a problem for years. Getting sent down from university was a common enough occurrence—

half the spoiled young bucks of London through it a rite of passage to get sent down—

Another thought intruded. Rite of passage. Ritual.

"Did you find any other marks on the body? Marks that could not be explained by the violent manner of her death? Anything strange or out of place that struck you?"

"Good God, Tanner. Everything about the death of an innocent young girl strikes me as strange, and out of place, and tragic as all hell. And it should strike you, too, you cool bastard." Jack's self-control was fraying around the edges.

Tanner brushed aside the implied slight. He knew that Jack meant nothing by it. And if he was as cold and aloof as people said he was, then so much the better. It was a sacrifice he gladly made to keep his mind keen and functioning more clearly than anyone else's. It was what made him cleverer. Clever enough to catch a murderer.

"Something different," he explained to Jack. "Some mark, or token, or sign that only you or I would see. Though I couldn't, though I looked. Think, man, something amiss. Eyelashes pulled out, or a fingernail, or a cut-off finger. Something—"

"Her hair. At the top of her nape, there was a hank of close-cropped hair." Jack pulled his notebook into his lap to find the remark. "A little bristle. I felt it when I examined her skull for fracture."

Clear, cold rage poured through Tanner like water over a fall, plummeting into him. This he had seen before. The words of the housemaid at Lowington House—the first time he had witnessed Lord Peter Rosing raping someone. Tanner hadn't interfered, much to his shame. But he heard her words now, the maid, Suzannah Miller. *Cut my hair he did, sir. With a little knife. As if the other weren't enough. He cut my hair.*

"It was Rosing. He'll have it. A trophy of his deed. A reminder of his sexual triumph. He may even take it out, and pleasure himself all over again while looking at it, reveling in the memory."

"Tanner." Jack's tone held both horror and alarm—alarm at the vehemence of his own tone. "That's one hell of an accusation to make against a peer."

"And I will prove it—I *must*—that he is the one who raped Maisy Carter, and then tried to rape Lady Claire Jellicoe, or he will go on raping and killing with impunity."

Tanner's cold, calculating rage pushed him into action, and he couldn't stand still. He began to pace back and forth across the chamber, with his fingers drumming against his mouth, the rhythm both calming and stimulating his brain as he thought out loud. "Rosing comes to the ball uninvited. As does his father, the Marquess of Hadleigh. Whose mistress, Lady Westmoreland, has a villa at Richmond, and a very passing acquaintance with my grandmother. Hadleigh must have been staying with Lady Westmoreland—perhaps she mentioned the ball—when he decided to invite himself. What butler would turn away a marquess? And he—the marquess—must have brought with him, not only his mistress, but also his bloody bastard of a son. Who rapes or attempts to rape two girls. But did he kill her? That's where my logic and the evidence part ways." The frustration was like a dull throb of pain at the back of his brain. "And if he didn't, why not? He—"

"Something else occurs to me, Tanner."

But Tanner had his metaphorical canvas spread before the wind and was sailing now. "I need to find how Rosing came across Maisy Carter—for I imagine that is exactly what he did; he's an opportunistic bastard, rather than a plotter and planner. He'll have simply prowled the less-populated hallways, trolling for a stray maid. That's what he'd have done. And—"

"Tanner." Jack broke in more emphatically.

"Yes?" He looked at Jack but didn't pause in his pacing. The rhythm helped him think, helped him see what he needed to see.

"I'm actually surprised you didn't bring it up." Jack's voice had changed tone—gone all careful and deadly quiet. "But it occurs to me how similar they are in appearance."

"Lord Peter Rosing and his father?"

"No, Tanner." Jack shook his head and closed his eyes, and Tanner could hear the carefulness in his friend's voice for what it really was—dawning horror. "Both petite. Both blond, and both blue-eyed. The maid Maisy Carter and your Lady Claire Jellicoe."

Chapter Twenty

After a long and gloriously hot bath, during which she scrubbed herself pink and listened very sympathetically and very, very attentively to the young maid's nervous chatter, Claire was summoned back to her parents, who, she was told, awaited her in her mother's silken sitting room.

Claire took the trouble and pleasure of dressing herself for the encounter first. *Herself* being the salient word— she didn't have the heart to ring for assistance. And it only seemed fitting that she dress herself in white muslin and arrange her hair in a simple style before she went to her hard reckoning in her mother's softly upholstered room.

Her father looked unhappy and primed for a fight. He did not disappoint but got straight to his point. "The Duke of Fenmore has offered for you, Claire. He said he was 'compelled to.'" Her father's tone was clearly one of distaste.

"Compelled?" That could be both good and bad. "In what way?"

Her father was brusque. "I did not ask, and he did not offer any explanation."

Claire looked to her mother for assistance, but the countess shook her head. So Claire tried another approach. "And what did you say?"

"Nothing." Her father paced before the empty fireplace. Evening approached, but in the long summer twilight only one lamp was lit for light. "Because I needed to speak to you first. And because your mother and I find ourselves at odds on the issue of Fenmore."

Claire looked back to her mother, who nodded encouragingly and explained herself. "I feel that you are old enough, and rational enough, despite what has happened, to make up your own mind. If you feel His Grace will suit, then I have no objection to an engagement, during which period the turbulent emotions of the past few days will fade and you may consider the matter more rationally still. And it will serve to quash the rumors."

"Despite?" But her parents were looking at her in expectation of an answer. "I—" Suddenly, despite the fact that she had thought about it—thought about him—and known, and hoped, a betrothal was coming, Claire felt as if the air were being squeezed out of her lungs.

She had never in her life gone against her parents' advice or approval.

And she had known Tanner only one long, exciting, calamitous day.

"He is rich. You will never want for material things." Her father's tone was emphatic. And unhappy.

"Why don't you like him, Papa?"

"I thought he had dishonorable intentions. I thought he had taken deeply dishonorable actions. And even if both you and he tell me his actions were honorable—that it was Lord Peter Rosing who acted so horribly dishonorably—it was still wrong of him to take you away, and keep you away for so long."

"But we had to, Papa, because of Maisy Carter."

"No." Her father made a slashing motion with his hand to cut off her argument. "He never should have involved you in that. Never. He should have seen you back to your mother's care immediately. His actions were not those of a gentleman, much less a peer of such rank as a duke."

"Papa, his actions to me were nothing but gentlemanly. I told you so. I have held nothing back." Nothing but a number of incendiary kisses. Hot, uncomfortable awareness flashed under her skin.

Her father saw her discomfort and took it for distress. "What did he do to you? What did he say or do? What hold does he have over you now?"

"Papa!" Claire tried to explain. "He has no hold over me."

But even as she said the words Claire knew they were a lie. Knew that he did have a hold over her. A hold of gratitude.

And of something entirely more. The Duke of Fenmore had not kissed her out of gratitude. Although certainly *she* had kissed *him*. But what might have begun as gratitude had rapidly become something else. Something much more persuasive than gratitude.

But she still owed him her loyalty. "Do you distrust him because of his background?"

Her father's chin went up in a way that told her she had hit a nerve. "What has he told you of his background?"

"I know that he wasn't always a duke. He told me himself."

"Did he tell you he was a thief? He spent his youth as a criminal, Claire."

"That was a long time ago. He was a child, Papa. And you cannot tell me that the Fenmore fortune was made and is maintained by stolen watches."

"Do not attempt to take that tone with me, young lady."

Her father's voice was as cutting as steel. "It's more complicated than that."

"Yes, it is. And if he is still a criminal—a thief—of a sorts, he now steals at the behest of the government, of which you are a part. Or is it his current involvement that you object to?"

"His current involvement? What lies has he fed you?"

"They are not lies." But she had no real way of knowing that. "But you have influence, and know people. You know people in the Admiralty." Indeed, ever since her brother Will had gone into the navy her father had taken a keen interest in the navy's political fortunes. "You ask the Lords of the Admiralty for yourself." Claire's voice had risen precipitously, and her tone was bitterly defensive.

And so was her papa's. "Indeed, I will do so."

Their tone had grown so acrimonious, her mother felt it necessary to hold up a conciliatory, cautioning hand. "We do not find his background at fault, Claire." Mama spoke in her calm, reassuring voice, speaking to her husband as much as to Claire. "Indeed the duke was raised by a very great degree by a man your father admires, Captain Sir Hugh McAlden, His Grace's brother-in-law."

"And a finer man I know not," her father admitted. "I put your brother Will into his care as a midshipman on Captain McAlden's ship, upon both my own assessment of his character and the recommendation of Sir Charles Middleton, as he was then, before he became Lord Barham. And I will say, Barham took a great interest in the young duke as well, however little good it did him."

"No." What her father said now made perfect sense— Claire recalled that Barham had been one of her father's set and a Lord of the Admiralty. "And why do you think that was? Because Lord Barham could make good use of him. And the Admiralty does still. But you will only believe it if the confirmation comes from someone other than His Grace or me. So ask Lord Barham's successor at the Admiralty. You must know whomever that is. Ask him"—she made a gesture, as if she were throwing the name at her father—"about Fenmore."

"Claire." Her mother's voice called her back to civility. "Are you quite sure? You must understand— Someone in your position, someone who had gone through what you have gone through, would be . . . susceptible. Open to influence by an exciting, mysterious, older man."

"Older man? He is but eight and twenty, Mama. And younger than that in many ways."

Her mother would not be drawn. "And you, who are older, in many ways, than your nearly twenty years, are going to help or change him? Are going to save him?"

Heat burned up Claire's throat and settled behind her eyes. "Mama, I am not going to save him. I could not. And the cold fact of the matter is that he already saved me."

"For which we are grateful. As I know you are. And such feelings can be blown all out of proportion during a time of heightened emotion."

"I do not have heightened emotions now," Claire lied. "I am entirely rational. And frankly, what choice do I really have? I thought you would be glad that I am happy to accept him. Happy that the scandal can be averted."

"Scandal be damned. Scandal can be managed." Her father's tone was as imperious and icy as winter. "I am Sanderson. You are the daughter of the Earl Sanderson. I will not allow my daughter to be scandalized into a marriage she does not want."

It came down to that. Managing expectations. Her father managing those expectations. Her father managing her life.

She had thought that by going in a boat with the Duke

of Fenmore she could escape from her circumstances for a little while. But the truth was that she could not escape. Not even for a little while. She could never escape who she was. And what was expected of her.

But she would not be a passenger in the journey of her life. She would not let life pass by her carriage window and never voice a change of direction.

Claire damned the tight fist of doubt squeezing her chest and rode the tide of her rising breath. "But what if I do want it?"

Her question was met with an utter cacophony of silence. Her father turned his face up to the ceiling, as he if could not even look at her.

"Papa?" Did he still think her at fault? Did he truly think that she had been stupid and so shameful in her conduct as to create the entire circumstance that she found herself in? The fist of doubt and self-loathing punched itself up into her tight throat. "Papa, please."

Her father shook his head and looked at her mother and shook his head again. "It is that you are my daughter. And you are everything good and right and beautiful. And he is . . ." Her papa took a deep breath and tried in vain to collect himself. But his voice was thin with repressed emotion. "He is sharp and clever and rich and terrifyingly resourceful. But for all of that, he is simply not worthy of you."

She had to find Fenmore. She had to find her Tanner. Claire squared her shoulders in her very fetching gown—a beautiful soft embroidered white muslin, put on especially to look lovely for His Grace. Because she loved him.

And she was most emphatically *not* going to cool her heels waiting for His Grace of Tanner, the Duke of Fenmore to come to his senses and discover he loved her. If he didn't know it yet, he should. Stupid, lovely, clever man.

But if he did not come to her, she would go to him. He

was in the house somewhere. All she had to do was think and keep her eyes open.

She found him just as the darkness pushed the late-summer twilight over the horizon. She traced him to the floor above by stalking quietly up and down the dark, silent corridors until she found a room with a light under the door in a place there oughtn't be any light—in the elegant chamber overlooking the lawns and the river, in which she had first been housed when she came to Riverchon.

She found him on one knee in the middle of the room, examining the rug. And though he was dressed in the Duke of Fenmore's finer tailored clothes, she could still detect the influence of the Tanner in the dark colors and practical boots he wore. Clothes for passing unseen.

"You shouldn't be here," he said, even as his hand reached out toward her. Such a strange, lovely amalgamation of bristling hostility and unconscious invitation.

Claire avoided his hand—for the moment—and leaned her back into the door to shut it. "What are you doing?" She looked around, half-remembering herself here before. Before her life had changed irrevocably.

"You've changed your perfume."

The nonsensical observation brought her gaze back to her Tanner. "I did." And it was gratifying that he had noticed.

"I liked the other. Orange blossom."

"I threw it out. It reminded me of before. It reminded me of Rosing."

Tanner's brows rose fractionally, as if he had not thought of such a possibility—of either her reaction or her subsequent action. As if he had only considered it from his own point of view.

Which was why she was still aggravated with him. She had an entirely different point of view, which he needed to take into account. "Where have you been?"

"Here."

"Why did you abandon me, just when I needed you most?"

"I didn't abandon you." He looked surprised at the suggestion. "You needed private time with your parents. And I knew you could handle the reunion far better without me there to arse it all up."

Claire crossed her arms over her chest. "I am still put out with you. Especially for being so rational. This is the moment when I wish I could make a witty, cutting remark to tell you what I think of your rationality."

And His Grace was looking at her with fresh eyes now. "I'll consider myself cut then, shall I?"

She tried hard to be arch. "Yes, do."

But neither of them could contain their smiles. Claire tried pursing her lips and then biting them, but she gave up the moment the corner of his mouth twitched upward. And then they were both grinning at each other for no other reason than it felt good to be together and sparring.

Lord, she had missed him. And it had only been an hour.

But she had questions that needed answering and news of her own to report. "My dear Grace of Tanner," she began.

His low rumble of a laugh faded, but his smile did not. It broadened. "Dear?"

"You heard me, Your Grace." She tried to disarm him with a smile of her own, the one she had often heard described as winsome. She didn't think he would be able to resist winsome.

He couldn't. He rose to his feet and captured her hand. "My dear Lady Claire. Don't you think we've come too far for the formality of 'Your Grace'?"

"My dear duke, haven't we come too far for the formality of 'Lady Claire'?"

"Yes. Far too far. But I have to admit, I rather like 'my dear duke.'"

"I'd rather call you Your Grace. But for reasons that have absolutely nothing to do with formality or title."

"Are—" He frowned over the top of his smile, as if he were suddenly not quite sure of himself. "Are you flirting with me?"

She looked at him from under her lashes. "Is it working?"

"God, yes." His voice was nothing but an urgent, elegant growl as he pulled her toward him.

She went willingly, moving close and then closer. His lips parted, ever so slightly, as if he could think of nothing but her kiss. She made him think a little while longer.

She leaned against the lean comfort of his chest and put her lips along the taut cord at the side of his neck to whisper into his ear, "We're a terrible scandal, you know."

"Yes." His agreement was tempered by the unevenness of his breathing. "But it's what you do after the scandal that counts."

"Does this count?" She wrapped her arms about his waist and turned her face up to his.

"God, yes."

Oh, excellent. His admission brought a sigh of pure relief to her lips. He was so ready, so poised on the very edge, all he needed really was a proper push in the right direction to fall rather hopelessly in love. Poor lamb, with all his cleverness. He had no idea that he was done for. But she could read the signs just as clearly as if he had written them out on a piece of parchment and handed it to her. "This is the part where it would be nice if you said you loved me."

"Why would I say that?"

"Because that's how you feel."

"Do I? How do you know?"

"Ah. I'm so glad you asked—I've been dying to take a crack at it." She rested her chin on his chest, right in the snowy folds of his cravat. "Because I owe my powers of observation all to you. I've learned my lessons, Your Grace, and I've learned them very well. And so." She stroked the back of her finger along the line of his jaw. "Your skin, Your Grace, is flushed. Just a tiny bit, here along the sides of your neck. And you breathed out when I came in, a lovely little silent gasp of greeting. And then, there were your eyes. They went obsidian dark. And then they narrowed, and then opened. Interest, I should think, that showed. Passion maybe even, in those dark, shuttered depths. And you went absolutely still. You don't do still, normally. Unless you're very, very interested. You try to be still, and invisible, standing along ballroom walls, being seen, but not *seen*. But you're always moving even then. Drumming your fingers against your sleeve, or tapping your foot, or moving your head ever so slightly to the beat of the music, as if you really, really want to dance. But you never do. But you are not still. So all those physical manifestations, as you called them, point me in the direction of a man who doesn't know how to properly express the pleasure that he feels in his gut because his head, that lovely, magnificent, terrifyingly brilliant head of yours, tells him—"

"Do shut up, Claire." He lowered his head to whisper against her lips. "When you talk like that, it makes it extraordinarily difficult to kiss you."

"But you like it when things are extraordinarily difficult, don't you? You—"

And then his lips—his lovely seraphic lips, with their perfect vee and the full pouty bottom lip—covered hers. And he was magnificent. He tasted like surprise and every taste and smell and feeling that she had missed in the past hour.

His hands came up to clasp her upper arms and pull her tight against him. One lovely burst of possessiveness, before his fingers spread wide and he released her. But he did not, she noted, stop touching her. Or stop kissing her. He ran his open palms down the length of her bare arms to enmesh his fingers with hers as he kissed her. As she kissed him.

On and on it went, giving and taking, tasting and nipping and wanting. Wanting more. What started as a little game, a punishment and exercise in her own powers, was so suddenly beyond her control. Heat, real, blistering heat, raced under her skin, and a hunger she did not know either of them had began to assert its insistent self, until she could hear their kisses, hear the slide of tongue and smack of lips and breathy gasping for air. "Tanner."

And she could feel his big, agile hands cradling the back of her head as he held her still for his kiss, and she could feel the smooth rasp of his chin with her own palms and feel the reverberating hum of excitement that awoke her skin.

And then the door behind her was whooshing open on its silent, well-oiled hinge, and Tanner quite literally set her apart—he picked her up and set her away—just as the bristle of taffeta skirts filled her ears.

Her mother was coming.

"Your Grace?" It was not her mother, thank God, but Mrs. Dalgliesh, the housekeeper, and the dowager duchess's right-hand woman.

"Ah, Mrs. Dalgliesh, thank you." His Grace her Tanner did not miss a beat. "Tell me about the room. Who found it, and where did they enter?"

Mrs. Dalgliesh made no demur whatsoever to Tanner's blunt question—he must have sent for her. "On the night of the ball, it was the Viscountess Jeffrey, Your Grace, who found the room in disarray."

"Disarray?" It was getting to be a habit, Claire thought,

this parroting of astonishing questions. A bad habit. "What do you mean?"

"Your room was ransacked," Tanner told her, in his blunt, factual way. "Go on."

"Lady Claire's sister-in-law, I understand, had come looking for her. She entered through the door, I should think." The housekeeper gestured over her shoulder to the door by which Claire had entered. "And when she saw that the room had been greatly disturbed, she sent for me."

"Was there blood?"

"I beg your pardon, Your Grace?" The housekeeper shot a mystified and slightly horrified look at Claire, who did not understand. She did not remember anything about blood. Maisy had not looked bloodied. But then again, the poor girl's body had been in the water.

"No, not *her* blood." Tanner had already interpreted Mrs. Dalgliesh's look and waved her away from Claire. "Think. Blood on the floor, or on the carpet, or staining anywhere." He opened the empty wardrobe where Claire's gowns would have been stored. "Anywhere in the room, or the corridor. Or the servants' corridor. Somewhere in this house. Large drops, I should think. A dark rusty brown. Maisy Carter's nose was broken, and there would have been blood."

"Oh. I see." The housekeeper blanched a bit, and swallowed, but she rallied and looked about the room as if she were trying to envision what it had looked like one night ago. "No, sir, there was no blood."

"Are you sure? Who cleaned the room? When did they clean it?" His questions came out in rapid fire, one right after another, as if his mouth were slow in keeping up with his clever brain.

"I did, sir," the housekeeper confirmed, as if it were a test of both her housekeeping skills and her loyalty to Riverchon. "I deemed it best to keep such a task private."

"Absolutely. When?"

"When did I put it to rights? Almost immediately, Your Grace, though I did show the room to both Her Grace, your grandmother, and the Earl and Countess Sanderson."

But Tanner didn't seem interested in either housekeeping or loyalty at the moment. "Tell me what you saw. Describe it. In detail."

"Every piece of furniture was disturbed—the bergere armchair cushions were on the floor, and one was smudged with ashes where it landed in the fireplace. Thank goodness the fire was cold—it was, if you remember, a warm night—or we might have had an even greater crisis on our hands."

"I recall, Mrs. Dalgliesh. The furniture?"

"The small chair was overturned as well." She pointed to the floor beside the bed. "The bed curtains had been ripped off the frame, and the bed linens overturned, and strewn about."

"And the bed linens?"

The housekeeper shot another glance sideways at Claire. A nervous, discommoded glance. "If it's all the same to you, sir—"

"Were the linens soiled?" Tanner's impatience for answers made his voice stronger than it needed to be.

The housekeeper's discomfort tightened her face into a moue of distaste. "Yes."

"On the top, or beneath, on the sheets? Top sheet or bottom?"

The poor housekeeper sent another desperate look at Claire and swallowed nervously. "On the counterpane, sir."

"And was there blood, as well as seminal liquor, on the counterpane?"

"Oh, good Lord!" Claire backed away instinctively. She hadn't understood what he was talking about. She only was thinking about poor, poor Maisy's nose and—

Claire felt her face heat and her chest tighten and her stomach flip all at once. But she must have made a sound of distress, because Tanner's incisive gaze shot to hers.

And then he stood, once again the cool, aloof Duke of Fenmore. "Forgive me. Perhaps . . ." He held out his arm, gesturing toward the door, as if she might like to leave the room. "Perhaps you might like to retire before—"

"No. No," Claire insisted, even as she wanted to do exactly as he suggested and bolt from the room. Or at the very least throw open the windows.

Which he did. The cool evening breeze helped. A little. "The room just felt a little close. But I'm not going anywhere. I won't be missish. I understand now." She made herself say the words matter-of-factly, though her face was both hot and clammy with discomfort. "You said there were no coincidences, and I understand now. Go ahead and answer His Grace, Mrs Dalgliesh. Was there any blood?"

Mrs. Dalgliesh's voice was the barest, choked whisper. "No, sir. Just the—"

In an instant, His Grace was back to the Tanner, like a dog with a bone. He all but growled at the housekeeper, "Are you sure? You examined them yourself before they were laundered?"

"I'm sure. But I— I hope you will forgive me, Your Grace, but I did not have them laundered."

He brightened. "Did you save them?"

"No, Your Grace. I burned them myself, in the fire in my sitting room. I thought it best. To keep everything . . ." She settled upon the correct word. "Private"

Claire could see the disappointment slide across Tanner's face like a cloud passing before the sun, and then he was past it and on to the next thought, the next clever idea. He turned a full circle in the room, his arms and hands outstretched from his sides. "So where then? Where did he kill her, if not here?" He went for the door.

"Did anyone hear anything? Any of the servants coming or going?"

Claire and Mrs. Dalgliesh followed him out. "The ball was under way, Your Grace." the housekeeper answered. "Most of the servants were attendant upon their duties and charges below."

"So the hallway is empty. Does Maisy come up?" It was as if he were seeing it unfold before him. "What would bring her back to this room?"

"My shawl." The realization sent an ache like a screw, tightening Claire's throat. "I was late for the dinner, and she had followed me as I hurried down, handing me my gloves so I could pull them on as we went. And she gave me my fan, as well. But I said I didn't need my shawl. It was too warm. So she would have brought it back up, and probably set about putting everything to rights, as we left in a rush—gathering up the loose pins and powder on the dressing table, and putting out the candles there."

"Mrs. Dalgliesh." His Grace of Tanner's voice whipped back to the housekeeper. "The candles on the dressing table. You've replaced them. How long were the candle stubs you replaced?"

Mrs. Dalgliesh frowned and closed her eyes to concentrate. And then she shook her head. "No stubs, sir. I sent the tweeny up this morning to dig out the wax. They were guttered."

"Just so." Tanner nodded and turned round once again in the hall, as he had done in the room, and Claire could see now that he was imagining it, standing there with his eyes wide-open, seeing the scene as Maisy Carter herself would have seen it. "So she had followed you down the main stairwell? So she would have come directly back up it. And she comes to the door, here." He stood on the threshold and pushed the door open. "But she does not go in to put out the candles, which continue to burn until they gutter." He went utterly, completely still. "Ah. He's here already, looking for Claire. But it's Maisy he finds instead."

The cool, damp air from the window chilled Claire's skin, prickling it into icy gooseflesh.

Tanner went on inexorably. "So she sees him, presumably on the bed with some token, and likely boxing the Jesuit. And what does our Maisy Carter do?"

"Token? And boxing the—" Claire hadn't the faintest idea what he was talking about. "Is that a nautical term? Like *boxing the compass*?"

He was too intent to do more than fix her with a solemn, pitiless look. "The seminal liquor. On the counterpane."

Claire would have gasped if she had had any breath left in her body. She was nothing but empty aching space— pity had hollowed her out.

Tanner was still intent and unmoved, turning in the other direction, toward the far end of the hall where three narrow doors faced out into the corridor. "She would have gone for the servants' stair."

Tanner strode down the hall and tore open the central door that led on to the steep, narrow service stair. "Have these been cleaned?"

"Of course, Your Grace." Mrs. Dalgliesh's tone was more than defensive—it was nearly outraged and definitely proprietary.

But Tanner was like a hound on the scent and would not be turned. "But the blood, Mrs. Dalgliesh. We're looking for the blood. Maisy Carter's lifeblood, seeping out somewhere in this house, or on these grounds. It's important, don't you see?"

"Yes, sir. I suppose I can ask the tweeny who cleans and mops the stair, sir. But—"

"But what?" He nearly growled his question. The poor man was barely holding his irritation in check.

Mrs. Dalgliesh stiffened her spine. "But she's a child, Your Grace. Just as I've known you since you were a child. You came here about the same age as the tweeny—twelve years old. So if you could, *please,* not upset her. These poor girls are frightened enough, thinking someone is out to murder them, without you adding to it with your talk of blood and *seminal liquor.*" If she pursed her lips any harder, Mrs. Dalgliesh was going to turn into a woody lemon tree.

Tanner straightened. "Ah. I see. Forgive me, Mrs. Dalgliesh." Once again, Claire could see the straight, chilly mantle of the Duke of Fenmore descend upon him like a cloak. "If you would please, ask the child yourself. So we can be sure that I won't upset her."

"Yes, then. Thank you, sir." The older woman inclined her head and bobbed a shallow curtsy. "If you'll just let me pass by, I'll see to it immediately, Your Grace."

His Grace the Duke of Fenmore flattened himself against the wall of the narrow stairwell, and let his grandmother's housekeeper pass by down the stairs. In her wake, he came out of the narrow space. "Good thing I've grown so tall, or I think she might have slapped the words *seminal liquor* right out of my mouth, the way she did when I was a child and said distressing things."

Claire's heart ached for him anew. What a strange unfrightenable boy he must have been when he became the duke. "And did you often say distressing things?"

"Always." His eyes slid to hers before he turned his head to regard her fully. "But you're not distressed."

"Oh, I am, certainly. I'd be lying if I said otherwise. And you, I'm convinced, would know. It's only that I'm determined not to give way to my distress. I'm determined to learn from this. Learn how to see things like you do, and protect myself."

He nodded, and though he didn't smile, the corners of

his eyes warmed just a little. "You made a good enough start on that before."

"Yes." She felt her own mouth curve in answer and felt the sense of naive distress fade just a bit. Just enough.

He nodded again. "Good. Then you come." He steered her a few steps back along the corridor and turned her to face the open servants' stair. "Show me what you see. Show me what Maisy would have seen."

"But she knew this house, did she not? She'd been here for several years. She would have known this was the servants' stair, and that this was her best escape, wouldn't she? And she was clever—cleverer than I. She would have known that Rosing was up to no good. She would have run straight for it."

"Yes." He agreed with her, but his eyes were regarding the two even-more-narrow doors that flanked the door to the servants' stairwell. "But what if she didn't make it?" He looked back at the door to Claire's chamber from whence they had originally come, as if to gauge the distance. "What if he caught up with her? Where would he take her?"

"What's there?" Claire pointed to the door on the right, keeping her voice as even as possible, even as the gorge rose in her throat at the memory of Rosing's strong, merciless hands upon her. Perhaps they had been on Maisy as well. "He was right-handed."

Rosing had opened the door to the boathouse with his right hand while he shoved her along with his big, merciless left clamped around her upper arm.

"We don't know yet it was Rosing, Claire," Tanner corrected quietly. "But that is a very good observation. Made under duress. Well done."

"Yes, well. You said there are no coincidences."

"I did. And there can be no accusations without proof. So what we need is proof that— Hello."

It was a narrow broom closet unlit but by a very small window at the back such as maids and footmen would use for storage and supplies. There were copper tubs and buckets, an empty coal scuttle, whisk brooms, mops, and pails alike stored neatly on shelves and hanging on hooks.

But along the left-hand wall was a dark, smeared telltale stain that trailed down the to the very bottom of the beadboard wall.

Chapter Twenty-One

"Blood," Tanner said before she had to.

The wall was dotted with blood both above and below the heavy smear. Just as he had predicted it would be. Maisy's blood.

This was where Maisy Carter had been attacked. And most likely murdered.

Claire took a step back, and another, and another. She could hear the rising cadence and feel the panicked force of her own breathing, but she couldn't seem to do anything about it. "I think I'm going to be sick. Again."

He was at her side, leading her to a nearby chair situated against the wall and pushing her head down between her knees. "You didn't vomit the first time, so you won't do it again."

"Don't be too sure." His hand was drawing lazy circles on her back. It was distracting. "I might surprise you yet."

"You have done nothing *but* surprise me, Lady Claire," he remarked in a warm tone. "But you will not vomit. You're too determined. You told me so yourself."

She pulled a deep draught of air into her lungs. "Yes. I am, aren't I?"

"Annoyingly so." The back of his hand was cool along

the nape of her neck. "You've become entirely unsavable. Can you sit up yet?"

"Yes, I think so." She sat up slowly, trying to keep her breathing even. "Thank you. I am sorry. I didn't mean to come all over missish."

"If ever there were an excuse for coming *all over missish,* seeing the place where another human being was murdered is it."

"Yes. It's like there was evil trapped in there and it just had to get out."

"Perhaps." She could see that he didn't believe anything so strange, but he was being kind to her, rubbing her back so gently. Because he really was a nice man. A very nice man.

She would tell *that* to her father.

"So now we've found the place," she asked, "what next?"

"I need to bring Jack down here to take all his meticulous notes. This is the charge that has been laid against me—not Rosing's murder, but Maisy's."

She was too numb to withstand the fresh rime of fear. She was clammy and cold everywhere, from her skin to her bones. "Oh, God. How unfair."

He was still crouched in front of her, and he looked at her from under his brows, still and serious. "Thank you. Thank you for believing in me. Because I could have done it, I suppose. You didn't see me before we met in the boathouse—I could have been anywhere."

"Of course you couldn't. And of course I saw you. You were in the drawing room, standing next to the tall case clock, when I came down and Maisy departed. And then you were in the ballroom, propping up the north wall the entire time. You never moved. Of *course* I believe in you. I *saw* you."

He turned his face away sharply and then stood and moved away.

"Tanner, whatever is the matter?"

He answered her question with a strange, uncomfortable shrug. "Forgive me. False charges laid against one with a magistrate tend to have a rather dampening effect, don't they?"

There was the sly, dry humor. She peeked up at him through her lashes. "You don't seem especially dampened."

He closed his eyes and shook his head as if he could rattle his brain back into proper place. "Claire, we have to find a way to prove that it was Rosing. To put a stop to him once and for all. You'll never have a day of peace if we don't. Think about it. What will happen if you have to face Lord Peter Rosing across a ballroom? Or on Bond Street? It's a small world, the *ton.*"

The cold could not spread any farther—she felt clammy all over. "I had rather hoped you had crippled him enough that he would never again grace a ball with his hideous presence."

"Well, yes. So did I. But we can't count on that. Especially now that he's laid a charge against me. I'll be the one who is discredited, and unwelcome. Or worse. Not that I care particularly for myself. But I won't have your name besmirched as well."

Claire braced herself for the next numbingly cold blow. But she had to ask. "Is that the only reason you made your proposal? To save my name?"

"No. Not only."

"Claire you must know. You must—" Tanner stopped to listen to footsteps coming at a measured pace up the central staircase, beyond. "Bloody—"

Doggett appeared. "Your Grace. I thought you should know that we have a visitor. The Marquess of Hadleigh has come to call. For the Earl Sanderson."

Claire rose slowly from her chair as if pulled up by some invisible hand. "My father?"

"Thank you, Doggett. Where have you put them?"

"I showed His Lordship the marquess into the library, Your Grace, and have asked a footman to conduct the earl to him there. But I thought you should like to know."

"Yes. Thank you, Doggett."

The man bowed again in his stiff, elegant way, but Tanner was already taking Claire by the hand and leading her away, giving further instruction over his shoulder. "I want this closet locked, Doggett, and only Mr. Denman given the key. No one but he is to disturb it. No one is to clean it. Do you understand?"

"By all means, Your Grace."

"Yes, by any and *all* means, keep Mrs. Dalgliesh and her mop squeezers out."

"What could the marquess have to say to my father?" Claire asked the moment they were out of earshot. "Do you think he's come to make some sort of apology?"

"I doubt it." He led her upward to the third floor of the library wing and into his chamber, whereupon he immediately locked and barred the door. He wanted no interruption—not even from Jack—no noise that might give them away.

"What is this place?" Claire kept her voice low, already sensing the need for stealth in the moonlit darkness.

"My room. It connects with the library below." He laid his finger across her lips, and then he led her to the narrow stairway door

"We can't just barge in," she whispered in his ear.

"Don't have to barge," he answered at her ear. "The acoustics are such that we'll hear their every word."

And voices were already rising up from below.

"Sanderson." The marquess's deep voice was everything Tanner had expected—commanding and haughty, and sure of his precedence over the earl.

And then the earl's greeting, his voice restrained. "Hadleigh."

Tanner pulled the door open just enough so that he could peer through the slit between the panel and the jamb. A warm wash of light from the fire and the lamps in the library spilled in a hot wedge across the floor of his chamber, and Tanner urged Claire closer to him, deep in the enveloping shadow.

Hadleigh's tone was brash and overconfident. ". . . you must see?" Hadleigh was finishing.

"No, I don't, Hadleigh." The earl's deep voice was level but slightly strangled, as if his vocal cords had been worn nearly to bits holding his words back diplomatically. "Perhaps you will explain it to me."

"Very simple really. Came here this evening to put an end to this needless speculation and gossip about your daughter. My son is prepared to give her the protection of his name."

If Claire had not clapped her own hand over her mouth to stifle her shock, Tanner might have. But when she turned her wide, startled eyes to him in utter horror he could only draw her close to stop the little tremors of indignation and fear that shivered through her body.

"Protection? Of his name?" Her father's voice was still conversational and controlled, but Tanner could detect a fine-honed edge of perturbation sliding under the pleasantness.

"And mine of course." Hadleigh might as well have thumped his chest. "My son will be marquess someday, although not anytime soon."

"And what do you imagine this protection would be for?"

"Why, don't you know?" Even Hadleigh's voice sounded disingenuous. "I hate to be the one carrying tales, but surely you've heard some of the things that are being said?"

"I have heard a great deal of different things being said, Hadleigh."

"Then you will know that very few of them are flattering."

The Earl Sanderson waited a long, cold moment before he replied. "Then I should like to know exactly why you started those rumors."

"Me? Come, man"—Hadleigh tried to sound bluff and sympathetic—"let us be realists. My son did his best for her then, but . . . I understand she's made her way back, but she's clearly ruined. She was gone for some time."

To Tanner's ears, Hadleigh sounded about as sympathetic as a serpent.

Apparently Sanderson thought so, too. His tone was as cold as a March wind. "You are misinformed. My daughter is here, just as she has been these past few days, and whoever has been telling you these lies will be brought to account by me." That was steel running like a blade straight through the Earl Sanderson's voice.

Hadleigh tried his best to evade the sharp edge. "Come, man. You may be able to cozen the world, as well you should try to do for your daughter's sake, but you can't cozen me. My son was there, man. He tried to save her."

"From what?"

"From Fenmore."

"Really?" Sarcasm entered the earl's tone. "She did not mention that your son had done so."

"Oh, no? What exactly did she say?" Hadleigh tried to sound only casually curious, but he was too used to getting what he wanted to wait. "How did she account for what happened?"

"She found the body of a young maid who had gone missing." Sanderson was playing his cards very close to his chest. "It was entirely distressing for her, as I'm sure you can imagine."

"Drowned herself, did she?"

Alarm bells immediately began to peal in Tanner's brain, resounding like a steeple on Christmas morning. He had told no one—with the exception of Claire, Jack, and himself, no one knew that Maisy Carter's body had been found in the river. Perhaps Claire had told others, like his grandmother and her parents, although Tanner hoped they had enough sense not to let that information out.

And Claire was just as quick to find the slip. She put her lips to his ear to whisper, "My father never said that we found her in the river. How does Hadleigh know that?"

It was a very good question indeed. Tanner's guess was that Rosing must have told his father that he dumped Maisy Carter's body in the river.

"I beg your pardon?" There was something sharper and more incisive in the earl's voice as well, and Tanner had to let go of Claire to inch closer to the light, so he might see down through the brass railing to the faces of the men below.

Hadleigh was seated, slouching negligently against the high upholstered back of his chair. Sanderson stood across from him, with his hand on a chair's back.

"Your information is wrong. My daughter is not drowned," Sanderson clarified. "She is well, apart from being deeply distressed by the death of the maid."

Ah. The earl was fencing with the man—subtly probing for weaknesses and and holes in Hadleigh's armor of arrogance. Almost as if the earl, too, suspected Hadleigh of lying.

Tanner inched as close to the edge of the railing as he dared.

"I meant the maid drowned, man." Hadleigh's tone was still dismissive. He did not realize his mistake.

Another clanging gong echoed in Tanner's brain. If Hadleigh thought—or was told by his son—that the maid drowned, why had he laid a charge of murder against Tanner?

"I'm sure I couldn't say." Thankfully, the Earl Sanderson did not let out any more information. His face was a study in calm.

"Come, Sanderson." Hadleigh turned cajoling. His narrow, hawkish face wasn't particularly familiar to Tanner. But he would remember it now. "You needn't be so stoic around me. I'm a father. I understand. My son lies broken in a friend's nearby home due to the events of that unfortunate evening. What I propose will answer for both of them."

"A *friend's*. How tragic." The earl's answer was noncommittal. "How does the young man fare?"

Oh, well played—another subtly snide touch of steel from Sanderson in the veiled reference to Hadleigh's mistress, Lady Westmoreland.

Hadleigh pressed what he wrongly saw as his advantage. "I can pledge that my son considers himself engaged from this moment forward."

The earl held up a staying hand. "And yet I feel that would be a little too precipitous, especially as your son 'lies broken' nearby. I must give the idea some thought, for it is not the first proposal I have had the honor of receiving this evening."

"Not?" Hadleigh rose, finally hearing the earl's careful hostility.

"No." The earl was as cool as the river.

The Marquess of Hadleigh drew himself up and tossed his chin at Sanderson. "And may I ask who else may have asked for your daughter's rather soiled hand?"

Sanderson remained a canny tactician, and waited a long, considering moment before he answered. "You may."

Hadleigh's face was growing red with barely concealed ire. "And?" he demanded.

"Himself." The earl gestured to the tall portrait hanging over the mantle, looking down so severely upon them. "His Grace the Duke of Fenmore."

The air in the library was still with charged calm for only a moment before Hadleigh burst into motion. "How? Where?" He stormed toward the library doors. "Is he here?"

The earl did not follow. "I should think not, although I give little countenance to the rumors that he has fled, because of course I have seen him. But search if you like. This is his grandmother's home—I am sure the dear, influential dowager duchess will take no umbrage at your searching about like an unleashed dog after a bone."

Hadleigh turned back sharply, and Tanner very, very slowly withdrew into the dark of his chamber, making no sudden moves that would attract Hadleigh's eye.

"You mock me," the marquess spat at the earl.

Sanderson retained his calm. "I do not, my lord. I merely remind you that we are both guests in another peer's house, and need to behave as such."

"Save your lectures on how to behave for your daughter," Hadleigh roared back. "This is a matter of law."

"It is a matter of an accusation before the law only. But this is how you talk about my daughter, the young woman to whom, you tell me, your son already considers himself bound?"

Too late, Hadleigh heard the heat in the earl's steely tone. "He is a gentleman, sir. He has been taught what is right."

"But what of you, Hadleigh, with your heated words? To what purpose all this"—the Earl Sanderson made a gesture between them—"in service of? For it is certainly not in service of my daughter, of whom you speak so disparagingly. You spoke of not being coy and cozening, Hadleigh, so don't think to cozen me. What do you seek from an alliance between your son and your house, and my daughter and my house?"

"An alliance, such as all noble marriages bring. Nothing

more, nothing less. I have long sought just such an alliance between our houses. You know that."

"Nothing more? You will recall I have turned down your other offers of an alliance before."

"Perhaps now you will reconsider."

"Perhaps not. As I told you, I am not at all interested in joining the financial conquest of Britain. I am no gambler."

But Tanner had heard the well-chosen words—*financial conquest*—and pricked up his ears. Sanderson was talking of the gold aurei.

"And I will not gamble with my daughter's portion either," the earl was saying. "Or were you not interested in how much she will bring?"

"Don't be daft." Hadleigh moved closer to the earl to correct himself. "But do not imagine that I will need her money."

"And does your son? He has gambling habits, or so I'm told."

Hadleigh waved the suggestion aside. "As do most young men."

"He has other habits as well. I hate to be the one *carrying tales,* but surely *you've* heard some of the things that are being said. Of vices and predilections and indecent needs far beyond the realm of decent gentlemen."

Tanner felt himself smile in the dark. It was getting downright vicious down there, with all the veiled barbs flying about. Just the way he liked it.

"Wild oats, which are neither here nor there. He will be Hadleigh, for God's sake. Family is destiny. The marquessate is too important to let his petty faults get in the way."

Tanner had heard such tripe for years, ever since the first moment he had set foot at Eton. But he knew without a doubt that a man was only what he could make of himself. What he believed. The measure of a man was how he treated those who could do him no benefit. How he treated his fellow man when no one else but God was looking.

The Earl Sanderson apparently felt at least partially the same way. "It is very much here, Hadleigh. Very much. His *faults* are vices that are by no means petty. People *will* talk, even if it is in whispers."

Hadleigh absorbed that blow and struck another. "Yes, they will talk. And they will talk about young ladies, and they will ruin their reputations with far more viciousness than they will talk about healthy young men who live in the world. *She* will not be forgiven so easily. I can start talk far beyond what I have already."

Beside Tanner, Claire went absolutely, lividly still with hot rage. He could feel it singeing off her skin.

"So is that the real transaction here, Hadleigh? My daughter marries your son, or you will make it even more of your business to further sully her name?"

Hadleigh smiled like a wolf who thinks he has cornered his prey. "You put it so undiplomatically."

"It is an undiplomatic offer, sir," the earl said bluntly.

"Let us hope your answer is not undiplomatic."

"My answer to this proposal is the same as to the last."

Hadleigh stiffened, but his shoulders eased slightly when the earl went on.

"Your son will have to put his proposal to my daughter. And then we shall see if she will have him. But I don't think I will want him as a son-in-law."

"I will never have him." Claire's whisper was low and fierce. "Never. I want to go right now to Lambeth Palace and get a special license. I—"

Tanner pulled her back deeper into the shadows and spoke low into her ear. "You have nothing to fear. Your father said it was your choice. And it's Doctors' Commons for the special license. And I've already sent my man."

The thought seemed to calm her. She nodded against

his chest and relaxed the grip she had taken on his arm. "Yes."

"Because, my lord"—Sanderson's voice was as clear and sharp as a shard of glass—"I don't in any way want to be connected to you."

"Be careful where you make enemies, Sanderson. You ought to know I have power."

"I have seen and felt your power, Hadleigh. And I want none of it. I want nothing to do with you, and what I have come to understand are counterfeited gold coins."

Hadleigh was outraged, but his voice betrayed the first real glimpse of honest fear. "Who told you that? Come, man, I gave you the coin to authenticate."

"One coin, Hadleigh, does not evidence of a hoard make. And it is a small world we live in. And people *will* talk. People in Mayfair talk to people in the City. And people in the City talk to people in St. Catherine's Dock."

The earl's statement was met with livid, hostile silence. And then Hadleigh spoke in tones so low and so heated that Tanner had to strain to hear the words.

"I will bury you."

The Earl Sanderson did not so much as flinch. He looked up to the very top of the ornate spiral staircase and looked Tanner straight in the eye. And answered Hadleigh. "You may try."

Chapter Twenty-Two

Tanner shut the door carefully, even after the two antagonists had gone. "Your father loves you. I just thought you should know that."

"I do know that. But I thank you anyway."

Claire wrapped her arms around him, and his brain went all but blank. She was soft and sweet and pliant beside him, and he wanted more than anything else in the world—more than being clever and more than finding justice—to kiss her.

He ached just looking at her. His body all but vibrated, as if he were a tuning fork that only she knew exactly how to strike. Her very presence sent bursts of unhelpful sensations careering through his brain, disrupting his thought processes, hindering his progress and abilities.

And he liked it. He liked her. She was his. At least for as long as she offered herself to him.

And offering she was. Her wide blue eyes were shining up at him. Looking at him in that soft, unfathomable way. She was exquisite. And never more so than now, when she was flushed and naturally beautiful, and unadorned with all the usual adornments.

There he was repeating words. It was illogical. It was atypical. He didn't like it.

Oh, but he liked her. He couldn't be in the same room, the same city, the same world as her and not want to be with her. Not want to kiss her.

And so he did. He framed her extraordinary face with his hands, brushing aside the strands of silken blond hair that had fallen loose from her pins, and kissed her. Long and slow and sweet. Taking his time. Feeling pleasure and ease and satisfaction seep all the way into his bones.

She was soft and smelled of gardenia in the hollows behind her ear, and he wanted to lick the sweetness of her skin. He wanted to consume her whole. He wanted to run his fingers through her extraordinary hair and scatter the pins to the ground and spread it out glistening gold against the linen on his bed.

But there were things that needed to be done. Dots that needed to be connected. Thoughts that needed to be organized, whirling around the cage of his brain. "Claire. Before you fall completely under the spell of my skill at kissing—"

"Oh, you're not particularly skilled at kissing. I've had better."

He was so disconcerted by that particular backhanded insult that he stopped kissing.

"But now that we're not kissing anymore," she said as if they had been drinking tea or eating biscuits or doing anything other than kissing, "I have something in particular that I want to tell you. It just came to me. I mean, I had another thing, and they are related, that I wanted to tell you as well. Indeed that is the whole reason I sought you out."

He hadn't cared or thought she needed a reason to search him out. He only cared that she had.

"But with all your insight, and talk of *seminal liquor* and *blood*, you made me entirely forget my point."

"Which was?"

"This afternoon I talked with one of the maids, as you do." She fluttered her hands in front of her in a gesture meant to intimate femaleish things. "You will not credit this—"

"Then why are you telling me"—he really did like this teasing her—"if you know I will not credit it?"

"Because it is a turn of phrase intended to make you sit up and listen attentively. So do shut up, stop gaping, and listen attentively for a moment, Tanner, because I think I have figured it all out."

He was not exactly gaping at her—his mouth was closed, and he was far to clever a man to ever gape. So he nodded, very politely, and said, "Just so."

"You were right about them being invisible—the servants. And it frightens them now to feel that they've been seen, that someone amongst them has been killed. But the girl I was talking to, Parker—Nancy Parker—said most of the guests never even notice when they are near. She said she was going up that servants' staircase we were just examining, last night, when she heard someone coming down. And her being one of the lower servants, she pulled back into the passing alcove—and I didn't even know there was such a thing as a passing alcove. But a man—a guest— passed by her going down. And he was carrying someone all wrapped up in a white ladies' evening cloak. And now I see that it must have been Maisy's body he was carrying down."

Tanner was all attention now, the gears in his brain whirring and falling into place like well-oiled tumblers in a lock. "Yes."

Clever, clever girl. She was just as alert and still and alive as he had ever seen her. And he had never admired her more. "Who do you think it would be?"

"Tell me it was Rosing."

"I am afraid I must disappoint us both. It was not Rosing."

The urge to smash his fist into the nearest wall rose like a rogue wave from within, nearly propelling him up and out the goddamned window. There seemed to be this insurmountable wall in his brain, between what he knew ought to have happened and the evidence from Maisy Carter's own hand.

He had to find the way through the wall. He had to.

"Do you not want to know who it was?" Claire was staring at him, all wide, beseeching eyes in the moonlight.

"Yes," he said, though his voice was resigned. It would be another Layham or Edwards. Or—God's balls—her father. Let it be anybody but her father. "Tell me."

"His father. The Marquess of Hadleigh."

And there it was, a way straight over the wall.

"Ah." His Grace of Tanner went entirely still, the moonlight streaming through the dormer windows illuminating his tousled head like a Renaissance saint's halo. "Now I have to rethink everything." He brought up his hands in a little steeple in front of his mouth and drummed his fingers against his lips as if it helped him to think.

She stilled his fingers. "Not everything. Just the part from that closet upstairs." In her excitement, she gripped his fingers so hard, her own began to hurt. But he didn't care. "The maid—Nancy Parker—said that she told Mrs. Dalgliesh what she had seen, because it didn't seem right his being there, and the housekeeper said to keep her thoughts to herself, as it was only Lord Hadleigh taking home his mistress Lady Westmoreland, who had become ill from too much drink. Said she—that is, Nancy said Mrs. Dalgliesh said she knew it was Lady Westmoreland from her white evening cloak. But—and this is the damning bit—the housemaids saw Lady Westmoreland, who was supposed to have been taken ill, still in the ballroom dancing until the party broke up when Hadleigh found Rosing." She was nearly out of breath from her tumbling narrative. "So it was Maisy. What do you think of that?"

"I think, Lady Claire Jellicoe, that you are one of the cleverest women I have ever had the good fortune to meet."

"How clever you are to recognize that." She gave him her absolute best version of her winsome smile.

It worked just as it ought, making him look at her with something more than admiration for her cleverness. "Why, you, Lady Claire Jellicoe, are a minx."

"Oh, I do so hope I am." She still smiled at him entirely pleased with this description. "And so are you. Or whatever the male equivalent is. Listening at doors as if you're quite practiced in the art. Scandalous."

"Absolutely. I'll be a scandal and you can be the enigma. Beauty as well as intelligence. Which puts you beyond the reach of all mere mortals."

She smiled at that. How could she not? It was a compliment for the ages. Especially since he sounded so charmingly aggravated admitting it. "It is a very good thing that you are not a mere mortal, but I thank you, Your Grace. I live to serve."

That tease did not have the effect she wanted, but brought him up short. He reached out to put his hand overs hers where she still held his, as if he could pass some of his vehemence to her. But his words were soft kindness itself. "You should live to *be*, Claire. Live just to be your own, lovely self."

He was being his own self, deep and blunt and profound. And most endearing. "But the truth is, Your Grace, that I am my best self when I am helping others. Rather poor-spirited of me, I might suppose, but quite, quite true. But helping others need not be onerous. I like helping you."

He looked away for a moment, out the open window

over the river, as if he were trying to avoid responding. But he could not be untrue to himself. He had to speak the truth. Even if it cost him. "I like when you help me."

"Good. For I should very much like to continue to do so."

His eyes came straight to her, that dark blue-green of the fathomless ocean. "Do you truly?"

"Do you know me so little still that you think I would lie about such a thing?"

"I think I know you well enough to think that you are generous to a fault and commit to things which you might regret later."

"I have not regretted one instant of our time together." Of this she was now sure. "Well, perhaps the circumstances of our first instant together. But not the second. Because if you had not come to me—and you did come to me, did you not? You came there, to the boathouse, for the direct purpose of saving me?"

"Yes."

"Then I am glad for it. All of it. For I don't think I should ever have met you, otherwise. I should never have had the courage to ask to be introduced. And that would have been the greatest loss of all, never having met you. All the trouble has been worth it to know you."

"My God, Claire. That is the most generous speech I think I have ever heard anyone make. You have suffered terribly, and yet you choose to characterize and see the incident in a positive light. My God." He ran his hands through his hair in a gesture of rumpled frustration. "Your father said it, and I know it is true—I am not worth such a price."

"You will have to let me be the judge of that, Your Grace."

"I will let you be the judge of everything, Claire. If only you will stop calling me Your Grace."

He was so, so dear. "All right then, Tanner."

"And I must ask you to stop talking in this familiar manner, for if you do not, I fear I shall very much have to kiss you again."

She hoped her smile was blindingly brilliant—she needed to encourage this lovely teasing flirtation. "I was rather hoping you would."

"You, Lady Claire Jellicoe," he said as he tugged her hand to bring her nearer, "are a very clever minx."

"Your poor Grace. Are you only just discovering that?"

"Yes. But as you have noted, my dear Lady Claire, I very much like discovery."

Their lips met alone in the middle of space, in the middle of the room, in the middle of the night. She leaned toward him just as he leaned toward her, balancing themselves carefully, holding themselves in quivering check, lest they disrupt their tenuous conclusions with their rising passions. And passions there were.

The moment his lips met hers, she fell into the kiss just as if she were falling into a dream—plunging in headfirst, tumbling weightless in the dark, silken pleasure. He moved to angle his head, turning to fit himself to her, so she could take the taut, pillowed curve of his lower lip between hers and taste the brandied tang of his mouth.

She closed her eyes and opened to him on a sigh. But she was not passive; she did not wait for him to pleasure her. She took what she wanted as well, kissing and licking and nipping and sucking with fervor and skill and abandon, until he was on his knees before her.

"Claire."

"Yes." She was looping her arm around his neck, tethering herself to him so he would hold her the way she wanted to be held.

"I need to say, before there are any more fathers, and

lawyers, and men of business, and representatives to estates, that I would be honored—deeply, wholly honored—if you would consent to be my wife. I wanted you to know—you alone—that I should like nothing more."

Claire did not answer. She did not say "yes" or "of course." She was equal to the honor of the moment and only took his hands between hers.

"I want to do it properly," he said in another uncharacteristic rush. "Before anyone starts any nonsense about scandal, and having to because it's the right thing. It is the right thing, but I'm the Duke of Fenmore, Claire. No one could make me do anything that I don't want to do. So I wanted you to know that I *do* want to marry you. I do want it, with all my heart."

He was so solemn that she wanted to do him the honor of answering him properly. "Your Grace—"

"God's balls, Claire. I'm proposing. Don't you think you could call me by my Christian name?"

"Well, I hardly think *Tanner* qualifies as Christian. And I'd like to meet your sister. Perhaps we should invite her for the wedding?"

"Yes." His relief spilled out of him on a rush of air. "There will be a wedding, will there not?"

She was so happy she could only nod, and he rose and kissed her again to seal their bargain. "Good, because I very much fear I love you."

His words were a torrid whisper, falling like warm rain upon her face, emboldening her, encouraging her. But she inched toward him slowly. So slowly, like time pulled into taffy, stretching and stretching, until *she* was stretched as far as she could, up on her tiptoes to try to reach his lush, curved lips. Because she wanted this moment to last.

But the promise in his gaze was so sweet it was worth the wait, and when at last the first butterfly brush of her lips fluttered against his she closed her eyes on a sigh of sweet relief.

His lips were taut and yielding and moving only very slightly beneath hers. Waiting for her. Waiting for her to do as she wished. So she took her time. She kissed him slowly, pressing her lips onto his gently, and then not so gently. Exploring the plush firmness of his mouth. And when his lips fell open on a raggedy breath, she took the taut plushness between her own and tasted him just a little.

He tasted of brandy and coffee and cinnamon and rain. And hunger. Hunger for her. Hunger for her love.

This was Tanner kissing her, in all his raw earthiness, not the cool, cerebral Duke of Fenmore. This was Tanner trying so hard not to do too much, or press too hard. But his need—his need drew her near, even as his hands were clenched in fists by his sides.

But it wasn't that he didn't want to touch her. It was that he didn't want to frighten her. But without laying a hand on her, he took possession of her mouth with such thoroughness it took the breath from her. It was a kiss and more. It was a claiming. It was hot and wet and hungry and everything, everything that he was, and everything that he had so obviously held back when they had kissed before.

And she knew she was done for. He was it for her. If she lived to be a hundred and ninety, there would never be another person in the world who could come close to filling the Tanner-shaped mark upon her heart.

And because he would not touch her, she touched him. She let her hands slide up the smooth contours of his sleekly muscled arms, feeling the strength and pliancy of his flesh and bone. She caressed the warm skin of his neck. She looped her hands around his neck and at last—at last—as if he had been waiting for some sign, some signal from her, his arms cinched around the small of her back and pulled her flush against the warm wall of his chest.

"Yes," he said unnecessarily. "You are in charge."

She did not feel as if she were in charge. She felt at the mercy of the intoxicating pleasure that filled her up from the inside. But he was right. She was not an animal. She had a choice.

"I'll stop," he said at the corner of her mouth. And he pulled back from her, he stopped kissing her, just to prove it.

"No," she said immediately. "No, please." Kissing him, being in his arms, felt good and right and natural. And she wanted more than kissing. She wanted to be his and make him hers irrevocably. She wanted to exorcise the ghost of Rosing. "I want him gone. I want to replace every thought of him with something better. With a man so far his superior—"

He stopped her with the press of his lips to hers, and she tightened her hands around his neck, leaving him in no doubt that this was what she wanted. This was what she needed.

The warm scent of starch, from his evening clothes, rose and mingled with the warmth of their bodies finally touching. The chill was banished by the bonfire of his attention.

She pulled herself closer, turning her head, angling to get closer to him in every way possible. And then he picked her up and he was walking with her, moving backward until he came up hard against the edge of the bed a few feet away.

The force of their movement and the weight of their bodies carried them down until he was flat on his back. He settled into the soft cotton mattress with a sigh of glad relief, and the tempo of their kissing changed, to one of ease and slow delight. His hands traveled in an unhurried mean-der, up her back to her nape, taking their time, learning the feel and way of her. Savoring her like ripe summer fruit.

And she was savoring him as well, learning the brandy-bright taste of him. Exploring the shape and size of him. She was laid all along the length of him, from his chest all the way down the long length of his thighs, and even with her mouth next to his, her feet just barely passed his knees. He hitched himself sideways, and carried her with him, so that his boots were twining around her skirts. But all thoughts of feet and boots, and if she ought not let her sturdy half boots on the counterpane, were lost when his hand came up to cradle her jaw and turn her head to an angle more to his liking so he could kiss her again. And again.

The kiss went on and on and on—tongue and teeth and lips and love, and everything, everything she had ever thought she could want from him, was there, at her mouth.

His fingers were spearing through her hair, scattering pins onto the counterpane—scattering her thoughts and in-hibitions until there was nothing but feeling, and need and hunger.

He kissed her mouth and her lips and her chin and her cheeks, and she felt beautiful and cherished. She kissed his perfectly shaped lips and along the long line of his jaw, and down the length of his aristocratic nose, and felt powerful and curious. He smelled of soap and bay rum and cedar and spice. She drew her hands along the high planes of his cheekbones delighting in the smooth feel of skin over the slight rasp of his close-shaved whiskers.

Her hand was at the neck of his shirt, laying waste to his impeccable cravat, pulling his button so she could trace the long line of his collarbone with the tips of her fingers.

And then, she had the strangest, strongest urge to kiss him there, at the hollow of his throat. And so she did.

His skin felt cool after the heat of his mouth, but she

could feel his pulse beating strong and sure under the warm cover of his skin, and he made a sound of such pure animal pleasure and encouragement. And she found herself wanting to do it again, to make him sigh with her kiss, and explore the architecture of her body with his lips and tongue and teeth.

He turned his head to the side, as if to grant her an invitation to explore the long, long slide of his neck under the edge of the shirt. To nip and worry at the spot where the sinuous tendon met the broad plane of his shoulder. To lave the sensitive spot on the top of his shoulder.

The sound she engendered from him was a surprised rumble of a laugh that vibrated and tumbled through her, emboldening her, urging her on, until she had kissed her way up the side of his neck, and had taken the soft, vulnerable skin of his earlobe between her teeth.

She bit down gently at first.

"Claire," he said, and his voice was strained and happy and wondrous.

And then she bit him not so gently.

The sound that burrowed out of his chest was a low growl of satisfaction that accompanied first his coat, and then his waistcoat to the floor. And the next thing she knew, he had rolled her in his arms until she was below him and the force and weight and strength of him bore into her.

"No." The word flew out of her mouth before she could stop it or wish it back. Embarrassment and confusion singed her skin, but Tanner was true to his word—he stopped.

He didn't ask what was wrong. He didn't need to. He was the kind of person who saw and listened and watched with different eyes. He was the kind of person who understood.

Before she could say another word, he had reversed their positions once more, but this time he sat up, with his back leaning against the pillows at the head of the bed. And with his hands at her waist, he guided her up until she sat upon his lap, with her legs to either side of his.

But he kissed her so sweetly, and held her so lightly that she was too beguiled by his attention to think about the awkward exposure of her position. And with her seated thus, her hands were free to roam and play over his body, and delve beneath the open neck of his shirt. To trace the rather miraculous musculature of his shoulders and upper chest.

He was a lean man, long in the bone, and knit together in graceful, sinuous lines, flowing from one supple muscle to the next, and she wanted to see him as well as feel the sleek skin beneath her hands. She slid her hands under his shirt to drag her fingers up over the strong lines of his ribs, and as if he had been waiting for her signal, Tanner reached down, and in one fluid motion shucked the linen over his head.

There he was, bare from the waist, his skin as golden and glowing as a navvy who worked in the summer sun digging ditches all day. This strange duke of hers was beautiful in his wild, barely tamed way.

And he was wild in other ways, too. He urged her to lean into him. To let the weight of her torso settle upon him, and let the soft muslin fabric of her gown brush against the bare expanse of his skin.

"Yes," he praised her when she did. "Ah, yes."

And the delicious frisson of her body against his filled her with a sort of giddy, mad delight that urged her closer still. That urged her to let her body rub against him as she kissed him.

His hands fanned open against her back, encouraging her forward, holding her weight so she could play with

the unruly, tousled curls that fell across his forehead. So
she could kiss his temples, where his pulse beat against
his skin, and all along the wicked slide of his cheekbones.

His mouth was wandering down the side of her neck,
sending little pinpricks of pleasure shooting like wayward
stars under her skin. So she threw her head back, anxious
to encourage him, wanting the bursts of bliss to continue
to rain down within her.

And it did. Her skin was on fire with a hundred points of
fire and light. Everywhere he touched, everywhere he
kissed across the top of her bodice, her skin flared into
impossible awareness. Each spot was more sensitive than
the next. More full of exquisite feeling than she had ever
imagined.

She was, after all, nearly twenty years of age, and she
had kissed and been kissed by more than two fellows in
her day. She had thought herself quite sophisticated—
sophisticated enough to go walking with the likes of Lord
Peter Rosing in the dark.

She was in the dark now, but this was nothing like that.
This was nothing like anything she had ever experienced
before. This was her Tanner whose care and attention and
love could not be denied. Would not be denied.

Not by her.

Not now. Not ever.

His mouth roamed lower across the slight swell of her
breasts, and she all but held her breath. Beneath her layers
and layers of clothing, behind gown, and stays and chemise, her nipples contracted in anticipation, tightening into
exquisite peaks of sensation against the thin lawn fabric.

Her body was bending toward him of its own volition,
toward the glorious pressure of his clever mouth. Her
hands speared their way into his hair, and she was holding him there, silently urging him to please, please end
the lazy torture and—

His lips—his clever, clever, supple lips—found her nipple through the fabric of her gown and closed down around it, and she felt such blissful heat blossom out of her chest that she thought she might faint from the pleasure.

But she did not faint. She gasped in a useful lungful of sweet air, and let the pleasure cascade all the way through her, from the very edge of her skin all the way down to the empty center of her belly. She let the pleasure fill her up, like a cup filling to its brim and then over the brim, soaking her in the wonder that was his intimate kiss.

His voice came to her from far away. "May I?"

Whatever it was he asked, she was glad of it. "Yes," she said, though her voice was nothing but pieces of air. "Yes, please. Please."

His hands went to the laces of her gown, quick and nimble, loosening the ties and pulling the seams apart. The bodice sagged loose, and she was pulling it away, pulling her arms free of the tiny cap sleeves, so she could wrap her arms around his neck and hold her breasts tight against him, because when she moved, even just the tiniest amount, the glorious, ravenous pleasure surged anew.

But his hands were at her shoulders, urging her away from him so he could push down the straps of her stays, and brush down the short sleeves of her chemise. His lips were whispering over the upper curves of her breasts. But it wasn't enough. So when his fingers plucked at the laces of her stays she did not object. She encouraged.

"Yes, please. There. Get them off. Get them off so I can—"

And then the laces were loose, and she could push them away and free herself. His hands, his warm, callused, clever hands, and fingers were already there, cupping her breasts. Taking her tightly puckered nipples between his forefingers and thumbs, and rolling them gently against the cotton fabric. And then his mouth was on her, sucking at her nipples through the thin lawn of her chemise, wetting the fabric until it cooled and drew her sensitized nipples into ever tighter, more sensitive peaks.

Everything was pleasure. Everything was brilliant, brilliant delight. And bliss. And need.

And then his clever, clever fingers were pushing the chemise down to her waist and she was bared to him, arching back over the strength of his arm. Offering herself to him. The only gift she had to give was herself.

Chapter Twenty-Three

Claire gasped—a small but thoroughly satisfying sound of encouragement and benediction. He could hear her agitated breathing meld with his own, and all but feel the pleasure and excitement coursing through her veins. He could feel the delicate, rising heat of her body as she instinctively pressed closer to him.

Tanner's world narrowed to her and her alone. Her breasts were beautiful and white, her skin gleaming pale and silvered in the moonlight shivering through the windows, washing across the bed for a long second—long enough for the image to etch itself indelibly into his brain. Her nipples were the same warm, delicious pink as her lips, and her skin held the heady fragrance of white gardenia and deep green summer.

He would give her what she wanted—what she didn't even know she was asking him for, with her breathy sighs and plush, inquisitive mouth. With her soft insistence.

"Tanner?" Her voice held just the right amount of question to make him want to answer her with his mouth on hers. With his hands saying, *Yes, yes, whatever you want*, and his fingers whispering enticing secrets against her skin.

Because they had secrets, his clever fingers. They worked at the behest of his brilliant analytical mind, and he knew how to watch and what to think and when to act. If he knew nothing else, he knew each and every signpost along the road to her complete arousal.

He laid his hand gently along the side of her neck, testing the race of her pulse, gauging the level of her excitement. Was it enough? Was it enough to overcome both her scruples and any lingering fear?

He leaned away from her, just a fraction, just enough so his body couldn't press upon her or hem her in. Enough so if she wanted the sweet frisson of the contact of her body against his, she would have to move closer. Or not.

It was her choice—her need to be in control, even if she did not yet know it.

He knew it. He understood her. And he would act accordingly. For both of their benefit.

Because the truth was that however attentive he was trying to be in watching and gauging her reactions, he could not really think—he was suffering from the same unaccustomed heating of his skin as she. The same unruly rush of his pulse. The same mad thumping of his heart.

All she had to do was sigh or smile or lean the weight of her head into his hand, and he was smitten, over and over again—a wave rebounding upon his shore, more strongly each time.

The result was total unpredictability—he was becoming dangerously out of control. And the total ungovernableness of his physical attraction to her frightened him in a way that knives and guns and threats of hanging never had. Never could.

But she didn't seem frightened. She seemed curious and warm and interested in his mouth in a way that was inexplicable, except that he was just as inexplicably interested in hers. In the way her lips seemed to fit rather exactly against his. In the way everything she did was exactly designed to set his physical body on fire and muddle his brain.

He felt buffle-headed. And extraordinarily alive.

And determined to get it right. For her.

For both of them.

He knew well enough how to send a girl over the edge. The straightforward steps that would send a female careering breathily toward her crisis, tumbling gladly toward her oblivion, so he might find his own. So he might lose himself for those few fleeting, heady moments when his body triumphed over his brain.

He wanted that oblivion; he wanted to work toward it immediately. But she was taking her time, meandering from his lips to his earlobes and back, and he was having trouble concentrating on what he knew he ought to be doing.

He ought to be finding her secret places, the hidden swaths of sensitive skin. He ought to be touching her there, at the very edges of her nipples, making her skin heat and her knees knock and her heart beat too fast beneath her lily-white breasts.

But it was *his* skin that felt new. His knees knocking together beneath him. His heart that beat a wild tattoo within his chest. Because she was mastering the space between them. Pressing closer when he leaned back. Taking hold of him when he would not lay his hands upon her.

Ah, but he wanted to. He wanted to hold her, to wrap his arms around her, and hold her tight against his naked skin. He wanted it with a hunger that felt as if it might eat him alive if he did not give in and grip the delicate rounds of her shoulders, and take her nipples with his mouth.

Lightly. Lightly. Just enough to show he that he wanted

this slow death by delight, this slow teasing march toward cataclysmic physical climax, as much as she. That he wanted this excoriating brush of her peaked nipples against the bare skin of his chest. That he wanted her with every breath of his body and every fragmented thought left in his mind.

She wanted, too. "Tanner. Tanner, please. Again." Her voice slid away into irregular breathing. "Tell me."

Ah. Words. He would give her those, too.

He told her, "Yes. You want what I want, too. I can tell. You want to feel the pleasure." His words were terse, blunt even, he was having as much trouble breathing as she.

"Yes." She gasped her urgent agreement into his ear. "I want to feel—I want to feel it all."

He would give her it all. Every bit of it. Every last piece of pulsating bliss he could wring for them. "Are you a virgin?"

He thought he knew for a fact that she was—the signs were there for him to read. Had been there for him to read. But life was messy and stranger than fiction, and the analytic part of his mind needed confirmation of all the facts, so that he could proceed correctly.

"Yes." Her voice was hesitant, as if she were unsure of why he asked.

"It matters."

"Oh." That was disappointment in her voice now. And she pushed away, separating them, moving just out of his reach.

"No. Not to me." He tried to make her understand. "It matters to you. It matters as to how we proceed." His words sounded stupid and stilted to his own ears. He had to do better. "In how I touch you. In how I ask you to touch me."

"You don't need to ask me to touch you." There was

dawning hope in her voice—the return of physical excite-ment, building in her breathlessness, and she proved her point by kneading the taut muscles at his shoulders.

He felt himself stretch and move wantonly unto the sweet pressure of her hands. "Yes. Like that. And like this." He led her by the wrists, so her palms brushed across his chest, teasing his flat nipples into their own tightly furled peaks.

She needed no more encouragement, and immediately raked the backs of her fingertips across the sensitized tips, and he thought he would come out of his skin.

"Yes. Just like that." He reciprocated by thumbing her glorious pink nipples into tight, needy peaks.

She drew her breath in through her teeth, a long sugges-tive sound of urgency and provocation. "Yes. Show me."

"I should like nothing more. I shall show you," he promised her on a whisper that had gone dark and hungry, "all the ways to give pleasure. I will show you the places on your body that are made for the giving and taking of pleasure. I will show you the places on my body, for they are different from yours."

"Yes." It was her turn for quick agreement now. "Please. Please." She could not abandon her exquisite manners even now, when she was in the throes of needy, unthinking bliss. And he liked her for it.

"Do you want me to touch your sex?"

Her eyes widened at the bluntness of his question, but he wanted—he needed—to be sure. He wasn't one for couch-ing his words or obscuring his actions in confusing or misleading euphemisms. They were not yet married. They were in the throes of sexual excitement. He would be inside her *sex*. They would be engaging in messy, wet, exhilarat-ing, pleasurable, physically draining, blissful sex.

With the woman he loved.

But he was not blind or stupid enough to think that she really loved him, despite the way she sighed her encouragement into his ear. Despite the way she looked at him now—half hope, half fear, and all physical excitement.

"Do you?" she asked.

He felt his mouth curve into a hard smile. "Oh, yes. Very much. But I want to make sure you want it, too. I want to make sure that you don't feel forced or pressured or coerced in any way. It's important for you to choose."

Her expression softened, and her head tipped to the side, as if she thought him even more buffle-headed than he felt. But he had to make sure she understood. "And whatever you choose—yes or no—I will abide by your wishes. I won't force you. Or try to coerce you. No matter how much I want to be inside you, or how disappointed I might be."

She set her delicate fingers against the pulse in the hollow of his neck. "How disappointed might you be?"

"Enormously." His straining cock was proof enough of that. "Make no mistake. I want you, Claire. But I also want you to want me."

She smiled. That warm, open guileless smile that slayed him, and shot him clean through with heat and need and torturous bliss. "I do want you."

His heart slammed against the cage of his ribs, straining to be let loose. "What do you want most?"

Her answer was as quick as it was satisfying. "I want to kiss you again."

He closed the distance between them directly, but not at such speed as to overwhelm her, and set his mouth to hers. It leapt between them, the attraction, like an arc of electricity jumping between poles, the moment his lips touched hers. He was jackknifed back into arousal by nothing but the plush push of her lips against his, and the soft breath of her satisfied sigh whispering against his cheek.

And her hands were everywhere upon him, already circling around his neck so she might pull him close. He allowed himself the satisfaction of letting his hands grip her by the waist, but he resisted the urge to pull her against him. He forced himself to wait for her to lay her body flush against him, to press her breasts into his chest.

Only then did he allow himself the pleasure of opening his mouth to her kiss, to tasting her heady sweetness, and exploring the plush tartness of her tongue and mouth.

"Yes," she whispered, and he took that encouragement for the permission it was, to draw up her skirts as they kissed, teasing her with his tongue and his teeth, nipping and sucking and tantalizing her with new sensations. With more delight, if only she chose to come and follow his lead.

She did. She pushed forward as he leaned into the cushions at his back, never breaking their contact. Never letting her lips part from his for more than the time it took to change his angle of approach, or take her lower lip delicately between his teeth, and sweetly bite down with just enough force to send a jolt of unholy arousal careening through his gut. "Claire."

Her name was both a groan of entreaty and a plea. A plea for more of the wickedly divine caresses that spanned the divide between pleasure and pain so neatly, he was nearly poleaxed by the force of his response. By the force of his need.

His need for more of her.

He widened his knees and pulled her closer, so that the delicate heat of her body would press directly against his arousal.

But she was moving faster than he. She spread her knees wider on either side of his legs and moved against him while her hands speared through his hair, fisting and tugging the disordered strands. He leaded his head into her palms, and let her roll his head in her hands, trying desperately to exhaust the itchy need for skin to be against skin.

She kissed him again, filling him full of urgent, insistent need. "Tanner. Tanner, please."

His name was like a spur to his own hunger, urging him on. Her clothing was a bunched impediment between them, but he could not bear to set her away from him, even to bare her white, white skin to his touch and to his greedy gaze.

He crumpled up her gown and drew it up, up the length of her body, taking his time, dragging the soft muslin slowly across her skin in a precursor to his touch.

The action broke the kiss, but Claire didn't seem to object. Her head fell back, and she groaned her approval to the air over their heads, helping him draw the material over her head. She flung it aside as he reached for the tapes of her petticoat, pulling it free of her waist and following the same torturous path up her torso. "Tanner," she hissed at him, her breath full of insistence.

Her stays had already been cast aside, so there was only the thin lawn of her chemise left, and he tortured them both by slowly drawing the thin material tight against her skin. So he could tongue her breasts again through the veil of the fabric, kissing and sucking and laving her harder, showing her his hunger and need.

She was the one to pull the chemise off, to yank it over her head and collapse against him, so that at last they were flush against each other, skin to skin, heart beating against heart.

He plied his lips to the hollow under her ear, kissing and nipping his long way down the sensitive side of her neck, teaching her that a wealth of sensation could be evoked from thorough attention to this lovely swath of skin above her collarbone. All the while his hands were stroking up and down the curve of her waist, his fingers fanning across the sweet curve of her back and his thumbs making light sweeps against the side of her belly.

He urged her closer, rounding his palms over the taut flesh of her bottom, cupping her sweet arse, and pressing her against his achingly erect cock, still held in check by the thick cotton of his breeches. But he did nothing to appease his fingers' need to touch her sweet cunny or rake his hands through the soft blond curls at the entrance to her body.

Not yet. Not until she said so.

She had to be the one to ask or take the initiative. Each step of their physical intimacy needed to be made without any kind of force. He did not want the ghost of Lord Peter Rosing between him and his exquisite girl. He wanted her all to himself.

All his to worship. All his to tease and delight. All his to satisfy.

He kissed his way along the line of her collarbone, across the hollow at the base of her neck, and out again along the straight line of delicate bone, until she arched her back and scored his chest with the soft pebbled peaks of her breasts.

His own heart was hammering away like an anvil inside his chest.

He felt, more than he heard, the deep sound of satisfaction sighing out of her before she pushed away. Not with any great force, but just enough so he, who was trying to be vigilant to any such move, felt it instantly and let her go.

But she only pushed away enough so that she could duck her head down to kiss him on the mouth again. A decadent, slippery slide of a kiss that made him long to make her slippery and ready beneath him.

Except that that wasn't how it was going to go. He wouldn't put her beneath him. He wouldn't press his hunger into her and succumb to the weight of his desire, or stretch his body over her. Not this time. Maybe even never.

It did not matter. She would be worth any price.

The price of his sanity seemed an easy thing to pay when her hand scrubbed down the soft skin of her belly, telling him with her articulate instinct what it was that she wanted.

She wanted him to touch her.

"I am going to touch you, my Claire. I'm going to touch you, and finger your lush little cunny."

He couldn't tell if the sound that flew from her lips was excitement or distress. But she didn't pull away—she tightened her grip on his shoulders. He spread his legs wider, pushing her open, laying her bare and vulnerable before him.

He concentrated on the sweet slide of her body, combing his fingers through the soft hair that covered her mons and shielded the delicate pink flesh of her sex. He cupped her, pressing the heel of his palm against the edge of her cleft, rubbing just enough so she gasped and pulled herself tight against him, and just as quickly levered back, so he could continue to touch her so intimately.

She was light and heat and soft, slippery need, encouraging him with her breathy sounds of frustrated delight.

He eased his fingertip along her delicate folds and was rewarded for his patience with the slick feel of her body preparing itself for him. He slid his finger into her tight sheath, exploring her, watching her face for her reaction, but she closed her eyes and buried her head against his shoulder but made not a sound.

"Look at me." He needed to see her face—to see what she was thinking. "Look at me while I finger your lush little cunny."

Her answer was a gasp and the tight grip of her hand

around his neck. He could not tell if it was pleasure or disgust that drove her.

"Do you like that? Do you want me to stop?"

"No." Heat was blazing across her cheeks. "Yes. You shouldn't say that," she whispered.

"Why not? It is a crude, dirty word. But I'm a dirty man, Claire. I'm the Tanner."

"You're my Tanner." She kissed the edge of his ear, softly, gently, and then with more force as his fingers played upon her, and her body began to understand its rhythm. She rocked against the insistent pressure of his hand, enough that her body pressed itself forward, grazing against his cock, straining within his breeches.

"You're almost ready for me, my Claire. You're almost wet and lush enough to take me. Almost." He slid another finger inside her, exploring her, stretching her tight cunny, all the while, letting his thumb graze the nubbin of her clitoris to heighten her gratification.

And gratified she was. "Yes, yes, Tanner. Tanner, please."

He wrapped his other arm around her nape and pulled her mouth down to his, kissing her with all the heat and urgency and need he no longer wanted to hide.

"Open my breeches," he urged against her lips as he stroked her and stoked the fires of her passion.

She worked with focused energy, quickly dispensing with his buttons and shoving the flap down, out of the way, and his arousal sprang free of his breeches.

"Take me." He could hear his voice slipping into the old way, tumbling into the rough, guttural intonation he had tried for years to train out of himself. But it was no use. He could be no more than he was. "Take me in your hand. Show me where you want me—"

She already was, grasping the long length of him, to

press his cock against her mons, to show him unequivocally that she wanted them joined.

"Yes." The word was an exhalation through his teeth, but he could barely hear it for the sound of his heart in his ears.

She was there, open and pink and bare and his. Waiting for him.

He slid his hand out of her and grasped her as gently as possible by the waist, because he didn't feel gentle. He felt tense and taut and on the very very edge of something bigger and more powerful than desire. He felt as if he couldn't breathe and didn't need to, because his cock was pushing against the lush, slippery warmth of her entrance and easing into her sweetly tight body.

He made himself take a lungful of air, and then another, and he could hear the harsh cadence of his breath, and he tried, tried to go slowly and ease the way. But he was going so mad with the need for her, with the need for the tight friction of her cunny gripping him and the sweet bliss of the joining of their bodies, that he could no longer think.

He could no longer watch her carefully or touch her gently or take his time. There was no more time. There was only now, and the pleasure that ripped him in two when she rocked her hips to seat his cock inside her.

She gasped, and went still and tense, holding herself tight against him, as if she could keep him from moving again.

"Oh, God. Claire. Claire. Are you all right? Are you—" He kissed her open, gasping mouth and kissed her tightly shut eyes and pressed his care and concern and love against her pleated lips. "It will get better. The pain will go away. It will leave us, and leave the pleasure behind. I promise you."

He was babbling again, crooning the soft words into the delicate shell of her ear, kissing and stroking her to ease away her pain and stoke the embers of her pleasure back into flame.

But it was working. She drew in a deep, shaky breath, and then another, and kissed him back, just a little. And then a little more. And then more still when his hands stroked up her sides to cup and fondle her breasts.

He pushed her away from him so he could see—see everything from her flushed face all the way down the pale, pinked slide of her body to the triangle of golden blond hair that hid the joining of their bodies. So he could see her crush her lower lip between her teeth. So he could see her nipples crest into tight, pink peaks. So he could see the softening of her belly when she finally relaxed and began to move against him.

And then he wanted to see it all and feel it all, as she slowly began to undulate in a sweet, sinuous motion, sliding her body against his, sending him rocking against the hard edge of his pleasure, over and over, and over again.

He grasped the glorious round globes of her tight little arse, and quickened her pace, helping her move, adding force and strength to the dance of her body upon his. "Yes, Claire, yes. Just like that. Just like—"

Like that.

Heat and light and pleasure and pain and bliss burst behind his eyes and blinded him with the bright force of her love. And he was gone.

Chapter Twenty-Four

Claire had never felt so alive. And so very exhausted. And so very, very happy.

She was sure she ought to be embarrassed to find herself naked but for her garters and stockings, draped across Tanner's equally naked chest. But she didn't seem to care. It seemed the very nicest place to be.

She rolled her head to the side to look at him. His eyes were closed, and his mouth was open, slowly drawing in air as if it were an elixir. But he was the elixir. Quite magical.

"Claire." His voice was full of a slow wonder—as if he had just discovered her, naked and draped all over him—for the very first time.

"Yes." She heard the laughter in her voice and felt the happiness bubbling up from within. From the well that finally felt full.

"We should not have done that," he said. But there was no heat, no purpose, in his voice.

"Really?" She was too happy to do anything but tease him. He needed teasing. Poor lamb. "Did we do it wrong? Ought we try again?"

"Yes." His gaze finally focused upon her. "We ought to do it again, and again, and again." He brushed his hand through her hair and pulled her closer to kiss her forehead. "But not now. You'll be sore, and I'd be a brute. And we still have a killer to catch."

"Now?" Claire was too comfortable, and too tired, to want to do anything but crawl under the covers of his bed and sleep until next Thursday.

"Yes, now. Because I want to marry you. And do *that* again and again and again. But I can't marry you with a false charge laid against me. And Rosing must be stopped once and for all. It is, as you've continued to remind me, past bloody time."

"Oh. I wish you had killed him when you had the chance." The moment she said it she was ashamed of herself. "No. Forgive me. I don't really mean that. I'm just tired."

"I've wished I did, too. At least a dozen times since last night."

"Don't. And don't think I wish that on you. I don't. You did the right thing. Because you're not an animal, Tanner. You're a gentleman, and you did the right thing."

"If I were a gentleman, you, my darling girl, would not be naked on my lap."

"I prefer to think of it as *you*, my dear duke, naked under *my* lap."

Claire felt his chuckle reverberate through her as he slowly disengaged their bodies and set her gently off him. "Either way, we must wash and dress, and find Rosing while Hadleigh is astir. If he is not still downstairs ratting around to try to find me, he is no doubt trying to find a magistrate who will leave his dinner and bother himself enough to have me taken up on his charge. Or maybe he'll be lucky, and find one who can simply be bought."

"Can he do that?" Despite all that had happened—all she had seen of the world in the past day—Claire was still shocked. "It doesn't seem fair."

"Life is rarely fair, Claire. Not unless we trouble ourselves to *make* it so." He hitched his breeches up, and
disappeared into his dressing room, from which he returned with lamp and a basin and ewer. "I'm sorry it's not
warm, but needs must."

He handed her a soft flannel, and then began rather un-
affectedly to wash himself, dipping his cloth into the water
and running it over his lovely lean body, leaving droplets of
water to sheen off his beautifully golden skin.

"Stop ogling me, Claire, and get yourself washed and
dressed, or you'll find yourself flat on your back on that
bed, and then your father will see me strung up regardless
of any charges."

"I'm dressing," she groused. "Even though I *had* rather
ogle you." She did as he asked, though she was more mod-
est and withdrew to the dark dressing room to wash and attire herself in her chemise and stays. But as to the lacing—

"May I?"

He was at the door, ogling her this time. He was dressed
in his rough, dark rig again, and she imagined he'd have
another disreputable old redingote in his wardrobe to replace the one he'd traded away to Tilly Wheeler, to turn him
back into a highwayman.

"Are you going to draw your pistols and have Rosing
stand and deliver?"

"Nothing so obvious. I prefer a less visible approach."

"What about me?" she asked as she gave him her back
to tighten the laces. "I'm hardly invisible in that gown."

He turned to look at the muslin, draped over a chair
like an inanimate ghost in the fitful moonlight. "I do wish
you had something darker. But there isn't— Ah." His
eyes narrowed and then brightened, and his lips, those
clever taunting lips, spread wider in that marvelously piratical smile. "Actually, the muslin is perfect." He handed
it to her.

"Perfect for what?"

"Looking innocent." He had the back buttons done up in a flash and was striding back to his chamber. "While I shall look quite the opposite." He began to fill his pockets and belt with guns. "We'll use the difference to our advantage."

"What are we going to do?"

"Come, Claire. We're going to go visit your counterfeit betrothed."

It was a good night for some housebreaking. The moon danced in and out of the clouds, cloaking their approach, and Lady Westmoreland's villa stood quiet in the night.

Tanner had rowed them the three minutes upriver to the neighboring property in the silent little skiff. He tied the vessel off with a slipknot—two ways in and three ways out of every hole—prepared for a hasty escape should they need it. But they shouldn't need it.

He had something else entirely in mind.

But he did take the trouble to check the small stable to assure himself that the Marquess of Hadleigh was still out, and would not be there to interfere and protect and cover up for his son. Not this time.

Not ever again.

Lady Westmoreland's villa—so called as it was merely a small country house sent in small grounds with no extended farm or tenanted land attached—resembled a jewel box at night. Light spilled out of every window as if there were no concern for economy or the extravagance of keeping wax candles.

The villa was not a country estate, but a house for retreating from the worries and heat of town in the summer months. Rumor had always been that Hadleigh had bought the house for Lady Westmoreland, who had been made a widow at a young age, and been left without a jointure or recourse to her deceased husband's fortune by a strictly enforced entail.

Hadleigh must be a generous benefactor. The entire house seemed to be illuminated, as if someone within were afraid of the dark. The light presented a problem, in that Tanner would need to extinguish a great many candles in order to skulk about effectively, but it also provided him with a great deal of information.

From without the house, it was easy to see who was within. It was easy to ascertain that Her Ladyship had retired to her sitting room above, with the windows open to the drive so she could be apprised of Hadleigh's return. It was easy to see that the servants were for the most part below stairs, congregating in the small servants' hall with the shining basement windows.

Outside, the wide lawn stretched uninterrupted from the house all the way to the river without the relieving cover of any greenery save the grass. There was nowhere to hide.

Tanner checked his weapons again, running his fingers over the pistols and touching the knife in his boot. And then he headed Claire toward the torch-lit front door.

"Do you mean we're just going to knock and ask if we can search the place?"

"No. *You're* going to knock, and ask to see your betrothed. I am going to go in through that library window we just passed."

"What am I supposed to say?"

"Say you're here to see Rosing. That you want to hear his proposal from his own lips. Use some of that marvelously forcible charm of yours."

"Forcible charm?"

"Yes. Where you smile and people fall all over themselves to do your bidding."

"You've never fallen all over yourself to do my bidding."

He looked at her from under his brows and spread his arms wide. "Have I not?"

"But—" She fidgeted, and turned back the way they had come, and knotted her fingers into fists. "But I don't particularly want to see Rosing. In fact, I hope never to see him again."

"Courage, Claire. You can do what needs doing, even if you're afraid. I've seen you. Just get inside, and I'll help with the rest."

A deep, uneasy frown was scrubbed between her brows, but she nodded twice, As if she were still convincing herself. "All right. I can do it."

"Good girl. Clever, good girl." And he kissed her—a quick, heady stamp of his love and encouragement—and slipped away. "I'll be right behind you."

Tanner took a moment to put himself back into housebreaking mode. He had to change his brain—twist it round a bit to see things with a different set of eyes. Still, the knowledge he had gained by being the Duke of Fenmore would put him in very good stead. He knew the inner workings of a stately house, even a small one like Lady Westmoreland's.

Tanner crept low along the wall until he was directly beneath the library window, which had conveniently been cracked open to cool the south-facing room with the evening breeze.

It was the work of eight heartbeats to slide the window open and slither over the ledge. Another two heartbeats and the branch of candles was extinguished, the flames quickly and silently snuffed between his thumb and third finger. He left the window open behind him. Another way out, if need be, and the open windows would provide an easy excuse if someone noticed that the candles had been blown out by the breeze.

Tanner took a moment to let his eyes adjust to the dark,

and memorize the layout of the furniture, especially the placement of any chairs that could be moved easily. The layout of the interior was typically Palladian, balancing one side of the house against the other, which meant that the room configuration and stairways would be exactly the same. Music room and drawing room on this side. Dining room and library on the other.

Tanner paused at the double doors to the hallway listening as someone—a male servant judging from the sound of the heavy footfalls—went to the door.

"Good evening." Claire's voice was clear, but she sounded nervous, the edges of her intonation flicking sharply upward. But that should suit. If she were really a young lady who had come to see her betrothed at his father's mistress's house in the middle of the evening, she ought to sound unsure. "I'd like to see Lord Peter Rosing."

"His Lordship is indisposed."

"He is ill. I know. That is why I've come. His father said I ought—"

She broke off, either in a very well-played show of delicacy, or else because she had run out of lies. Either way, it worked.

"If you'll wait one moment, Miss . . . ?" The servant paused meaningfully, waiting for Claire to supply her name.

"Lady . . ." Claire made her own dramatic pause. "I'm sure you understand, but as we're to be betrothed, Lord Rosing and I, perhaps—"

"Lady Claire, isn't it?" Lady Westmoreland's amused purr pattered down from above. "What are you doing here?"

"I've come to see Lord Rosing. His father, the marquess, came to speak to my father tonight, but I needed to see Rosing myself, and speak to him, and— I'm sure you understand."

"Actually, I don't." Lady Westmoreland's voice grew stronger, as if she had at least partially descended the stair. "He's not fit for any visitors, much less a young lady. He's practically swathed from head to toe in bandages. And he woke up for the first time only this afternoon, and only for a short while. He's too weak to speak, really, done in with pain, and of course the laudanum."

"Oh." Claire's distress sounded all too real. "Nevertheless, I feel I ought."

"Suit yourself." Lady Westmoreland must have made some motion of acceptance, because in another moment two treads could be heard on the stair. "From what I understand he's lucid only for short intervals. But have your wish. For myself I can't stand a sickroom."

The voices trailed away, and the entryway was left in silence. And then Tanner was following after them, extinguishing wall sconces as he went and opening windows where he could. Lady Westmoreland was to be complimented on her housekeeping—every window and door was well oiled, and opened easily and soundlessly. A lovely house for the breaking.

And at the top of the stair he moved to the open door of the corner bedchamber, where Claire stood alone, staring at the bed in the low light of a single candlewick. Tanner closed the silent door behind him, and moved to stand next to Claire, and offer what little comfort he could.

And there he was, Lord Peter Rosing, stretched out in the bed like the veriest invalid, his body encased in a linen nightshirt. He was motionless, his head upon the thin pillow swathed in bandages, as were his arms—evidence of what must have been repeated bleedings to try to relieve the ill humors trapped in his concussed brain. Well they could try, but his shallow breathing and deep sunken cheeks meant that His Lordship did not appear to be recovering. And the fact that they had left him—the seat of the chair by the bedside was cold to the touch—meant that they did not fear his waking.

He had well and truly cracked the bastard's skull.

Tanner tried for a moment to feel some sort of remorse or pity, but nothing came. No finer feeling stirred in his breast. Nothing but the need to prove that this man lying in such a pitiful state was the lying, raping, murdering bastard both Claire and Tanner, and half the serving girls in London, knew he was. "He doesn't look so very dangerous now, does he?"

"Snakes look all innocent coiled up in the sun, too," she said.

"Good. He doesn't deserve your pity." Tanner looked round the room. "I'll check the wardrobe. See if you can rouse him."

The wardrobe between the curtained windows held a well-tended valise, folded and laundered clothes neatly stacked, as well as a pair of well-polished boots and a pair of evening slippers. The evening slippers Rosing had been wearing when he stepped on the back of Lady Claire Jellicoe's train, and shoved her face against the wall.

Tanner's vision went blank and black and red. Funny how the simplest things could trigger such unmitigated rage. But the shoes didn't matter; the waistcoat did.

Tanner flipped through the careful stacks. Only a few shirts, four cravats, and two pairs of breeches. Rosing had not intended to stay in Richmond long. And there were only two waistcoats. The first was the sort of crisp, warm lemon-colored linen that would look good at a garden party or in a drawing room. But the second. The second was evening wear. A starkly white silk designed to be worn with a dark coat, like the superfine from Schweitzer and Davidson, and white satin evening breeches.

Plain white silk. No gold threads. No twilled weave. No rip or sign of repair on the slit pockets. Not the man

Maisy Carter had scratched at in her desperation. And not a married man, with a ring upon his finger.

Two pieces of evidence that said Rosing was not a murderer.

But there was something else. There was a small, round leather box—the sort of thing in which a man might keep his ornaments, like a cravat pin. Or a watch fob.

There was no fob, but then Tanner hadn't expected one—Rosing's fob would likely be the one in his possession. Except for the contrary evidence of the waistcoat. So, for a long moment Tanner stared down into the box, too intent upon what he didn't see to take note of what did lay coiled in the bottom. Hanks of blond hair. Tokens of Rosing's conquests. And amid them was a simple gold cross, studded with garnets. Just the sort of humble piece of jewelry a girl like Maisy Carter would have been given by a former mistress as a parting gift. It was worn and well used. dirty even, as if she touched it often and never took it off.

Rosing might not be a murderer, but he was certainly a vicious rapist. He had strangled Maisy when he raped her. He would have had this cross on him, in his pocket, when he went back downstairs to find Lady Claire Jellicoe, and put his filthy hands upon her, and drag her down the garden, and try once more to satisfy himself with violence.

The man in the bed didn't look like a rapist. He looked small and diminished, swathed in a bandage that wound around his head like a dowager's cap. But he looked like he was coming round, as Claire waved a vial of strong-smelling salts close under his nose.

"Wake up, Rosing," he growled close to the bastard's ear. "I've come to finish what I started."

It would be an easy thing to kill him here and now. Tanner had told himself that if given another chance he would kill him. He had come here with just that intention riding like a whip at the back of his mind. It would be all too easy. And no one would ever know.

"Tanner."

Claire would know.

But killing Rosing now would be a mercy, and save the man the ironic horror of recovering just so he could be hanged. And it would certainly satisfy the savage blood-lust coursing through Tanner's veins. But choking the life out of Rosing just the way he had choked the life out of Maisy Carter would only serve to push Tanner closer to the noose.

"Tanner," she said again, stronger this time. "Look at me."

It was enough. Enough to remind himself that he was not an animal—a ravening beast with no brain to guide his heart. No matter his savage lust for revenge, he could choose.

He could choose, he had told Claire. And so he would.

He would choose the right course.

Tanner shifted his focus to Rosing, staring up at them with a muzzy combination of fear and disassociation that must come from the laudanum. "Tell us what you did."

Rosing transferred his wide, startled gaze to Claire. In the dim light from the single candle her white muslin dress was illuminated, making her look like an avenging angel come down to take God's vengeance.

She said, "Tell us about Maisy Carter. I know what you did to me. But now I want to hear you admit what you did to Maisy Carter."

Rosing's gaze darted unevenly back and forth between the two of them and then at the door, as if he might find some salvation there. But perhaps he realized he wouldn't, because he looked back to Claire before he said, "I don't know what you're talking about."

His voice was a dry, weak scrawl, and Tanner saw

Claire, being the kindhearted person she was, transfer her gaze to the glass of water on the table. "Should I give him water, Claire, for his dry throat?" Tanner asked. "Or should I break his other leg, so he tells you the truth?"

She flinched a little at the violence in his voice. But not as much as Rosing, who looked like he was trying to crawl out of the bed. Tanner leaned his weight onto the sheets, trapping the man beneath the linen. "What's it to be, Claire?"

"The leg."

Ah, that was his girl. His immaculate avenging angel.

"No." Rosing's protest was stronger. "No, please. I don't know who you're talking about."

"The maid," Tanner clarified for him. "The maid you raped before you tried to rape Lady Claire Jellicoe."

Rosing's wide, dark gaze swung back to Claire.

"Tell me why you killed Maisy Carter," she said again.

"I didn't, I swear. I didn't. I didn't mean to. She was alive."

Tanner leaned down even closer, looming over the stricken man. "But you did rape her, didn't you? Her cross—the cross you strangled her with while you raped her—is right there in your valise, in your wardrobe."

"I swear, she was alive," the puling bastard croaked.

"For that alone, you deserve to die." The vehement whisper came from Claire's lips. "So you can never do it again. Never shove another girl up against a brick wall."

Tanner stood and looked at her. "We both wished we had killed him when we had the chance. Well, now's your chance, Claire." He pulled that long, wicked blade from his boot, and nimbly reversed it in his hand in front of Rosing's wide, glassy eyes, holding it out to Claire hilt first. "Kill him now."

She looked at the knife for such a very long time, Tanner was afraid that he had overplayed it, and that she might not understand that if she truly wanted the man dead, he would do it for her.

"Or if you like, I'll kill him for you. I'll do it right this time. I'll just stand on his leg, and while he's convulsing and writhing in pain the way he made you, and made all those girls, girl after girl, writhe in pain, then I'll slide my blade right through his ribs, and turn it until he's bled dead and dry."

Tanner didn't know who was more shocked, Claire or Rosing. But the color came back to Claire's cheeks—two high spots of ardent color. She rallied, his brave, avenging girl. "I'll do, Tanner. If you'd be so kind as to stomp on his leg again, I'll—"

"No. No, I swear I didn't kill her," Rosing gasped, tears of fright seeping from his eyes. "Please."

"Why did you rape her?" Tanner pressed. "Why didn't you just leave Lady Claire's room, and let her go?" He had asked himself this question over and over. And he had thought he knew the answer—that Rosing raped her because he could. Because he liked it.

"She would have told Lady Claire."

The rage was a ravenous thing that was consuming Tanner from the inside out. But he could not let it. He had to think. He had to use his brain and ask the next question. The question he hadn't liked to ask himself.

"Why did you go to Lady Claire's room in the first place? Why didn't you just wait for her at the ball, and do as you did then? And steal her outside, and down the lawn?" What had been the impetus? Why had Rosings picked his Lady Claire Jellicoe and not another?

Rosing's admission was a desperate whisper. "I was supposed to ruin her."

Ah. The tumblers in Tanner's brain aligned, and the bolt fell free. Rosing meant to rape Claire instead of Maisy

Carter up there in that bedroom. He was supposed to. Someone wanted him to.

Someone else—someone with a heavy ring on his left hand, and an ancient Roman coin fob, and the cold-blooded conscience of a snake had crushed Maisy Carter's windpipe.

Somebody with a reason to keep Maisy Carter from naming Rosing, so he could go on to ruin Lady Claire Jellicoe as he was supposed to. Someone who wanted an alliance with the House of Sanderson.

"Hadleigh." Tanner looked at Claire. "Hadleigh killed her, and then took her body out, and dumped her into the river, just as you supposed."

Chapter Twenty-Five

There was only one place left to look for the evidence to support their answers.

"I'm going to search Hadleigh's chamber."

"I'll come with you."

Before he could object, Claire shook her head, silently telling him she couldn't be brought to stay with Rosing for any reason.

Tanner's gaze went to the bottles on the table. "Pour out some laudanum. That'll keep him quiet."

Tanner forced the dose past Rosing's crying mouth, and waited for the opiate to take effect. Once the man had slipped under the influence of the drug, Tanner took up the candle, and he and Claire slipped down the corridor to the opposite side of the house, to the room that would adjoin Lady Westmoreland's sitting room. Light blazed from under her door, but the adjoining room, facing the back of the house and the water, and which would most likely be Hadleigh's, was dark.

Tanner snuffed out the sconces as he went—relit candles would be a clear indication of movement in the house—and paused for a long, careful moment outside the door, listening, making sure there was no sound of

Hadleigh's valet within. There was only the faint sound of movement below, the low, droning summer sounds of insects in the night, and the occasional shuffling of paper from next door, as if Lady Westmoreland were amusing herself by reading the scandal sheets.

Within the room it was dark and quiet. The windows were closed, the curtains drawn, and the bed turned back—all in preparation for Hadleigh's return.

Tanner wasted no time. Claire went to one side of the room while he went directly to the small dressing room. Hadleigh kept a larger portion of his clothing at Lady Westmoreland's house than did his son—clearly he was very much at home there. There were many different coats and shirts and cravats. And many different waistcoats.

But Tanner thought, as he ran his hands across the fabric, he sensed a connection—old-fashioned, twilled silk fabrics, and fine metallic threads woven through.

But no sign of a ripped waistcoat of white and gold metallic threads. Not unless—

Tanner's eyes fell to the small valise stored on the bottom shelf of the wardrobe. A valise such as a valet would pack, if he meant to take an article of clothing back— He stopped thinking and simply looked.

Ah. "Claire."

There would be no need to canvas London's tailors now. At the bottom of the bag was the torn waistcoat, no doubt waiting for the valet to take back to London for repair.

Hadleigh.

Hadleigh had been the one. Rosing must have told him what he'd done, and Hadleigh had gone to the closet where his son had left Maisy Carter concussed perhaps, or half-dead from the effects of the rape and semi-strangulation and the broken nose.

Hadleigh had gone there, and either taken the barely

conscious girl somewhere else, or more likely strangled her there, on the spot, hidden from view in the closet. And then he moved her body, wrapped up in his mistress's distinctive white cloak.

A chill, like a cold breeze from an open window, coursed through Tanner.

It must have been—right from the beginning—a ploy to see a marriage made. To cement an alliance between the House of Hadleigh and the House of Sanderson. That was why Hadleigh and Rosing had come uninvited to the ball in the first place. Because his father had not been able to interest the Earl Sanderson in a previous alliance—in joining his scheme.

Lord Peter Rosing had gone upstairs to Claire's chamber to find her before the ball had even started. He had meant to compromise her then and there, while the rest of them waited below in the drawing room. While Tanner propped up the wall.

And Claire had foiled him by rushing downstairs to be on time. And Maisy had come back to the chamber and paid the consequences.

Tanner could see it all now, the deadly sequence of events. The greedy error compounding upon greedy error. And there was more greed still. There was the fob.

He could hear his sister's voice now—*it always comes down to the money.*

Tanner needed more evidence. He needed those counterfeit coins. Or better yet those cylinders that had been cast to stamp the blanks.

Would Hadleigh keep such a valuable but incriminating possession with him?

Tanner began systematically turning out the wardrobe, shelf after shelf. He rifled through the valise again, searching for a false bottom, running his hands around the edges of the wardrobe's wooden frame, feeling and searching for a hidden catch.

Nothing.

But Claire was already ahead of him. "Tanner."

She was standing next to the writing table, upon which sat a large rectangular carrying case of burnished York tan leather, the kind important papers, or jewelry, were carried in. A locked carrying case. Just waiting for him.

"Can you open it?" she asked. And then asked, "*Should* we open it?"

"Yes." A case like that he could have open in a few seconds. He wasted no time on explaining his moral failings but moved the candle closer to the keyhole, fished his picks out of his pockets, and set to work.

Hadleigh was a smart man and had chosen a well-made case, with interior hardware—hinges and clasps on the inside where they couldn't be pried apart with force. And there were two brass-plated keyholes—Tanner would have to pick each lock individually.

Tanner's encyclopedic mind was already sorting through the catalogue of locks in his mind, remembering successful approaches, reminding him of failures, warning him of possibilities like a sequential lock, where one side might have to be half-set and then the other follow before both sides would release. Or the need to have two keys, and the locks to be turned simultaneously.

He set to it gingerly, feeling his way carefully with the pick, counting the tumblers, sorting out if they were equal to a side, before he attempted to rake the first set. And he was glad he had gone gently when the first lock clicked to half-set.

He repeated the pick on the left side and then thumbed the latches to half-set. Then he raked them both again, until the tumblers fell with a satisfying click.

"Ah." He positioned his thumbs on opposite sides of the latches, and simultaneously pushed the brass buttons outward.

The latches snapped open.

Claire crowded close and held the candle up so they could see into the interior as he lifted the lid.

At first there didn't appear to be anything within but a neatly organized leather tray with some writing utensils—metal pens, an old penknife, and a bottle of ink.

But beneath the tray were a small collection of flannel pouches. Tanner plunged his hand in, and felt through them until he found the shapes he was searching for. He pulled open the drawstring and spilled the objects into his palm.

He felt Claire's sharp intake of breath beside him. "Oh, my God."

And there they were—the cylinders. One for each side of the counterfeit coin. Brass and steel gleaming in the candlelight.

"Should we take them with us, or the whole case?" Claire was looking at him with a clear mixture of excitement and relief chasing across her face.

"No." He had left the evidence—the tokens and Maisy's cross—in Rosing's wardrobe as well. He needed them found here. He needed them found by somebody else. By the law. "We'll leave them for—"

He heard it then, the jangling sound of coach harness, followed by the telltale crunch and clatter of gravel that meant Hadleigh was returning.

Tanner felt his face curve into a nasty smile. Right on time.

He snubbed out the candle with his fingers, and waited for their eyes to adjust to the dark. Next door, Lady Westmoreland stirred, and made her swishing silken way out of her room, and then paused at Rosing's room—presumably to check for Claire—before she went to the stairs, to greet Hadleigh.

As soon as she was past, Tanner set the cylinders back in their flannel pouches, replaced the leather writing tray, and flipped the latches shut. "Put it back exactly where you found it."

"Here. It was here, on the desk." Claire positioned the case just so.

Below, voices sounded from the entry hall. "Why isn't there any light?" Hadleigh sounded irritated and even angry.

"Hadleigh." Lady Westmoreland's voice from the stair-well, snide and soothing. "You'll never guess who came to call."

"Who?"

But outside there was another sound—the jangling din of a second carriage running up Lady Westmoreland's semi-circular drive. With any luck, it was the law, come to call. Just as Hadleigh had likely desired.

The urge to run from the law was nearly as strong as the urge to confront Hadleigh. But Tanner disliked postponing justice. He disliked having to hold himself back and wait for the slow legs of the law to catch up. His own brand of justice had always been more sure and more swift.

But he knew to free himself—to free him to marry Lady Claire Jellicoe—the Duke of Fenmore had to publicly and legally discredit the Marquess of Hadleigh, and expose his schemes before justice could follow.

But Claire was feeling the urge to run as well. Especially when Hadleigh's voice, incredulous and demanding, roared up from below, "Who? Where is she?"

"Tanner!"

Tanner drew Claire to the window, flipped over the latch, and shoved the silent sash open. "You'll have to go out the window. The roof to the conservatory is right there; you can walk right onto it. But stay low. Don't try to get

down until you hear that everyone is inside, and the coachmen have gone to the stable."

"How will I get down?"

"You'll have to jump."

A sort of frenzied excitement gripped her. Her heart was
pounding in her ears, but she felt no panic. Tanner was with
her.

But he meant her to go on alone. And she couldn't do it
without him. "What about you?"

"I need to cause a diversion to make sure you get away
safely. But I'll be right behind you. Just the way I was
coming in. Now go." He put his big hand on the top of her
head, and propelled her over the sash and onto the roof.
"You can do it," he assured her. "I know you can. Just like
the wall in Chelsea. You're clever and resourceful. Just get
yourself well away, and promise me you'll wait for me to
come out."

But a diversion made no sense when they could get
away clean now. "But what if—"

"Do you promise?" He reached through the open window, and gripped her shoulders, and gave her a hard little
shake, pressing his vehemence into her.

"I promise."

And then his big hand snaked around the back of her
head, and he pulled her to him for a kiss that was as thorough as it was fast. Heat and devastating emotion in under
a heartbeat.

And then he set her away. "Good girl. I love you. Now
go." And he shut the window behind her.

With no other choice, Claire did just as he'd told her
she could. She slinked her way across the conservatory's
painted metal roof, and slid down the steeply pitched side
of the mansard roof until she could find the lowest point.

But the coach and four was rolling slowly by, the

coachmen and footmen chatting as they went, so she stood, and flattened herself as best she could against the white-painted brick of the house's wall, so her dress would blend in, instead of standing out against the conservatory's dark roof.

But it worked, or no one noticed her anyway. It didn't matter. All that mattered was that lamps and candles were being lit and turned up within the house, and she had to get away before the spill of light illuminated her.

And so she pretended she was back at Downpark or back in that alley in Chelsea with the Tanner, and she tied her skirts up so she could use her legs, and she jumped.

The moment she hit the ground she rolled and came up running, straight for the tree line, secreting herself in the darkness to wait. But when her heart stopped pounding in her ears she realized she'd made a mistake.

The surety hit her hard in the chest—he wasn't coming with her. He wasn't waiting to cause a diversion. He wasn't coming at all.

No. She had to be wrong. She could see him through the well-lit windows, walking calmly across Lady West-moreland's chamber, headed out the back of the lady's room, moving toward the servants' stair.

Claire counted out the steps, going back again when he should have emerged at the bottom to recount and think of where he might be. Counting and wishing and praying. Hoping against hope.

But she knew. Claire blinked into the night, and knew deep down in her bones that he was staying within to confront Hadleigh. That Tanner would face him down and demand justice.

But he was alone.

Poor clever, stupid lamb. He had not learned how very much he needed her.

Claire picked up her skirts and pitched herself toward the skiff.

It was a game. The same game he had played day in and day out as a child—plan what you want to happen. Play a role. Brazen it out, but make it real. Make it convincing.

He would make it convincing. Because the alternative was all too real. The alternative was a noose.

And so he ignored the throbbing of his pulse in his ears, and watched Claire make her careful way across the roof. Then he latched the window.

One less way out. But he wasn't going out.

He was going downstairs, sneaking his way through the dark to the connecting door, and then through Lady Westmoreland's chamber to the servants' stair, so he could make his invisible way through the house.

He was going to Lady Westmoreland's well-lit library to sit and take his ease—perhaps help himself to a drink—and wait calmly for the Marquess of Hadleigh, and his guests, to find him.

It was a matter of some minutes before Hadleigh did find him.

"Forgive me," the marquess was saying to someone in the entry hall. "It seems Lady Westmoreland had an intruder. I'm her guest, of course, but I've checked the house, and assured her . . ."

Tanner took a deep breath and let the jangling excitement, the keen sense of physical and mental readiness, fill him up. If ever there was a moment he had wished for the Duke of Fenmore's sartorial precision, it was now. But needs must while the Devil drives. He would use the duke's precise rapier-sharp words instead.

Outside the door, the voice gained in volume. ". . . on my way to the country now that my business in Lords is done. Why don't we come in here—"

Lady Westmoreland's footman opened the door, and Hadleigh strode through first. And stopped in his tracks.

"How do you do?" Tanner minded his manners and doffed his wide-brimmed hat with an elegant bow. "I'm Fenmore. We've not met, but I understand you've been looking for me."

If looks alone could kill, Tanner would be bleeding his life's blood into the plush carpet. Hadleigh's eyes bored into him, and though the man did not move so much as an inch, the muscle along the edge of his jaw hardened, like steel annealing.

Behind the marquess, Tanner recognized the face of the local magistrate, Lord Bartholomew Bennet, an old card-playing crony of his grandmother's.

A shiver of sly relief slid through him. Hadleigh had chosen badly. He had chosen an honest man. And Tanner could only hope the two men with Lord Bennet—either lesser magistrates of some kind or constables—were just as honest.

Unlike Lord Bennet, Hadleigh was not an honest man. The Marquess of Hadleigh was as powerful and controlling and evil as his son was criminally rapine. They were quite a pair—the House of Hadleigh's bad blood ran deep.

Though the marquess was a man Tanner had never had occasion to cross, he was someone Tanner instinctively and very logically distrusted. He was known to be both political and politically dirty. He shifted his allegiances as often as the weather, depending upon who was in power and whose allegiance he could buy, beg, or steal. He was a man whose skills Tanner might have been tempted to admire, but for the fact that he was known to have no loyalty. No sense of morals. No sense of what was truly right.

And he was a murderer.

So Tanner kept his eyes on Hadleigh, who crossed to the desk and took up his position of power, though he also looked as if he would like to stab Tanner with the gleaming penknife so conveniently left upon its surface. Tanner would have to mind himself, lest he find himself stuck in the ribs. Murder could become a habit just as easily as rape.

But the marquess was no fool, and would make the best of this situation. "There he is," Hadleigh crowed. "There's the man who is wanted on a charge of murder. Arrest him."

To which accusation Tanner smiled. "Ah. As you say. Good evening, my Lord Bennet." Tanner made his bow to the magistrate. "Which is why I have come. To prove my innocence, so you may dismiss the charge. Which"—he smiled in Lord Bennet's direction—"I should very much like to do at your earliest convenience, my lord. You see, I'm getting married."

"Felicitations," Lord Bennet murmured politely.

"Prove your innocence?" Hadleigh scoffed. "Good God, Fenmore. You can't imagine that we'll be proving anything over my library desk."

"Ah. Then perhaps we can do it over Lady Westmoreland's library desk. And thank you, but I have already poured myself a drink. Although coffee would be acceptable, if you have it. Lord Bennet?"

His Lordship nodded and settled himself into a chair opposite Tanner. "Coffee, if it looks for us to have a long night."

Tanner made one of his ducal gestures to Lady Westmoreland's footman, who was still hovering at the door. "Thank you." Tanner then sat and turned conversationally to his accuser. "So, Lord Hadleigh. What is all this nonsense?"

"Nonsense, Duke? A charge of murder has been laid against you."

"By whom? I should like to know the scurrilous rat who has done so much to waste your time. And mine."

"By Lord Peter Rosing, sir, my son. Laid evidence last night with the Bow Street Magistrates' Court. Been looking for you ever since."

"Apologies." Tanner made another elegant little bow of his head. "I've been traveling. But Lord Peter Rosing could not have laid evidence against me."

"The devil you say," Bennet murmured.

"Bow Street have his complaint, signed and sealed, sirrah," Hadleigh countered.

The footman—no doubt not wanting to miss a word—was already back with a tray of coffee. No doubt at least half of the servants were listening at the door. Good. It would be best to have an audience. More witnesses.

"Then that complaint is fraudulent. Quite a fraud." Tanner took a very long, satisfying draught of the hot coffee. Just the way he liked it—strong and dark. Already he could feel the stimulating effects coursing through his veins and sharpening his brain.

"How so, sir?" Lord Bennet obligingly asked. "This is an astonishing charge. How so?"

"Because Lord Peter Rosing was until late this very afternoon in a state of coma, a word I have learned in consultation with a learned surgeon and professor of anatomy, Mr. Jackson Denman. Do you know him?" Tanner adopted Claire's breezy sympathetic style of speech. "He consults with Bow Street and the Old Bailey on a frequent basis. But the coma is a state of unnatural heavy, deep, and prolonged sleep, with complete unconsciousness and slow, stertorous, often irregular, breathing, due to pressure on the brain."

"Egad," said Lord Bennet.

"Do you come to lecture me, sir?" demanded Hadleigh.

"No, Hadleigh. Only to state to you that I am innocent, and that the charge made against me is false, because Lord Peter Rosing could not have made any charge, as he was insensate. I have had it from Lady Westmoreland's mouth, as I'm sure the servants who have been nursing him will confirm."

"This is your explanation? You do not dispute the truth of the charge, only the legality of who has made it, when my son lies *insensate*?"

"Ah. Thank you for confirming it. And absolutely not. I deny all of the charges. I have not committed murder. Nor an abduction, and what it more, I can prove it. I only ask that you see the charge is pure conjecture, Lord Bennet, because I must assume it was made by Lord Peter Rosing's father, Hadleigh here, on his son's behalf."

"And if I did? Nothing wrong with that," Hadleigh asserted.

Tanner drew back, and invested himself with all of the chilly hauteur of the Duke of Fenmore. "I beg your pardon. It is a manifest conjecture on the part of the marquess, who was not present, in an attempt to clear his son of the very crime of which he accuses me."

It took a long moment for Lord Bennet to grasp Tanner's accusation. "And this is your testimony? But I imagine Lord Peter Rosing will say the opposite."

"I imagine he will. I imagine he will say anything to clear himself. For he is the guilty party."

"Guilty of what?" Lord Bennet queried.

"Of the vicious rape of a maid. And complicity in her murder."

"That is ridiculous," Hadleigh thundered. "How could my son have done any of those things? He is the one who has been viciously assaulted. He is the one who lies mortally injured."

Lord Bennet turned his steady regard back to Tanner.

"And can you explain, or should I ask if you were responsible for the injuries to Lord Peter Rosing?"

"Yes." Tanner made his statement as easy as it was unequivocal.

"You see," roared Hadleigh.

Lord Bennet was not yet satisfied. "And may I ask why?"

Tanner judged it best not to engage in an argument in which he had no defense, "the bastard touched my woman" not generally being accounted as an acceptable excuse.

He could feel the nasty sick tension snake through his body. He had thought he would have the advantage with Lord Bennet. He thought he would be able to make it clear with science and fact and evidence, but all of a sudden he could see that there were other, stronger factors at play here. And for the first time in all his deserving years, he saw that he just might end up being undeservedly sent to prison, and from there to await trial.

It gave him some small comfort to know that he could remarshal the forces of truth and fact and science to his side should the matter come to trial, but it would be a grimmer battle. He would already have lost so much by that point.

And he could not involve Claire.

He found his voice somewhere at the bottom of his worn boots. "The young woman who was murdered, Miss Maisy Carter, was in the employ of my grandmother, the Dowager Duchess of Fenmore, at one of her dower properties. I'm sure you will appreciate that I have a responsibility to the people in my grandmother's employ. Miss Maisy Carter is dead. But I did not murder her. The Marquess of Hadleigh did."

The room went absolutely and unequivocally quiet for a long, long, sick moment.

"He can't make such an accusation," Hadleigh said directly to Lord Bennet.

Tanner kept his voice careful and mild. "But I just did. And what's more, I should like to make it formally. I have proof. I should like to lay *my* evidence and *my* charge against the Marquess of Hadleigh."

"I will crush you, Fenmore" was Hadeigh's answer. "You and anyone else you try to bring against me."

"Will you? How predictable you are, Hadleigh, for you said the same to me last night."

The wide double doors to the library were opened to admit the Earl Sanderson. And behind him was calm, up-standing Jack Denman. And the Countess Sanderson, as well as Tanner's grandmother, leaning on Doggett's arm.

And behind them all, pushing to the front, was Claire, looking like God's avenging angel.

His angel. His Claire.

Chapter Twenty-Six

"Ah. Lovely." He beamed at her, as if it had all been arranged. As if he didn't want to shout and tell her to go while she had the chance. Go before Hadleigh turned his accusations on her. "You are all here. All armed with evidence. How kind."

"You have no evidence," Hadleigh stated. "Only jumped-up lies to save your own neck, while my son lies prostrate from your assault."

He had no argument to make against assaulting Rosing, so he made none, and concentrated upon what he did have. "That is for my Lord Bennet to decide. This is England, my lord, a nation of laws. Laws that stand, and must be met, whether you try to bend them to your will or no."

Tanner moved quickly on, so Hadleigh could not interrupt, and force him to surrender the high ground. "I have evidence that the maid, Maisy Carter, who was a good and dutiful servant, was brutally assaulted by Lord Peter Rosing, who choked her, broke her nose, and raped her—all injuries which can be attested to by the eminent surgeon and professor of anatomy from the Royal College of Surgeons, Mr. Jackson Denman, who is present with his report"—Jack, God bless him, held up his notes—"in a closet at Riverchon House. At which point Lord Peter Rosing stole a necklace—a religious cross that had been a gift from her former employer, Lady Harriet Worth—and has since kept it in his possession, here at Lady Westmoreland's, upstairs. I would suggest you send your man to Lord Peter Rosing's chamber, Lord Bennet, before the marquess can charge his people to make off with it."

The entire room swiveled toward the marquess, who reddened with dangerous ire. "How dare you—"

"I dare because I saw what you and your son did to that young woman. I pulled her body out of the cold water of the river Thames where you had so callously dumped her."

"She was a slut."

Though he might have anticipated such a predictable slur, Tanner felt his precious control slipping from his cold palms. "She was a small, vulnerable woman."

Hadleigh countered with an even more predictable attack. "You thieving bastard, I know all about you, Fenmore. You're nothing more than a lying sneak thief, whose word can't be trusted, and—"

"Enough, Hadleigh." Lord Bennet's voice cut into Hadleigh's rant.

Tanner quieted the room his own way. "There is more— much more. There is the murder itself. Which took place in that same closet on the upper floor of Riverchon House. The blood of the victim still stains the wall where the housekeeper, Mrs. Dalgliesh, a servant above reproach in the employ of the Dowager Duchess of Fenmore for some twenty years, found them and brought them to the attention of Mr. Denman, who was investigating the matter at my behest."

"This changes nothing," Hadleigh insisted. "Nothing."

"It changes nothing of the fact that you then murdered Maisy Carter in cold blood. Cleaning up the mess your son had created when he raped her, you thought. Crushing the life out of the struggling girl"—he was obliged to raise his voice over his grandmother's pitiful cry of anguish—"as she fought you. You wrapped your hand around her windpipe, and choked the life out of her as ruthlessly and completely as if she had been hanged."

There were more gasps from the ladies, and even the Earl Sanderson closed his eyes and turned away.

"But you left your mark, Your Lordship. The impression of your ring, sir. That crest of the House of Hadleigh upon your left hand. It left a mark and a bruise upon her body for the world to see." Tanner gestured imperatively at Jack, who did his bit and held up his notebook, as if the pages within contained that very fact.

But Tanner also caught the stern eye Jack leveled on him, as if to warn him he was laying it on too thick. But Lord Bennet was the only one who mattered now, and he was caught openmouthed and slack jawed, staring at the Marquess of Hadleigh with new eyes.

"And then Hadleigh wrapped Maisy Carter's body in the white velveteen summer cloak of his mistress"—Tanner forbore from making any further reference to the lady, as the name of one lady would invariably lead to another and *that* he would not countenance—"and spirited the dead girl's body out of the house, and down the lawn to dump her unshriven into the river."

Tanner held them all spellbound with the tale, and for one fraction of a moment Hadleigh looked well and truly caught, stripped bare of all his layers of cunning and influence and money. And just as quickly it was gone.

"Preposterous. This is all a . . . a fantasy, a story he has concocted to save his own neck from the noose. His neck that should have been stretched years ago, for it is well known that Fenmore is nothing more than a thief himself, born and bred."

Lord Bennet swung his troubled gaze back to Tanner.

"It is an old accusation," Tanner assured him with calm certainty. "You may be assured that the House of Fenmore made quite sure that I was the true and rightful heir, despite my unfortunate and dreadful childhood at the hands of a kidwoman." God forgive him for abusing poor old Nan so, but he had to press his advantage; he had to strike while Lord Bennet was growing hot, and wanted such a contentious case removed from his desk and passed on to a Grand Jury. "I have spent the past sixteen years of my life in atonement for my youth. And that atonement has been a dedication to English justice that many here are prepared to attest to."

"Hear, hear," said the Earl Sanderson. "I will attest to that."

"They're all in it together. You can prove nothing," Hadleigh spat.

"I can prove everything," Tanner roared back at him. "I can prove that the deceased, Maisy Carter, fought you with her very last breath, because she took something from you. Took it in her hand, and held it tight while you strangled her. She clawed and ripped at you, while you choked the life out of her, didn't she? She ripped your waistcoat—and held tight to the threads. She took the only thing that she could reach, which was your watch fob, and she held it tight until the surgeon Mr. Jackson Denman pried the trinket from her cold, stiff fingers."

"You murderer! You murderer." The Countess Sanderson could not contain her horror.

"Your watch fob, my lord," Tanner continued, "the token of your financial power. The symbol of a syndicate of investors you have gathered for the purpose of the financial conquest of Britain. A syndicate of investors in a horde of gold aurei from Pompeii. But not even your investors"—here he turned to nod to the Earl Sanderson—"know that the coins are all fakes."

He tossed the clipped, leaded forgery onto the desk where it rolled and clattered to a stop. *"Male fide,"* he intoned. "Made entirely in bad faith, of lead barely covered in gold. The evidence of which lies in this very house. Upstairs in the Marquess of Hadleigh's traveling case."

Lord Bennet turned to one of his men. "Go now. Secure it immediately."

"He put it there," Hadleigh accused. "He was in the house. He planted it there to accuse me."

"A case with your initials stamped into the leather? Come, Hadleigh, you should know there are records, records of everything, that will prove me true. Bills of sale, or an entry into your household accounts for the purchase of such an expensive case. Your man of business will have made an entry into a ledger. His Lordship will not have to take my word for it."

"But I will. For now," Lord Bennet confirmed.

"No," Hadleigh roared.

"Yes." Tanner rose and advanced upon him, ready for any trick he might try. Ready for a gun to be brandished. Ready for the wicked slice of the letter opener. Ready for anything.

"Like a house of cards, sir, all an elaborate, fraudulent show. As is everything that the Marquess of Hadleigh has charged. It has all been *male fide,* in bad faith. Now he adds lying to a magistrate"—Tanner swept his arm toward Lord Bennet—"to his crime of murder."

Hadleigh was nearly shaking with some frightful combination of fear and rage. "What about my son?" He played his last card. "What can you say to your assault on him?"

Tanner chose his words carefully, for he knew well he was treading on dangerous ground. "I can say nothing. I can say nothing but that he is a rapist. And a habitual, flagrant one at that. And that he deserved the brawl that ensued when we met."

"Ha-ha! You see," Hadleigh crowed. "He admits it."

"I am happy, my Lord Bennet, to stand the charge of assault. It is my duty as a peer and an Englishman to face my actions before the law. I only ask that you see fit to do the same to Hadleigh."

The eyes of every person in the room swiveled from Tanner across to Bennet.

It all hung in the balance, whether the magistrate had been swayed, or whether he would toss his hands up, and let a jury of Tanner's peers hear his story before the King's Bench.

"It all comes down," Bennet said cautiously, "to the word of one man against another."

"Indeed," Tanner intoned. "One marquess against one duke. Rather a play on the old expression *put up your dukes*. But along with my word, I have evidence. And witnesses. I do not make conjectures."

Lord Bennet could not make up his mind. "Be that as it may, in the end it is still one man's word against another's."

"And one woman's." A clear voice spoke from the back. "I should like to speak on behalf of the duke."

Claire could hold her tongue no longer. Even if Tanner was content to let it all come out in a trial, she was not.

"No," Tanner said, furious and panicked. "No. Take her away from here," he said to her father, and anyone else who would listen.

"No," said the magistrate. "Why should she not speak? What do you think to hide?"

Claire stepped past her father's protectively restraining hand. "He thinks to hide my part in this tragic affair."

She stepped forward, holding her chin up high, as cool and serene as ever the lofty Duke of Fenmore could be, because she would be his duchess and learn to walk like that if she chose. And she chose now to go to him.

"And who are you?" the magistrate asked.

"I am Lady Claire Jellicoe, daughter of the Earl and Countess Sanderson. And I am the lady whom Lord Peter Rosing was attempting to . . ." She faltered, frozen for a moment by her shame and regret under the eyes of so many strangers. But here was only one man whose eyes counted, and so she looked to him for strength.

Tanner shook his head back and forth, silently begging her not to speak, not to expose herself to their condemnation. But she had no choice. It would not stop until someone with an unassailable reputation stood up and spoke, he had said. And so she would.

"I am the young woman whom the Duke of Fenmore aided by striking Lord Peter Rosing down. I am the young woman whom Lord Peter Rosing was attempting to compromise and force into marriage against my will. I am here"—she turned to acknowledge Hadleigh, but she would not look at him, for fear she would not be able to withstand the hatred in his eyes—"to refute each and every one of the charges laid by the Marquess of Hadleigh."

Hadleigh's response was as instant as it was vicious. "You can't believe her. Look at her—she's in love with him. She'd take his part, the little slut."

The room gasped around her, but she would not let it stop her. "That is the second young woman you have declared a slut"—she could not stop her voice from choking over the word—"this evening, my lord. One might think you thought all women to be such, when that is not in fact the case."

"You can't believe a word she says."

No one refuted Hadleigh's accusation. But neither did anyone give it credence.

"Why not, my lord? Why is my word as the daughter

of a peer any less valuable than yours? Because it is not what you want these good people to hear?" Claire pressed her whisper-slight advantage. "But I should like to speak to my Lord Bennet, who presides here, and not to the marquess. It is Lord Bennet who must weigh the evidence and the charges, and he from whom I seek permission to speak as the daughter of a peer, and as a victim of Lord Peter Rosing."

The magistrate bestirred himself to rise. "Yes, of course. I am obliged."

"Thank you, sir. And my statement is this—that it was Lord Peter Rosing who was guilty of assaulting me. It was Lord Peter Rosing who pulled me by the arm from the dance floor and down the length of the Dowager Duchess of Fenmore's garden in Richmond and pushed my face into the brick wall of the boathouse." She turned her cheek so Lord Bennet might see. "Lord Peter Rosing assaulted me, and would have . . ."

Claire took a deep breath. It had not happened. It was well and truly over.

"He would have continued, if the Duke of Fenmore had not come to save me."

Her mother came to her side, and put her arm around her, but did not say anything. Lord Bennet looked from her to Hadleigh, who pulled back his lips in a sneer that told her he was about to speak.

She preempted him. "The Marquess of Hadleigh will counter this by dragging my name, and that of my father, through the muck. He will say I am a flirt and worse, much worse. But all will be lies in the service of all his other lies. The Duke of Fenmore is guilty of nothing more than defending my honor, and there is no charge against that."

The Marquess of Hadleigh edged slightly back, and

tried an entirely new gambit. "The accused can't lay evidence against another man while he is under a charge."

"Am I in custody, Lord Bennet?" Tanner asked quietly. "Are you going to recommend I be bound over for trial?"

"If the Duke of Fenmore cannot lay evidence, then I will." The Earl Sanderson spoke. "I will lay all of this evidence against the Marquess of Hadleigh, and I will bear witness to the fact that the marquess's son assaulted my daughter with the express purpose of ruining her and forcing her into marriage."

Tanner faced the magistrate. "What is it to be, my lord?" Tanner prided himself on not holding his breath. But he almost did when Lady Claire Jellicoe reached out to take his hand.

"I find no evidence except hearsay laid against the Duke of Fenmore. But I will see the Marquess of Hadleigh taken up for a charge of murder."

They came out of the villa into a fine drizzling rain that was soft against her skin. The night seemed even newer and more different than it had last night, newer and fresher, splashed and washed silver white in the light rain.

Hadleigh had been taken quickly. Tanner and Jack Denman had seen to that. It was over. And it was just beginning.

Her father and mother hovered nearby with the dowager, leaving Claire to speak to Fenmore privately.

"Why did you come?" was all Tanner said to her.

"Why did you stay?" she asked instead.

Tanner took a deep breath. "Because when you run all your life, you get tired. And you learn to stop and face your accusers, or whatever it is that's chasing you. You learn to face them all down. I wanted to face them all down for you."

"Ah. Poor lamb. The reason *I* came is because you

stayed, and I felt we had not settled satisfactorily between us, you and I, about whether you are, or are not going to make me your wife?"

That slow, wicked smile began to curve across one side of his face. "I rather thought I did so this night, Claire."

Claire could feel heat singe her cheeks from the warm rasp of his voice along her skin. "Properly."

"Did I not do it properly?"

Another huge surge of warmth insinuated itself deep into her belly as his smile slowly curved along his lovely, wickedly carnal mouth. "I welcome another chance to do it properly," he added. "You know you have only to command me, and I will—"

"Stop it. You know what I mean."

"After what transpired between us tonight, I consider you my wife. And that is an end to it."

"That, Your Grace, is only a beginning. My father stands ready nearby. So as I see it, you have two choices. You can either arm yourself—which I should not like to see, since you are both excellent shots, and I love you both—or you can perform some one of your feats of back-alley magic and conjure up a parson. But choose. Now."

Desperation colored his voice—a raw emotion that he took pains never to show. "Claire. You must know how I feel. You must. I told you."

"You told me you wanted to protect me."

"I do. Desperately."

"But do you love me?"

"Desperately."

Claire put her finger up to her chin. "Ah."

"Ah?"

"Yes. Ah. *Desperately.* Being desperately in love is something altogether different from being merely in love."

"*Different* as in better, or merely different?"

"Better. Desperately better. Infinitely better."

"Better." Breath seemed to be filling his lungs again. "Better is better."

"Infinitely so." She took pity upon him, and smiled at him, and enlaced her fingers with his, so he would know unequivocally how she felt. So she could draw him nearer.

Near enough to kiss, softly and solemnly on the corner of his mouth, where she knew he liked it. But still, he needed to be sure.

"So have you decided whether you will do me the infinite honor and very great personal favor of becoming my wife?"

"Yes, I'm quite de—"

"Determined, yes. It is one of the things I admire excessively about you."

"Do you?" She looked up at him, in that hopeful, guileless way that always, always absolutely slayed him.

"Yes. Desperately," he added for good measure.

"Another compliment?"

"Yes." He could only hope he did not look as stupid and juvenile and exposed and in love as he felt.

The corners of her wide blue eyes turned up ever so slightly. "Are you only saying that so I'll kiss you?"

Tanner felt his breath go quiet. "Would it work?"

"I think it might." The pleasure transferred from the corners of her eyes to the corners of her mouth. Her blue eyes lightened and sharpened and danced as her gaze fell from his face to his lips—she wanted to kiss him.

And he wanted to kiss her. With heat and passion and all the pent-up desire he had kept so savagely behind his wall of restraint.

Her voice was an encouraging whisper. "Is this better?"

"Oh, God, yes." His own voice cracked a little, as if it were under a great strain, and had finally giving way. "Yes. Please."

He kissed her then. A wholehearted, nothing-held-back, pick-her-up-and-walk-her-into-the-sunset sort of kiss that would not keep for later. He kissed her hair, and inhaled the lovely scent that was her, as if they were just a fellow and his lass lost in the simple pleasure of each other's company.

Lost to everything of the world but themselves. Not as if he were a duke and she his duchess—although he was surer than ever that he was about to make that plan a reality—but as if they were simply people who had chosen to be together for no other reason than mutual company and pleasure.

A new feeling welled within him. A feeling he had not felt since the day his sister had married her captain, and put her hands on Tanner's face, and looked him in the eye, and said it was over—that they were safe.

They hadn't been really, for safety was a mutable, fickle thing, but he had believed her then. And she had been partially right; he had never been that cold, or that desperate, or that hungry again. But he had been lonely. And lonelier still.

But not this morning. Not now. Not ever again.

He had always watched her—watched the inestimable Lady Claire's beautiful wide blue eyes sparkle, and her glowing porcelain face light with smiles for others. He had followed the bright shine of her golden blond hair as she had twirled and whirled around the dance floor with other, more worthy, less guileful men.

But now she was real, and his.

Tanner wasn't worthy of her, of course, his self-possessed swan. He was only an accidental aspirant to her world—an interloper who would never really feel at home in their glittering mansions and on their palatial estates. Even when the palatial estate in question was ostensibly his own.

But his swan would guide him, as she did now. "May we please go get married now? Surely you're rich and influential enough for that special license. Or are you a flat with the ecclesiastical crowd?"

"A complete flat. You'll have to manage it for us, my duchess."

"My duke. My Tanner."

"Yes." He took her by the hand and led her toward her carriage, and felt, for the first time in a very, very long time since he had become a man and understood all the responsibilities and people who depended upon him day after day, as if all were right with the world. As if there were nothing more he could hope or wish for.

"Should you like to get married straightaway, or wait, to show the world the lofty Duke of Fenmore answers to no man, and will not be rushed, but does things in his own sweet time?"

She was teasing him, smiling up at him with her open, guileless face, and he could only smile back. "Right away. I should like to begin telling the world you are my duchess straightaway. Especially your father. I don't expect he has liked a delay in clearing your name."

"My father will like what I like. And I think my father and his countess— Oh, I shall outrank my own mother. How very odd. I hadn't thought about being a duchess."

"Then you shall be different and eccentric duchess and do as you like."

"Yes. And I think we should get married as soon as possible, in a few days, or a week's time, only so my mother can order up enough ribbons and white soup for a wedding celebration that will not cause a scandal."

Tanner took a deep, easy breath. It was remarkable how

he stopped thinking when he was around Claire. He had always thought such a thing—to not think—would be a disadvantage, a hindrance to his life. But now it felt like a much-needed respite.

Such a respite that he wanted to kiss her still. He wanted to consume her whole. He wanted to revel in the remarkable fact that she was so much more than the porcelain doll he would have painted her to be. He was the luckiest man in Christendom to have Lady Claire Jellicoe at his side, accepting him for who he really was, not a cardboard cutout of a Duke.

He pulled her closer and kissed her forehead, but said nothing else as they made their way through the night, just as he had said last night, like a fellow and his girl with nothing but love to feed themselves.

Epilogue

The wedding of Lady Claire Jellicoe and His Grace the Duke of Fenmore did not, as it ought, take place deep in the bosom of society at St. George's, Hanover Square. Instead, the marriage of the season, of the popular and only daughter of an earl to the enigmatic and aloof duke, was celebrated in the less rarefied but comfortable confines of Mayfair Chapel, directly across the street from Sanderson House.

He had done her the honor and courtesy of courting her openly, of walking with her in Hyde Park or Green Park every afternoon, and chatting only with her at every soiree, ball, and rout. He intimidated hostesses into seating her next to him, and he ignored the entirety of the other company, as he had done for years, and talked and looked and smiled only for her.

He was, he heard them say, a new man. A man utterly besotted.

A man in love.

He did not mind. Nor did he correct them. For they were entirely correct. He was a new man.

And he and Claire would make something new between them. And he would have her in his house, to have and to hold. To kiss, and to do many other various and erotic things as well.

Both the chapel and Sanderson House were abloom with flowers—even the wrought-iron gate fronting Curzon Street was decorated so gaily that the street was nearly overrun with gawkers. But not only society came to gape and celebrate the unlikely nuptials—the pavement outside the venerable old church was crowded with the oddest and unlikeliest collection of revelers anyone could ever remember seeing.

Street thieves and beggars, highwaymen and magistrates alike shared the pavement until the crowd swelled so large, Curzon Street became impassable. And in further defiance of custom, the bride and groom did not retreat in solitude to the opulent fortress of Fenmore House but threw the grounds open for a masked ball, where Tanner Evans, ninth Duke of Fenmore, astonished the world by doing what he had never, ever done before.

He danced with his bride.

He kissed her hand, and led her out upon the lawn where a patchwork parquet floor had been laid, and he swept the new Duchess of Fenmore into a waltz so close and sensual and flagrantly romantic that dowagers standing by the sides of the floor fell unconscious in swooning faints.

But the duke and duchess never noticed. Tanner and Claire were too busy making up for lost time. Too busy making the promise between their hearts and their bodies sing its way from the present all the way to tomorrow.

He had stolen her fair and square, and he had managed to keep her, though it had taken every last ounce of stealth and guile and luck that he had ever possessed. But she, with all her innocence and simple, honest grace and desperate bravery, had proved more larcenous than he, for she had well and truly stolen away his heart.

Author's Note

The characters in my Reckless Brides books tend to come from other books I have written: Secondary characters in one book are destined to become the heroes or heroines of the next. This is doubly true of *After the Scandal*. Readers of my previous books will have met our hero, Tanner, before. The story of how he and his sister, Meggs, lived as thieves in London is found in my RITA-nominated book, *The Danger of Desire*. Our heroine, Claire Jellicoe, was first introduced to readers as a secondary character in the story of her brother Will Jellicoe and his true love, Antigone Preston, in the award-winning book *A Breath of Scandal*. The story of Will's navy service is found in *Almost a Scandal*. The story of how Claire's other brothers, Thomas Jellicoe and James Jellicoe, Viscount Jeffrey, find their happily ever afters is found in *Scandal in the Night*.

Coming soon…

Don't miss the next Reckless Brides novel by
Elizabeth Essex

A Scandal to Remember

Available in September 2014 from St. Martin's
Paperbacks